BLACK DOUGLAS

It was almost inevitable that, in the 15th century, the new Scots royal House of Stewart would have to come to conclusions with the great and puissant House of Douglas. When the subject is mightier and more princely than his monarch, however loyal, trouble looms. Young Will Douglas, 8th Earl, greatest and most illustrious of his famous line, was born to almost unbelievable power, influence — and trouble. With a boy king on an uneasy throne, and scoundrels ruling Scotland, the death of Will's curious father pitchforked him into destiny. An unwilling paladin, he was nevertheless cast in the heroic mould, a quietly decisive young man of action, with a conscience, in an age when might was very much right, and the end justified the means.

Foremost noble of Scotland, and military commander of the realm while still in his teens, Will Douglas fought his strange and lonely battle. For though the Black Douglas could call on thousands of men at the merest crook of his finger, and moreover had five brothers close at his back, he was a lonely man. And when he wed the greatest heiress and most famed beauty of the land, The Fair Maid of Galloway, his loneliness was hardly lessened.

His struggle was complicated by the demands of vengeance. His cousin, the 6th Earl, had been decoyed and shamefully murdered in the presence of the young monarch, by no less than Crichton, Chancellor, or Prime Minister, and Livingstone, the king's Guardian. Douglas, for centuries had been a name to tremble at, in Scotland and well down into England. Douglas blood and the Douglas name cried out to be avenged. Yet Will was not a vengeful man. Moreover, his ancestors, generation after generation, had served Scotland — and Scotland was badly in need of serving.

Black Douglas

Nigel Tranter

CORONET BOOKS
Hodder Paperbacks Ltd., London

Copyright © 1968 by Nigel Tranter
First published 1968 by
Hodder & Stoughton Ltd
Coronet edition 1973

Printed and bound in Great Britain for Coronet Books,
Hodder Paperbacks Ltd., St. Paul's House, Warwick Lane,
London, E.C.4, by Cox & Wyman Limited, London, Reading
and Fakenham

ISBN 0 340 16466 2

Hush ye, hush ye, little pet ye,
Hush ye, hush ye, do not fret ye,
The Black Douglas shall not get ye.

(Traditional Lullaby)

PRINCIPAL CHARACTERS

In Order of Appearance: Fictional Characters in *Italics*

WILLIAM DOUGLAS, MASTER OF DOUGLAS: eldest son of James the Gross, 7th Earl.

JAMES DOUGLAS: twin second son of the 7th Earl.

ARCHIBALD DOUGLAS: twin third son. Later Earl of Moray.

HUGH DOUGLAS: fourth son. Later Earl of Ormond.

Pate Pringle: James the Gross's steward at Abercorn.

LADY MARGARET DOUGLAS: eldest daughter. Later wife of the Chamberlain of Galloway.

LADY BEATRIX DOUGLAS: next daughter. Later wife of Hay, the High Constable of Scotland.

LADY JANET DOUGLAS: next daughter. Later wife of 1st Lord Fleming.

LADY ELIZABETH DOUGLAS: next daughter. Later wife of Sir John Wallace of Craigie.

JOHN DOUGLAS: fifth son. Later Lord Balveny.

JOHN CAMERON, BISHOP OF GLASGOW: Former Chancellor.

LADY BEATRIX, COUNTESS OF DOUGLAS: Wife of the 7th Earl.

WILLIAM ST. CLAIR, 3rd EARL OF ORKNEY: brother of the Countess.

SIR JAMES HAMILTON OF CADZOW: chief of the Hamiltons, and grandson of Livingstone, King's Guardian.

SIR WILLIAM HAY OF ERROLL: Lord High Constable of Scotland.

KING JAMES THE SECOND: aged thirteen, son of assassinated James the First, and fourth Stewart monarch.

SIR JAMES LIVINGSTONE: eldest son of the King's Guardian, Keeper of Stirling Castle. Later Chamberlain.

SIR ALEXANDER LIVINGSTONE: King's Guardian. With Crichton, co-murderer of 6th Earl of Douglas.

DAVID LIVINGSTONE: another son of above.

ROBERT FLEMING OF CUMBERNAULD: later 1st Lord Fleming.

SIR WILLIAM CRICHTON: Chancellor (or Prime Minister) of Scotland.

SIR ANDREW CRICHTON OF BARNTON: son of above.

SIR JOHN FORRESTER OF CORSTORPHINE: a powerful knight.

LADY EUPHEMIA, DUCHESS OF TOURAINE: mother of the murdered brothers, and of the Fair Maid of Galloway.

Meg Douglas: tiring-woman to the Fair Maid; an illegitimate grand-daughter of Earl Archibald the Grim.

LADY MARGARET DOUGLAS: The Fair Maid, Lady of Galloway in her own right, sister of the murdered brothers.

JAMES KENNEDY, BISHOP OF ST. ANDREWS: Primate of Scotland. Later Chancellor. Grandson of Robert the Third.

ALEXANDER LINDSAY, MASTER OF CRAWFORD: later 4th Earl of Crawford, known as Earl Beardie, or The Tiger.

DAVID, 3rd EARL OF CRAWFORD: father of above. Justiciar of the North, and Lord High Admiral.

Sir Patrick Hamilton of Dalserf: a veteran jouster.

GEORGE DOUGLAS, MASTER OF ANGUS: later 4th Earl thereof.

JAMES, 3rd EARL OF ANGUS: brother of above. Chief of Red House of Douglas.

PRINCESS JOAN: eleven-year-old sister of the King.

PRINCESS MARY OF GUELDRES: Queen of James the Second.

Wattie Scott: personal servant of Will Douglas.

HENRY DOUGLAS: youngest son of 7th Earl. Later a priest.

POPE NICHOLAS THE FIFTH: born Tomasso da Sarzano.

AENEAS SILVIUS PICCOLOMINI, BISHOP OF TRIESTE: papal aide, later Pope Pius the Second.

RICHARD PLANTAGENET, DUKE OF YORK: Lord Protector of England.

SIR HERBERT HERRIES: brother of Laird of Terregles, a sheriff-deputy of Galloway.

SIR PATRICK MACLELLAN: uncle and Tutor to young Laird of Bombie; another sheriff-deputy of Galloway.

SIR PATRICK GRAY: brother to 1st Lord Gray. Captain of the King's Guard.

WILLIAM TURNBULL, BISHOP OF GLASGOW: Founder of Glasgow University.

SIR WILLIAM LAUDER OF HATTON: a royal courier.

PART ONE

CHAPTER ONE

"JAMIE — you fool! Back! Back, I say! Here — to me! Quick!"

Above the high excited baying of the hounds, the deeper rumbling lowing of the cattle and the shouting of lesser men, that yell rang out, vehement, urgent. The youth on the shaggy short-legged garron turned in his saddle, to look back towards his brother, questioningly.

"Quick, man! He'll charge. God, Jamie — he'll have you trapped!" As still the other hesitated, uncertain, the shouter pointed downhill in a sweeping gesture, below his brother. "The edge, see you — the scarp! No space to jouk. He'll see it. Charge you. Back here . . ."

James Douglas glanced downhill. Fifty yards below him the short heather mixed with deer-hair grass ended in an abrupt lip of bare basalt rock, where the hillside fell away. It was no cliff or precipice, but there was a steep drop of forty feet or so, with a bouldery base, before the slope eased off again — a long minor escarpment typical of the many which scored that sunny, tree-dotted south face of Fastheugh Hill. No garron, however surefooted, could negotiate that scarp.

The youth was already reining round his horse as he changed his glance to peer in the other direction, uphill — for his eyes were not the strongest of Jamie Douglas, and the slanting late-March sun of mid-afternoon that blazed over all the Forest of Ettrick from a cloudless sky, helped nothing. The stocky, wind-twisted Scots pines which grew out of the heather up there were closer together that most of the scattered trees of the long hill-side, and the barred shadows they cast made it difficult to distinguish the bull amongst the other milling cattle which the hounds had chivvied into taking up panting stance there, white as was its hide. Jamie saw no urgent need for alarm, but he dug his heels into the barrel sides of his mount, just the same; of all the Douglas brothers he was the one least apt to argue with Will's admittedly sometimes autocratic commands.

But he was too late. With a bellowing roar that shook the warm heather-scented air, as its pounding hooves seemed to shake the hillside itself, the great white bull charged, head down, tail up, sweeping aside the frightened cows, knocking over two stiff-legged calves, and scattering the yelping deer-hounds which encircled the herd — only one of which stood its ground and attempted a snarling leap at the bull's heavily-maned neck, to be caught and skewered in a lightning jab of a long, wickedly-curving horn, and tossed high in the air, to crash in the heather yards away, a twitching mangled carcase.

James Douglas's eyesight was not so poor as to offer any doubts but that the bull was making directly for himself. There were plenty of other targets — his three brothers and half a dozen foresters and herdsmen irregularly spaced around the clump of pines. An ordinary domestic bull might have been diverted; probably would not have had the wit to perceive the youth's dangerous position, in the first place. This however was no ordinary bull but a wild-born killer, massive, great-shoul-dered but lean of rear, shaggy-coated red of eye, auroch-horned veteran of fights innumerable, as cunning as it was savage. There were many of these wild bulls in Ettrick Forest, relics of the great wild herds of ancient breed which once had roamed all these southern uplands. They were a menace to man and beast, attacking at sight, often stealing the cattle herds which grazed the lower slopes — as this had done — and spawn-ing treacherous and unprofitable offspring on honest men's cows; but, for all that, they provided the most exciting and man-sized sport to be had in all the Forest, far outshining the chase of even the greatest hart or the occasional boar which still sur-vived.

Will Douglas saw that his brother would not, could not, get out of the brute's way in time. There was not more than seventy yards between Jamie and the trees — and more than twice that distance of broken ground before the escarpment tailed away and gave room for manoeuvre. The bull could string the bow, swing over at a tangent. The garrons they all rode were broad-hooved and sturdy, for the hill, but not fast, and the uneven heather and outcropping stone made bad going. Jamie would have been better to turn and face the charge, jouk at the last moment, then spur off uphill before the bull could turn round again — but of all the brothers Jamie would not think of that. Now he would be caught sideways-on, and helpless. He was tug-ging out his sword – but what use was that, in Jamie's hand . . .

Will shouted again — but not to his brother to hasten, or to turn and dodge, or to fight. The cry that burst from his lips now was a crazy one, in the circumstances, however potent it could be on other occasions. "A Douglas! A Douglas!" the terrible slogan that could strike fear in the stoutest Scottish heart — or Northern English, for that matter — rang out wildly, involuntarily, as he kicked furious heels into his own garron's sides, and positively flung beast and self forwards, to cut that tangent between brother and charging bull.

It made a strange, mad race. Three headlong courses converging — or not quite converging, for while Jamie rode for him and the bull charged for Jamie, he, Will, headed half-right, to distract the bull if he might, to shorten its course if he could. With a shrill scream his short, broad-bladed stabbing-sword was whipped from its sheath, to belabour the horse's rump with the flat — for the beast's reluctance was manifest.

It was a close thing. Jamie, who almost inevitably had tended to slant away half-right in his dash for safety, closer to the escarpment's edge, to gain every precious yard and moment, when he heard his brother's cry and saw him ride forward, swung his mount's head half-left again, towards him — whereat Will cursed explosively; for however natural a reaction, not only did it shorten the gap but it left less space in which Will himself could operate; and with a charging bull space was the prime requirement.

But there was no time to be wasted on direction to his fool brother. It was all a matter of seconds now, and split seconds. The pounding of six pairs of hooves merged into one drumming tattoo, accompanied by the unchancy snoring roar that the bull emitted as it thundered down. The brute did not change its direction, whether or not its red eye had perceived Will's advance; it continued to drive directly at Jamie.

Will had to make a lightning decision. They were all desperately close now. If the bull did not swing on him at the last moment, it would be best that he drove in *behind* it, try to crash his garron into its rear quarters, to throw it over, or at least deflect its course. But was there time? In the instants longer that this would take, might not the bull reach Jamie, broad sides-on, and those wicked horns do their fell work? Will chose that he must insert himself between, if he could.

The decision was scarcely taken before it was implemented.

Even so, the bull would probably just have won the race and struck the younger man, or his horse, before Will could drive in. But in the final few yards it seemed to recognise the menace of attack as more worthy of its fury than the fleeing original quarry, and with an extraordinary swift and nimble action for so massive a creature, threw up its hindquarters, pivoted round on its forelegs, and without loss of momentum, hurled itself instead at the advancing Will.

Knowing his bulls, that young man had been prepared for some such behaviour — but scarcely for the speed at which it was executed. He wrenched his garron's head round to the right, reining in savagely at the same time. The horse reared high, pawing the air, but could not sufficiently check its impetus. It neighed with fright. Only by superb horsemanship did the rider not only keep his seat but ensure that the animal kept turning away, even as its weaving forefeet came down to the heather again. By merest inches the lowered gleaming left horntip of the bull missed Will's thigh, and the garron's haunch, as the animals hurtled past each other.

Without letting up on his fierce rightwards drag, Will wrenched his mount completely round. But the creature was terrified, no fighting charger this, trained for the tourney and the lists, but a humble hill-pony bred to round up herdsmen's flocks. It did not respond as it might have done, it stumbled on an outcropping stone, it pecked and staggered and sidled. It did come round in the full half-circle required — but it took a few seconds longer about it than it should, a fatal second or two longer than did the white bull to complete the same reversal.

Will Douglas found himself in the most unenviable position of any contender in a mounted encounter, face to face with a head-on charge, with no immediate momentum on his own mount either to meet the onslaught or to avoid it in time. He knew, even before the garron reared up again in whinnying panic, that there was no hope, no possible escape. He might conceivably save himself; the horse he could not save. He kicked his feet free of the stirrups.

Rising on its hind legs, the garron was at its most vulnerable, its unprotected underparts completely exposed to those cruel horns. With a vicious tearing upthrust the bull bored in, ripping open the bulging belly like a punctured bladder, even as the

13

force of its charge overbalanced the horse and sent it reeling over backwards.

The young man part jumped and part was flung from the saddle. It was an unstable, collapsing stance from which to launch himself, but he was trained to the lists and knew how to fall, how to roll out of the way of trampling hooves, how to keep sword and sword-arm in action. He landed more heavily than he might have done, because of the backwards roll of the horse, but not sufficiently to injure himself. He took the heather on a tucked-in left shoulder, rolled over and over to that side, away from the animals' feet, holding his right arm and weapon out and free — and almost before he had stopped rolling had his knees drawn up under him to aid him to his feet again. Reeling dizzily, he stood up and staggered round, to face his fate.

Mercifully, the bull was temporarily preoccupied. Too clever to waste time on savaging the dying horse, it nevertheless could not avoid, in its rush, getting itself entangled with the garron's fallen body and flailing legs. Bellowing, it was forced to check, heading aside its disembowelled victim to free itself.

Will did not hesitate, however dizzy. He had an unexpected second or two, and had no doubts about how he should attempt to use them. The bull's tail-lashing rear was towards him. Running the two or three steps towards it, not away from it, he hurled himself in a great vaulting spring up on the brute's heaving back.

He knew that there would be swift reaction, but he was scarcely ready for the immediate and violent convulsion, as the animal arched its back steeply, thrust down its head and threw up its hindquarters. Only the shaggy mane saved him from being tossed forward right over those weaving horns, providing something for him to grasp with deep-clutching fingers, while he dug in thighs, knees and ankles with all the tenacity that was in him. Even so, he sprawled forward over the brute's neck, slewing sideways as it bucked and shook itself. He all but lost his grip on his sword, as he clutched at the mane, only just saving it. Face buried in the creature's coarse, strong-smelling hair, he clung.

As well, in being thrown forward, his legs had been forced higher, however unhelpful this was towards his ability to cling — for the bull was lashing its head sideways, now left, now right, in an attempt to hook him off with its great horns, and would almost certainly have been able to reach his legs otherwise. As he sought to straighten up, Will saw that he dare not lower his legs to a more secure and natural position.

He saw more than that. He saw that anything he might do he must do quickly, for the chances of maintaining this position on the see-sawing, heaving back, for more than a few moments, were negligible. Sprawling there, he took a grievous chance. Releasing the grip of his right-hand fingers, which clutched mane as well as sword-hilt, he tossed the sword up, to grab it again part-way down the blade — and almost bungling it, thought himself for an evil moment as good as carrion, with his horse and hound. But his fumbling clasp enclosed the steel again. The sword had been too long, before, to use effectively in his present contorted position. Now, twisting sideways, so that he could strike further back, he drove the stabbing blade down with all his power.

He felt the bull beneath him wince and quiver to the wound. But he felt also the jar of steel on bone, and groaned aloud. He had not struck far enough back. That would be the shoulder blade.

The brute's jerkings and lashings and twistings reached new heights of frenzy, and its assailant would probably have been off had he not now something else to cling to — the sword itself, half-buried behind the creature's shoulder. Hanging there like a limpet, he gasped deep breaths before seeking to make another attempt. He was aware of horsemen milling around him now, but aware also of how little anyone else could do in the situation — save only perhaps distract the bull's attention a little.

It may be that this was to some extent achieved, for Will thought that there was a momentary relaxation in the beast's furious efforts to dislodge him. Not wasting an instant of it, he sought to withdraw the sword — but found it more difficult than he had bargained for, in maintaining his awkward position. Cursing, he tugged. His right knee was cramping.

He got the sword out, and reaching further back still, but with a more forward-probing thrust, drove in the blade again, deep as he could.

The bull heaved, staggered a little, and coughed hugely.

That was the lung, he guessed — not the heart. Will sobbed another curse. Should he try somewhere else? The throat? In at

15

the ear? Or the eye? He could not risk that, on the tossing jerking head. There could be little of the required accuracy in such stabs. Anyway, he was too far back, and dare not edge forward.

He was tugging out the blade again, his fingers sticky with the blood that was flowing from his hand, lacerated by his own steel, when he perceived that there was a new motion in the brute beneath him. It was running now, bucking and tossing head and hindquarters as it ran, but running. And in a more or less straight line, not turning and pivoting in circles. Tripping too, and coughing and roaring, sore-wounded; but there were still great reserves of strength in that massive body.

The creature was heading uphill again, back towards the huddled cows and calves. Will Douglas did not require his brother Archie's shouted warning to inform him that the bull was not bolting, running away, seeking refuge in the herd. It was the tree that it sought. This was a forest bull, bred amongst trees. It would use them to rid itself of its enemy, to brush him off against the pine trunks.

In no doubts that if the animal once got him amongst the timber it would be the end of him, the young man recognised equally clearly that, if he threw himself off into the heather, the bull would almost certainly round swiftly upon him and he would be at the mercy of those daunting horns. The foresters were carrying bows and arrows — but could he rely on any of them, once he was off the brute's back, to put an arrow accurately into a vital spot of a running bull, before it could gore him? He knew the answer to that, also.

There was only one advantage left to him; with the beast heading determinedly for the trees, it had stopped lashing its head from side to side. He could risk sitting up, instead of half-crouching, half-lying — and so be in a better position to use his sword. He raised himself almost to the upright. In that improved posture he could wield his blade much more effectively. He drove it down vehemently into the body beneath him. Again and again he struck, seeking the heart.

When the bull started to lash its head again, and to circle in its tracks once more, triumph began to swell within Will Douglas. He had to raise his legs again — but he could feel that the animal was stricken. Its rush, as well as losing direction, had changed both momentum and character. Its motion was now a scrabbling unsteady run, constantly tripping in the heather. The great head, though swinging still, drooped now; heavily. One of the thrusts must have reached the brute's vitals.

The end came suddenly, without warning. One moment, the bull was still running and heaving, the next its forelegs had buckled under it. Over and down it crashed, its horns ploughing into the heather and peat, hindquarters still upright.

No amount of tenacious clutching could hold Will on that collapsing back. He was thrown violently forward, and hit the hillside more awkwardly than in his previous fall. But the tough, springy heather saved him. Shaken, the air knocked out of him, he sprawled there.

But only for a few seconds. He was already rising when eager hands reached down to help him up. Roughly he pushed them aside and staggered to his feet unaided, gasping for breath. He turned to stare. The bull lay a couple of yards from him, sides still heaving but mouth open and a scarlet stream of blood flowing from it. Even as he gazed the red-rimmed, angry eyes seemed to lose their heat. With a choke and a great shudder the brute died.

His three brothers were round Will, loud in exclamation; James anxious, apologetic, declaring that he was ashamed of himself, asking if Will was hurt; Archie, the twin, laughing, clapping him on the back, vowing that it was well done — but why in the name of all saints hadn't he hamstrung the creature before he jumped on its back, that time? And young Hugh, only fifteen, choking with mixed excitement and adoration, gabbling praise.

Will Douglas ignored the last two, but swung on the shame-faced Jamie. Dark eyes blazing, he threw down his dripping sword, and clenching the bleeding hand, swept his fist up in a fierce buffet towards his brother's cheek. Only an inch from the other's face he managed to check the blow—and the fist quivered there for moments on end, scattering red drops on James's flinching jaw. Then the obvious effort succeeded, and the hand dropped to the other's shoulder and half-shook, half-patted it. Then thrusting his brother aside, and ignoring the other two, Will strode off. He was like that, a young man of vehement impulse, not always effectively controlled.

Pausing for a moment beside the bull, he looked down at it,

biting his lip. He stooped to touch, almost to stroke, the great horned head, not in any naked triumph now but with a sort of compassion, regret. One of the foresters spoke, in respectful congratulation. Will answered nothing, stalking off across the heather. A hound, which came near to fawn on him, he kicked away savagely.

He made for where the sorry remains of the dead deer-hound lay in a shambles of blood and guts. Kneeling down, he raised the dog's shaggy grey head, putting his arms around the neck, regardless of the gory mess which fouled him.

"Luath! Luath, my hero!" he cried, rocking the carcase like a baby. "You only! You only of them all dared the onslaught. You only put courage to the test. I might have known it, old friend." Tears streamed down his darkly handsome, almost swarthy features, unchecked. He did not try to hide them. "Great Heart — we will hunt together some other day, some other where, you and I! . . ."

His voice broke. He laid the hound down gently, and rose to his feet, dashing the tears from his face now, and strode back towards the others. That also was Will Douglas.

Young Hugh brought him his abandoned sword, almost reverently; Jamie had torn a strip from his shirt to bind up the bleeding hand; and Archie made a somewhat offhand offering of his own garron. Will accepted all without comment, as his due, almost impatiently. He shouted to the chief herdsman.

"See to all this carrion, Wattie. I want the bull's horns. Bring Luath to me at the castle, treated honorably. These others will bring down the cows and calves." He mounted the garron a little stiffly, for he was bruised, and turned to his brothers. "Come, you."

Archie mounted on Hugh's beast — though making the younger boy ride pillion — and the four Douglas brothers on three horses rode away from the scene of the encounter, down the long slope of Fastheugh Hill, eastwards, the sun at their backs now.

"Will — do not be sore at me," James pleaded, spurring alongside. "I am sorry. I did not see yon edge. I was watching the cattle . . ."

"Your folly cost me Luath!"

"Aye. But that was scarce my fault. If you had left the bull to me . . ."

The elder youth's bark of laughter was mirthful rather than sour — but it brought a flush to the other's cheeks nevertheless. "You? Leave the bull to you, Jamie? Sakes — it would have eaten you! I would still have had to slay it — but one brother short!"

When James did not answer, Will turned to glance at him — and seeing the dark stain of humiliation on those comely, sensitive features, he reached out a swift hand to grasp and shake the other's arm.

'Man, man — take it not so hard!" he exclaimed. "You are something slow with the eye. And the sword. Likewise the spur! That is all, Jamie. With the pen, now — or the tongue, i' faith — you have us all beat!"

"Say it!" his brother cried. "Say that you had to save my foolish life. That I would be dead now, like Luath and the garron, but for what you did. Say that you must ever watch over men, like a bairn!"

"Have I ever said that? . . ."

"I will say it for you, Jamie — if you must hear it!" Archie declared from behind them, laughing. "Not a bairn, perhaps — but a clerk. I swear that you should have been a priest. You would do better, 'fore God, in a cloister, than on the hill. And with a missal than with the sword! Aye — and it is not too late. You could be an abbot, yet!"

James turned to look back. Twins are commonly notable for their sympathy, close in feelings as in looks. Not so this pair. They had a superficial similarity in appearance; both were dark — all the Douglases were that — and well built, though Archie was the taller and broader, even if Jamie the more delicately good-looking. But in the natures they were poles apart. Archie was bold, brash, forthright, seeing all in black-and-white, where the other was quiet, retiring, hesitant, introspective. That neither knew which was first-born was another barrier between them — for in that family such primacy could mean much. Not that the meditative James would have wished for it; but others were concerned, and to the out-going, vigorous Archie it was a matter of continual nagging moment.

"What is wrong with being clerkly? With learning? With books?" James asked. "In the end, is it not men skilled in these that rule this realm? All realms? Who make the laws? Is not the good Bishop Kennedy the greatest man in Scotland? . . ."

"Save us! You, a Douglas, say that? Kennedy, that whey-faced priest! Only because he has king's blood in him rides he so high. He does not rule, besides. Nor do law and parchments, his or others. The sword rules, here and always. Ask Crichton, that murderous hound! Ask the Chancellor what rules in Scotland. Ask Livingstone, who holds the King by his sword . . ."

"For the moment these seem to triumph. But the pen will triumph over the sword, in the end. Always it does. Holy Church will still prevail when Crichton and Livingstone are as dead as our cousins . . ."

"Holy Church! Think you prayers and mouthings will bring down these butchers? You are a fool, Jamie. Only a sharper sword, more stoutly and shrewdly wielded, will cleanse Scotland of the like. Pray God it will be a Douglas sword!"

"There! You pray despite yourself! . . ."

"Aye — a Douglas sword!" young Hugh joined in. "You can have your missals and prayers and books, Jamie. See what good they will do! When Douglas rides we will have no need of such, I say!"

"*When* Douglas rides — heaven pity us!" Archie said, with something between a snort and a groan. "When! In that day, when we can raise our heads again and look other men in the eyes, it will not be learning and law that wins the day, that is certain!"

"In that day, nevertheless, Douglas may be glad to have the support and prayers of Holy Church," James insisted. "Call me fool if you will . . ."

"I do! And worse, man. It is such talk and such feeble flinching that has brought up to this pass. Such spineless, craven sloth that had made the name of Douglas a spitting and a byword! You are little better than, than . . ."

"I say so, too!" Hugh yelped excitedly.

"Quiet Enough! All of you." Will turned in his saddle. "That is no way to speak — and you know it. Enough, I say. Archie — you have a tongue like a bell-clapper! Mute it — or I will mute it for you! Hughie — there are words which should never be spoken. Our father is . . . our father. And none speak so of him in my presence. Mind it. Mind it well. Jamie — all agree that you are a fool! The more so that you must provoke your still more foolish brothers! A God's name, be quiet — all of you!"

Frequently the eldest brother had to speak thus. And when he did, in that tone of voice, it was seldom indeed that the others, even Archie, disobeyed. He was, after all, Master of Douglas.

From the skirts of Fastheugh Hill they crossed over on to the flanks of Newark Hill. They were out of the heather now, and down amongst the open glades of birch and oak and hazel, where the russet of dead bracken was just beginning to show a rash vernal green, with April only a day or two off. At the burnside below the hill they turned along the track there, and Will, in the lead, kicked his beast into a heavy canter. There was no more opportunity for unsuitable talk for a while.

The brothers had emerged into the broad open cattle-dotted haughlands of Yarrow, and could see the tall grey keep of Newark Castle, chief stronghold and messuage of all the vast Ettrick Forest, rising on its mound above the river half a mile ahead, when they saw something else. Three horsemen were riding by the waterside towards them, from the castle's direction, not on any shaggy garrons these but handsomely mounted on tall horses — which looked weary by their pace however. The men wore morion helmets, and steel breastplates, with red hearts painted on them, front and rear, over the blue-and-white livery of Douglas.

"That is Pate Pringle, the steward at Abercorn, I think," Will said. "What brings him to the Forest? And in some haste, by the looks of him."

"No good, you may swear!" Archie declared sourly. "From that airt blow only snell winds."

None disagreed with him, on this occasion. For years the brothers had more or less run wild, here at Ettrick in the Middle March of the Border. Seldom indeed was there any communication between them and their parents, at Court or at the Earl's favourite house of Abercorn in Lothian — and when there was, it was not usually to their liking. For too long they had been neglected and left to their own vigorous devices, to take kindly to any fiats of far-away authority.

As the two groups drew near, it could be seen that the three newcomers were indeed travel-stained and weary, their horses sweat-streaked and flecked with spume. One was a big, burly, grizzled man of middle years, the other two ordinary men-at-arms.

Warily the Douglas brothers eyed them. Pate Pringle, the big man, drew up a dozen yards off, and dismounted stiffly, heavily, to come forward on foot, while his companions sat their mounts impassive. The steward paced to Will's side, took off his morion, bobbed his head, and awkwardly got down on one thick knee before the youth.

"My lord," he said hoarsely.

Will, unused to such respectful greeting, nodded uneasily. "Aye, Pate. Well? . . ."

The man cleared his throat. "My master, the Lord Earl your father, is dead," he jerked, flat-voiced.

"Dead! He . . . our father . . . is dead?" Will stared at the speaker, and then at his brothers.

"Aye, my lord. He died last night. At Abercorn. We have not been in our beds. We rode before dawn, nor stopped on the way." He rose to his full height again, and stepping closer, reached out to take Will's right hand between his own two. Holding it thus, to the youth's embarrassment, he bowed grey cropped head over it, and made a gesture at kissing it. "I am your lordship's man, now," he said.

"But . . . how did he die? What does it mean? Was he . . . slain?"

"Aye — was this more murder? Treachery?" Archie demanded. "Was it Crichton and Livingstone again?"

"Not so. My good lord died in his bed. He has been ailing, mind. This long while . . ."

"Nobody told us so."

The man looked down. "Maybe no'. But . . . my lord was sair burdened. For long. Yokit by the flesh. He hasna been the man he used to be, these many years . . ."

That at least the boys knew sufficiently well. James the Gross, formerly first Earl of Avondale, for the past three years 7th Earl of Douglas, had been for almost as long as any of his sons could remember little more than a mountain of flesh, a man so hugely fat, heavy and lethargic as scarcely to merit the description of man — and fantastically, ludicrously to represent the greatest house in all Scotland. No one in the kingdom was ignorant of that. But that he should be ill enough to die of his grossness had never so much as occurred to any of them.

No single tear came to any of the boys' eyes. Their father had meant nothing to any of them save a distant authority in

22

whose name they were occasionally inconvenienced — that, and a burning and constant humiliation, the bearer of the proud name at which all the land pointed the finger of scorn, the man who could have split the kingdom in two, yet who had been too lazy, too inert, or perhaps too involved, to attempt to avenge the shameful murder of his two grand-nephews, the 6th Earl and his brother, by the Chancellor Crichton and the King's guardian, Livingstone — by which deed, in fact, he himself became Douglas. How could they, or any, weep for James the Gross, second son of the mighty Archibald the Grim, 3rd Earl, descendant of the warrior race that had upheld the Crown in their hands so often and been custodians of the hero-king Bruce's heart that now emblazoned their coat-of-arms and glowed on their men-at-arms' breastplates?

"Our mother? . . ." Will asked.

"Your Lady Mother sent me here. She bids you all to attend her at Douglas Castle tomorrow. By noonday. She brings my lord's body there. For burial."

"Tomorrow? So soon?"

"Aye. She leaves Abercorn this day, early as may be. She thinks to sleep at Carnwath tonight. Winning to Douglas tomorrow by noon, it may be. She would have you there, my lord — all of you — to greet your Sire's corse."

"Is this not something hasty, man?"

The other shrugged his shoulders. "It is my lady's command."

"It were better that we had gone to her at Abercorn. To escort her . . . and the body. To Douglas. Than that she should do this alone. A woman.

"She . . . the Countess will have sufficient escort, my lord. Her commands are that you attend her at Douglas."

Will considered the man levelly for seconds, before nodding his head. "Very well. This means that we must ride tonight."

"That is so." The steward sounded as though he did not relish the prospect — but greater men than he were careful not to question orders from the Countess of Douglas. He remounted his tired horse.

They rode on to Newark, the brothers quiet, subdued for so essentially lively a band. Without any deep and probing contemplation of the situation, all were aware that a chapter had abruptly ended in their lives, a fairly carefree and comparatively independent chapter. Whatever the future held for them, it would not be the same, they recognised; possibly life would never be the same again.

At the castle they were greeted anxiously, in kindly if misplaced sympathy, by old Abbot George Douglas, the ineffectual and distinctly woolly-headed far-out relative who had once been abbot of the Douglas abbey of Holywood, in Nithsdale, and now was in theory the youths' tutor and governor at Newark — but in fact a mere cipher in the hands of his masterful charges, with Jamie the only satisfactory and approximately obedient one.

"My sorrow, Sir Will — these are sore tidings," he quavered, wringing his hands. "An ill thing. Very grievous. Your poor father, my good cousin. But . . . God's will be done. My heart is wae for you laddies . . ."

"Aye. To be sure, Master George. But we will manage well enough, I have no doubt," Will said, briskly. "There is much to be done. It seems that we must ride for Douglas tonight. Johnnie and our sisters also. They must make themselves ready. And quickly. If we leave in an hour or so, riding by Megget and Tweedsmuir, we should win as far as Sim Tweedie's house of Oliver, where we may bed. Then cross the high hills to the west, over Clydesmuir into Douglasdale, in the morning light."

"It is a long, rough road, lad. No' for lassies, in such haste . . ."

"They will do very well. They are Douglas queans, not bower-ladies! Margaret will see to them. Where is she? Tell her to come to me."

"Aye, Sir William." Abbot George, no less than the brothers, knew better than to argue with Will Douglas when he used such voice. His insistence on calling the young man Sir William was something of a joke in the family — although it was, in fact, an accurate appellation, even though few others ever used it. Will, along with sundry other eldest sons of great nobles, had been knighted by King James, first of that name, of puissant memory, at the tender age of five, on the occasion of the baptism of the monarch's twin sons. That was nearly fourteen years before, and much blood had flowed in unhappy Scotland since that extravagant day, the King's amongst it.

"I am here, Will," a girl's voice said, behind and above him.

24

The Great Hall of Newark Castle contained a minstrels'-gal-lery-cum-oratory skied halfway up one stone wall towards its high vaulted ceiling, reached by a narrow mural stair and pro-vided with its own window, aumbries, garderobe and little fire-place — a favourite haunt of the girls. She who called down from there now was more than just a girl, a striking and well-made young woman of high colouring, raven hair and great dark eyes, bearing a marked resemblance to Will himself. They were good friends, these two, only eleven months separating their ages, with the twins a further year behind.

"Good, Meg," Will called, raising a hand. "You have heard? All?"

"Yes. All. It is ... God's will. We have said prayers. For ... for his soul."

"M'mm. Aye. That was right. I had not thought of it, I fear."

"No. We could do no less. Do you come up now, also? Here? To pray? ...'

Archie snorted eloquently.

"I say we should," James declared.

"It would be meet. Suitable. Dutiful," Abbot George said. "Pleasing in God's eyes."

"No." Will shook his head. "Time enough for that. At Douglas. There will be prayers in plenty, I warrant! If we are to reach there by noonday tomorrow we have more to do than pray today! It is fifty miles, across the roof of the land. Mostly lacking any road ..."

"Must we go so soon?" That was Beatrix, the second daugh-ter, aged fifteen but ever a rebel. She leaned over the gallery parapet, less good-looking as yet than Margaret, but the pale colouring denoted no pale nature and the strong features and flashing eyes might well presage a fierce and dramatic beauty, one day, similar to their mother's own. "Why such haste?" she called down.

"It is our mother's command, Pate Pringle says. To be there by noonday. To meet ... him. As he comes to Douglas for burial."

"He will wait, well enough. My lord was good at waiting!" Beatrix cried.

"Lassie! Lassie!" Their tutor raised a protesting hand. "Here's no way to speak..."

"When Douglas comes back to Douglas, we should be there to meet him," Will cut through the old man's quaverings. "It is seemly. And our mother has commanded it."

"But *you* are Douglas now, Will! Are you not? It is you who commands, is it not? You are the Earl of Douglas. *You* are the Black Douglas, I say!"

The sudden stillness which the girl's high-pitched words produced, in that lofty stone hall, was notable. It was as though all held their breaths for a moment or two, at the sound of that potent name. All eyes turned on Will, as though suddenly seeing him in a different light. For centuries, until these last years, those had been the most effective, dreaded, terrible three words in all Scotland — The Black Douglas. Undoubtedly the full implications of their father's death had not really reached any of them until that moment; certainly the thing had not truly formed itself in Will's own mind. He was the Earl of Douglas.

He stared up at his sister for long seconds, mind plunging deep into the meaning of what she had said. Then, as almost with a physical effort, he roused himself, throwing up his head in typical and distinctive fashion.

"We ride for Douglas within the hour, nevertheless," he said. "Be ready, all of you. Margaret — where is Johnnie? He is not up there?'

"He is at the stables, I think Will . . ."

"Hughie — get him. See that you are dressed your best, all of you. It is necessary. I will attend to the horses. Master George — food and drink for us all. But for Pate and these others first. Now go . . .'

*   *   *

Riding down the shadowy glen of the Talla Water towards the infant Tweed, in the strange half-light of the gloaming, the long cavalcade was strung out for hundreds of yards — for the cattle and sheep track it followed was insufficiently wide to ride more than two abreast, and not always that. Besides the nine Douglases — five brothers and four sisters — there were the Abbot George; the Newark captain, Dod Scott; the Chief Forester of Ettrick, Wattie's Tam; Pate Pringle and the two Abercorn men; and perhaps half a dozen other servants. Archie, as usual, rode well ahead, claiming to be on the watch

26

for robbers and outlaws—but though outlaws there were in plenty amongst these empty, forested uplands, none would in fact dare to attack any company wearing the colours of Douglas.

Will rode beside Margaret, Beatrix rode alone, then James came with the younger sisters, Janet and Elizabeth, while the two younger boys, Hugh and John, kept their distance from such female company — but equally eschewed the vicinity of their tutor. They had already covered over twenty rough miles, from Newark. Five more should see them at Oliver Castle, on upper Tweed, where Simon Tweedie, a Douglas supporter, would give them shelter. It had been considering how Big Sim would look when he saw so many descending upon him, to bait and bed, and wondering if he would have to remind the laird that he was his father's vassal, which brought up Will's mind, with a jerk, to the recognition that Tweedie was no longer his father's vassal, but his own. From now on such recognitions must become a constant feature of his life. As the night settled over the great heather hills and the velvet gloom deepened in the valley, Will Douglas, lost in a brown study, made his sister but indifferent company.

To be the Earl of Douglas! What did it mean? What did it actually make of him? To perceive that his whole life would be utterly altered was the least of it. His mind reeled at the prospect, at the vastness and complexity of the implications. Admittedly the earldom was in poor shape, neglected, shorn of some proportion of its power and greatness and glory, by political manoeuvres, the spleen and envy of the Crown and of other nobles, as well as by James the Gross's years of inertia. The mighty Lordship of Galloway, with the Earldom of Wigtown, had been divorced from it on their cousins' murder, and was now held by a mere girl, sister of the murdered Earl; as was the Lordship of Bothwell and much of Clydesdale. Annandale had been forfeited to the Crown at the same time, by a piece of Privy Council chicanery. But despite these, and lesser losses, the main Douglas earldom was still an impressive heritage, the greatest in Scotland. It was not one earldom, indeed, but two, for Will was now Earl of Avondale as well as of Douglas. Moreover, he was feudal Lord of Balveny, in Moray, and baron of Boharm, Avoch, Brackly, Edderdour, Kilmalaman, Petty, Strathderne and part of Duffus, in that same province; of Oberdour and Rattray, in Aberdeenshire; of Ardmannoch and the old earldom of Ormond in Ross; of Abercorn and Inveravon and Strathbrock in Lothian; of Petinain and Strathavon in Lanarkshire; of Stewarton in Ayrshire — and many another which he scarcely knew of. All this in addition to the vast entailed properties of Douglas itself, of Douglasdale and Liddesdale and most of the West March of the Border, of this Ettrick Forest and the adjacent Forest of Selkirk. Moreover he was titular Duke of Touraine and Comte de Longueville, in France — although the French king had seized the opportunity to resume the valuable lands of these for himself, of recent years. Douglas held the superiority over literally hundreds of lairdships, such as this Tweedie of Oliver's, scattered over all the kingdom. And as well as all these territorial possessions and titles, there were certain offices of state which were more or less hereditary in the family — although Will knew little of these. But the Earl of Douglas, he did know, was always Warden of the West March — and often the Middle also — even though he frequently appointed a Deputy to carry out the duties.

Will could not really contemplate or comprehend the magnitude of all this. He had not been brought up as the heir to it should have been. His father had only been Earl of Douglas for three years, previously having had no expectation of succeeding to the major title, a second son with brother, nephew and two grand-nephews to carry on the main line. But the death in battle, in France, of his brother, the 4th Earl, in 1424; of his nephew the 5th Earl, Lieutenant-General of the Kingdom, unexpectedly of natural causes, in 1439; and the judicial murder of the sixteen-year-old 6th Earl and his brother the following year — these had thrust the representation of the almost princely house upon a man who was already too old, bloated and obese to bestir himself. Too late then to take in hand the family abandoned to run wild in the Ettrick Forest — just as it was too late to make the effort to avenge the name of Douglas. James, the 7th Earl, had done nothing, nothing at all, for three years. And now William, 8th Earl, at eighteen years of age, was face to face with overwhelming destiny, all unprepared.

But Will Douglas was a young man of spirit, vigour and initiative, even though these might be marred at times by impulsiveness and violent temper. There was more to contemplate than unwieldy possessions and overwhelming responsibility. There was opportunity. Power to be wielded, men to

28

be led, deeds to be done. Above all, there was the name of Douglas to be redeemed, and vengeance to be taken. Vengance . . .

The youth's dark good looks were sombre as he splashed his mount across Tweed's dark shallows — and only belatedly remembered to turn back to ensure his sisters' safe crossing.

CHAPTER TWO

THE church of St. Bride, at Douglas, rebuilt and enlarged by Archibald the Grim — like his founding of Holywood Abbey, no doubt, as counter-balance for some of his other activities — was large and stately; but it was packed so full of people that they were even sitting on the recumbent effigies of sundry previous notables of the house of Douglas. Such perchers were perhaps fortunate, however cold and knobbly the seating, for everybody else had to stand — save the Countess, who sat in the great chair usually reserved for the Bishop, today brought down to the chancel steps for her use. The Bishop himself did not require it meantime, for he was conducting the funeral obsequies — a circumstance which surprised Will Douglas, as it did many another; for although St. Bride's was a prebend of Glasgow Cathedral, and Douglas town probably the most important place in the diocese, this haughty and ambitious prelate, former Chancellor of the realm and the late King's secretary, was not the man who could be summoned at short notice to officiate at services, however illustrious the summoner. Presumably Bishop Cameron's presence there that day was one more tribute to the Countess Beatrix's position and influence at Court — for he was a courtier and political churchman, was John Cameron, rather than any kind of pastor.

Moreover, the Bishop had not come alone. He had brought what amounted to a court of his own, officials of the diocese bearing the renowned relics, purchased at enormous cost it was said, from all over Christendom, the pride of Glasgow and the envy of the metropolitan see of St. Andrews itself — the image of our Saviour, in solid gold; the silver crucifix encrusted in rubies and diamonds and inserted with a fragment of the True Cross of Calvary; the silver casket containing some hairs of the

Blessed Virgin; the phial of crystal, holding a small quantity of the Virgin's milk; another phial containing saffron liquid said to have leaked out of the tomb of Glasgow's own Kentigern, of St. Mungo; two lined bags with mixed bones of Mungo and his mother, St. Thenew; a square silver coffer containing the scourges of Mungo and St. Thomas of Canterbury; and hides displaying parts of sundry other saints. Never had the like been seen assembled together outside Glasgow Cathedral — and only John Cameron could have occasioned it. These, with the magnificent jewelled copes and vestments of the Bishop and his subordinate dignitaries, added to the forest of pastoral staffs, croziers, maces and the like, all gold and precious stones, created such a blaze of scintillating brilliance and colour in the light of hundreds of candles, as to be almost overwhelming; while the smoke of the said candles, and that of the dozen and more swinging censers, added to the exhalations of the tight-packed and excited concourse, produced an atmosphere which was almost suffocating. James the Gross had never managed to produce in life one tithe of all the resplendence which now surrounded his final exodus — however overshadowed in consequence was the vast and rather oddly-shaped lead container which enclosed his substantial remains.

There was a great deal of coughing in the church, what with the clouds of incense, the candle smoke, the varied smells and the general lack of air, so that the Bishop's rich intonings, and the choir of singing boys' responses, were apt to be drowned at times; but there was at least no sniffing and weeping. Not a damp eye glistened in all the candlelight — except perhaps for Abbot George's, which tended to run anyway. If any expected the widow to be prostrated, they were unaware of the quality of Beatrix St. Clair. Certainly Will did not look for such emotion, nor any of her children.

The woman who sat in the Bishop's chair was of a great and striking beauty — despite the nine children who stood near by, and the youngest, Henry, elsewhere. Still under forty, she had kept an excellent figure; she had suckled none of her offspring herself. Unlike her dark Douglas progeny, she was very fair, thanks perhaps to the Norse in her ancestry, with great grey eyes, a noble brow, proud chiselled features and a firm chin. She sat now, richly but fairly simply dressed, her fine eyes slightly averted from the leaden coffin just in front of her at the chancel steps, with the still but pregnant calm for which she was famous. She had moved hardly so much as a muscle in all the forty minutes of the ceremonial, since she had sat down, however much of a stir there was around her. Not everyone, by any means, looks the part which birth calls on them to play. The Countess Beatrix did so. She appeared every inch the daughter of high St. Clair, of the Earls and Princes of Orkney, and great-granddaughter of a king. Eyeing her, at her right hand, her eldest son knew afresh the accustomed sensations she ever inspired in him; the strange mixture of pride, respect and something that was almost repellent.

On the Countess's left stood the splendid figure of her brother, the 3rd Earl of Orkney and Lord of Roslin, a man whom his nephews were inclined to look upon as the epitome of dignity, and little else. William St. Clair was a spare, dry, early-ageing man, only a year or two older than his sister but looking nearer a score, upright and stiff as a stick in carriage, unsmiling, unbending, apparently devoid of emotion. In the disrespectful opinion of the young Douglases, this Earl was even more meet for a funeral than their father, their attitude being that he had been more or less dead for years.

There were numerous other illustrious, dry-eyed and magnificently garbed mourners. Amongst them all the new Earl of Douglas and his brothers and sisters stood out like daws amongst peacocks, so plain not to say shabby were their clothes, their best as these were. A great many of the burghers and tenants present were clad much better than they were. Nevertheless there was a quality, a dark, lean, almost arrogant style to them which spoke louder than any mere apparel.

Bishop Cameron at last reached the end of his sonorous Latinities, and after a noticeable pause in which he stared round with every appearance of contempt upon the entire congregation, raised a beringed hand to point almost accusingly, first at Will Douglas and then at the huge leaden coffin. A flick of the hand sideways then set off the choristers in a slow chant.

Will had been primed for his part, however unwillingly. He stepped forward, jerked a bow beside the coffin, and reached out to pick up the small silver casket which sat on the top of the plain leader lid. With this in his hand he stalked on, up towards the altar, with a stride more apt for the heather than the

31

chancel. He halted before the gorgeously-robed prelate, and held out the casket to him. It was not very large. Compared with the rest of him, James the Gross's heart was evidently of quite modest proportions.

The Bishop took the thing in his own time, and with considerable ceremonial turned and paced slowly to the altar, and there, after raising it high for a few moments, placed it between two of the candlesticks. There were other similar caskets sitting there already, mostly much more elaborately fine, flanking that of the Good Sir James. It had been the Douglas custom, for many generations now, to extract the hearts from the corpses of their leading figures and to preserve them separately — presumably in token of the said Good Sir James's fulfilment of his friend Robert the Bruce's dying wish, when he had taken the hero-king's heart to the Crusade which its owner had never got round to conducting in his busy lifetime.

Will went back to his place, self-consciously set-faced. His mother had changed neither expression nor direction of glance. Margaret and Jamie gave him sympathetic looks, and Archie grimaced.

The Bishop now made a new series of signs. From the side of the church, husky men-at-arms, with staves, came clanking out, to the number of about a dozen, not a few with somewhat sheepish grins. They pushed through the throng unceremoniously, to the coffin. There, after shuffling and jostling each other, and looking doubtful, at a further peremptory signal from the altar, they set to, with hands and staves, to push and lever the enormously heavy affair over the stone flags and down the chancel steps. Watching the straining and puffing, Will wondered how it could have been transported all the forty miles from Abercorn.

The next stage of the interment was slow, awkward, but much more interesting than anything which had preceded it. In fact there was a general crowding forward of the packed congregation, with much thrusting and commotion, manoeuvring for position to see better; also excitement, exclamation, even argument. The choristers in consequence chanted the louder.

As well as the sheer weight of the remains, body and lead, there was a further difficulty. The chiefs of Douglas were never buried; they were deposited in an underground crypt of St. Bride's here, directly beneath the high altar, in leaden rows, while their magnificent carved stone effigies and monuments multiplied above, to decrease the size of the chancel. Which was all meet and fitting. Only, in redesigning and enlarging the church fifty years before, Archibald the Grim, or his masons, had rather underestimated the problem of getting heavy leaden coffins safely down below. The fairly narrow and steep stone stairway, which opened from the side aisle, was adequate for people proceeding on their feet, or even for coffins carried on men's shoulders; but for thirty stone of corpse and more than that of lead, it was a different matter — especially as this particular container was almost as broad as it was long.

By dint of much heaving and leverage — with no little advice from nearby mourners — the straining men-at-arms got the thing as far as the stairhead. But there it stuck. By no means could they lift James the Gross up on to their shoulders. Even with volunteers pushing it on all sides it was impossible to get enough shoulders actually under the thing to support it; anyway, even if that had been feasible, there was insufficient width to the stairway to accommodate the coffin and men at the sides as well.

Considerable argument took place. Bishop Cameron, at the altar, raised his eyes heavenwards, managing to look patient, detached and deploring all at the same time. The Countess Beatrix altered neither her position nor her expression. Lord Orkney sniffed. Will Douglas went to see what should be done.

Pate Pringle was already taking charge. "He'll no' carry," he announced. "No' doon thae steps. We'll need to push him, just."

Will nodded. "Yes. But can they hold it on the way down? The weight? . . ."

"Och, aye. Some at the head, some at the feet. Fine, that." The steward sent three or four of the men round in front, a few steps down, to hold and steer from below; the others to push from above — but to be ready to pull back strongly also, if necessary.

With no one at the sides, it proved difficult to overcome the massive inertia and friction. But after mighty efforts, the coffin inched forwards. When it reached the lip of the first step, it stuck once more, lead being only an indifferent sliding agent. Much restricted in their movements, those above, aided by all who could get a hand on the thing, pushed heroically, while those below tugged as best they could. Gradually the coffin tilted forwards, and began to slide.

"Hold you! Hold — for guidsakes!" Pringle cried. "Hold — or he'll be awa'!"

But there was not really much on the leaden lid and sides for restraining hands to grip on. The coffin continued to move onwards and downwards. Indeed it began to gather speed.

The men below were not slow to perceive their danger. Shouting, and with one accord, they exchanged pushing upwards in favour of headlong flight downwards. Leaping the steps three of four at a time, they went hurtling down into the crypt, none hindmost.

No amount of clawing and clutching could halt or even slow the deceased now. Gaining momentum inevitably, impressively, the remains sped off, free of all restraint, downstairs, with a strange thudding rumble and high whimpering sound, mixed. There were perhaps six seconds of this, and then a crunching, very solid and final crash. James the Gross, for better or for worse, had finally joined his ancestors — and with an alacrity unequalled in a score of years.

There was a stunned silence in the church — for even the singing boys had faltered in their chanting as the drama unfolded. John Cameron, ever an opportunist, coughed, raised two fingers and delivered a sketchy benediction. He turned, paced to the nearby vestry door, and passed through, out of sight, a man outraged.

Pandemonium broke out in the prebendary church of St. Bride's.

"My God — did you ever see the like of that!" Archie Douglas shouted happily.

The Countess Beatrix stirred at last. She rose from her chair calmly, laid a hand on her brother's arm, and turned to her eldest son. "Come, Will," she said quietly, and proceeded to walk, with queenly and unhurried tread, to the side door.

Belatedly her two trumpeters, flanking the doorway, brought up their instruments and blew a slightly ragged fanfare.

*   *   *

Douglas Castle was vast, massive, menacing in its lovely valley, an unpleasant place of dungeons and donjons, bartisans

34

and machicolations, triple moats and multiple baileys; thirty-foot high curtain-walls, topped with timber hoardings and gallerys for defence, enclosed a huge and ugly square keep, ninety feet to its parapet, lit only by tiny cross-shaped arrow-slits. Compared with Newark, or indeed any of her other Douglas castles, it was a frowning prison. All the young Douglases hated it. In fact, none of its lords had ever found it to their taste, all preferring to live elsewhere. There was no other castle quite like it in all Scotland — which was not strange, for it was the English who had built it. During Bruce's Wars of Independence the enemy had taken Douglas Castle while the Good Sir James was away supporting his king elsewhere. Hearing of the shameful happening, the Douglas had made a swift and temporary return, besieged and recaptured his own original fair castle, and put the English garrison to the sword, every man. Thereafter he gathered together all its furnishings, tapestries and woodwork piling them in its Great Hall; on top he heaped all the food in its larders, all the carcases of the cattle in its parks, all the barrels of wine and spirits from its cellars, and crowned all with the bodies of the slain English. Then he set all alight, and marched away to rejoin King Robert, assured that no invaders should again defile Douglas walls. In due course Edward of England gave orders that the present fortress be built up on the burned-out ruins of the old castle — but it still was known as the Douglas Larder nevertheless, and it found no favour in the eyes of its lords. One hundred and thirty years had not mellowed it.

In the vast and gloomy stone Hall of this barracks — the Lesser or Private Hall, though it was — Will Douglas was caught by the Lord Bishop of Glasgow, as he went to answer the summons, by a servitor, to his mother's private room above. John Cameron, divested of his magnificent canonicals, was now dressed in the height of secular fashion, with nothing to indicate his clerical calling save the mitred arms of the See of Glasgow, outlined in gold filigree and tinctured with jewels, which adorned the short velvet cloak above his crimson satin doublet.

"My lord," he called, with a nice blend of authority, condescension and even a hint of flattering respect, as he moved forward from the great table where the principal funeral guests were refreshing themselves. "A word in your ear, I pray."

Will hesitated. He did not like the prelate, had in fact been avoiding him. "My mother calls for me, my lord Bishop," he said.

"Your lady mother will spare me one minute of your precious time, my son, I am sure." Cameron took his arm, and led him some way aside. Will could hardly break loose.

"In God's good providence, you have been raised to notable and high estate," the Bishop said, lowering his voice. "I trust that you have given much thought to it, my son? And, h'mm, prayer."

"I have had little time to do so, sir. As yet."

"No? Then a word, perhaps, from an older well-wisher, with some little experience in matters of rule and state — and of course, your father-in-God — may not come amiss."

"M'mm." Will did not commit himself.

The other sank his mellifluous voice still further, confidentially. "As you are no doubt aware, my young lord, our realm of Scotland is in a sorry state. In the past, the house of great Douglas has moved mightily in the guidance of this realm. In his earlier days your excellent sire did great things likewise. Great things — but then he was not Douglas. But of later years he has been but a sick man, with God's hand, er, heavy upon him. He has been unable to play the part to which he was called by name and nature. To Scotland's loss, to be sure. Now — there is a new Earl of Douglas."

The young man waited, silent.

"It is important, my son, that if you elect to play the part for which you, too, were born — and I pray God it may be so — it is important at this early stage that you choose the right and proper course, with great care. You have little experience, I think, of the ways of courts and governance, and of the scheming and grasping men who seek to wield the power. To my sorrow, I have — overmuch. Happily, such experience, dear-bought as it has been, is at your young lordship's service and command."

"Er . . . thank you. I shall not forget."

"I counsel that you do not, my son. For you will be beset by rogues — nothing is more certain. There are over-many such in Scotland today — not a few of them in positions of power and consequence. It is ever the way when a child is king. And the worst of all, 'fore God, is he who sits in the seat that once was

36

mine — the Chancellor of this realm! That foul spawn of Satan, the upstart William Crichton!" The Bishop's voice trembled. "Of all the festering sores on the body of this land! . . ."

"I have reason to know something of the quality of Sir William Crichton, my lord Bishop," Will interrupted.

"Eh? . . . You? What can you know of the evil of the man, the depths of his infamy, boy?"

"He, and Sir Alexander Livingstone, treacherously slew my cousins."

"M'mm. Yes. To be sure. But that is a mere drop in the ocean of his iniquity. He . . ."

"He raised his hand against Douglas!" Will said, between his teeth. "A treacherous hand. That is enough for me!"

"Ha! Yes, yes. That is so, of course. You are entirely right, my son." The Bishop looked at his companion with a new and speculative eye. "Such sentiments do you much credit, my lord. Aye — Livingstone! Livingstone too is a dastard. Almost as great a rogue. That he, an unlettered and ruffianly mountebank, no more, should hold the young King and his mother in his hands, and so hold the kingdom also, is beyond all bearing. It must *not* be borne much longer, boy! Two up-jumped scullions ruling this roost! . . ."

"And none to say them nay?"

"Aye — there's the rub. There are plenty who would say them nay — but lack the power to say it loud enough! A strong hand is needed in this realm again. A strong, sure and true hand . . ."

"I fear that mine is scarce sure enough, my lord. As yet!" Will said, with a flicker of a smile.

"H'rr'mm. No. Not so. That is not . . . what I intended. My meaning . . . otherwise." For so assured a man, Cameron looked a little discountenanced. "I meant that *I* might supply that hand. In all humility, of course. But . . . it is an experienced hand. I have been Secretary of State, Privy Seal, Chancellor. I would have most of Holy Church behind me. With God's help — and that of Douglas to be sure — I could teach these rogues a lesson, and do the King notable service."

Will did not answer.

"Your opportunity is great my lord," the Bishop added.

"Is it? Or yours, sir?"

The other coughed. "Would you question the need, my son? With Scotland in the hands of scoundrels and self-seekers? You would not withhold your hand, Douglas's mighty hand, in the realm's need?"

"I think not. But you must give me longer to discover that my hand is indeed mighty. I will think on what you have said. I lack experience, you declared. You said that I must choose the right and proper course, with great care. I shall seek to do so . . . with your good advice in my mind, sir. But meantime, I must to my mother . . ."

Breaking away, Will strode across the Hall to the private stair in the thickness of the walling. He had the door to it almost shut when it was pulled open behind him. Another richly dressed gentleman confronted him, much younger and more dandified than the Bishop, but with a hard thin-lipped face. It was Sir James Hamilton of Cadzow, head of that family.

"Sakes, Will — you are in a great haste!" he declared, with a kind of joviality, panting a little because of his own hurrying from the table. "Not so fast, lad. What was that old fox Cameron at? Little good, I warrant!"

"'He was keeping me from my mother's summons, sir. As are you now, I fear. You must excuse me . . ."

"Tush, boy — not so fast. I want a word with you. See — in here." He stepped within the stairway's narrow space, and pulled the door to behind him. "There are weighty issues to consider, see you."

"I said my mother calls me, sir. Already I have been held. Later, it may be. My mother is . . ."

"But a woman, lad! What I have to say is man's talk. And you are Douglas now, are you not? To be tied to no apron strings!"

"Aye sir — not to be tied to *any* strings, I think! But my mother is still my mother, and a woman of some consequence, as you know . . ."

"She will wait. Women are good at waiting. I' faith, they were made for it! Even women of consequence. I should know, should I not, having one to wife? Hear me, before you run to her."

Will frowned, but hesitated. Hamilton was a man of some renown in the land, chief of a widespread family, lord of large lands, and moreover grandson of Livingstone who held the young King. He had married Euphemia, the widow of Archibald, 5th Earl of Douglas, mother of the murdered brothers — who still called herself Duchess of Touraine, her late husband's French title. Hamilton was not a man to offend lightly.

"What should I hear, sir?" Will asked.

"Much. I was your father's friend. That is why I am here — unlike some! I would be your friend also. So long as you follow as wise policies as he."

"Wise? ... Did my father have any policies, sir? I never heard of them."

"Ha! There can be policy in not doing, as well as in doing, boy. James Douglas could have done great harm and scathe. And did not. Many urged him to. That Bishop, for one. He would have had him rebel against the King's government. But he was wise, and did not."

"The King's government, since the King is but a boy of thirteen years, is Sir Alexander Livingstone, the King's keeper! Is it not? Your own mother's father, sir. He and Sir William Crichton, the Chancellor."

Hamilton pursed thin lips. "That puts it over-simply. But how can you know it all, who have been no nearer to Court than Ettrick Forest! My grandsire is the King's Guardian, yes. But it is the Privy Council which rules, in the young King's name."

"And Sir William Crichton rules the Privy Council, as Chancellor! Even in Ettrick Forest, sir, we know that much!"

"Crichton is strong, yes. But Crichton can be brought low. And must be."

Surprised, Will stared at the man. "*You* say that? Livingstone and Crichton are a pair. Friends. They work together. In all things. Together they betrayed and slew my cousins. And you ... you wed their mother!"

The other narrowed pale eyes, then shrugged. "I wed their mother, yes. So have all the more reason to see justice done. That slaying was Crichton's work, planned by him alone ..."

"Livingstone consented sufficiently to attend the banquet to which they were invited. With the young King. Was there when

39

the bull's head was placed on the table before them. Watched my cousins seized, there at table. Took part in the mockery of a trial. Voted against them. Watched them taken out to the courtyard and beheaded, there and then. Two boys younger than myself — and one of them Earl of Douglas!"

"Yes, yes. It was an ill business. My grandsire saw it done. As did many another. But what could he do? The young Douglases were there at Crichton's invitation. It was in his Castle of Edinburgh, mind — not Livingstone's Stirling. Crichton's men were everywhere. My grandsire had the King's Grace to think of. He dared not oppose Crichton then and there — or the King would have been seized, taken from him, and this realm plunged into still sorer straits. That was not the time when he could counter Crichton. But ... the time is perhaps come now!"

Will waited.

"Throughout the land there is a stirring against Crichton and his black deeds. As never before. Men will rise, now. But they require a leader."

The other almost smiled again. "I think that I have heard this before! This leader, sir? Is it to be yourself? Your grandsire will never lead against his friend?"

"He is not his friend. Livingstone has never loved Crichton. They have on occasion worked together, but uneasily. He would bring Crichton low but he is getting to be an old man, now. He will support me, rather than lead himself. And that means the King. The Crown's favour and authority."

"Then you are like to win, are you not? Especially if you seek the Bishop of Glasgow's aid. For he would have Crichton down likewise. Then you would have Holy Church behind you, also."

"That snake! Cameron would but be Chancellor again — from which the saints preserve us! Moreover, he hates my grandsire. He will never work with Livingstone — or Livingstone with him. Besides it is warriors we need to bring down Crichton — fighting men, not clerks! And, Will — Douglas can raise fighting men, by the thousand!"

"Aye. I wondered when we would come to that, Sir James!"

"See, lad — you likely do not rightly know your own power. If you but give the order, you can field more lances and swords

40

than any other man in Scotland. It may be that John of the Isles can field more men, more bare-shanked savages — but in horsed and sworded men-at-arms no two other lords in the land can look at Douglas. Once let it be known that Douglas is entering the lists again, that Douglas is behind myself and Livingstone — then Crichton's days are numbered. His friends and toadies will desert him. He is no great noble, no chief with large numbers of his own people at his back. He is just a cunning upstart laird that the late King raised too high. He depends on the levies of his friends, for men. Denied the royal authority, and his friends leaving him, Chancellor though he is, he cannot fight, he cannot stand. Raise the standard of Douglas, my good lord — and see it happen. Hamilton was a little breathless with enthusiasm, and his long speech.

"And see whom in Crichton's place, sir? As Chancellor?"

"Why, myself, lad. Who else? My grandsire is too old. His sons have scarce the wits. I shall be Chancellor. And you — why, you could have what office you desire. You are young — but I could guide you. Hamilton and Douglas! Aye, Hamilton and Douglas together could do great things, Will. Hamilton and Douglas could rule Scotland — and rule it surely. I was your father's friend — I would be yours. And our friendship will serve the realm."

The younger man spoke slowly. "My father's friendship did not turn over to you, or to any man, the power of Douglas!"

Hamilton's jaw tightened perceptibly, and for moments he seemed to hold himself in. Then he smiled, laughed, and nudging Will in man-to-man fashion, actually turned to pat the young man's flat, taut belly.

"There's why, lad!" he cried. "Why *your* friendship and support should do greater things than ever your father's did. Why he let the power of Douglas languish. Did they tell you? In digging for his heart, they took four stones of tallow out of James the Gross! Four stones! You are something different, are you not?" Sir James raized quizzical eyebrows. "I wonder what they did with it?"

Will swallowed, moistening his lips. He stared, for the moment wordless.

"Something of a lesson, is it not? . . .' the other was going on, when the younger man interrupted him.

"Sir — you will excuse me. I shall not forget . . . what you have said." He turned abruptly on his heel, and ran off up the stairs.

Hamilton called after him, but he did not pause nor answer.

* * *

The Countess Beatrix sat before the fire in the upper chamber that had been the English governor's room, with Will's Aunt Elizabeth, the Countess of Orkney, and other of her ladies. Will, bursting in, halted at sight of them all, and jerked a bow or two slightly agitated. None of his sisters was included in this company, he noted.

His mother rose, and actually made a graceful half-curtsy. "My lord," she said gravely. Perforce the others had to rise and do likewise.

Confused, Will cleared his throat. He did not realise how blackly he frowned. "You sent for me?" he said.

"I asked the favour of your presence, my lord," his mother corrected, gently.

If her son eyed the Countess with something like suspicion, it is hardly to be wondered at. In all the years of his childhood and youth, Beatrix Douglas had paid but little attention to him, or to any of her children. She lived in a different world, the world of the Court and palace and power; no doubt rightly, she conceived these as no suitable worlds for the bringing up of children. So her offspring had been banished, first to the Clydesdale estates of her husband, and later, on his succeeding to the earldom of Douglas, to Newark of Ettrick, where they had grown up uncontaminated by Court life indeed, but also unguided by any more decided hand than that of the Anxious Abbot George. For the Countess had not seen fit to share their banishment. It was hardly devotion and concern for her obese and lethargic husband, probably, which dictated her choice. Her father had been James the First's principal friend and tutor, the 2nd Earl of Orkney, and she had grown up with the King's sisters as an intimate. She was all St. Clair, was the Lady Beatrix, in sheer overweening pride of line the most vaunting in all Scotland. Small wonder, then, that Will Douglas found this sudden respectful deference unmanning.

Perceiving his confusion, the Countess gestured towards a door which led to a small tower chamber. "There are certain

42

matters to discuss and decide," she said. "Shall we speak priv-ily, in there?"

Nodding, he strode for the door, and held it open for his mother.

The circular apartment was small and bare, devoid of furnishings. But there were stone benches flanking the deep window recess, and on one of these the Countess went to sit. Will remained on his feet.

His mother's still, calm beauty by no means put the young man at his ease. She eyed him levelly but closely, almost as though seeing him properly for the first time, sizing him up. Not being able to return the scrutiny, in the circumstances, with any comfort, he gazed out of the half-glazed, half-shuttered window. He could not remember when last they had been alone together. He cleared his throat but did not speak.

The woman did not seem to find the silence uncomfortable, at least. When at length she spoke, it was reflectively. "You are a man now, Will. A tall, goodly man. And by the dark looks of you, all Douglas."

"Would you expect otherwise? Desire otherwise?" he blurted. "I am near nineteen. And Douglas by name!"

"No. It is not strange. I but . . . had not realised what you had become, Will. I am glad of it." She gave the faintest smile. "You are very like your father."

He started, to turn and look at her. "What . . . do you mean?"

"You wonder? Long ago, when I married James Douglas of Balveny, he was a young man, not unlike you. Dark, slim, full of life." She did not sigh, or speak with any emotion, much less sentiment; just simply, factually, her voice as fine as the rest of her. "Do you doubt it? He was not James the Gross in those days, Twenty years ago, he was all a man. And I was a bride of fifteen."

Will blinked. "I did not know. Always to me he has been old. Fat. Half-asleep. Not that I saw him much. Or ever knew him."

"No. Perhaps it was better that way. For your father was a sick man. Sick in many ways. He is, I think better gone." She stirred a little on her stone seat. "How think you he got ten bairns out of me, in eight years? Before I was twenty-five."

Embarrassed the son looked away, wordless.

43

His mother went on, unhurriedly. "But I am glad, Will, to see you as you are. I might have wished that there should be something of St. Clair, of Orkney, about you — but it is probably best that you are all Douglas. Since you *are* Douglas now. Have you considered what this means?"

He almost snorted. "If I had not, I would have learned something of it, today! Coming to you, I have been learning, fast. From two who would teach me. That is why I was held back. Yon Bishop, and Sir James Hamilton — they made it clear what it meant that I was Earl of Douglas. Severally. What it meant, for them!"

"Aye. They both have their ambitions. They sought your help?"

"They sought armed men! Douglas support. Towards power. For themselves. Each would be Chancellor, in place of Crichton."

The Countess nodded. "This was bound to be. Many others will come to you likewise, Will. That, no doubt, is why my lord of Glasgow came here. Not out of love for me or mine. As for Sir James, this I had foreseen — for he was ever at your father, on the same errand. He has been swifter than I thought, that is all." She shrugged slightly. "What did you tell them, Will?"

"I told them that I would remember what they had said. As I will. Remember well! That was all."

"Good. That is best, at this stage. But I hope that you did not offend them. Either of them? Both are men it would be foolish to affront. Men who could be of use to you, men who could help you to where you must go."

"Go? Where must I go? Where such as these can aid me?"

"You must go, Will, to where Douglas should ever be. To the lead in this realm of Scotland. To be the King's right hand. And, if it be that aught should remove the young King — more than that!"

Will stared at her. "What . . . what are you saying?" he demanded. "What do you mean?"

"I mean that you, by birth and blood, are destined for great things, Will. Your father was less so. He never thought to be the Black Douglas. It came to him by chance, and he failed to rise to the challenge. You, I hope, will not so fail. For you, whatever your looks, have the blood of Orkney in you also. You are Douglas, and have the blood that has upheld the kings of this

44

realm; but you have the blood of the Norse Kings also. You must not fail."

It was his mother's quiet and authoritative but far from emphatic manner, as much as her words, which held the young man. Her statements as to his blood was not news to him, of course; old Abbot George had not failed to inform his charges from whom they were descended. The Douglases had upheld the Crown of Scotland by more than their swords. The late King's brother, the murdered Duke of Rothesay, had been married to Mary Douglas, Will's aunt, sister of James the Gross. His father's brother, Achibald Tyneman, 4th Earl, had married the Princess Margaret, daughter of Robert the Third. His other uncle, the illegitimate Sir William of Nithsdale oddly enough had wed Egidia, a daughter of Robert the Third — which princess's own daughter, another Egidia, marrying Orkney, was again his own mother's mother, a strange tangle which he had never quite unravelled. The throne of Scotland, therefore, was more than somewhat involved with the house of Douglas. Moreover, King Haakon of Norway had publicly recognised the St. Clair Earls of Orkney as scions of the Scandinavian blood-royal, through the older Norse princes and Jarls of Orkney. If blood meant anything, his was rich enough. It seemed that blood meant a lot to his mother, at least.

"What, then? What would you have me do?" he demanded, a little hoarsely. "Everyone, it seems, would have me busy! Douglas should do this, do that! This concern for what I do is something sudden!"

The Countess nodded. If she sensed any bitterness in her son's voice, she did not react to it. "Sudden, yes. As many things in life are sudden. And in death. Yesterday, what you did, Will, was much your own concern. Today it is all Scotland's."

"So it would seem. And who do *you* wish Douglas to draw sword for?"

"The sword is not my concern," she said. "There are many, over many, to advise you on that. I only say, be in no haste to draw it — so that when you do it shall be a mighty sword indeed. Make Douglas great again first, I say. Then the sword may make Douglas greater. There is much that you can do, must do Will, before you draw steel."

"*Must* do . . ."

45

"Must," she repeated, but equably, almost pensively. "For Douglas to be weak, inactive, laggard, is to this realm's hurt. While the lion sleeps, jackals snap and snarl. The lion has slept too long, and the jackals have drunk deep of the life's-blood of Scotland. They must be sent whimpering back to their dens. But first, the lion must stretch himself, brace his muscles, summon his strength . . ."

"What would you have me do, in this? Talk plain, a God's sake! What *can* I do? As I am?"

"You can do much, Will. You can wed Margaret of Galloway, for a start."

"Wed! . . ." Involuntarily he stepped back against the walling as though his mother had struck him.

"Aye, wed. It is time, and past. You are nearly nineteen. And there is only one bride for Douglas. Your cousin Margaret. Wed her, and you unite again all the great lands riven from your earldom three years ago by Crichton. After the murder. All Galloway. The earldom of Wigtown. The Lordship of Bothwell. Most of Clydesdale that you do not already hold!"

"But . . . but . . . I have no desire to wed her! Her, or any other. I have not so much as seen her. When I take a wife, I shall choose her differently from this, I swear!"

"Choose? What choice is there? You are not some bonnet laird, Will, to pick on any wench that takes your eye. Not to *wed*. You are Douglas. Next to the King, you bear the greatest name in the land. You must wed accordingly. Margaret Douglas of Galloway is the greatest heiress in Scotland. And she holds what should have been yours. Moreover, she is very fair."

The young man gazed at his mother without seeing her. He knew of the Fair Maid of Galloway, of course, reputed to be the most beautiful creature in all the realm. Who did not? He knew that she queened it over the large and populous province of Galloway, the south-west corner of Scotland, with a dozen castles in her white hands and ten score of rich baronies. Not that the thought had ever concerned him. She was the young sister of two murdered youths, daughter of Archibald, 2nd Duke of Touraine and 5th Earl of Douglas, and on her brothers' execution, this vast slice of the Douglas patrimony had been slashed off and vested in the twelve-year-old girl — not out of any sympathy with her situation, but that the mighty earldom itself should be thus drastically weakened. That had been Crichton's doing also, and Crown and Privy Council had played his game. James the Gross had done nothing.

"She is little more than a child," Will objected. "Fourteen."

"Almost fifteen," the Countess agreed gently. "And at fifteen, a girl can be woman enough. I was but fifteen when your father wed me — and I served him passing well."

"That may be so. But *I* do not seek a wife . . ."

"Will — see it this way. If *you* do not marry her, another man most assuredly will. And gain Galloway, Douglas land, with her. Would you relish that? Many will have their eyes on this rich prize. Wed this girl and you double the power and wealth of Douglas without a blow. Allow another to wed her, and you raise up a rod for your own back. Raise another to power almost equal with your own."

He shook his head. "Is she not to be considered? Herself? This Margaret Douglas? She may have her own choice for husband!"

"She is a Douglas. She will not refuse the Black Douglas himself. Besides, her mother, the Duchess, is now married to Hamilton. And Hamilton desires your support, it seems."

"You would have me begging that one's aid, to gain a wife I do not want?"

"Douglas does not beg. Douglas lets it be known — and wise men perceive and act accordingly. Sir James will be glad to assist you, at no cost to himself."

"The girl — she is too close related to me for marriage, is she not? In cousinship. Within the Church's forbidden degree?" Margaret of Galloway was in fact the granddaughter of James the Gross's brother.

"Holy Church makes such decrees — and can unmake them. Never fear. Bishop Cameron also seeks your support? Make him earn it, then. He will petition the Pope for you, and due remission will be made."

"I will not be beholden to that arrogant prelate . . ."

"No, no Will — there is no need. You are too direct. Lacking in subtlety. Let it be known that you seek the aid of his rival — of Bishop Kennedy of St. Andrews, the Primate. Then my lord of Glasgow will come beseeching you to let him approach the Holy Father on your behalf. You need promise nothing. You must learn how these things are managed by great lords. Such as Douglas need be beholden to none."

This time he eyed her directly. "I think, madam, that you might have left it less late in teaching me such lessons! I have been your son for some time now! And heir to Douglas for three years. I could have been learning these things before this."

The Countess inclined her fair head. "That is true, Will — to my sorrow. You should have been prepared for the position you would hold. Many times I spoke to your father. Pleaded with him. But he would do nothing, and have nothing done. In this as in other matters, I think . . . I think that he feared you. Saw you as something of a threat. A finger, pointing. A reproach to his own sloth. He would not permit that I do anything. In this, as in much else, his commands were that he be not troubled. It was all part of his sickness. Can you understand, Will?"

"I understand that I was begotten by a slug, rather than a man!" he cried.

"Not so." She was quietly patient. "He who begot you was no slug. Then. Was it a slug who took Berwick town from the English, in 1045, and burned it to the ground? Was it a slug who fought and slew Sir David Fleming, one of the most notable knights in Scotland? Was it a slug who could hold the offices of Warden of the Marches and Justicier-General of Scotland? My lord was all man, once. His son must not forget it. As I do not."

Will did not speak.

"There is more that can be done to restore Douglas to its rightful place, Will, than wedding Margaret of Galloway," his mother went on, after a slight pause. "Much more. Without recourse to the sword. There are your brothers and sisters. They must play their part. There is another great heiress in Scotland. Elizabeth Dunbar of Moray, Countess in her own right. One of your brothers should marry her. Gain with her the earldom of Moray. It is a rich heritage. Elizabeth is only young — twelve, I think. But girls have married younger than that. And my brother, Orkney, is one of her guardians."

Her son drew a deep breath, but did not venture on words.

"One of the twins. Which should it be? You know them best, Will. Which shall be Earl of Moray?"

He shook his head, in wonder, exasperation and a kind of

helplessness. "This is crazy-mad!" he exclaimed. "What are we? Cattle, to be traded? Bulls for heifers!"

Levelly she considered him. "You are the representatives of the greatest house in Scotland — that is what you are. You have run free too long, I think. Now it is time to act the man, not the child. Jamie and Archie also. Margaret and Beatrix likewise — they must play their part."

"You would marry them off, too?"

"It is their destiny. And by the looks of them, they are ready for it. Wisely wed they can contribute greatly to the power and glory of Douglas. For Margaret, I have no doubts. The great Lordship of Dalkeith is one of the most potent branches of Douglas. Unhappilly its present lord is little more than an idiot, fatuous. But he has a brother, Harry Douglas of Borgue, unmarried and of sound mind. The lordship placed in his hands, and married to Margaret, he could serve you well — for Dalkeith disposes of much of Lothian, as well as the Morton lands flanking Galloway."

"You have thought of it all, I see. Nothing overlooked! Save *our* wishes in the matter! Our desires!"

"I have had long to think, Will. Years. I knew this day would come. And someone must needs do the thinking. As to wishes and desires — what do you, any of you, know of what is best, fitting, possible? In this new situation. In this you are all still but bairns. Lacking all experience, you must be guided by me. You will perhaps thank me, one day. Desires, at your age, Will, can change with the moon. Only this desire would I vouch for — that you would, that you *must*, desire revenge for the hurt done to Douglas by Crichton and Livingstone. Your cousins' blood cries out for vengeance. Is that not your desire?"

"Aye," he said. "That, at least."

"Then, believe me — here is how you may best achieve it." The Countess actually reached out to lay hand on her son's wrist, a rare gesture indeed. "You have not told me — which of the twins had best be Earl of Moray?"

He took a pace or two into the little room, and back. "Why ask *me* who shall be saddled with this child of twelve, for wife! It is your notion, and they are your sons. Choose you!"

She refused to be roused. "There is more to the choice than just the marriage, Will," she told him. "You know their natures better than do I — and much could hang on this. Have you thought of it? Until you have a son of your own, one of them is heir to Douglas. You have to consider this. If you are taken — which God forbid — who would you have to succeed you as Earl of Douglas? This choice, I say, should be yours, not mine."

That brought him to a halt in his pacing. "Surely that falls to him who was first born? They are twins — but one must have been born before the other?"

"No doubt. But who knows? I was in a swoon. As babes they were very alike. The chamber-woman confused them. None knows which came first. It mattered little, till this. Now it is important. You should make the choice. One shall be Master of Douglas, the other Earl of Moray."

"Saints aid me — here is a hard thing! Archie has the spirit. He would ever take the lead, but not always in the right direction! Jamie is gentle, but true. He would make a better priest than an earl, I think."

"Archie, then, would be best on the battlefield. But battles are fought but rarely. Who would be best in the council-chamber?"

"There, Jamie. Aye, Jamie, to be sure. I would trust Jamie's head, to Archie's, any day."

"Very well. Then the choice is made, is it not? Let Archie play Earl of Moray and husband to Elizabeth Dunbar. Jamie will be Master of Douglas, your lieutenant, and meantime your heir. It is, I think, the choice I would have made myself — for lacking your stronger hand, Douglas would be safer with him than with headstrong Archie. So be it. I shall declare that Jamie was the first-born twin. None can assert otherwise."

"Aye. So all is settled! To your satisfaction."

His mother ignored the sarcasm. "Almost all, Will. I must think of a husband for Beatrix. One I had in mind — but he is not strong enough, I think. She is going to need a strong hand, that girl, if I mistake not. An older man. A widower, belike. But there is time for that."

"No doubt your wits will not fail you in such small matter! Now — have I your permission to retire?"

"Permission? You are Earl of Douglas. The only permission you need ever seek is the King's. Go, if you will." She sighed just a little. "Do you hate me, Will?"

"Eh . . .? Hate? Save us — no! Why should I hate you? I . . . I scarce know you!"

She looked away quickly. It was the woman's turn to be silent.

"Shall I send your ladies to you?"

"Thank you — no. Where . . . where are you going, Will?"

"Why — home. Where else?"

"Home," she repeated, and there was an unusual hesitation in her normally calmly melodious voice. "Where is . . . home?"

"Ettrick, of course. Newark, in the Forest. Where else?"

"The Earl of Douglas cannot hide himself away in Ettrick Forest. Amongst the deer and outlawed men. Your father hid you there, yes. But now . . ."

"Where would you have me go, then?"

"I had hoped, back to Abercorn with me. To be near the Court."

"No. Thank you — but no. Not yet. You must give me time. I am not ready for that. I must consider. My head is too full, now. I must have time."

The Countess rose. "You are your own master now. Mine also, indeed. You will do as you will. But remember always — the proudest name in all this land is in your keeping. You cannot avoid it, escape it, even if you would. You have greater opportunity than any other in Scotland — even the young King. He is a deal less free than are you. If you will take it."

He nodded shortly. "I shall not forget it, never fear." He crossed to the door, and opened it for his mother. The chatter of women's voices beyond died away.

"I thank you, my lord," Beatrix St. Clair said clearly, as she passed him. "All shall be as you say."

Will strode through the outer room without a glance at its highly interested occupants. He made for a narrow servants' stairway in the thickness of the keep walling which would take him down to the courtyard without having to pass through the Hall beneath. He wanted no more interviews or advice that day.

CHAPTER THREE

WILL DOUGLAS rode through the blithe and sparkling April morning whistling to rival the larks which soared and shouted all around him, while he gazed about him eagerly, over the wide-spreading rolling countryside, appreciating, approving all that he saw. It was a scene which he had never actually looked on before, much as he had heard of it, intimately as he knew it at second hand. He picked out the various green knolls and grassy mounds, cattle-dotted and peaceful now, that rose beyond the wide valley of the winding burn, as though recognising them all. There, on that long brae, with the red roofs and grey walls of St. Ninians village showing behind — that would be Brock's Brae, and on its summit would lie the Bore Stone where the standard of Scotland had flown so proudly that day, one hundred and twenty-nine years before. The round lump west of the village would be Cockshot Hill, where his great-grandsire, the Good Sir James, had besought Bruce to let him ride to his friend Randolph's aid — and then stopped short when he saw Randolph prevailing, lest he should rob him of any of the glory. The forerunner, that small victory, that was to herald the mighty victory of the next day. There, near the burn itself, was a mill, the Park Mill it would be, opposite which the Scots centre had based itself that great June day. So that, to its left, in the morass, still reeds and bog, the left wing, commanded by Walter the Steward and his great-grandsire, must have waited. Waited to good effect. There stood while wave after wave of English chivalry beat through the quagmire to reach them, and went down into it until it was more blood than mud. Stood unyielding through all the livelong day, while the battle raged and surged this way and that on either flank. And then, at even, with fifty thousand English dead, Gloucester slain and Edward himself so dazed with fatigue that he had to have his bridle taken and be led off the field — then Douglas had moved at last. Moved forward now, and chased the proud English king no less than forty grim miles, killing all the way, towards Dunbar and the Border. That was the day of days, when Scotland's freedom was forged anew — the Scotland which the jackals now rent and snarled over.

As Will rode over the Bannockburn braes, the whistling died on him. Emotions surged within. Pride, anger, doubts, confusion — and determination. Determination most of all. Those days, the days which culminated in Bannockburn, might not be wholly gone yet. The blood was still the same, surely? Ran in the veins of men. Not only in his own veins but in those of all the descendants of the men who fought so gloriously that day? Could that blood not be roused again, to cherish and uphold what Bannockburn had so dearly bought? To purge the corrupt body of the realm? To unite the nation again, and drive out the jackals? Could Douglas play the part that Douglas once had played? . . .

The young man stared on, beyond the foothill braes and knowes, northwards over the land that sank in great green waves and folds to the level plain of Forth, out of which abruptly rose the majestic tall, fortress-crowned rock of Sterling, Scotland's stern but lovely heart, challenge and guardian in one, proudly fronting the fertile carselands, the green bastions of the Ochils, the wide blue estuary of the Firth of Forth, and all the serried purple infinity of the Highland mountains. Fronting all — and held by one of the jackals. Narrow-eyed, aware, Will Douglas rode on to Stirling.

It was three weeks since his father's funeral. He had had opportunity to think, to talk with his brothers and with Margaret — since Beatrix alone had decided to go back with her mother to Abercorn and the high life of fashion, elegance and the Court, the other young Douglases choosing to return that same evening of the funeral the long, hilly road to Ettrick, with Will. There had been time, and occasion, for great talking, argument, declamation, discussion, and out of it all some decisions — not all of these spoken decisions. It was as an outcome of the undeclared sort that Will now made his way alone, well-mounted, well-armed but clad more like any poor Border lairdling than a great lord, on the road to Stirling.

He was well aware that what he did was open to criticism; dangerous, according to Jamie, downright foolish according to Archie, lacking in dignity according to Abbot George. Even Margaret had advised against it. But Will could be stubborn, and, the decision made, nothing would budge him. He would ride alone, unattended, to the King — but not unawares or unprepared. After all, he knew what had happened to his cousins

This was the way he must commence his warfare. For warfare it must be; of that he had no doubts.

From St. Ninians village he rode down through ever more populous countryside to the low land flanking the great river, out of which towered the mighty citadel and the grey narrow-streeted town which climbed the skirts of the castle rock. He was interested in all he saw — and there was much to see, for at St. Ninians he had joined the road that roughly followed the Forth, linking the two seats of government in Scotland, the King's — and, more important, his guardian's — seat of Stirling; and the Chancellor's and Secretariat's seat of Edinburgh. There was inevitably traffic between these. Indeed, soon after leaving the village Will suffered, not altogether humbly, the experience of being shouted at and hustled out of the way by a hard-riding tight-knit group of men-at-arms in steel and red and white livery, who swept all lesser folk clear of the road for a richly clad, fine-looking man who rode behind, attended by two esquires and a further following troop of men. Slightly flushed, and cursing indiscreetly, Will was passed without a glance. That, it seemed, was the way for lords to travel the King's highway.

A mile nearer Stirling, it was his turn to seek passage. He was not really hurrying, as the others had been, but even so he found himself held up behind a pacing procession that quite filled the roadway — which in this low-lying riverside area was something of a narrow causeway built across undrained water-meadows where cattle stood knee deep. There were more men-at-arms here, but on foot, strolling along unhurriedly, halberds over their shoulders, chatting and laughing together. Ahead of them, Will could see two white jennets pacing side by side, with a canopied litter slung between them, and led by a couple of servitors in white surcoats over chain mail. There were further armed men in front. Will was assuming that this must be some great lady's entourage, when he perceived that, at the front of the procession, was carried a tall cross on the end of a stave, gleaming golden in the April sunshine. Enquiries from the rearmost file of the escort as to which prelate this might be, elicited stares, facetious remarks and scorn, that anyone should be clodhopper enough not to know that this was Master Adam, sub-Abbot and Steward of the Abbey. Will's question as to which abbey, brought forth considerable hilarity before he gathered that Cambuskenneth Abbey lay just ahead, in an almost islanded bend of the river, below the castle rock. Since by no means would the churchmen move aside to let him past — and he was damned if he was going to plouter through the mire for them — Will had time to ponder over the fact that if even sub-abbots took the road in such style, then he himself must make a notably unimpressive figure. It occurred to him, as he paced his horse, with only moderate patience, behind the clerical company, that it would have been informative to have seen how the fast-riding lordly troop had got past; possibly Holy Church would concede where pressure was sufficient.

In the busy narrow streets of the town itself, however, the lone traveller was content enough to follow on behind the sub-Abbot's party, for however crowded the causeway, the folk all pressed respectfully aside — as well they might considering the way the escort laid about them with their halberd staves. When, at the foot of the steep ascent to the castle, the abbey party headed straight on towards Cambuskenneth and the bridge, Will found it altogether a different matter to make his individual way upwards through the idle, gossiping throng, none of whom showed any inclination to stand aside for him. All Stirling seemed to be congregated in the streets this sunny forenoon, apparently with little to do. It was as well that it was a typically breezy spring day, or the smells would have turned a stomach reared in the clean air of Ettrick Forest.

At last Will, having worked his way up and up, stood on the high platform of open space before the great gatehouse of the outer bailey of Stirling Castle, under the frowning regard of battlements, bartisans, curtain-walls, gunloops and towers, from the topmost of which flew the Royal Standard of Scotland's Lion Rampant. This was the most powerful fortress in the land, and even to Will, used to castellations, it looked daunting, not so much a castle as a bristling walled city up there crowning the summit of the mighty rock. But if the architectural impression and siting was of fierce authority, at the moment the human atmosphere was otherwise. The open forecourt was full of stir, but an easy stir. Men-at-arms strolled and chatted and laughed. Groups of horses were tethered here and there, pulling at bundles of hay. Booths were set up, like any fair, and townsfolk came and went, while children played and dogs barked. Though the great gatehouse tower looked form-idable to a degree, the portcullis was up, the gates wide, and the drawbridge down over the broad ditch. All looked entirely peaceable. After noting how men passed in and out through the gatehouse pend, apparently without question, Will rode on and through. None sought his business.

He found himself in another wide space between the outer and inner baileys, evidently used as a tilting-yard, for there was quite a thick carpeting of crumbled peat strewn on the ground, no doubt very necessary for the hooves of charging horses on the naked out-cropping rock. There were lean-to buildings around this area, stables, barracks for men-at-arms, kitchens storerooms and the like. Beyond was another deep ditch, backed by a barrier of wall, in which a second large gatehouse opened, surmounted by a parapet and walk, a sort of open de-fensive gallery. Just now, however, it was being used as a grand-stand. Many people thronged it, above the gateway and the second lowered drawbridge, looking down. Many others crowded round something that was going on below.

Will moved foward to the edge of the crowd. Being still mounted, he could see over the heads. A baiting was in pro-gress. A composite baiting. A bull and a bear were involved, as well as sundry dogs. The bull was not like one of the wild forest creatures Will knew, but a big, black, heavy brute, com-paratively short of hide and of horn — horns that were red-tipped now, and hide stained with sweat and in some places hanging off in bloody strips. The bear was big but very lean, its shaggy coat patchy and seeming to hang too loosely. There was a great gaping gash on the animal's massive shoulder. Both bull and bear were shackled with iron and chains, the former on all four legs, so that it could not move freely, the latter only on the hind legs.

There was a considerable noise, men shouting and urging on the protagonists, dogs yelping. The combatants, however, paid as little attention to the one as to the other — though there was one dead dog lying almost flattened near by. The bear, growl-ing deeply with a steady rumbling, was slowly circling the bull, on its hind legs, great forepaws, with huge white claws, ex-tended and weaving. The bull, head down, snorting and grunt-ing, turned and backed and sidled awkwardly because of the shackles, breathing hate. The dogs nipped in here and there

56

snarling, to bite at one or other of the principals — but mainly at the bull's hindquarters, that being the least dangerous target.

Obviously the fight had been going on for some time, for both bull and bear were showing signs of weariness and loss of blood — and the watchers were clearly less enthralled than they might have been. Every now and again, however, the lumbering bear would lash out, with almost unbelievable swiftness, with one or other of those great claw-armed paws, sometimes scoring a hit which left deep parallel rents on the sweating black hide. Less frequently the bull would make a violent, vicious twisting lunge with a short straight horn — none of which actually touched the bear while Will watched, though one sideways sweep did catch and eviscerate an already limping mongrel, to the glee of the audience.

Personally, Will Douglas did not think much of the entertainment. After fighting wild bulls on their own ground, this shackled contest was as dull as it was unsavoury. The bear was clearly half-starved, and the bull in bad condition, and too hampered to put up a good fight. As for the dogs, they were a foolish intrusion. After only a minute or so of it, he rode on over the drawbridge and the gatehouse arch.

Three guards in half-armour were here. They, in fact, were all standing on the stone porters' bench that flanked the archway, the better to see over the heads of the crowd round the baiting. As Will rode up, however, they turned to challenge him.

"Where away, fellow?" one demanded.

"In yonder," Will nodded. "To speak with the King's Grace."

"Ha! You say so!" The spokesman eyed him up and down. "To speak wi' the King's Grace, quo' he!"

"That is what I said, yes."

"On what business? Eh, my cock? None pass here without good cause."

"My cause is good enough. And my business is with King James. And the keeper of his castle. Not with you, sirrah. I am Douglas. Let me past."

"Guidsakes! Hear him! Business wi' the King! Him! . . ."

"No horses past this gate," a second man jerked, older than the first, as Will began to heel his mount forward. The speaker reached for his halberd, alean against the wall.

57

"Very well." Will dismounted, a little stiffly from long riding. "Take my beast."

"Hold his nag for him, now!" the first guard cried. "Hark to the cockerel!'"

Will held himself in. "I will wait, then. Go tell you whoever is your master. Tell him that Douglas seeks audience with His Grace. I will wait — but not overlong!"

"You will wait, will you! A pox — you will not! Off wi' you — if you ken what's good for you! D'ye think the likes o' you can come chapping at Sir Alexander Livingstone's door? . . ."

"The King's door, is it not?"

"Ha! Watch your tongue, laddie! If you would keep it in your dolt's head. Be off, now — before you go feet foremost!" The guard took a threatening step towards him.

Will Douglas's dark eyes flashed in a fashion that his brothers knew well, and respected mightily. He leaned forward just a little, swaying on the toes of his long riding-boots. "Fool!" he said softly. "I told you. I am Douglas. I will see the King. See to it, or . . . Stop you!" That was a sibilant but menacing whisper. "One hand on me, and you will rue it! . . ."

The man's hand dropped to his sword-hilt. He came on.

Will acted with explosive speed. Instead of reaching for his own sword, which hung at his hip from a shoulder baldric, he jumped further forward, to grab the guard with both hands, pinioning his arms, and in the same movement, jerking him nearer, hard against himself. As he did so, his left leg kicked round behind the other's knees. With a fierce burst of strength, in the opposite direction, he thrust the other way again, backwards. Over the bent leg he went, feet going from under him. As he floundered, toppling, Will let him go, and drawing back his right fist, smashed it hard under the unprotected chin. The guard went over like a ninepin, to hit the drawbridge timbers with a hollow crash. His helmet went clattering.

It was all the work of no more than three seconds.

Even so, it had taken almost too long. The other two guards had not stood still. One was tugging out his sword, while the older man with the halberd, had it couched like a lance. He came rushing, with it levelled, spear-point stabbing.

Will leapt aside, for his life. The point of the halberd nevertheless thrust in through the baldric, ripping the good homespun of his best doublet at his left side. The force of the thrust

58

spun him round so that he almost overbalanced. Had the third guard been quicker at unsheathing his sword, all would have been over then.

Grabbing the six-foot long shaft of the halberd, Will jerked it violently towards him — and the wielder, clutching, was pulled stumbling with it. Twisting the thing over and round, the younger man wrenched it right out of the guard's grip.

He had no time to adjust his hold on the weapon, to use it as a pole-axe, for the third soldier was running at him now, sword out. Grasping the handle like a quarter-staff before him, with both hands, he flung it and himself on to its onwards-staggering owner, and locking himself against the other, swung both round so that the fellow was between himself and the advancing swordsman, masking any thrust.

He kept up the impetus, while his present victim was still off-balance, pushing and circling. There was only limited space on that drawbridge. The sworder had to back and skip sideways, or he would have been forced over the edge — for such bridge could have no parapet. Using the same device as he had done with the first guard, Will thrust his left leg behind the older man's knees, and heaved. The unfortunate halberdier collapsed backwards, and falling bodily, hit the edge of the drawbridge. Clutch as he would, nothing could save him. He plunged over, into the ditch twenty feet below.

Will, only too well aware of his danger from the third man, was flinging that halberd round in a wild windmill-like swing from the very moment that he thrust its owner away — all but capsizing himself in the process. As well that he did, or the steel would have had him. As it was, the flailing pole knocked the sword aside, and its wielder had to leap back swiftly, morined head ducking, to avoid the axe-head's sweep.

For the moment the odds were evened. By the time the swordsman could come dancing in again Will had the swinging halberd under control, and his own footing steadied. Panting, he faced the other.

He was no expert with a halberd, an unwieldy implement at the best. But he had no time to cast it aside and draw his own sword. At least, its six foot length gave him the advantages of range. They circled each other warily, weapons feinting and probing.

But the interval was brief indeed. The first guard, though

shaken, had got to his feet, and was lurching for his own halberd, left leaning beside the porters' bench. Worse, men-at-arms were now coming streaming from the baiting ring. Will was vaguely aware of the change in the shouting, and that the attention of the watchers, above and below, had been transferred to this more lively contest. He had only moments to improve this situation, before he would be overwhelmed by sheer numbers. But what opportunity had he left to exploit?

His horse! The animal, though it had sidled away alarmedly from the clash of steel, was still standing near the drawbridge end. There was no other horse in the vicinity.

Will backed, in their tense, cautious fencing. He could spare only two or three seconds. Suddenly he raised the halberd high, horizontally, and launched it like a javelin at the sworder. Deliberately he hurled it at the fellow's left side — which meant that to avoid it he must sidestep swiftly to his right. And at that side he was near the edge of the bridge. Aware of it, the man flung himself as much back as sideways, a complicated movement which made for stumbling footwork. The halberd missed him by inches, and its top-heavy iron head plunged into and splintered the bridge timbers.

Will, the moment the weapon had left his hand, swung about and raced the few remaining paces to his horse. Shouts arose all around. His flapping sheathed sword was an impediment, but he could spare no hand for it meantime. A yard or so from the nervous beast, he sprang, projecting himself forwards and upwards. He could not actually vault so high as on to the animal's back, but he managed to fling himself bodily over the saddle, on his stomach, clutching at the mane. Again the sword got in the way, and for a moment it was touch and go whether he could maintain position and balance as the horse pranced and backed. But at least this was no deliberately bucking, horn-lashing bull. Kicking the dangling sword away, he flung his leg up and over, and with a supreme effort steadied and raised himself. As the beast cavorted round, Will sat approximately upright in the saddle, his toes feeling for the stirrups.

Men were all around him now — but keeping heedful distance from those flailing hooves. Confusion reigned, the two advancing guards being somewhat lost in the crowd from the baiting. Other swords were out, and varied orders and advices with them.

Will managed to draw his own sword at last. At the screech of it, the nearest throngers pressed backwards — for few men on foot would choose to cross swords with one mounted. In a bent figure of eight motion, he slashed the blade downward, right and left, sweeping one side then the other. Savagely he dug in his spurs.

'A Douglas! A Douglas!' he yelled, and drove the rearing, curveting horse back on to the drawbridge, straight towards the gatehouse arch.

Undoubtedly this move took most by surprise. The bridge was no more than ten feet wide — which gave little enough space for sharing with a frightened horse and sword-lashing rider. Such as found themselves that side of the intruder had to do something about it very quickly. One or two managed to dart round to the side, but those actually on the drawbridge, including the two original guards, could not do this. The ditch was twenty feet deep and sheersided. They turned and ran. A heavy six-foot halberd being little aid to running, the first guard tossed it into the ditch as he went.

The drumming of hooves on the bridge planks changed to a clatter as the horse's shoes struck sparks from the cobblestones under the gatehouse pend. Like rabbits into their holes the four or five men before him darted or fell into the open guardroom doorways on either side. In only a few brief seconds after his slogan shouting, Will Douglas was through, and cantering up the steeply-rising slope within the inner bailey towards the tall buildings which flanked the great courtyard of the castle.

There were men about — but none in a position to know what had transpired below, however surprised they may have been to see the single horseman's drawn sword. There was shouting behind — but there had been shouting at the bear and bull baiting for some time. No one attempted to halt Will at any rate. Sheathing his sword, but not greatly slowing his mount, he drove on up and into the courtyard. At the most important-looking doorway therein, in the side of a splendidly lofty and decorative range of building, he drew up, and dismounted, before another trio of steel-clad guards.

"Douglas to see the King's Grace," he panted. "Take my horse."

These men were of a different kidney from those below. One

came down the few steps, at once, to take the horse's bridle. Another spoke respectfully.

"His Grace is down at the gate. With Sir James. Sir James Livingstone. Did you no' see him sir? Watching the sport. Sir James has a bear yonder, they say. If you have letters for Sir Alexander? . . ."

"The King? Down there? Watching? . . ." Will gulped, frowning.

"Aye. But no' Sir Alexander. I'll take you to him, sir. You have letters? Papers? No doubt Will's breathlessness and general dishevelment gave the impression that he had ridden far in great haste, a courier with urgent tidings for Livingsone.

"No. It is the King. I would see the young King." With a swift glance over his heaving shoulder, he drew himself up. "Take me to His Grace, man. Quickly. It is important."

"Aye, sir." The spokesman jerked his head to his third colleague, and leaving the man with the horse one on either side of him, they escorted Will back whence he had come. That young man was aware of a greater trepidation now than he had known throughout the entire proceedings. He frowned the blacker.

Turning out of the courtyard again, to face the cobbled slope to the inner bailey, they found themselves confronting a climbing crowd. Scores, possibly hundreds of people were coming up the hill, on foot, with haste and urgency most evident, filling all the roadway.

"Here comes Sir James. And the Constable. With His Grace," the guard said. "The sport must be by with."

Will cleared his throat — and sought to clear his head likewise.

Though there were many men-at-arms, soldiers and servitors amongst the throng, there were not a few richly dressed walkers. In the middle of the front row, a boy hurried, chattering and obviously excited, between two men. There was nothing kingly about his appearance, manner or behaviour. He was not particularly well apparelled. He was short for his thirteen years, but stocky. And though he had eager darting eyes, he was plain-faced to a degree, with a great red birthmark on his cheek — which gave him the nickname of Fiery-face. The men on either side of him were both tall and splendid. The younger, garbed in the height of fashion was handsome in a dissipated way, slender, arrogant of manner. The other, in early

62

middle years was the lord who had passed Will in cavalier haste at St. Ninians, still wearing his travelling cloak.

"It is he, I tell you!" The shrill boyish voice was crying. "Have these two taken him? Unhorsed him? I do not think they could. See — he still has his sword. But sheathed . . ."

Neither of his companions appeared to be answering their monarch. Both were looking doubtful, one grimly, the other fleeringly. As Will approached, they paused, holding the boy back. All around them, hands were on sword-hilts, but no steel was drawn. Only the High Constable of Scotland might draw sword in the King's presence — and the Constable forbore.

Not so Will Douglas. As he neared the waiting company, unfaltering of step however unsure within himself, he reached down to draw his sword once more — and the shrill sound of it bred a swift intake of breath from many present. But in the same movement, the young man tossed the weapon up, hilt foremost, into the air, to catch it round the blade halfway to the pommel. Holding it before him so, he strode ahead of his escort the few paces, to sink down on one knee before the eager-eyed nervous boy.

"Sire," he said, "My sword. Take it. Yours. My sorrow — I did not know that Your Grace was there. To draw sword. In your presence. I crave mercy. Forgiveness. I did not know . . ." The words came out jerking, awkward, not as he would have said them.

James, King of Scots, second of that name, stared at the sword-hilt held up, almost thrust under his nose, and bit his lip. He looked from one to another of his companions.

"Do not touch it, Sire," the tall slender elegant rapped out. "Leave this insolent rascal to others." He reached down, and himself grasped the proffered hilt. "Guard — take this . . ."

His words broke off abruptly, as he was jerked forward. The weapon was pulled vigorously out of his clutch, and presented towards the young monarch again.

"My sword is only for the King!" Will exclaimed, looking up with an expression anything but humbly dutiful.

"God damn you! . . ."

"Touch it, Sire," the older man, on the boy's left, said quietly but clearly. "But touch the hilt. That is all. Have no fear. This fellow may be a rogue — but he means no ill, now, I think."

63

The boy put out a rather hesitant, nail-bitten and distinctly grubby hand, touched the sword-hilt as though it had been red-hot, and thrust the hand behind his back thereafter, saying nothing.

"This is folly!" his younger adviser cried. "Giving recognition to a brawling bravo . . ."

The clatter of the sword on the cobbles drowned his strictures. Now, without changing his half-kneeling posture, Will held out his two hands, palms together but an inch or two apart.

"Sire," he said, "I am Your Grace's man. I would do my homage."

James coughed. "Yes. Homage, aye. Homage. I . . . I . . ."

"By the Rude — this is beyond all! The rascal is crazed! A madman!"

"He fought well, Sir James," the boy said. "He fought . . . not as though crazed! Did he? Sir William — what shall I do?"

"Have his name, Your Grace. Before you give him your royal hand. Your name, sirrah? And what you do here?"

"He shouted Douglas! . . ."

"Aye. But there are many of that name. Over many!"

'I *am* Douglas," Will jerked.

"Of where? From whence, man?" Hay, the Constable, demanded. "Who are you who comes swording and fighting into the King's presence? Only nobles may claim to do homage . . ."

Will was not of a character to conduct conversation with any man, king or constable, on his knees. He rose, picking up his sword as he did so, and sheathed it, without undue haste. "I told His Grace," he said, looking at Sir William Hay. "I am Douglas. Himself. Commonly called Black. You will have heard, sir, of the Black Douglas, I think?"

The Constable's sudden intake of breath was to be perceived rather than heard amongst the gasping from all around.

It was the young King who found words most quickly. "You mean . . . you mean, sir . . . that *you* are Black Douglas? Yourself? The Earl? You?"

"Since my father's death three weeks past, Sire, I am. William Douglas, his eldest son." He amended that, a little self-consciously. "*Sir* William. Earl of Douglas. The 8th. Come to do my fealty to my liege lord, the King of Scots."

The boy's prominent jaw dropped slightly, lips parted, but he found nothing to say.

"God's eye — is this truth, man? You do not jest? . . ." the Constable exclaimed, thickly.

"Did I seem to jest back at the gatehouse, sir? When I sought entry to this castle, to pay my duty?"

Hay was eyeing him up and down, much as the guards had done. "How . . . how could any know? Coming . . . thus?" As an afterthought he added, almost as though it choked him, "My lord."

"I said my name and asked to be brought to the King's Grace. Your ruffians at the gate would have none of me . . ."

"Not mine, my lord — they are none of mine. Livingstone's men." The Constable looked over the King's head at the other man.

Sir James Livingstone, eldest son of Sir Alexander, the King's guardian, was having difficulty with his facial expression; also with his breathing. He looked at Hay and the King, not at Will. "How were they to know? How any of us to know that this was not . . . an impostor! A young man. Dressed so. With no attendants. Not so much as a servant. And no banner. No arms blazoned. Nothing to show his worth and quality. To come to Stirling Castle thus! . . ."

"Would His Grace have preferred that Douglas came with a thousand men at his back?" Will demanded. "Or two thousand? Or five?" If that was hot, and not a little vaunting, Will had been sorely tried — and moreover he found the speaker obnoxious.

Young Livingstone did not answer. Hay cleared his throat.

"The point is taken, my lord," he said carefully.

"He . . . my lord of Douglas . . . showed his worth. His quality," the boy James exclaimed. "Back there with the guards, Sir James. It was good fighting, was it not? The best we have seen . . ."

"It was rude fisticuffs. Brawling, Sire. Like common wrestling at a fair! . . ."

"My father was a wrestler, sir!"

Livingstone all but choked. James the First had indeed learned wrestling during the eighteen years of his imprisonment in England, had in fact become renowned as one of the finest wrestlers in that land — as well as runner, athlete, poet, lutist and, later, iron-handed ruler.

"May I have your hand, Sir?" Will asked levelly. He did not intend to make it sound almost like a command.

The boy thrust out his hand, at once. Will took it between both his own, in the traditional gesture of homage. He jerked his head over it , and muttered something perfunctory. He did not, however, resume his kneeling stance.

"Why did you come dressed so? Like a merchant?" James asked. He sounded interested, enquiring, not in any way censorious. "And with no train? I have never seen a lord look like you."

Will looked down at his dusty, travel-stained garb. There was nothing wrong with it, except for the tear made by the halberd-point in his doublet. It was not fine — but nor was it ragged or badly soiled. "I did not know that clothing was so important. I have no better than this. I have never lived at Court, Sire. Where I live we esteem the man within, not his clothing."

"Yes. Yes — you have the rights of it, my lord. So think I!" James glanced down at his own apparel. He was not notably fine himself, though his clothing had been plainly good once. He was much less handsomely clad than most of those around him. He switched his gaze to the magnificence of Sir James Livingstone and the quieter richness of Sir William Hay, and grinned at Will.

The other answered with a fleeting glimmer of a smile. There was something of rapport established between them, from that moment. They were, after all, cousins of a sort, and only five years apart in age.

Sir James cleared his throat, frowning. "My father," he said stiffly. "I think, Sire, it is time that we saw my father. With . . . with this lord of Douglas!" There was more than a hint of threat in that, barely disguised.

Will looked from King James to the speaker, over to the Constable, and back. "I will perhaps see Sir Alexander Livingstone on some other occasion," he said harshly. "I have matters to discuss with him. Notably regarding my cousins. Who . . . died! The 6th Earl, and David his brother. Sir Alexander was present, was he not?"

The stir all around was immediate, almost electrifying. Livingstone bit thin lips, eyes narrowing. James Stewart looked appalled. He had been present also, of course, those three years before, at the fatal dinner, arrest, trial and execution of the two Douglases, however unwillingly.

When no one found anything to say, in reaction, Will went on. "Another time. For Livingstone. I have ridden far, Sire. I am of a sweat and I have not eaten. I'd esteem it a favour . . . in this your house of Stirling? . . ."

"Yes. Yes — to be sure. You must come to my tower. I have quarters in the old Ballengeich Tower." Young James looked quickly, almost defiantly, at Livingstone. "You will come to my room, my lord of Douglas. My own room."

"I thank Your Grace." Will turned, and without waiting for other lead or invitation, began to move back, up towards the lower courtyard. King James hastened to walk at his side. Perforce, Livingstone and the Constable had to fall in at their backs, and the rest followed on.

"You served those men, the men at the gate, the guards — you laid about them splendidly!" James said admiringly, the words tumbling out. "It was good, excellent sport. Much better than the bull. And the bear. They were very poor. You are strong and quick. I wish that I could fight like that. My father would have taught me. You would not have beat *him*, my lord! He was the best fighter there was. It took six men to kill him. Nobody here will teach me. They say it is not kingly, not knightly, to fight with the hands. Only the sword and the lance. Would . . . would you teach me?" That came out with a rush.

"I have not been trained, Sire, I have but learned, by experience. In many fights. I have five brothers! And the men of Ettrick are great fighters. With their hands. I am less nimble with the sword . . ."

"Then *I* will teach you that! If you will show me the other. I have been taught swording. Will you?"

"You are the King, Sire. Your wish is my command. If you will have it so."

"Yes. That is well. Good. My tower is the old one. It is part a ruin but it has a little garden on the side of the rock where you could teach me. Over there, through the pend."

Will noted that Sir James Livingstone, behind them, had betaken himself off.

*　　　*　　　*

67

As they sat down at the table in the bleak little room with the magnificent prospect over the flat Carse of Forth and the Flanders Moss, towards the Highland mountains, Will eyed the plain fare set forth, and smiled grimly.

"No black bull's head for Douglas, today!" he observed.

The boy-king, who had scarcely ceased to chatter in half an hour, swallowed audibly and said nothing.

"That was an ill deed. But an old story, my lord. And no responsibility, no concern, of His Grace." Hay, the Constable, who remained with them of all the company — and who obviously was not going to leave the visitor alone with the monarch — spoke shortly.

"It was the concern of all in this land, sir. Especially all who bear the rule. In any degree. Since it was done in the King's name and presence."

"A child of ten! Forced to watch while, while . . . others did what they would."

"Aye — others. Evil men. One of whom still holds this royal castle, it seems. And another who rules the realm in His Grace's name."

Hay glanced about him, in something like alarm, as though the stone walls of that meagre chamber might have ears. "Watch what you say, a God's name!" he jerked, voice lowered. "Remember where you are! Who you speak with. Men have died for less words than these."

"Men are forever dying, my lord Constable. Sometimes even the evil men die! For myself, I scarce think that Livingstone will risk to slay another Earl of Douglas eating in the King's presence! It is said that lightning strikes but once in any place!"

"Nevertheless, my lord — I say, watch your words. Watch well every step you take in this place. However you may wish it otherwise, Sir Alexander Livingstone holds this strength, and all within it. On the authority of His Grace's Privy Council. You have seen fit to put your head into a noose, here. Why, I know not. But see you — beware lest Livingstone decides that he must pull the noose tight!"

"He will not do that — since, I think, he is not a fool as well as a knave! This is His Grace's castle, not Livingstone's. His Grace has asked me to his table. That is as good as safe conduct. Is it not, Sire?"

"Yes. I . . . I suppose it. Yes." His Grace did not sound altogether confident.

Will laughed shortly, "I am content," he said.

As they ate, Hay put the question bluntly. "What brought you here, my lord? Like this. Alone. Unsupported. You must have had a reason. When you might have come . . . so differently."

"Would I have gained entry to Stirling Castle had I had thousands at my back? Would I have been eating at the King's table, sir?"

"Perhaps not. Not with thousands. But with some style, some circumstance. Seemly in a great lord."

"I did not know that style and circumstance meant so much in Scotland. But I came so of a purpose, yes. Already men have been seeking that I take sides in this land. That I take one's part against another. Use the Douglas power thus, or thus. All think to enroll Douglas's thousands. How was I to judge aright? Had I come with a great company. I would have learned but little. Save that men respect Douglas swords — which I knew already. This way, I learn much. I *have* learned much. Which it is good for Douglas to know."

"I say that he is right," King James exclaimed. "I am glad that he came."

Hay was less enthusiastic. "Such knowledge might cost you dear, my lord."

"That I thought of. But I wanted to learn something of the state of this realm, with my own eyes and ears and wits. Not just what others would have me believe."

The Constable grunted. "And you learn apace, my young lord?"

"Aye."

"For example?"

"If you will. I learn, amongst other things, that the King of Scots is held prisoner in his own castle." He glanced around him. "And not in the best quarters of it, I think! And that the Lord High Constable of Scotland, whose duty it is to guard and protect the King's person at all times, is helpless to do anything!"

Hay drew a hand over mouth and chin. "You are less than careful with your words, by the Mass!" he said, but heavily, not fiercely.

"Perhaps. But they are true words, are they not?"

"Only part true. Only part. You are young, my lord. It is easy for you to speak, to make your swift judgements! What know you of the dangers, the difficulties, of the balance that must be maintained in this Scotland today? Weighing this force against that. Think you, man, that I would have it this way?" The Constable spoke with a restrained passion now. "I would serve His Grace better than this if I might. I am Constable of Scotland, yes. I bear the sword of state. My authority is great. But where lies my power? I bear that sword all but alone. *I* cannot field thousands, my lord!"

"This Council? His Grace's Privy Council? Is it not for them to give you the power you need?"

"The Council! The Chancellor calls a Council. Who, think you, attend? Who will walk into his Castle of Edinburgh? Not those who fear that they might not walk out again." Once again the involuntary glance around him, even at the young king, as that came out.

"Yet there must be many of the Council who are leal? No friends of Crichton?"

'No doubt. But they are not united. Scattered over the land. they need a lead. A powerful lead."

"Aye. I have heard *that* before! Who make up the Council?"

"Many creatures of Crichton's. And Livingstone's certain of the greater prelates. Officers of state, as myself. The Chamberlain. The Treasurer. The Secretary. The Justiciar. And of course, the earls . . ."

"All the earls? Then I am of it also?"

"Aye, my lord — you are. And much good may it do you! Or His Grace! Few earls ever attend. Your father was of the Council, both as earl and as Justiciar. I cannot mind once seeing him there!"

"My father was a man sick," Will said briefly. "I am not. To summon this Council? Can only the Chancellor Crichton do that?"

"The Chancellor summons. In the name of the King."

"Aye. But it is the *King's* Privy Council, is it not? As other than the great council of a parliament. It is not the Chancellor's Council. His Grace could summon it himself? Without the Chancellor?"

'My lord — you tread dangerous ground! As well that I am no creature of Crichton's! His Grace is young, not of age. He cannot act the king, as you would have him do."

'As I *would*, my lord, if I could!" the boy interposed.

"It may be that you are less helpless than you think, Sire. Than Sir William thinks."

"Would *you* help me, my lord? Would Douglas help?"

"I have done homage, have I not? Said that I am your man. I did not come to utter mere empty words . . ."

He stopped as, without a warning or a knock, the door was flung open. Sir James Livingstone stood there, holding it wide for another and older man.

King James half rose from his chair, fear writ large on his eager features. The Constable, as required when the King stood, stood also. Will Douglas, though he knew the custom, remained seated.

The newcomers came in, leaving the door wide. The older man though most evidently Sir James's father, was an unlikely sire for so tall and slender an elegant. Small, twisted, stringy, a sandy ferret of a man he looked not so much old as ageless. Of no appearance, presence or dignity, and overdressed like a fairground monkey, he nevertheless still impressed by his sheer latent vitality, acuteness, and the shrewd penetration of his darting weasel's eyes. Beside him, his fine son was no more than a walking clothes-horse.

Ignoring the others he looked directly at Will. "This, then, will be the new young Earl of Douglas?" he said, and his voice was as thin and lacking in quality as the rest of him. "And a lad o' parts, I'm hearing — hey?" That ended on a cackle, almost a giggle.

It had been Will's intention to ignore the man, and to ask the Constable who was this who presumed to burst into the monarch's presence without warning or acknowledgement. But he found himself rising, to answer, nevertheless, and though he managed to halt the uprising he could not withhold response.

'I am Douglas, yes. Come to the King. And you — are Sir Alexander Livingstone? Who helped slay my cousins!" That was not what he had meant to say, at all.

"Ha! That way the cat jumps! Na, na, my lord — you mistake. Chap you at another door, man. Yon was Crichton's ploy — no mine." The other grinned.

"You consented, sir. The invitation. To visit Edinburgh Castle, to meet the King. That was sent in your name, as well as Crichton's."

"The invitation, aye. For the young Earl o' Douglas to come take his due part in the conduct o' the realm, to be sure. No' the deaths that followed, lad. That wasna Alec Livingstone! I'm a man o' peace." Again the whinny of high laughter. "His Grace here will tell you so. And Sir William, the Constable. Eh? Eh?"

James nodded quickly, anxiously. Hay inclined his head, expressionless, but said nothing.

"I have heard of your peace, sir!" Will said shortly.

"Aye. As well you might, lad — as well you might! No' that your own entry to this Stirling Castle was that peaceable, I'm told! Eh? Swordery. Riot. Cauld steel out in the King's presence!"

"Your bullies denied me entry. To the King's presence. Attacked me. Douglas defends himself. *This* Douglas!"

"Ooh, aye. Worthy. Aye, worthy. Me — I'm an auld done man, but I defend mysel' also. And defend His young Grace here, likewise, see you. Frae all assaults. By whomsoever. Be they named Stewart! Or Hay! Or even Douglas! By orders o' the Council." There was no attempt to disguise the threat of that, despite the chuckle.

Will drew a deep breath. "Or . . . Crichton?" he asked.

The little man's glance was keen, probing. For moments he did not answer. Then he nodded. "Aye — or Crichton," he agreed. "Assuredly. If he came chapping at the gates o' Stirling."

"If he came, *he* would not come as I have done, I think. Alone."

"Maybe no'. Think you he is like to? *I* wouldna think it."

"You know him best, sir. You work with him. You together rule this realm, do you not? But . . . if Crichton could hold the King's Grace in *his* hands, where would Livingstone be then?" That came out less calmly, certainly, than Will would have wished. He had a mental picture of how his mother would have carried it off, and strove to emulate — but knew himself to fall far short.

The other sniffed. "If! . . . If! . . . Seven years I have been guardian and governor. Think you he wouldna have seized His

Grace before now? If he could! What difference is there now?"

"This difference." Will swallowed. "Douglas."

"Eh? . . . What do you mean, boy?" That was almost a squeak.

"I mean that, before, there was not a Douglas who was ready to act. Now, there is."

"God's death! You say that! You sit here, in my castle, and threaten me! Livingstone!"

"I sit at the King's table. Having eaten his salt. And threaten none. I but tell you that it is time that Douglas acted . . ."

"Acted! See you, boy — there are deep vaults below you! Pits! Where bonnier men than you have rotted! Aye — and women too! . . ."

"If you speak of His Grace's mother, the Queen Joanna — I know of that shame. And of her husband, Sir James Stewart of Lorn. But . . . you will not put *me* in your dungeons, sir!"

"No? Why?"

"Because, unlike my cousin, Earl William, I did not bring my brothers with me! He had only one brother — and you took and slew them both. I have five, sir!" Will was on his feet now, and the effort to keep his voice steady, level, was enormous. "Five! All of hot blood. All straining to try their strength. Another reason why I came alone!"

"Christ God! I told you. You'll no threaten *me* in Stirling Castle! . . ."

"And I told you, I do not threaten. I but remind you. In case you have forgot. Besides, if I had thought to threaten you, sir, would I not have gone to *Edinburgh* Castle? And Crichton? Not Stirling, and you?"

That seemed to give the little man pause. He turned, and slammed the door shut behind him, then came forward and leaned over the table towards Will. There might have been none other in the room. "What are you here for, then?"

"To offer His Grace my homage. And my sword."

"Aye. But on what terms?"

"I do not bargain with my liege lord!"

"Do not fence wi' me, man! I am the King's guardian. I speak wi' the King's voice. Until he be of age. Speak you plain. Do you sell your sword?"

"Douglas does not sell his sword. He has no need, but many

have come to me, seeking to borrow it! Other than your daughter's son, Sir James Hamilton of Cadzow!"

Livingstone muttered something thinly savage. Then he pointed again. "Others? Crichton?"

Will sought to meet the other's glare. "I came to Stirling," he said, "Not Edinburgh."

Seconds passed in a tense silence.

Young Livingstone broke it. "He but cozens you . . ."

"Quiet!" his father snapped. "Think you I need *your* guidance?" The little man hirpled stiffly round the table, behind the King, to Will's side. "My lord o' Douglas," he said softly. "You would lend your sword to me?"

"Not so. Only to His Grace. But . . . *Your* sword is lent there also, is it not?"

"A-a-aye! But . . . who wields this two-handed sword, my lord? Who wields?"

"This man." Will pointed at Hay, who still stood at the other end of the table. "He is the Constable. It is his place to wield the sword of state, is it not? For the King's and the realm's weal. With Douglas power. And your statecraft."

"Ha! So that's it? An alliance! An alliance — against Crichton?"

"That was in my mind, sir."

Hay still did not speak.

The old man brought down his crooked fist on the table, to make the viands jump. "Here's a bone to chew on! I' faith — I think I like the taste o' it! Young man — I'll think on it. Aye, I will. As do you, Hay. We will speak o' this, again." He looked at Will, grinning now. "You will not be leaving this castle, my lord?" That was only ostensibly a question.

"I will go when I choose, sir. With His Grace's permission. But . . . I had not thought to go until this thing was decided."

"Aye — do not, my lord. And you wise!" The old man's high cackle resounded as, slapping Will on the shoulder, he made for the door — which his son hastened to open for him. Passing out, the Livingstones left it wide behind them.

James Stewart himself hurried to close it.

"My lord, you were brave. Very brave. To front him so," he declared, admiringly. "Was he not, Sir William? I have seen none do that. So starkly. I was . . . afraid for you. He is a hard man. You had best have a care, my lord."

74

"Too many have been having a care in Scotland, I think, Sire. For too long."

"Yes. How did you learn it? How to deal so? With Sir Alexander?"

"My father did not breed us for Courts, Sire. But there are other kinds of learning. In Ettrick Forest we learn much about how to deal with hard strength. I find Livingstone none so different from an Ettrick bull. Of the wilder sort!"

"Bull? Wild bull! . . ."

"Aye, Your Grace. We gain some sport from these. There are many in the forest."

"You hunt bulls? Wild bulls? In your forest? I would wish to see this. Will you show me? Take me, my lord? To hunt wild bulls . . ."

"If Your Grace wishes. Ettrick is your own. A royal forest. Douglas but keeps it for you."

"Yes. You hear, Sir William? We will go hunting wild bulls, in Ettrick. You hear?" Suddenly the boy's eager face fell. "If . . . if Sir Alexander will permit it."

The silent Constable did not look optimistic, or even very interested in bull-hunting. He nodded briefly. "I hear, Sire. My lord of Douglas — you spoke of Sir James Hamilton. Did he put you up to this?"

"Not so. He sought my sword — that is all."

"Against Crichton?"

"Yes. But I would better think, *for* Hamilton!"

"Aye. And others have done the same? Against Crichton?" Will nodded.

"Who are these others?"

"That is my affair, sir."

The other shook his head, but not in anger. "I think not. If we are to be allies, my lord, it is mine also."

"Then . . . then you agree? You will fight Crichton, sir?" Will could not keep his voice level.

"It seems that I have no choice. And if others are ready to rise against the man, then I shall not, cannot, hold back. Yon William Crichton is, I think, the Devil himself!" There was a quivering intensity in those last words which were all the more startling in coming from so sober and quiet a man.

They caused Will Douglas to catch his breath, at any rate, and the youthful elation to fade from his dark eyes.

"Now, my lord — who do we know is prepared to rise against the Chancellor? Besides Douglas and Hay? And Hamilton?"

"And Livingstone! . . ."

"Livingstone! Put not too much faith in Livingstone. Others have done, to their cost. And Scotland's. Watch him — watch all the breed — as you would a snake. His every move. He who walks with Livingstone treads slippery ground! . . ."

CHAPTER FOUR

"Hold! Hold, Cousin!" King James cried, panting. "You go too hard. You beat me down by main force. Because you are bigger, older. It is not fair. Besides, it is not the way. Swording is a finer business than this! I am not one of your bulls! Hold, I say."

Will put his sword-tip down into the turf of the little garden perched high on the ledge of Stirling rock below the Ballengeich Tower, and laughed. "So ever you say — when I have you beat!" he claimed. "I fear we see this differently. I see swording as fighting to win. No dancing-master's ploy . . ."

"You would name me dancing-master, my lord! *Me* — your King!"

"No, no, Sire," Will schooled his features to gravity. "I' faith — not that! You are a very lion for the assault, for fighting. It is but that you are too fine for me. That I look only to the end, while you pay more heed to the road thither."

Mollified, James nodded. "It is the knightly way," he declared, somewhat smugly.

The fact was that young King James was no very notable swordsman, however lofty his teaching, being much too concerned with flourish and posture. From the first, Will had had the greatest difficulty in not defeating him, despite the fact that he it was who was supposed to be receiving the lesson. His own methods were swift, vigorous and unorthodox, but effective, based on vehement attack from start to finish, not tournament duelling but sheer combat. And in the enthusiasm of the moment he sometimes was apt to forget his role.

In the ten days that Will had stayed at Stirling, however, despite this, his relationship with James had developed apace

They were constant companions — almost too constant for Will, who would have relished greater freedom and privacy both. But the young monarch, starved of youthful company and with an enormous admiration for physical prowess, attached himself to the newcomer with alacrity and determination — and since the part Will had come here to play implied that the King's wish was his law, any holding-off process was difficult. He lodged in James's broken-down tower, ate with him, would have had to sleep in the same room had the small vaulted chambers available been large enough. The boy now called him Cousin, save when he was hipped, when he reverted to my lord. These occasions were fairly frequent, though of short duration — for James Stewart, though cowed in the presence of those who controlled him, was of a spirited nature, and indeed had a notably hot temper.

Will found the constant proximity cloying, the confinement trying, and the time slow of passing. With the King, he was a virtual prisoner in the castle. To one who had been used to the free life of Ettrick, the leadership of his brothers, and the constant stir and turmoil of a large household of young people, this period of constraint and comparative inaction was galling. They could not be practising wrestling, fisticuffs, quarter-staff and swordsmanship all the time — and other diversions were scanty. Baiting, cock-fights and similar contests were not for everyday occurrence — and were by no means put on for the royal amusement. Indeed, the Livingstones and their hangers-on largely ignored their youthful sovereign, save when he was required to sign some edict, charter or pronouncement. He had a tutor-cum-priest, a man-servant, and constant guards. And when Sir William Hay was in the castle, he waited on the King assiduously.

Will's relationship with Livingstone had, on the face of it, made little further headway. He had seen the old man only two or three times, and then not alone or in circumstances where either policy or strategy could be discussed suitably. Unfortunately he saw rather more of the son, Sir James — but between them only a mutual arm's-length antagonism persisted. Will had sought to use Hay as go-between with Sir Alexander, but so far without much success. With the Constable himself he was on satisfactory terms, although it was hard to get close to that silent, soldierly man; but Hay lived half a day's journey to the north-east, at Erroll in the Carse of Gowrie, and spent only part of his time attending on the Monarch.

The Douglas was learning patience, however unwillingly.

James was explaining to his pupil the nicer points of what he had been doing when the other had crudely battered down his blade, when they were interrupted. A hail from the tower above caused them to glance up.

"Lord of Douglas," a young man cried down to them, standing beside one of the ever-watchful guards. "My father desires your presence." It was David Livingstone, this time, a younger son, one of the many indeed, though only three were in residence meantime at Stirling, the others being strategically placed as captains of various royal castles.

Will opened his mouth to speak, then thought better of it. He turned back to James. "Your Grace was saying? . . ." he asked loudly enough to be heard from above.

The King glanced away, alarmed. "Nothing. Nothing," he said. "I . . . I . . . Sir Alexander! . . ."

"Did you hear me, my lord? My father desires your presence."

"Then let him seek it, sir," Will declared shortly. "As you see, I am engaged with His Grace."

"I was told to bring you, Forthwith."

"Your father may tell *you* what he will. Douglas he does not tell. You tell *him* so. If he would see me, of a sudden, let him come."

David Livingstone stared down at him, nonplussed. Then red-faced, muttering something, he turned away.

"You should not have done that, Cousin," James said, his voice a little tremulous. "He will be angry. Very angry, Sir Alexander."

"I care not that for Livingstone's anger!" Will said, and snapped his fingers. If it was not quite literally true, at least it was an affirmation of principle.

"He will make you pay for it. He is an ill man to cross. He can do what he will, in this castle."

"Not with me, Sire. Nor with you, from now on. We must let him see it. Now — you were showing me the way of this feint to the shoulder? . . ."

But James had lost his interest in sword-play meantime. If,

for a high-spirited boy of thirteen, his fear might seem irrational, his background and experience were calculated to account for it. His father, James the First, had been stabbed to death seven years before, in his own bedchamber, before his wife's eyes, by knightly assassins. He himself had been seized at Edinburgh and confined in the castle there by Crichton, a year or so later. His mother, the lovely, widowed Queen Joanna Beaufort, being denied access to his person, had enlisted the aid of Sir Alexander Livingstone, who was then captain of her dowry castle of Stirling. By a stratagem Livingstone had got the child-king smuggled out of Edinburgh Castle in a wardrobe and carried by boat to Stirling. There Livingstone had showed his true mettle. Holding the King himself, he had entered into a pact with Chancellor Crichton, to share the rule of Scotland between them. The Queen Mother had been cast into Stirling's dungeons, where he had already immured the Stewart of Lorn husband she had hurriedly married in an effort to rally that great clan to her side. Then, at a hunt in Stirling's neighbourhood, while Livingstone was absent at Perth, Crichton had gone back on his crooked partnership to the extent of kidnapping the boy once more and taking him back to captivity at Edinburgh. Guile had eventually got him to Stirling once more, and a renewal of the compact — but now James was kept close indeed. He had been forced to attend the fatal Black Dinner to the Douglas brothers, and to watch their execution. And others similar. His mother now languished in Dunbar Castle, as prisoner, ill-used by a brutal Hepburn minion of Crichton's. She was said to be dying, although still a beautiful woman in her late thirties. His stepfather was banished overseas. Young James Stewart had reason to be apprehensive.

Presently David Livingstone returned. This time he came down to the little garden itself. "My Lord of Douglas," he declared flatly, after coughing. "Sir Alexander Livingstone, my father, guardian of His Grace and governor of this castle, seeks your lordship's advice on certain urgent matters. He says that he is troubled today by old bones, and would esteem it an honour if you would wait on him, rather than he on you."

"Aye." Will nodded. "Just so. I think, in that case, if His Grace permits, I might pleasure Sir Alexander."

"Yes. Oh, yes," the King agreed hurriedly.

In silence the two young men proceeded through the fortress

precincts to the notably finer state apartments occupied by the governor and his retainers. Will was well aware that this conceivably might be a walk that would end in a dungeon.

He was shown into a small over-heated chamber off the Lesser Hall, where Sir Alexander sat, in a furred robe, over a well-doing fire of logs. The old man was alone. Looking round, he greeted Will with wheezing amiability, and with a lightning-swift change of expression, flicked away his son.

"Come away in to the fire, my lord," he urged, indicating a bench opposite. "It's cauld, cauld. Or maybe it's just my auld bones. Aye. It's good o' you to spare me o' your precious time!" He tee-heed high laughter.

Will did not take the proffered seat, and kept his distance from both fire and man.

"The years dinna come alone, lad," Livingstone went on. "You'll find out, one day. If you live long enough! Hey? Sit man."

"I prefer to stand, sir."

"You do? Hech, hech — uncomfortable. Like the loon who built yon wee pit under the East Tower. You ken it? Uncomfortable, aye. Fell deep it is — fourteen feet, they say. In the living rock. But only eighteen inches wide, mind. So a hannie held in there has to stand, lad — since he canna sit! Hee-hee! I'd no' like it, mysel'." Without pause or change of intonation, he went on. "How many men have you assembled? And where?"

Taken by surprise, Will blinked. "What? What do you mean?"

"No' a hard question, my lord! How many men has Douglas mustered to arms? Now. And where? How near to Stirling?"

"Why, none, sir."

"Fool! Do not lie to me!" the old man shrilled. "You came, threatening Douglas power. You'll no' tell me you've no men?"

"I came alone. Of my own decision. Threatening none. To discover the realm's state before I . . . acted. Douglas can field thousands — that you know. But I have not assembled. Why do you ask?"

"I do not believe that," Livingstone snapped. "You'd no' come here naked. Think you I'm witless, boy, because I'm auld? Forbye, even if you did, you'll have been sending to gather men, these past days. For our project. Aye, our mutual project. Have you no'?"

"I have not. These days I have waited, to discuss with you further. You have not spoken of it. How could I gather men? Here? I have been with the King, waiting."

"Have you no' heard o' paper and pen? Messengers, man? Hay, coming and going, seeing to it. You've had word wi' Hay."

"I have ordered no assembly, sir — and there's an end to it."

"God's curse — so you have wasted near on two weeks! *Wasted!* Playing fool games wi' yon laddie! By the Mass — is this the quality o' Douglas! Is it?"

"I'll thank you not to rail and rant at me, sir!" Will gave back, hotly. "Or you will learn the quality of Douglas soon enough!"

"That I'll be glad to know! Lest it is all words, all belly-wind!" The old man leaned forward. "So you have no men? No power mustered, to make a showing? And William Crichton challenging us, demanding that we meet at Linlithgow. *He'll* no come tailless, I'll wager you that!"

"Crichton? Linlithgow? . . ."

"Crichton, yes. He's got word o' this some way. Of what is proposed. Och, he has his spies everywhere. He kens you're at Stirling. Wi' me. He kens what's to do . . ."

"Who told him? Since only you, Hay, the King and myself know it? . . ."

"I tell you, he has eyes and ears a' place, that one. Yon's the cleverest carle in this realm, boy! He kens — and wants a meeting. At Linlithgow, tomorrow. And he'll no' come alone."

Will stared. "Wants a meeting? Crichton? To talk? Then — why does he not come here? To Stirling?"

"Cha! Here — that fox? Poke his head into *my* den! Guid-sakes — *he's* no' an eighteen-year-old laddie! I told you — he's clever. He doesna step foward where he maybe canna step back! Na, na — you'll no' see Crichton in Stirling Castle. Any more than you'll see Livingstone in Edinburgh! But . . . Linlithgow's half-way between, see you. The Court is there. He rides to Linlithgow tomorrow."

Will had heard something of this strange arrangement, this fictional Court — an arrangement that, however ridiculous, was nevertheless necessary in unhappy Scotland. Linlithgow town and palace was in West Lothian, midway between Stirling and Edinburgh. It was not a fortress or stronghold, but a residential palace. Theoretically it was the King's home, the royal domicile — even though the monarch was prisoner in Stirling and his mother in Dunbar. In name it was the seat of the Court. A Court of sorts did subsist in Linlithgow, where decisions of state were taken and ambassadors were accredited — since Crichton would not accept Stirling nor Livingstone Edinburgh. Most of the country's great nobles had residences near by, or town-houses in the burgh. It was at Abercorn, not far off, that Earl James the Gross had lived, and died, and where Will's mother and sister Beatrix now dwelt.

Will paced the floor. "Crichton may ride to Linlithgow. But need we? Need you play Crichton's game?" he demanded.

"He asks a meeting. If we do not give it, we proclaim before all that we are for fighting him. Before we're ready. Christ-God — before you have a single Douglas troop mustered! We give him warning. Time. And that one will ken how to use both! He's the Chancellor, mind. He speaks for the Council. He holds the purse, the realm's gold. He can *buy* men. No — we must meet him, play him. Till we are ready to strike. Or he strikes first. Is that in your head, boy?"

"Then let us talk. What need of armed men?"

"Saints save us — use your wits! To demand this meeting, Crichton has heard something. Is already on his guard. He'll bring five hundred men with him, if he brings one. Think you we can thrust our heads into that, and get out again, lacking men?"

"Surely Livingstone, the King's Guardian, has men and to spare?"

"Na, na. No' me. I have a puckle men only — enough to guard this castle and other royal castles, for His Grace. That is all. I'm no great lord, mind. Just an honest bit laird, working for King Jamie! Hay can raise two hundred. I've sent for him, to have them here by tomorrow's dawn. Erskine, too. And Ruthven. Aye, and Gray. But Gray's no' a man to trust . . ." Livingstone jabbed a sudden finger at his companion. "*You* have the castle o' Abercorn. No' far frae Linlithgow. Your father's house. The Countess bides there yet, does she no'? How many can you raise there? For the morn?"

Will shook his head. "I do not know. I have never been to Abercorn. It is not my house. My mother's . . ."

"Tush, boy — you are Earl o' Douglas! All is yours. Your sire would keep a wheen men there, I'll be bound. Send you a message, my lord. Forthwith. That every man the Countess Beatrix Douglas can raise rides for Linlithgow. To be there by midday. Bearing Douglas colours. Write you, I'll see it is delivered."

"But . . ."

"But nothing, man! You wanted an alliance against Crichton. Did you no'? You talked about acting! Act now, by the Mass! Or Crichton will ken what to do wi' you! Go — write your mother. She'll ken what to do, that one, I'll wager — Orkney's daughter. The pity there's no other Douglas lands we can reach in time. And you had ten days! Wasted! . . ."

Will found that he was moving to the door, despite himself, at the other's sheer authority. He was halted, nevertheless.

"And, laddie — tomorrow wear you some clothing more like a lord's a God's name! Here's no way to dress . . ."

"Damn you!" Will cried, eyes blazing.

"Aye. Just that." The other cackled his high laughter. "If you canna do better, here, likely my son Davie'll find you some wear o' his. You're much o' a size . . ."

Furiously Will strode to the door, and out, slamming it behind him. He could still hear the tee-heeing as he rushed down the winding stone turnpike stairway beyond.

*   *   *

It was twenty miles from Stirling to Linlithgow, and a fairly early start was necessary. When Will presented himself, in a thin drizzle of rain, at the wide forecourt of the outer bailey next morning — dressed, needless to say, in the same clothes as before — it was to find a large mounted company assembled, under Sir William Hay, and the same Master Adam, Steward of Cambuskenneth Abbey, whom he had been forced to travel behind on the day of his arrival here. Hay said that they totalled about three hundred and fifty, with his own people, the

Abbot's men, and small contingents from Erskine and Ruthven. It was intended that they should pick up some more at Callendar, the Livingstone lairdship near Falkirk, en route. Hay sounded depressed about the entire expedition.

Although Sir Alexander had been stern about the hour of assembly and move-off, he kept them all waiting in the rain for the best part of half an hour before he himself put in an appearance, wrapped in a huge cloak and coughing and complaining about sundry ills of the flesh. He had only his younger son David with him, leaving Sir James in charge of the castle and monarch. The King waved them farewell from the gatehouse parapet, having been curtly refused permission to accompany them.

Once on the move, there was little or no conversation, this grey morning, between the three principal architects of Chancellor Crichton's downfall. Livingstone treated them only to bouts of coughing and groaning. At Bannockburn, no further, he called a halt, declaring that he was a sick man and should be in his bed. He could go no further. They would have to proceed without him. They would be little better than babes in Crichton's hands, but it couldn't be helped.

Much concerned, Will and the Constable debated whether or not they should turn back also — but Livingstone would not hear of it. That would but play Crichton's game. He would put it about that they dared not face him. It would gravely prejudice their chances with those who wavered in taking sides. Forbye his grandson, Sir James Hamilton, would be meeting them at Callendar.

This was the first they had heard of Sir James Hamilton being involved. But Livingstone coughed and spluttered aside all queries. Abruptly, with his son, he reined round and rode briskly back for Stirling.

It was a very doubtful pair who rode on southwards, at the head of the jingling cavalcade. Hay was still of the opinion that it probably would be wiser to turn back. He was sure that Livingstone's sudden chest affliction was entirely fraudulent, and the old fox, having launched them on to this dangerous course, was prudently backing out until he saw how things would go. He could deny all connection with them, if advisable. He had sent no men. No other Livingstones accompanied them. Hamilton, if he did indeed make an appearance, was head of a large and independent family. He could be claimed, or disclaimed, as the situation warranted.

Will saw all this. But he thought that they must press on, nevertheless. To turn back would be to be beaten before they had begun. If a lead was to be given to the King's leal supporters everywhere, they could not resile now. Livingstone's physical presence would have strengthened their hands; but it could have been a handicap too, since he would have taken charge, and perhaps manoeuvred them into a false position. Undoubtedly he would have done most of the talking.

Hay wanted to know who was going to do the talking, now? And what they were going to say?

The younger man was not too happy about that, himself. But he pointed out that it was Crichton who had called for a meeting. It would be for him to make the running.

Even so, Will Douglas rode onwards in a distinctly uneasy frame of mind. He seemed successfully to have raised the Devil — but laying him might prove less simple.

At Callendar, on the far side of the little burgh of Falkirk, they found Sir James Hamilton awaiting them with a further fifty or so men — and all Hamiltons so far as they could see. Any notion that he was involved in Livingstone's probable deception was promptly dispelled by his obvious surprise and alarm at his grandsire's absence, and clear if unvoiced disbelief in the ill health story. He gave the impression that there was skulduddery afoot somewhere, and that Will and the Constable were by no means innocent in the matter.

Three less enthusiastic and mutually trustful allies could have been hard to find, as they trotted the few more miles to Linlithgow.

That long narrow grey town amongst the green braes that enclosed its wide loch, was already a hive of activity as, just before noon, the newcomers clattered in over the West Port cobblestones. The rain had stopped falling, and men-at-arms in a great variety of colours thronged the streets. The place indeed was much more like an armed camp than was Stirling — to Will's surprise. He had not foreseen this assembling of miscellaneous forces. When he asked Hay who all these men might represent, the other shrugged.

'Many lords," he said shortly. "Sexton. Maxwell. Lindsay.

85

Lyon. Cunninghame. These colours I have seen. Waiting to discover which way the cat jumps."

"But . . . how do they know that there is anything to wait for? All these? . . ."

"Scotland is like a powder-barrel — that is why. All men's ears are stretched. To hear the faintest hint. When rogues rule, and there is no sure authority, this is the way of it. Every lord has his spies. Think you that half the land does not know by this that the new young Earl of Douglas came to Stirling to see Livingstone?"

"I came to see the King . . ."

"I give you credit, my lord, for listening to my advice at Douglas Castle, that day," Hamilton said stiffly. "For taking my guidance. But you would have been better to come to me first, rather than my grandsire . . ."

"I did not follow your guidance, sir. Nor any man's. Or woman's!" Will interrupted. "I followed my own. Only that." He knew that that sounded sour, boastful, immature. But it was true, and he had to say it.

As they rode on in silence, Will, though he looked, saw no Red Hearts of Douglas amongst the many emblems painted on breastplates and morions, and had to admit to a certain disappointment. Whatever their colours, however, the crowd fell back respectfully enough before the tightly-knit four hundred who trotted in close file behind the banners of the High Constable and Hamilton.

Where the long High Street swung away from the lochside, a smooth grassy mound rose between. On its summit were set both the palace and the fine church of St. Michael. A fairly steep but broad alley climbed thereto. As the newcomers turned into it, not only Will gave a gasp. The entire length of the alley was lined, on both sides, by motionless horsemen, their serried ranks turned in on each other. Any approach to the palace had to be made through this corridor of steel. And on every breast, the Red Heart of Douglas was vividly emblazoned.

His companions swung on Will.

"What is this?" Hay demanded. "How came these here? . . ."

"My lord, you are more cunning than you seem!" Hamilton exclaimed. "Is this a trick? . . ."

Will shook his head, and did not trust himself to speak.

They rode up between the ranks of silent inscrutable men, still even though their horses fidgeted. At a swift assessment, Will reckoned that there were no more than fifty on each side — but marshalled and spaced like that, they seemed far more. They had a quiet authority that was almost unnerving. Four times as many men rode behind, but they did not create the same impression as these.

As the newcomers neared the alley-head and the palace gates, a single horseman urged his mount forward to confront them. It was Pate Pringle, the Abercorn steward. He carried a tall pole, from which he was unfurling a great silk banner as he came. Its folds billowed out in the April breeze, to flaunt the Bloody Heart beneath three white mullets on an azure chief — the undifferenced arms of the Black Douglas himself. As he raised this on high, those silent ranks of men erupted into sound, harsh, strident, vibrant sound.

"A Douglas! A Douglas!" they shouted. It was ragged at first, but quickly settled into a rhythm, stirring, indeed menacing. "A Douglas! A Douglas!" they cried, and went on crying.

Pate Pringle spurred forward, dipped the banner briefly in front of the embarrassed Will, in a symbolic gesture of deference, and then reined round to take up a position just behind his lord, jostling Sir James Hamilton in the process. The Douglas banner now flew between the other two, higher than either and larger.

Will coughed, "Aye, Pate," he said.

Half a dozen Douglas men-at-arms moved out from the ranks, to flank the steward and standard. The rest remained still, but vocal.

"A Douglas! A Douglas!"

So the visitors rode on into the forecourt of the Palace of Linlithgow. And none in palace or town could be left in any doubt as to who made entry.

Will frowned as he rode, saying nothing to those by his side, a prey to conflicting emotions. While a fierce and elemental tide of pride undeniably surged within him, he knew anger also. This was not his doing, not as he would have it. Presumably it was his mother's work — although his message to her had merely said to have as many men as possible at Linlithgow by midday. Possibly, even, Livingstone's hand was behind it all;

he might well have sent a letter of his own, with his courier. Will had deliberately sought to manage things differently from this, not to become just an influential cat's-paw in the dire and selfish power-struggle which was ruining Scotland, whatever his mother, Hamilton, Bishop Cameron, or other proposed. Now, here he was, manoeuvred into this false position, playing his mother's game, possibly Livingstone's game, with Hamilton by his side.

The outer court of the palace was full of men also, though these were not drawn up, but dismounted and at ease. There were the liveries of many different houses here also; how many of them were under Crichton's authority was anybody's guess.

The palace was a great quadrangular structure of warm brown stone work, and, though not a fortress, it had a low gatehouse tower over the arched main entrance, midway along its south front. On the flat platform roof of this, now, a colourfully-dressed group stood watching. There were not many women there, but easily to be discerned was the Countess Beatrix of Douglas, an almost regally beautiful figure. Will made no sign that he had noticed her as he and his companions came close, and passed under the archway into the inner courtyard. The mass of their supporters remained in the outer yard; only Hay and Hamilton, with their esquires, rode on and in — until Pate Pringle perceived that Will had no such aide, and thrusting the banner to one of his men, followed the other five.

Apart from servitors, only gentry were to be seen now, a superficially gay and chattering throng which, if it hushed itself for a little at the sight of the newcomers, quickly resumed its buzz of exclamation, speculation and comment. As Will dismounted, he could not but be aware that he was the target for all eyes, and for a flood of remarks and witticisms. If his humdrum costume had been kenspeckle at Stirling, it was notably more so here, amongst all the richness and colour.

Hamilton took charge now, as to the manner born, a resplendent figure himself in multi-hued broad cloth and goldinlaid half-armour. He led the way inside the guarded main doorway demanding that they be taken to Sir William Crichton.

Amongst the dense and noisy high-born crowd inside, they were caught up at once, and could make but slow progress through. Will was comforted to see that Sir William Hay looked just about as out of place and uncomfortable as himself, a stiff soldier, suspicious and ill at ease. Soon Will felt his arm taken, and there was his mother at his side. She had with her a good-looking and well-built young man in his early twenties, who eyed Will interestedly.

"My lord," she said. "I rejoice to see you here. Come to Court. And in good company."

He nodded, more curtly than was suitable. "I have not come to your Court. Only to speak with Crichton. He is here?"

"Yes. Has been this hour. He had to ride through your Douglas guard to win entry. I have no doubts he noted it well!"

"Not *my* Douglas guard — yours!" he grated. "I did not ask you to make such gesture. Shake the Douglas fist in the face of all." His voice lowered, he spoke tensely. "I'll thank you to leave the gestures to me!"

She looked at him thoughtfully, unruffled. "As you will, my lord. But, as you were not here, and the men you sought had to be disposed in some fashion, I deemed this best. Most telling. With the numbers I could gather. To best effect." As always, she sounded entirely reasonable, correct. She turned. "Robert aided me. Will — here is Robert Fleming of Cumbernauld and Biggar. He would . . . serve you."

Will's quick breath and quicker glance was more tell-tale than he knew. If Fleming was a stranger to him in person, he was far otherwise by name. To the chiefly house of Douglas, the name of Fleming held overtones of shame. Archibald the Grim had ruined this young man's grandfather; his father had been slain by James the Gross in an ambush; his brother had been executed by Crichton and Livingstone along with the Douglas brothers.

"My lord," he said, bowing. "I am yours to command."

Will searched the other's face, an open, strong and attractive face, fair without being actually handsome. He supposed the man was indeed his vassal — for the small remnants of the once great Fleming lands he held were held of Douglas now.

"I . . . I have no commands for you, sir," Will said. "But I wish you well. Your name is known to me."

The other nodded. "I am at your service nevertheless, my lord."

The Countess was looking at Hay the Constable. "I am glad that you have brought Sir William," she said. "He is a good man. But I fear that he has not the wits to match Crichton's. Nor indeed has Sir James Hamilton. You will be careful, Will?" It was not often that Beatrix St. Clair sounded anxious or unsure.

"I will be careful, yes."

"He is a most clever man. And, and . . ."

"And I am not! Well I know it. But perhaps cleverness is not all in this matter. We shall see."

A superbly dressed gallant came pushing his way through the throng. He raised a mellifluous voice. "Constable — the Chancellor will see you now. Come."

Hay and Hamilton began to move forward.

"No!" Will barked out abruptly.

All eyes turned on him. The chatter in great groin-vaulted hall died away.

"Would you so answer this man's summons?" Will went on, thickly. "As though he was the King!"

"He is the Chancellor," Hay said.

"And you are the Constable. Great Constable of Scotland. Under the King's Grace, does any hold higher office? Chancellors come and go, do they not? But Hay is Constable, and ever will be." Sir William was in fact 7th hereditary Lord High Constable since Bruce had created the office.

Hay looked uncomfortable. Hamilton coughed. The magnificent emissary looked appalled.

"Tell Sir William Crichton that we will see him, yes." Will jerked. "But here." He glanced round the crowded vestibule. "Or . . . or somewhere else," he ended, distinctly feebly.

"There is a small chamber, my lord. Beyond that door. Part of the chapel." That was Robert Fleming, speaking quietly at Will's back.

"Aye. Let it be there, then. Tell the Chancellor, sir, we will see him there. The Constable. Sir James Hamilton. And Douglas."

There were moments of silence, and then the elegant turned and went whence he had come, wordless.

Immediately a great buzz of talk broke out. Nodding to Hay, Will set-faced, pushed on towards the small door Fleming had indicated.

The other two entered, none too confidently, but their esquires held back, waiting. Will found that Robert Fleming had come along behind him. On an impulse, he gestured to him to come in with them. He shut the door.

"Fleming of Cumbernauld," he said shortly to the other two, as they stared. "Who, if he had his rights, would be Earl of Wigtown! Sir William Crichton slew his brother."

Hay looked doubtful, but did not comment. Nor did Hamilton, but he pursed thin lips in obvious disapproval.

Will, looking around that little bare room with its dusty table and some spare chapel furnishings, spoke again, "My ladymother, out there, reminded me. That Crichton is a cleverer man than any of us. Not to forget it. *He* asked for this encounter. He wants something, therefore. Let him talk, I say. The less *we* say, it may be, the better. At first." Hay was unlikely to talk too much, but Hamilton might be otherwise.

Will had expected that Crichton might keep them waiting for a salutary time. But he had barely finished speaking when the door opened, and the same elegant as before announced the Chancellor of the realm.

The man who came in, edging past the speaker, was almost laughably different from anything that Will had imagined. He had been prepared for arrogance, pride, dominance, vehemence, ruthlessness. He could perceive no sign of these before him now. William Crichton was a tall, spare, rather sadlooking man of middle years, with the ravaged face of an ascetic and the stoop of a scholar. Pale, stiffly formal, almost diffident in manner, only the heavily-hooded eyes gave any indication that he might not be all that he seemed. If Livingstone had been a surprise, Crichton was more so. Soberly but richly dressed, he inclined his greying head towards Hay.

"My lord Constable," he said, and his speech was flat, colourless, and with the faintest impediment. "Sir James. My lord ... of Douglas, I understand?" He looked at the well-turned-out Fleming, not at Will. "And who is this? Not Sir Alexander Livingstone, whom I had expected."

"Alexander's regrets," Hay jerked. "He was taken ill. At Bannockburn. Had to return to Stirling. It is ... unfortunate."

Crichton looked unhappy. "Ah. Very."

"And *I* am Douglas, sir. This is Robert Fleming of Cumbernauld. A name that will be known to you!"

The older man inclined his head, almost as though in acceptance of a distressing fact. But those heavy-lidded eyes were considering him very thoroughly, Will was certain. "A day of surprises," he sighed.

They waited, in a rather embarrassed silence. At least, Will and his companions did; Crichton appeared to be lost in a sort of pensive melancholy.

Hamilton it was who cracked first. He cleared his throat loudly. "We have come a great way, my lord Chancellor," he said, "to see you."

The other moved slowly round the table, touching its top with long delicate fingers. When he turned, he had the window's light at his own back and in their faces. "Is that so, Sir James? I am flattered. But ... to what may I ascribe the honour?"

Hamilton frowned. "You sought to see us. Asked for this meeting. Came here to speak with us."

The Chancellor spread his hands. "The pleasure is undoubted. But I came to Linlithgow to meet my old friend and colleague, Sir Alexander Livingstone of Callendar. On the realm's affairs. In which we are both, alas, concerned as officers of state." The inference in that was plain.

"The Constable is also an officer of state," Will said.

"That is so. Have you come to see me on state business, Sir William? If so, perhaps my chamber would be more comfortable than this."

Hay shook his head. "Cease this beating of the air, sir, of a mercy!" he exclaimed. "Let us be at what we have come for.'"

"With all my heart, sirs."

They waited, and exasperation grew.

At length Hamilton burst out. "'Fore God, Crichton — come to the bit! *You* sought this. What have you to say?"

"I sought talk with Livingstone, sir — not with his grandchild.' That was sorrowful rather than tart, and the emphasis on the final syllable was so slight as to be barely noticeable.

Hamilton noticed it, nevertheless, and grew purple in the

face. He was a man of nearly thirty, his mother, Livingstone's eldest daughter, having been only sixteen at his birth. He took a step forward, hand dropping to sword-hilt.

Fearing complete failure, Will spoke quickly. "You have not spoken with him for many months, so Sir Alexander says. He holds that you would speak now, only because of myself. Douglas." Flushed, Will was talking with anything but the calm care he had determined to employ. "Douglas strength it is that has brought you here, I think! Is it not so? You have something to say to Douglas?"

The Chancellor shook his head, as though in wonderment. "My good young lord," he said. "What is this? Of what strength is this you speak? I fear I do not rate Douglas strength quite so highly, as do you . . ."

"You feared it highly enough three years ago, to slay the Earl of Douglas my cousin! And his brother. And Fleming's brother likewise. To slay, when your invited guests, in bloody murder!"

No single sound stirred in that stone-vaulted chamber, as men held their breaths for long seconds. Will himself stood appalled at what had escaped his lips.

Crichton's long fingers reached out to touch the table-top, and the tap-tap of them at last broke the utter silence. "You . . . you are young, my lord. Very young," he said, and there was steel behind that level voice now. "Else, I swear, I could not permit the tongue that so spoke to speak again! After this day. No man speaks the Chancellor so! But . . . you are scarce a man yet. So I must be patient. But be warned, my lord of Douglas — be warned!"

"We are both warned, then!" the younger man said harshly. "I am not my cousin. Nor yet my father! And I have many brothers. Seek to silence *my* tongue, and others will speak the louder! And many will listen!"

"So you threaten me, my lord? Me, the Chancellor!"

"Yes," Will agreed, simply.

Hay intervened, "Such talk serves nothing. We did not come for this. We came believing that you wished to talk, sir. For the good of the realm."

"For the good of the realm?" Crichton sighed, himself again. "You, my lord Constable? Hamilton, Douglas. And, it seems, perhaps *not* Livingstone! Your concern for His Grace's realm

93

touches me. The Council will rejoice to hear of it also, I think!"

"The Council will watch how the cat jumps. As always!"

"The Council have not failed, as yet, to support their Chancellor and preses. As I recollect it. As is right and proper."

"The Council may think again. When they perceive the forces supporting the King."

"But we all support the King's Grace, Sir William. Am I not his chief minister? While His Grace remains under age, those who rise in arms against the authority of his Chancellor and Council are in rebellion. Guilty, Whoever they claim to support."

"You say so? Even if they include the King's governor. And the High Constable?"

"Even so. Since the Council can annul these offices, Sir William. And would, I promise you!" Crichton added that, after a slight pause, almost regretfully.

"You are very sure of your Council, sir!"

"He should be less sure," Will put in shortly. "Has he forgotten Holy Church? How many bishops sit on the Council?"

The Chancellor swung on him, more swiftly than in any of his previous movements. "Bishops? ... What mean you by that?"

"How many bishops may attend your Council? The Lords Spiritual. Twelve, is it? Thirteen?"

"My lord of St. Andrews, the Primate, is ... sound. He attends. Few others. *He* speaks for Holy Church."

"Not for my lord of Glasgow, I think! Nor others. Incuding kinsmen of my own. Bishop Cameron was Chancellor once. He does not love you, sir!"

Crichton went very still, seeming to gaze down at the streaked dust of the table. "I see," he said, at last He glanced up. "No, Cameron does not love me. But others do. And there are those who do not love Cameron. Eh, Sir James?"

Hamilton looked embarrassed.

"So! Ambition makes strange bedfellows!" He turned back to Will. "Did you come to Linlithgow with anything more to say to me, young man?"

Will swallowed. "We came, rather, to hear what *you* had to say, sir."

94

"Yes, indeed!" Hamilton blustered. "Since you it was desired the meeting. Out with it, sir!"

Crichton shrugged, with apparent acquiescence. "I came but to talk with Livingstone. My friend. To inform him of certain matters. He has not attended the Council of late. We have been considering. The office of Lord Treasurer is like to fall vacant. The Council considered that Sir Alexander might worthily fill it, if it is not too great a burden. You are of the Council, my lord Constable. Perhaps you will seek Sir Alexander's view on the matter?"

His hearers stood all but dumbfounded. In a few short words he had changed the entire situation. All knew it. Livingstone, although he had made himself immensely powerful, had always lacked money, wealth. He held the King and most of the royal castles, but these were a drain on his resources rather than a source of profit. An unscrupulous man, as the realm's Treasurer, could line his pockets at will. Crichton had always kept this key position for his own disposal. The present Treasurer was a minion of his own, Sir Walter Haliburton of Dirleton. If the Chancellor was prepared to buy Livingstone with the Treasurership, there was no question as to how Livingstone would react. Avaricious to a degree, he would grasp at it. All else would go by the board. Crichton knew his man. Any alliance between his hearers and Livingstone was as good as shattered. And Livingstone, holding the King, alone could lend the vital air of authority, legality, to any rising against the Chancellor.

Once again there was complete silence in that little chamber. No talking would change this situation.

Crichton coughed in his diffident way. "The Wardenship of the Middle March is at present vacant. Owing to the late lamented death of the Earl your father, my lord of Douglas. You are young for so onerous a task on the realm's behalf — but there is an able Deputy-Warden in Sir Walter Kerr. The Council must make the appointment shortly. I ask myself whether to suggest your lordship's name? . . ."

So there it was, the second stroke in this shrewd attack to detach Douglas from the others by flattering Will with this lofty appointment, to keep Douglas power busy patrolling the Border instead of threatening his own hegemony.

"No!" Will cried. "No, Sir. Keep your Wardenship. I do not want it."

The other inclined his head. "So be it. I was in doubt as to the wisdom of it, since I have seen your style! In that case, sirs, I have no more to say." Crichton bowed stiffly, and moved round to the door. "A good day to you. You will convey my concern to Sir Alexander, over his health? My deep concern! And not fail to inform him of the matter of the Treasurership?" With a levelly significant glance round them all, he left them.

The putative allies eyed each other starkly. In the chaos of their reactions they had one urge in common requiring no discussion. They all wanted to be away from Linlithgow, without delay. Outmanoeuvred, dismissed and made to look foolish, their immediate concern was to be gone. They streamed out, practically wordless.

It is to be feared that Will Douglas was less than the dutiful son when his mother sought to question him, as he pushed his way through the crowded hall. With only the curtest of answers to her queries, he thrust on. She had little better response from Hay, but Hamilton was more eloquent. She was not alone in her interest.

In the inner courtyard, Will found that Robert Fleming was still at his back, with Pate Pringle. "You choose no goodly cause to support!" he jerked. "Better back to your Cumbernauld!"

The other shook his head. "I said that I wished to serve *you*, my lord."

"My service looks to be barren, does it not? Profitless!"

"Nevertheless, I would come with you. If you will have me. You have no esquire?"

"Why, man? What have I to offer you?"

"You are my lord. What I have I hold of you."

"My mother put you up to this?"

"Not so. I sought her aid, to come to you." Fleming's voice changed a little. "I see your service as the best road to my desire, my lord. Vengeance on Crichton. For my brother."

"Ha! And you still think that, after what you heard in there?"

"Yes."

"And what of vengeance for your father? Your grandsire?"

"That is by with. An old story. All who played part in that are dead. So I would ride with you, my lord."

"As you will. Pate — find Cumbernauld a horse."

"Aye, lord. And the troop? The men I brought? Out there?"

"They were loud at shouting Douglas!" Will said grimly. "Let us see if they can do more than shout. Let them ride with me. To Stirling."

"Aye. Good, my lord."

"There speaks Douglas indeed!" Fleming exclaimed. "I thank God to hear it!"

Will turned to look at him, but said nothing.

Later, as the enlarged company, of nearly five hundred, rode out of Linlithgow westwards, Hamilton spoke. "At least it shows how high he rates our threat. This Treasurership. To give up that will cost Crichton dear. We must have troubled him sorely."

"*We* have not. Only Douglas," the Constable said. "These at our backs. Douglas swords and lances. That is all that troubles Crichton. The rest he can deal with. You saw — he did not seek to buy *us*. With offices. Only Douglas. And Livingstone."

"Livingstone," Will repeated. "Can we keep this matter from him? Meantime. Tell him nothing of it?"

"Crichton will send messengers, never fear. He will not leave it to us."

"Could we not waylay his messengers? Keep them from Sir Alexander? Watch for them. We have men, now. To give us time."

"Time for what?" Hamilton demanded. "What can we do? With my grandson? He will do nothing, until he knows Crichton's views. And when he learns of the Treasurership, he will take it. Nothing more sure."

"Aye. So say I. But still we need time. It is not Livingstone we need look to now, I think. Only that he should remain ignorant, so long as may be. He cozened us today. It is our turn, now! . . ."

*   *   *

Will at least wasted no time. That very evening, in the Ballengeich Tower of Stirling Castle, he all but importuned young James Stewart.

"Your Grace," he cried. "Do you not see it? If you are ever to get out of the clutches of these scoundrels who hold you fast, and spoil your realm, you must act now. Act the man. The king. Before it is too late."

"But what can I do?" the boy exclaimed. "I *am* held fast. They will never let me out of this castle. What can I do?"

"You can do what only a king can do. What they hold you here to do. For them. Sign decrees. Which are then the law. The royal warrant. I say such decrees need not always be written by Livingstone and Crichton!"

"But, if I signed some paper contrary to their wishes. They would make me pay for it. Sorely."

"Only with their tongues, Sire. Can you not face that? Others will be hazarding more than that, in your cause!"

"Yes. But, even so, they would not let it stand. A decree that I had signed. Not of their making. They would annul it. Make me sign another, declaring it void."

"To be sure. But that would take time. They would require a meeting of the Privy Council to annul a decree bearing your royal signature. Would they not? Livingstone himself could not do it. Nor Crichton. And that time could be well used."

"What would you do, Cousin? What would you have me to sign? What difference can it make? Since I cannot leave this castle?"

"*You* can not, Your Grace. But *I* can. Livingstone will not try to hold me now, with a hundred Douglas lances in his forecourt!" That was the situation. Livingstone had by no means permitted the great company of Douglas, Hay, Hamilton and other supporters that had ridden from Linlithgow, to enter the castle proper; but even in the outer bailey they represented a threat. Will felt a deal safer than he had done before.

"But what will you do?"

"I will raise your standard. The King's Royal Standard. Against Crichton. If you will let me, Sire."

The boy stared, biting his lip. He glanced over at Robert Fleming, who sat there quietly listening. "How . . . how shall you do that?"

"I shall need Your Grace's help. I can raise men. The Douglas power which all talk so much of. But it must not be *only* Douglas. Others must rally to your cause. Otherwise it will be proclaimed rebellion. Treason! And that will frighten many.

98

The Constable's authority is not enough, he says. For he is only responsible for Your Grace's person and safety, he tells me. So we need *your* authority. Your royal decree. There is only one man who may raise the Royal Standard of Scotland. Other than the King. That is the King's Lieutenant-General. Lieutenant-General of the Realm!"

"But, but there *is* none. Is there?"

"Not since my cousin died. The 5th Earl. Archibald, Earl of Douglas and Duke of Touraine. Father of those who were murdered. He was Lieutenant-General. You could make another, Sire. And only you can!"

Even Robert Fleming cleared his throat nervously.

James almost whispered it. *"Me?* Make *you* Lieutenant-General? You? Could I do that?"

"Why not? You are the King. And being held here, you need a Lieutenant. I am young, but at least I am loyal. Make me Lieutenant, and all leal men can rally to your standard."

"They would annul it. Crichton. The Council."

"They would wish to. But could they? The King's Deputy? Appointed by himself. They would not confirm it — but could they annul it?" Will looked at Fleming.

"I do not know, my lord. Your Grace. But it would seem a most special office. Not for the Council to appoint to. This would much confuse them I think."

"So think I. Which gives us time. If I have such decree written, Sire, will you sign it?"

James hesitated, darting uncertain glances, the red strawberry mark on his cheek red indeed. Then he nodded. "Yes, Yes, I will. So be it you win me free out of this castle. Soon. I will sign it."

Will sighed his relief. "That is our purpose, Sire. Now, this very night, those Douglas men-at-arms out there will turn messenger! To ride to every corner of the realm where there are Douglas lands and Douglas vassals. To muster. To assemble, and ride for Stirling. Pate will see to it. Pate Pringle. He will know how it should be done and where to go — for I do not. This Douglas power — we will see what it amounts to!"

"It will take time, my lord," Fleming warned. "There has not been an assembly of Douglas might for many years. Men will have grown slack. Forgotten their duty, perhaps. Time it will take . . ."

"And time we have not got, I tell you. There must be no holding back. No delay. You — you will go to Angus. To the Red Douglases. The Earl of Angus, at Tantallon. He can field a thousand, they say. And near to hand, in Lothian. Tomorrow . . ."

CHAPTER FIVE

To the high shrilling of a trumpet, Will Douglas spurred his heavy charger to a canter, and rode, clanking and clattering, up the serried ranks of armed and mounted men who sat waiting, that sunny morning, on the Burghmuir of Stirling; and the cheer that rose at the bottom end of his quarter-mile ride swelled and deepened as he went, and gradually changed its tempo and quality, as the chant of 'A Douglas! A Douglas!' mingled with it, permeated it and finally overbore the rest. Not much more than half of that host wore the Douglas colours, but these, in their troops and companies, formed the entire forward portion of the long and wide column, so that, as the Earl came pounding up the line, that ominous, pregnant slogan, two words that in the past had struck more of dread in Scots ears than any others soever, grew and prevailed. The young man who occasioned it all would have been less than human had he not been affected, excited, enheartened by it — and Will Douglas was very human. It was his nineteenth birthday.

He was, indeed, glad of the heavy, clumsy and restricting armour that he wore — since, within it, his actual trembling eagerness could not be discerned. Armour, of course, should be made for a man, tailored; and Will had had no time for that, amongst other things. What he wore, indeed, had been built up from various pieces, mainly provided by Sir William Hay from the Erroll armoury, some fitting, some not, and all tending to look slightly old-fashioned. But the open, loose linen surcoat over it at least was his own, sewn by a Stirling tailor, with the Red Heart of Douglas embroidered front and back. He rode bareheaded, his black hair streaming in the wind, the great battle helm with its rude crest of a salamander's head, carried at his esquire's saddle-bow behind. His mount also was armoured and heraldically caparisoned, a massively-built brute more meet to pull a plough than lead chivalry, but necessary to carry all its weight. Its great hooves spattered turfs from the Burghmuir as it cantered heavily.

Close behind, two others rode, both armoured likewise. Robert Fleming carried, as well as the helmet, Will's lance and great blazoned shield, hastily painted with the quartered arms of Douglas and Moray, while Pate Pringle bore aloft the fluttering banner of the Bloody Heart. Some way further behind, the trumpeter trotted.

The trio came to the head of the array, where the Constable awaited them, under his own red and white banner, amongst a group of knightly supporters. They made a glittering and impressive-seeming leadership to a noteable cohort. But none there was deceived, least of all Will Douglas, however momentarily uplifted.

He raised steel-gauntleted hand to Hay. "No more come," he said, a little breathlessly "No sign of any parties from north or west. From the topmost tower Hamilton has failed us."

"Aye. I expected it," the Constable said curtly. "And Livingstone?"

"He has not shown face. Keeps his room. But interfered nothing. His two sons never leave the King's side."

Hay nodded. "We have been fortunate with Livingstone, at least. He can know nothing, or he would never have let us go, like this. Without railing on us. We ride now, then? Forward?"

"We ride, yes." Will signed to the trumpeter, who sounded his clamant ululant advance. Like a great monster laboriously stretching and shaking itself, the long array stirred into movement, southwards.

"God go with us and cherish us!"Master Adam, the somewhat smug Cambuskenneth sub-Abbot said piously — the only churchman present.

"Amen!" the Constable grunted feelingly. "Else we were wise to turn back now. While still we can!"

Hay was no optimist, of course, but the situation was indeed less heartening than it might seem. There were fifteen hundred men in that goodly company, eight hundred of them Douglases — but that was nothing like the numbers that they had looked for. From most of the Douglas baronies and lairdships, the response had been disappointing and tardy; from some, not at all. Admittedly the time had been short, but even so, enthusiasm for the new earl's summons had been markedly absent. No single great Douglas baron had come in person, and most had sent only token forces. Notably, the Earl of Angus, after a cool reception of Robert Fleming at Tantallon, had sent not one man; so that, significantly, the Red branch of the house was totally unrepresented. Apparently James the Gross's inertia had been infectious, and here too, men waited to see which way the cat would jump. As for others than Douglas, it was the same story, only more so. Basically, only the Constable's friends and neighbours from the Carse of Gowrie and south Perthshire were represented. And apart from the local Cambuskenneth contingent, Holy Church looked otherwhere. Even Hamilton evidently had had second thoughts.

Had they been able to wait longer, months instead of a week or two, it might possibly have been different, for the assembling, arming and despatching of large numbers of men was a slow business — or so the excuses went. On the other hand, delay could have aided the other side equally. Moreover, Will had come to the reluctant conclusion that men, if they sought excuse to hold back, would continue to find it.

What had forced their hand, however, was the information from Dumfriesshire that the Chancellor was urgently assembling men from Crichton lands of Sanquhar and Upper Nithsdale, and was strengthening the defences of Edinburgh Castle. So he was preparing for hostilities — and still having the nation's purse to pay for it, he could gather support. The only blessing in the situation had been their evident success in keeping from Livingstone and his sons the offer of the Treasurership. Three of Crichton's couriers lay languishing in the cellars of Cambuskenneth Abbey, their messages undelivered. Sir Alexander had been informed only of the proposed bribe of the Border Wardenship for Will, and the Chancellor's belief that Livingstone dared not move against him. So the old man, who seldom emerged from the castle, was lying low, waiting. But he had other sons, elsewhere, and sooner or later Crichton would approach them.

The muster on the Burghmuir had gone on. Livingstone had done nothing to try to stop it, but neither had he acknowledged its existence. He would claim credit if they were successful; if not, he would repudiate them entirely.

Will fretted, now, at the slowness of the pace the great lumbering horses imposed upon them. It was thirty five miles to Edinburgh. All Scotland would know that they were on their way, before they got there.

Nevertheless, at Bannockburn, a mere couple of miles on their road, he had the trumpeter sound the halt. There, on that ground sacred in Scotland's history, he ordered the troops and companies to break ranks and gather round. He handed the precious parchment to Hay to read aloud — which in stiff embarrassment that man did.

"To all lords, spiritual and temporal, barons and landed men, burgesses, lieges and leal men of this my realm of Scotland — greeting!" he jerked forth in a flat monotone. "I hereby decree and declare that I have this day, in my castle of Stirling, for the better governance and weal of this my realm, appointed and established my right trusty and well-beloved cousin and servant, William, Earl of Douglas and Avondale, to be my Lieutenant-General of the said Realm, as was the Earl Archibald and others before him, to wield in my royal name and stead the sword of state, and to require of all lords and lieges soever that they offer the said William all support, strength and service as they would my royal self.

Signed by my hand, this twenty-ninth day of April, of our Lord's year the fourteenth hundred and forty-third, at my castle of Stirling,

JAMES."

If Will had expected a great wave of excitement and enthusiasm for this announcement, he was disappointed. Surprise there was to some extent, but by and large its significance passed over the heads of the vast majority of its hearers. The few of the lairdly and knightly class who led the host, of course, perceived something of its vital importance, but by and large the thing was accepted as some sort of clerkly formality irrelevant to fighting men. Even the ceremonious unfurling of the splendid red Lion Rampant on gold, the Royal Standard of Scotland, to take pride of place between the banners of Douglas and the Constable, raised not so much as a cheer. It was six grim years since James the First's assassination when that standard had meant anything in the land.

It was Will Douglas's firmest intention, however, that it

should mean something hereafter. Under its once-proud folds, he led on southwards. It might all seem like mummery, play-acting, as Hay himself tended to think, for someone still lacking two years to being of age, but he at least was determined to prove it otherwise.

*　　*　　*

There were no crowds present at Linlithgow, that late after-noon as they rode into the grey burgh by the loch. They paused there only long enough to dismiss the acting Constable of the palace and sheriffdom, in the King's name, and to install in his place Douglas of Mains, an elderly man and one of the few substantial lairds of the name who had rallied to his lord's banner in person. Then Will self-consciously read a brief proc-lamation, his first official act as nominal Lieutenant-General of the Realm, declaring that he had taken over Linlithgow, the King's personal house, in His Grace's name, and commanding all loyal men to rally here to the Royal Standard. The said Standard was run up from the palace's topmost tower, and leaving a scratch garrison of about one hundred of the least active men to hold the place, they moved on eastward. It was all only a gesture, a token, but with its own significance and probably worth the hundred men. There was a certain satisfac-tion for Will, at least, in thus making good the humiliation of their previous departure from Linlithgow.

Six miles more brought the weary host to Abercorn, where monastery, village and castle all huddled together round a small tidal estuary of the Firth of Forth, about ten miles from Edinburgh. Will had never been here before, to his father's chosen domicile, and saw it at once, in the sunset light, to be a place of ease and comfort rather than strength, a soft and rich establishment of scattered undefended buildings, orchards, pleasances and gardens, strange seat for the head of the warlike house of Douglas. The castle itself was hardly to be dis-tinguished from the monastery occupying a low green promon-tory of the firth. Here was no base, as he had hoped.

But at least there was ample provision for the tired and hungry warriors to camp for the night, Pate Pringle and the Prior taking charge. The Countess was at home, with Will's sister Beatrix, and gave them fair enough welcome — even though she seemed less than enthusiastic over her son's present venture. Undoubtedly, in her ambitions for Douglas advancement, she preferred less warlike and straightforward methods. Some indication of this was evidenced when, later that night, after he had come back from the encampment, she came to Will's room.

"This adventure, Will," she said. "Were it not for the Constable, I would think it ill-advised. And he, I fear, is less than sanguine."

"You have been talking to Hay? I'll thank you to leave him to me. As Constable, he is necessary to give me something of the authority I need. I have been at pains to keep him at my side. I do not want him made the more doubtful." Will was always at his most gruff and uncomfortable with his imperturbably beautiful mother.

"I do not seek to weaken your hand, Will — only to strengthen it," the Countess assured. "You are young, and like to run where you might better walk, I think. I would but counsel care. Using your head rather than your right arm. As for Sir William, I would bind him closer to you, not turn him away."

"How that?"

"He is a good man. Honest. And a widower. With broad acres. I had thought to wed Beatrix to Robert Fleming. To ensure that he makes no trouble over the Wigtown earldom. But I think Sir William would serve her better. He is stronger, older. And Beatrix needs mastering . . ."

"Older! I' faith — he is old enough to be her father!"

"No harm in that. I was twenty years younger than your father. He will make her a good husband. Safe. And it would bind him surely to Douglas. Robert can wait . . ."

"And Beatrix? What of her? It this all you think your daughters are for?"

"They have their part to play, in the restoration of our house. And suitable husbands must be found for them. That is my concern, Will. Leave it to me."

"Gladly! Myself, I would restore our house on the field rather than in the bedchamber!"

"So says nineteen summers! And where is your first field to be fought, Will? And when? Crichton shuts himself in Edinburgh Castle, they say. You will not take that. Any more than he could take Stirling."

"No. But we can strike at Crichton other than in Edinburgh Castle . . ."

They were on the move early next morning, following the coast eastwards, by Queen Margaret's Ferry and Dundas. Little more than an hour's riding brought them to the mouth of the River Almond in its leafy valley. And breasting the green slopes of Cramond beyond, they saw ahead of them only a few miles further, the smoking ridge of Edinburgh, rising above lesser hills and culminating in the soaring, proud castle-crowned rock, so like Stirling's, that shook its fist in the face of the morning. Silently the leaders at least stared at it.

Robert Fleming, at Will's back, leaned forward to touch the younger man's steel-gauntleted elbow, and pointed, half-left. Much nearer at hand, from gentle, rolling, cattle-dotted braes, a tall and handsome grey stone towerhouse rose amongst the grasslands, a fine sight in the early sunshine, against the sparkling blue of the isle-dotted firth.

"Barnton Castle," he said.

Switching his gaze between the great frowning fortress on the far ridge, and the goodly fortalice a bare half-mile away, Will nodded. "So that is Crichton's house. Aye. It will serve very well, I think. How say you, Sir William?"

"A notable bait," Hay acceded. "But . . . can we spring the trap? With this?" He jerked his head back towards their following host.

"We have come to try. To put it to the test, at least. Come."

They rode directly towards the fine house. Soon they could see signs of activity about it, hurrying men coming and going, some cattle being hastily driven away. Presently a couple of horsemen were seen to ride out from its enclosing courtyard, and spur off eastwards in the direction of Edinburgh.

"Let them go," Will said, when Pate Pringle wanted to order pursuit.

By the time that the column reached the home parks and infields of Barnton Castle, the place was shut up against them. Though no great stronghold, it was a fortified building, as was every lord's and laird's house, rising from a mound around which was a wide and deep dry ditch, which was commanded from the high encircling curtain-walls, of the courtyard. The drawbridge across this had been raised, at the gatehouse.

Within this enclosure, the towerhouse itself rose five storeys to a parapet and walk surounding the gabled attic storey. The thick stone walls were pierced by small iron-grilled windows, and provided with many splayed apertures for shooting from.

Ordering the men to be drawn up just beyond bow-shot range of the walls, Will and Hay, with a few supporters, rode forward to near the bridge-end, under the Royal Standard. People could be seen watching them from windows and the parapet-walk. The trumpeter sounded a flourish.

Will, helmet on but visor open, raised his voice. "Douglas speaks. Appointed Lieutenant-General of this kingdom, by the King's Grace. Who holds this house shut against the Royal Standard of King James?"

There was no reply.

"I speak in His Grace's name," he called again. "Who holds Sir William Crichton's house of Barnton shut against the King?"

From the parapet walk a voice replied. "I see not the King's Grace there. I know naught of any Lieutenant. This is the house of the Chancellor of Scotland. I, his son, Sir Andrew Crichton, hold it, in his name. If you would see my father, go you to Edinburgh." Sir Andrew did not see any necessity to mention that he was only an illegitimate son.

"I have come to Barnton," Will returned shortly. "I demand that you open to me, in the King's name."

"I know you not. And will open nothing. Go to my father."

"Hear this, and think again, Sir Andrew." Will nodded to Hay, who once more read out the royal decree and command that all obedience and aid be accorded the Lieutenant-General by every one of the King's lieges.

There was some delay before an answer was shouted to that. "I know not whether your paper be true or false," Crichton's son asserted. "I know none of you."

"You refuse to yield this house to the King's command?"

"I do. I refuse to yield anything but to the King himself. Or on my father's order."

"Then we must take it. And the worse for you!"

"Take it. If you can!"

Will looked at the Constable, and shrugged. There was no

more to be said. It was only what they had expected, indeed planned for.

They turned their horses and rode back to the waiting ranks.

Prepared as they were for this development, there was an inevitable sense of anti-climax. Despite threats, there was remarkably little that they could do that would be effective, meantime. They had no artillery or siege-engines, and without such there could be no breaching of the walls. Any attempt to rush the curtain-wall with scaling-ladders, by day, must be immensely costly in men; and even if successful, could leave the attackers exposed in the courtyard to decimating fire from the tower itself. It would have no ground-floor entrance, save to vaulted cellarage, the doorway being at first-floor level, reachable only by a removable timber stair. It would be scaling-ladders again, hammering at an iron-barred outer yett, and under murderous fire from above. These towers of fence were not called that for nothing. There might be slightly better chances after dark.

Hay now took charge. A spate of orders sent the host to various tasks and stations. The castle was encircled, camp was pitched, horse-lines staked out, forage gathered, all still-available cattle rounded up. But this activity was not for all, or indeed for the majority. Will and Fleming took the main body and rode up the gentle slopes to the south-east. There, on the long, low grassy ridge, they could see all the lie of the land round about, and all the way to Edinburgh. Will, from much hunting in Ettrick Forest, had an experienced eye added to a natural flair for country, and he quickly perceived the possibilities and hazards of the site, tactically. Without any training in soldiering, it was nevertheless quite evident to him where men could be disposed to best effect, where numbers could be hidden in reserve, where ambushes could be laid and flanking moves made. Pate Pringle and Robert Fleming translated these notions and dispositions into commands and instructions. Troops and parties of men moved off to their appointed places.

When Will returned to the red and white campaigning pavilion Hay had had erected, out of the fourteen hundred men only perhaps one-third were concerning themselves with besieging Barton Castle. The rest were facing Edinburgh.

There was nothing for it, now, but to wait. It seemed dull and spiritless employment for so puissant a company. But all day they did just that, while the larks shouted, the cuckoos called and the gulls wheeled around Barnton braes.

As darkness fell, braziers were lit all round the curtain-walls of the castle. There were to be no undetected night attacks, it seemed. Not that anything of the sort was planned.

Will slept but little that night. There are few hours of deep darkness of a May night in Scotland, and he spent them moving round the perimeter positions of his little army — although Hay declared this quite unnecessary, and himself retired to bed. Will was much concerned lest a swift and unheralded attack from Edinburgh should take them by surprise. He was only too concious of the fact that William Crichton sat only four miles away, with the resources of the great fortress and city at his command.

But no attack transpired. Men who had stood to arms all night slept late into the forenoon, and still there was no sign of a move from Edinburgh. The besieging force settled down to a routine — which included great eating, for quite a herd of Barnton cattle were discovered in a hollow to the north, and it would have been a poor armed force which failed to spoil the enemy and nourish itself at the same time. Will Douglas, however, of an energetic and impatient temperament, disliked the idleness and waiting intensely. Unsuitably for the lieutenant-general of a kingdom, he made himself quite the most active man in his host. Hay, who had a great capacity for patient inaction, lectured him briefly on the essential military virtue of delegation of authority.

At least, Will's restless perambulations produced one possibly useful result. Prowling around, he discovered, to the west of the castle, a little grassy dell where a small but brisk streamlet disappeared underground. Probing established that the line of flow went on in the direction of the castle; and further exploration revealed the burn emerging again on lower ground some distance to the north-east, approximately on the same line. He guessed that this might well represent the castle's water-supply, since the line seemed to pass beneath the establishment, yet without flooding the dry surrounding ditch. Presumably the water was reached by a well-shaft sunk in either the courtyard or the basement chamber of the tower. Will, therefore, set men to work damming and diverting the stream. If they could not produce artillery to batter the defenders into submission, at least they might be reduced by lack of water.

The second day passed as uneventfully as the first, with not so much as a messenger approaching from Edinburgh, or any move made by the castle inmates. The second night passed as had done the first.

On the third day, however, there was a diversion. About midday, scouts reported that an armed force was approaching from the south. But it was not a great array, only about four score men, and under a single banner of three black hunting-horns on white.

"Three hunting-horns? That is the device of Forrester of Corstorphine," the Constable said. "A notable baron."

"That is all?" Will demanded. "No other follows? None ride elsewhere, in support?"

In due course the newcomer arrived, warlike in aspect but proclaiming adherence to the King's Lieutenant-General. He was indeed Sir John Forrester, a powerful knight, of middle years and substantial reputation, whose lands lay just to the west of Edinburgh only three miles away. He came offering his sword and strength.

Will made much of him, mightily pleased. This was his first unsummoned recruit, and one of worth. He had not come in any hasty enthusiasm, but on the third day. He had waited, most evidently, to see how matters would go, and only now had decided to throw in his weight against Crichton. It was a hopeful sign. Forrester brought interesting tidings, as well as support. He informed that people of his, in Edinburgh the night before, reported no large assembling of men in the city — which nevertheless was agog with rumours of a great army's approach, led by the dreaded Douglas. The only unusual activity was a further strengthening of the castle's defences, and a great intaking of provisions. It looked as though the Chancellor anticipated being besieged, like his son, rather than himself making more aggressive moves. Although Sir John did not say so, this was obviously what had made up his mind for him.

With sentries well posted, Will felt it safe to sleep most of that third night.

By noon the following day, Will's scant store of patience was exhausted, however long the Constable was prepared to wait.

He approached the drawbridge-end, with Hay and Forrester, under the Lion Rampant, and had the trumpeter blow loud and long.

"Sir Andrew Crichton," he called. "Do you hear me? Douglas. Aye. Then, see you. No help comes to you from your father. He has shut himself up in Edinburgh Castle. Here is Sir John Forrester of Corstorphine. You know him."

Forrester raised his voice. "It is true. The Chancellor makes no move. He shows not his face in the streets of Edinburgh. He deserts you here. I counsel you to yield. With honour."

"Surrender this house now," Will went on. "And you may go free. Take what you will from it. Keep your sword. All within will be spared. Resist further and you will receive no mercy. As a rebel against the King, you and all your house will suffer the penalty of treason. Think well on that. In the King's name, I order that you yield. Forthwith."

There was a pause. Then Crichton's voice sounded thinly from a tower window. "Forrester. This of Douglas? Is it true? That he is made the King's Lieutenant?"

"True, yes. I have seen the decree."

"And Livingstone?"

"Livingstone is still with the King. At Stirling."

Another pause. "If I yield, you swear that I go free?"

"I swear," Will shouted. "You and yours."

"Aye. It is the water. We have no water. The well is dry. I. . . I yield, then. And hold you to your oath, my lord. Before all."

So Barnton Castle fell, a bloodless victory. Sir Andrew Crichton rode out, with his people, about thirty of them, men, women and three children, well laden with goods and belongings. A sandy-haired foxy-faced youngish man, he made sour token surrender of his sword to Will, and then led the way off towards Edinburgh with scarce a word spoken and never a backwards glance at his deserted fine house.

Will now came into major disagreement with his colleagues. The general attitude was that this goodly house was the legitimate spoils of war, and should be sacked and then held against Crichton, its owner. Will was not against a certain amount of sacking, but declared that he had neither the men nor the inclination to garrison and hold castles. Taken once, it could be taken again. Crichton might win it back, and wipe out the blow to his prestige. It should be destroyed entirely. That way, the Chancellor would suffer the greater harm to his name, and authority. Pull down his house, so close to his citadel of Edinburgh, and he was not able to lift a hand to save it.

Will had his way, and presently, after some ransacking, large numbers of men were set to the task of demolition. It was no light undertaking, with all that massive stonework and iron-hard mortar. But at least there was no lack of labour, and the men discovered a fiendish pleasure in the destruction, after long idleness. They went at it with a will.

At length, aided by some gunpowder discovered in a cellar, the once-proud fortalice amongst the green knowes was reduced to a vast heap of rubble. On top of this they piled all the woodwork and most of the plenishings, unused hay and the like, and set all alight. Under the great column of black smoke the array eventually formed up in its troops and companies, to ride away from Barnton braes, in the early evening.

They proceeded in the same direction as before, eastwards.

Despite Sir John Forrester's assurances about the reactions in Edinburgh, it was with considerable trepidation that Will approached that ancient proud city between the hills and the sea. Their host, at Barnton, or even on the Burghmuir of Stirling, might seem large and powerful; but against the capital city it was a mere handful. Yet, if their attempt was to achieve anything of lasting value, be more than a mere flash-in-the-pan, something like what they now proposed was necessary. They could by no means turn back yet.

They met no opposition, at any rate, on their four-mile approach. As they neared the city, villages, demesnes, mills and the like clustered ever more thickly. But no crowds congregated to greet them either, although it was evident that their presence and identity was well known — indeed their outriders reported that everywhere the dread name of Douglas was on every lip. People peered, as they passed, from windows and behind walls.

Forrester was concerned about timing. They had taken too long in demolishing Barnton, he said. The gates of the walled city closed at sunset. It was no part of their policy to raise the citizenry against them by assaulting gates and walls; on the other hand, if they had to camp outside until morning, it would give the enemy time to make dispositions, and also to ascertain just how small, in fact, was their strength. In the narrow streets and wynds, this would not be so apparent.

They sent forward an advance party to try to ensure that the gates were kept open for them.

When they reached Edinburgh, with the sinking sun behind them, it was to find the West Port still open. The advance party, waiting there, declared that there had been no attempt to close the gates. The townsfolk knew well that they were coming, and were apparently not in a mood to offend Douglas.

Will had mixed feelings about this evident dread, by the common people, for his name. In theory, he knew that it had existed; to experience it, however convenient in these circumstances, was another matter.

Unlike the villages, the city streets were crowded as they rode in. Everyone seemed to have come out to watch, or were thronging the windows of the tall thrusting tenements and lands so lofty and close-huddled that they almost blocked out the sky. The streets were so narrow that the upper storeys of the houses, projecting in top-heavy fashion one above the other, all but met at seventh and eighth floor level — indeed neighbours could converse comfortably up there, window to window, across the street, and washed clothes hung on lines between. Will felt suffocated, the more so as the cobblestones of the streets themselves were the receptacles for all filth and garbage, with pigs rooting amongst the crowds and poultry pecking. If this was city life, heaven preserve him from it.

However interested, inquisitive, the Edinburgh crowds were not welcoming, open gates or none. In silence they watched the long columns of armed men ride through their deep ravines of wynds and alleys. There were no cheers, no smiles, no wavings. Crichton might be unpopular, but Douglas was certainly no less so.

Will was in a fever of uneasiness. The latent hostility of such numbers of people was daunting. Moreover, the narrowness of the already crowded streets ensured that no more than three horsemen could ride abreast — and though this had the effect of attenuating the column to the impressive length of well over half a mile, it meant that any attack from a side lane could cut the force up with the greatest of ease.

The Grassmarket was wider, and here they rode directly

under the towering cliffs of the castle. It was a strange sensation to parade along so close below and in fullest view of so much hatred and entrenched strength up there, and yet to be, for the moment, comparatively safe from any harmful expression of it — for the fortress's cannon could by no means be depressed sufficiently to shoot down at so steep an angle.

Winding up the narrow hill of the West Bow was different, again — and Forrester, who of course knew the city well, was anxious now. At its head they would come out on to the high Lawnmarket, on the very spine of the ridge on which Edinburgh was built. This was just below the castle's forecourt approach, and in fullest view of its gatehouse and battlements. If so decided, cannon could open fire there and clear the streets. Worse a swift and sudden sally from the fortress could attack and overwhelm the head of the invading column while its long tail was still far off, and so deal with the rest piecemeal. He, Forrester, would have preferred to do what they had to do down in the Grassmarket.

But Will was adamant, however alarmed. This thing must be done properly, and with no appearance of fear or haste. The Market Cross, beside the High Kirk of St. Giles, was the place for official pronouncements. There it must be, if humanly possible. In this Hay agreed with him.

The emerging on to the open Lawnmarket was one of the most unpleasant experiences of Will's life, to be so exposed to danger and yet to be so incapable of protecting oneself or striking back. On the left they were now looking straight at the frowning ramparts and yawning gun-ports of the citadel. To turn their backs on that, and ride right-handed down the High Street, was an exercise demanding strong nerves. The street was wide and devoid of cover.

Only a couple of hundred yards down the High Street was the great cathedral-church of St. Giles, with its mighty ribbed lantern-tower, the biggest church Will had ever seen. In its shadow was Edinburgh's Market Cross, its tall ornate unicorn-crowned shaft rising from a platform-turret. They reached this, at least, without any cannon-fire or indeed any sign of activity from the castle behind them.

There followed the trying business of waiting for the rest of the company to arrive, under the distant scrutiny of the populace, which here held well back in the mouths of pends and entries and under the arcading of the merchants' booths, only too well aware of the menace from the citadel. Hay sent for the city's Provost.

At length all were assembled around the cross, in their steel-clad ranks, completely filling the High Street right up to its junction with the Lawnmarket. Will was certainly not going to wait longer, for any provost or civic dignitary. He mounted the steps of the cross, with his party, under the Royal Standard.

This time he did his own announcing — since it seemed that the Douglas name was so potent here. When the trumpeter had finished, he spoke into the hush.

"I am William Douglas, the Earl." He paused, looking round him. "I greet all leal citizens of Edinburgh, in the King's name." Another pause. "His Grace, for the good of this his realm has appointed me his Lieutenant-General. Here is his royal warrant."

Will read out the decree. Almost he could recite it, by heart, now.

When he had finished, Hay plucked at his armoured arm. "Here is the Provost, my lord."

A little plump man, in a furred robe, all eager smiles, bobbed and scraped before him, rather like a pigeon.

Will nodded, and went on. "I Douglas, hereby declare that, by the King's royal command, a parliament of his realm will be held, at Stirling, on the first day of July next, at which all lords, spiritual and temporal, all officers of the Crown, all representatives of the shires and of royal burghs, and all others meet to attend, shall compear. At which parliament new Lords of the Articles will be appointed, for the governance of this kingdom, and a new Chancellor will be sworn in, in the room of Sir Willam Crichton who is hereby declared forfeit and without the King's peace. This I, Douglas, Lieutenant-General of Scotland, declare to you, in the name of James, King of Scots, and in the presence of Sir William Hay, High Constable of Scotland. God save the King's Grace!"

Hoarse and self-conscious, Will glared around him, in the fading light. He felt a fool mouthing this sort of clerk's talk. But nobody that he could see looked in the least amused or mocking, least of all the Provost. In fact, most of his hearers seemed to be distinctly grim-faced, if not agitated, over the implications of what he had announced, whatever they may have thought of his manner of announcing. For a youth still in his teens, even though Douglas, to declare the formidable Chancellor forfeit, and therefore the chancellorship vacant, was to challenge fate indeed.

Will thrust a paper at the Provost. "Master Provost — you will see that this summons to the parliament is published. Before all. I charge you. See to it."

The little man looked anxious, doubtful and ingratiating, all at the same time.

Will nodded to the others, signed to the trumpeter, and clanked down the cross steps and back to his charger. "It is enough, he said, to Fleming. "Let us be away from this city."

So the long, slow and winding return journey was made, in the evening's dusk — and in the narrower streets it was already night. The crowds had disappeared, and though many still watched from lighted windows, the general effect was eerie and strange, and the sense of latent hostility by no means lessened.

They found the gates closed for the night, but the Town Guard was swift to open for them, thankful to see the last of them. The lengthy column rode out into the darkling countryside, not without sighs of relief of their own. Three miles they went further, westwards, to the parks of Forrester's castle of Corstorphine, to camp for the night.

It would be back to Stirling in the morning, with not a man lost — but with how much gained remained to be seen.

CHAPTER SIX

IN very different company and on a very different mission, Will Douglas rode through the high summer day, southwards. Gone was all the clanking armour and warlike trappings. Gone the host of men-at-arms, the heavy chargers, the Lion Rampant standard. It was only a very tiny party indeed, of half a dozen men, four of them servitors. But at least its principals were well-dressed, better than ever before in their lives. Will was resplendent in black velvet doublet and trunks, slashed with silver, his long thigh-boots of softest doeskin, a flat velvet bonnet with jewel-clasped curling ostrich-feather on his dark head. His brother Jamie was only little less fine, as befitted new status of Master of Douglas. It was an occasion for special dressing.

This was the second day of their riding, from Ettrick, and the North Galloway countryside looked very fair under the August sun. They had not far to go, now.

Jamie, despite his increase in dignity, sang in tune with the glad morning, and in time with the clip-clop of their horses' trotting; he was a great singer, when he was happy. Will did not join in. His was a less tuneful voice, admittedly, and today he did not feel like singing, anyway.

In fact, considering everything, his feelings were unsuitable. Undoubtedly he should have been of a very different frame of mind. Many would say that he should have been the most cheerful young man in Scotland. He had achieved great things — even though by no means all that he had planned. In name, at least, he occupied the second place in all the kingdom. He had crossed swords with the two astutest characters in the land, and for the moment at least appeared the victor. His name was on everyone's lips, and in the main with some degree of respect to add to the traditional dread. Even though he had miscalculated, and the parliament called for July had had to be postponed until November, on account of the difficulty of persuading the great of the land to attend, still Crichton's Privy Council had not officially met in the interim, and the former Chancellor had lain notably low. All of which should have been inspiring to any young man. Moreover, he was on his way to his courtship.

Will Douglas was perhaps insufficiently grateful.

At the village of Carlingwark, by its loch, they turned away westwards across low grassy pasture ridges dotted with whins, where much cattle grazed. In little more than a mile they saw the topmost tower-head of Threave Castle, flag fluttering, appearing above the green brae ahead — a peculiar sight in that this Threave was alleged to be the greatest stronghold in all Galloway, built by their grandfather, Archibald the Grim; and yet its surroundings, though rich and verdantly lovely, were gentle rather than strong and defendable. It was not until they breasted the last of the little ridges that they perceived that the Earl Archibald had not been untrue to his name. Threave was vastly larger than their first impressions had suggested, and further away. An enormously massive single square keep, it rose abruptly, seven storeys, from a low green island formed by the temporary splitting of the wide River Dee. Indeed it almost appeared to rise from a loch, for the river here flowed but sluggishly, and greatly overflowed the low marshy land. The usual double curtain-walls surrounded the keep, with round flanking towers at all angles, to enclose an outer bailey and an inner courtyard. A narrow and twisting stone causeway reached out from the shore, only just above the surface of the water now, so that at most seasons of the year it would be, in fact, slightly underwater and forming a hazard indeed for all approachers save those who knew exactly its turns and bends. This was itself cut, part-way, by a wide gap over which was thrown a drawbridge. When the bridge was up, Threave would be well-nigh impregnable. Above it all, the banner of the Lordship of Galloway flew proudly.

The horsemen were challenged twice before reaching the causeway, but the Red Heart on the servitors' livery ensured that this was more or less a formality. They rode on heedfully over the slimy stones. The drawbridge remained lowered for them. At the gatehouse of the outer walling, under the high frown of the keep, guards halted them.

"What lords come so lightly to Threave?" somebody demanded, deep-voiced.

"The lord of Douglas. To pay respects to the Lady of Galloway."

"Douglas? ... Lord? ... Douglas himself!"

"Himself."

There was a great shouting of orders and clashing of arms and bolts. The heavy iron gates swung open.

Demanding to be taken into the presence of Threave's chatelaine, they were informed by the doorward that the Lady Margaret was in the water-garden beyond the outer bailey. They would summon her . . .

Will forbade it. Surely it was for them to seek their cousin. Lead them to her.

Dismounted, the brothers were crossing the courtyard diagonally towards a small postern door which stood open in the northern curtain-wall, when they were hailed from a first floor window of the mighty keep. Evidently one of the guards had hurried directly within, with his news.

"My lord — the Duchess welcomes you. She bids you attend on her in her bower."

Will paused uncertainly, frowning. He knew that the Lady Margaret's mother often stayed with her here, but he had not thought of her as present and had not schooled himself to a meeting — for she was said to be a tiresome woman. Since she was not chatelaine of Threave, it was right and proper that he should first pay his respects to her fifteen-year-old daughter, the Lady of Galloway. On the other hand, brusquely to ignore this summons was hardly to be considered — and the co-operation of the mother was advisable if the daughter was to be secured.

"Go you to the Lady Margaret, Jamie," Will decided. "With my duty. I will come so soon as I may."

He climbed the timber forestair to the first floor of the keep, where an aged manservant took charge of him and led him across the Great Hall to a narrow private turnpike stairway in the thickness of the eight-foot walling. On the floor above, he was ushered into a pleasant tapestry-hung chamber.

The Duchess sat in a window-seat, and pretended to be much startled by his arrival. "A mercy!" she cried. "How you affrighted me! I was deep in thought. Mercy me!" She fanned herself with her ring-encrusted hand, as though Will was responsible for a sudden rise in temperature.

He bowed stiffly. "I was told that you bid me to come to you, my lady," he said.

"Yes. Yes, to be sure. But you came so swiftly. You must have run, I vow! Run to an old woman's call!" She simpered. "Come, my lord — here, where I can see you. My eyes are not so bright as once they were!" She fluttered her eyelids nimbly enough at him, nevertheless.

Will moved one pace forward, looking at her askance. Her appearance, manner and talk did little to improve on the mind-picture he had formed of her — although, despite all this talk of age, she was very much younger than he had thought to find her. He had imagined her as fat and old, regal in bearing as became Scotland's only Duchess, something of a dragon. In fact, she was only in her late thirties, like his own mother — but like her in nothing else. She was fussily nervous in manner, and desperately thin, a large-eyed, faded, gaunt woman, without dignity or calm. She made Will see his mother as a woman to esteem — a recognition that was overdue on his part.

"So you are Cousin James's son," she said. "A deal more handsome, I vow! My daughter is fortunate, I think!"

Will cleared his throat, but found nothing to say.

"You look strong," she went on. "Very strong. Come closer, my lord."

"I must go pay my respects to the Lady Margaret," he jerked.

It did not fail to cross his mind to wonder what the daughter might be like if this was the mother — even though she was known as the Fair Maid of Galloway. Hamilton did not rise any higher in his estimation for marrying thus, and a woman ten years his senior, however great the riches she brought him. Yet, she was the mother of those two cousins he had sworn to avenge.

Euphemia Graham, sister of the deposed Malise, Earl of Strathearn, and great-granddaughter of King Robert the Second, still styled herself Duchess of Touraine, the French title of her late husband, there being two other Countesses-Dowager of Douglas — for her son had wed a fifteen-year-old bride, Janet Lindsay, daughter of Crawford, just months before his murder.

"Margaret will wait. You would desert me so soon? The old woman for the young! Out on you, cruel my lord!"

"This is her house . . ."

"Aye — and you would have it yours again, and quickly, I have no doubt! And all Galloway with it. Your mother made that very clear."

"My mother does not speak for me," he answered shortly.

"Nevertheless you have come!" She smiled again, archly. "And coming, I am well content. I think we shall be friends, my lord." She held out her thin hand to him.

Will bit his lip. Completely to ignore it would be discourteous in the extreme. He stepped forward quickly, and taking that hand, raised it to his lips perfunctorily, seeming to accept it as a gesture of dismissal. "I go see the Lady Margaret," he said, and turning about hurried to the door, and out.

Thankfully he ran downstairs, across the Hall, and outside. Through the postern door in the courtyard he found himself between the outer and inner curtain-walls. But beyond was a small arched pend through the basement of one of the round flanking towers, and this led out into the northern tip of the low island not occupied by the castle buildings. Here were a few acres of grass and reeds and willow-scrub, cut up by little channels of the river. It had been turned into a pleasance, a water-garden, with tiny canals and pools created here and there, and banks of flowers and shrubs planted. It was a woman's place, which would have endangered Archibald the Grim's blood-vessels, but it was very attractive of a summer's day.

There were paths laid, winding amongst the creeks and bushes. Will took the largest of these. And rounding a willow-clump he came face to face with a young woman coming walking in the other direction.

She was a laughing-eyed comely creature, generously made, with a lot of red-gold hair, not over-tidy, her skin honey-coloured, her eyes sparkling blue. Her mouth was too wide and her nose too short for real beauty, and there was a vigour about her unusual in ladies of quality, but her shapely, lissome grace was undeniable, her full firm breasts magnificent, and her smile frank and friendly. She was dressed simply but effectively in a short homespun gown of dark green, its bodice only rudimentary, over a white lawn blouse wide at the neck almost to uncover the shoulders, with round her throat, and hiding but little, a silken scarlet kerchief. Will knew with sudden entire certainty that he had never seen a female that pleased him better.

He entirely forgot to bow or make any suitable saluation — voluntarily, that is. "Are you . . . are you Margaret Douglas?" he demanded.

"I am," she agreed, with a tinkle of laughter. "Though I am usually called Meg."

"Meg," he repeated. "Aye — I like Meg. Better. Sweeter. I am Will Douglas."

"So I understood, my lord. Threave is the happier, I swear! All here are your servants I came seeking you."

"Kind," he said. "I was with the Duchess. She . . . I . . . h'm."

He caught her eye — which was not difficult — and she grinned. "Yes, my lord. To be sure."

"I came so soon as I might. You saw my brother? James?"

"Oh, yes. And a most proper young man. But . . . other than you, I think."

Sensing some signficance in that, he challenged her. "And I? I am not a proper young man?"

"Less proper, perhaps! And less young!"

"M'mmm." He paused. "And so you left him. To come seek *me?*"

"He was well content to be left, I think. They are not far. There is an arbour beyond those bushes. A pretty place."

"No doubt." Will found himself in no hurry to investigate. "So you found my brother too proper? And too young? For your taste, lady!"

"Myself, I prefer men to boys, my lord! A matter of taste, as you say!"

"Yes. You, yourself, seem older than I had thought."

She sketched a mocking curtsey. "Is that flattery? Or otherwise? But . . . I would not have believed that you could have thought anything of *my* age, sir. Since I am less than the flower you crush beneath those fine boots!"

He glanced down, to discover that he was indeed standing on a small patch of pimpernel, bruising the tiny scarlet flowers. Hurriedly he stepped aside. "No," he said. "Not so. I have thought much of this. It has troubled me. I am much . . . comforted. To find you . . . thus. I had feared it might be different."

She raised arching brows at him. "Can it be, my lord, that you mistake? Take me for what I am not? I am *Meg* Douglas, as I said. Not the Lady Margaret Douglas of Galloway. Only her tiring-woman. Sent to seek you . . ."

"Save us!" Will swallowed, staring at her. "I thought . . . I believed! . . ."

"I am sorry indeed to disappoint, my lord Earl!" she murmured modestly — although her smile was less so. "To be only a serving wench!"

He stood there glaring at her, adjusting his mind and emotions.

Meg Douglas considered him closely, thoughtfully. "You are angry? Think yourself deceived?" . . ."

"I am not angry. Only . . . only, as you said . . . disappointed." That was simply stated.

"For that I thank you," she answered, and this time she did

not smile. "Come, my lord — I will take you to the Lady Margaret. And, and naught said of this mischance."

He walked just half a pace behind her along the further path. "Who are you, woman?" he jerked, at the lovely column of her neck. "You are no common serving-wench — that I vow!"

"Then you vow amiss, sir," she answered, without turning. "My mother was maid to the Countess-Duchess before this one — the Tyneman's wife, daughter to King Robert. And my father — he was a by-blow. Of Earl Archibald's."

"Ha! I thought as much. Something of the like. So . . . i' faith, you are my cousin! For *my* father, also, was a son of Archibald the Grim. In blood we are cousins."

"In blood only, my lord. And if you were to acknowledge all such cousins — why, you might find yourself with over-many! For Archibald, our grandsire, was a potent lord, they say!"

"That may be so. But I swear not many are like you! . . ."

"Hush, sir! Here is my mistress. And your brother . . ."

Round a denser clump of willows they had come to a sizeable pool formed from a widened inlet of the river. At its head a rustic shelter had been contrived out of rough-hewn logs, decorated with seashore shells. On a bench before this Jamie and a girl sat.

Will paused for a moment, and perceiving it, Meg Douglas did likewise. There was no question now that before him was the Fair Maid of Galloway. The girl who sat there listening to Jamie and idly shredding leaves from a willow-wand to drop into the water, was the very picture of fragile loveliness. Slight, graceful, upright, herself as willowy as the growth around her, she had hair paler than flaxen above a high clear brow and delicately narrow features, perfectly formed. She was dressed in a high-necked, close-fitting gown of palest blue linen, longer than the other girl's, and cunningly cut lovingly to mould her small-breasted slender long-legged figure. As she sat listening to James Douglas, her expression was sweetly grave.

"So-o-o!" Will breathed out, on almost a sigh.

"She is very beautiful, is she not? A meet bride for the Black Douglas!"

He turned to his companion, and their eyes met. "Aye," he said, "Beautiful. But . . . a child."

"More woman than you think, perhaps," Meg answered him. "Beware lest you misjudge, my lord."

Jamie, at least, did not look as though he was concerned over the immaturity of his hearer. He was leaning forward and talking as Will had seldom seen him talk, never for a moment taking his eyes off the girl's face. They made a pretty picture as the others came down to them by the waterside.

When she saw Will, the girl rose slowly to her feet. She gave an impression of height, standing, though in fact she was not tall. He saw that her eyes were large, serious and grey. It came to him that she was like a cornflower — which was strange thinking for Will Douglas.

There was no introduction, almost no greeting, in words at least. They stood and considered each other. Will moistened his lips. Undoubtedly she was the most beautiful creature that he had ever seen, or imagined — but he had no urge to tell her so.

"I met my lord of Douglas on the way," Meg said, to break the silence.

"Aye," Will nodded. "I come with my duty. Respects."

"Yes. You come to wed me also, Cousin, I think. Do you not?" Her voice was low-pitched, almost husky, strangely deep for one so young.

Startled at this directness, he coughed. "No. Not that. Or . . . not just so. To see you. To see if you . . . to seek your views. To pay my court . . ." Unhappily he floundered.

Gravely she listened to him, as though to words of deep wisdom. "You are kind, my lord," she said, when he had faltered to a stop. "But you came to wed me, even so, did you not? Since Douglas must have Galloway again. And Bothwell. And Wigtown. Nor dare let other have them." That was stated as a matter of fact, not in any rhetorical fashion, or challenge.

He shook his head. "It need not be. I have much land without Galloway. It was not of my devising. It would be a notable match. But . . . not necessary. Not for Douglas."

"But I am Douglas also, Cousin. And would not have it otherwise."

"Oh." Blinking, he looked away — and it was Meg Douglas's eye which he caught again.

Jamie sighed heavily at Will's other side.

"Sit , my lord?" Margaret said, indicating the bench. "Or are you hungry? Would you eat? . . ."

"No. This is very well." Will now shared the bench with the girl, sitting on the edge of it, while Jamie stood near by looking melancholy. Meg Douglas moved a little way off. Will found himself turning his velvet cap round and round in his hands.

"When will you have the marriage, Cousin?" Margaret asked calmly.

"Eh? *When?* I . . . I do not know. I have not thought so far. I was nowise assured that you would wish it."

"Is not the matter decided? My mother believes it so. With *your* mother."

"Mothers!" Will all but snorted. "They scheme and plot. Others' lives. *I* am not my mother's chattel — if you are! Her interest in me is over-sudden!"

Thoughtfully the girl eyed him. "Yet, you came."

Aye. I came. I could do no less."

"You mean that you came looking, my lord? Seeking the style of me? Before you declared yourself. You are careful, in this matter!"

Will wriggled on the edge of the bench. "No. That is not the way of it. You misjudge me. I came to see you, yes. To discover how it was with you. Your mind in this. Marriage is a serious matter. Not to be decided by the toss of a dice. Or the length of a rent-roll. Nor yet by two widow-women! . . ."

"And yet, my lord, your prayer to the Pope has gone in — or so says my mother. For dispensation to marry me. Since, it seems, we are within the prohibited degree of blood relationship."

"What?" Will cried. "What do you say? The Pope? I have done no such thing. I know nothing of any prayer."

"Yet my mother told me of it weeks past." The Lady Margaret spoke simply, quietly, not in any way accusingly. "The Bishop of Glasgow sent the letter. Seeking the Holy Father's permission for our marriage. With a large payment, she says . . ."

" 'Fore God! Cameron! That fox! This is too much!" Will was on his feet now, pacing. "Devil take him — here's an insolent priest! But . . . you say payment? A large payment. For the Pope? Cameron would not do that. Not of his own. It must be my mother's doing." He rounded on his brother. "Did you know aught of this?

"Nothing." Jamie looked reproachful. "Or I would have told you, Will. Besides, I have not seen her since the funeral."

"You are angry, my lord?"

He halted in his pacing, to look at her. This was the second time, in a short while, that he had been asked that question. Was he acting ill, being a fool? "I ask your pardon," he got out. "Here is no fault of yours."

She shook her head, eyeing him levelly, with a sort of quiet understanding. And looking at her, he knew what it was that had kept niggling at his mind about her. She was like his mother. Of the same mould. They were alike. They were related, of course, for his mother was half Douglas herself, great-granddaughter of the same Archibald the Grim.

She may have perceived the change of expression on his face, the sudden shadow of hostility. She turned to Jamie, a little wistfully, almost appealingly. "I am sorry," she said, small-voiced.

The other did not fail to respond. "Will means you no unkindness, Cousin," he said. "He has much to think of. He is not hard."

"No."

"I told you — you have nothing to fear from Will." Jamie went to sit beside her on the bench, close.

His brother looked from one to the other, and rubbed his chin.

From further round the pool Meg Douglas hummed a snatch of song to herself, gently.

Will drew a long breath. "You must bear with me,' he said. "I would seek my own road, for Douglas. Not my mother's. Each way I turn, she is there. God save me from masterful women!"

"And you think that I am on your mother's road, not yours?"

"She has prepared this road for me, has she not? Prepared well. All the way to Rome!"

"Her road could be your road also, could it not? It is the road also to Galloway, Wigtown, Bothwell and the rest. To greater power for Douglas."

"Yes. But . . ."

Those grey eyes held his own steadily. "I think, my lord, that you are less than honest with me. I think what ails you in this matter, now that you are here, is *me!* Not your mother, and mine. Me. Seeing me, you want nothing of it. Is it not so?" There was nothing coquettish or arch about that, just a sort of fact-facing, tinged with regret.

"No. That is not true." Almost he shouted at her. "You have it all awry. You are beautiful. The most beautiful I have seen. Too good for me. Too fair. And young . . ."

"You find me too young? It is my age? I am sorry for that. But I am fifteen. And growing older, Cousin! I believe that, that I would serve you . . . kindly!"

Jamie's choking breathing did nothing to help his brother. Will flushed hotly. "Have done, a mercy's sake!" he cried. "It is none of this. Not as you think. I swear it! I am a fool. None of this is as I would have had it. Believe me."

"How would you have it, then, my lord?"

He shook his head. He could hardly spell out to her what was wrong with him. That he found her too like his mother. That something in him was affronted that all was done for him, that there was to be nothing of a man's wooing of his bride, that all been settled without him. Least of all could he say that his masculinity had responded too fully to the other young woman, whom he had met first, to see the Lady Margaret as more than a child being forced on him, however wise and beautiful a child. In his frustration he turned on her, almost accusingly.

"And *you*? What of you? How would you have it? There is two to a marriage. You have feelings also, have you not? Desires. What of them?"

She nodded. "I told you, my lord. I am content."

"Content! What means that word? From a girl of fifteen! For her marriage. Content!"

"Very well. Say that I am pleasured. Well pleasured. At this match."

"With *me*? Why? You spoke of honesty. I cannot think that you are full honest, now!"

"It is the truth. I did not say that I was pleasured with you, my lord. But with this match. Because I am Margaret of Galloway, you are Earl of Douglas."

"And that means much to you? A mere girl."

"Yes. Is it so strange? Have you forgotten who was Earl of Douglas before you? Or before your father. My brother, Cousin. I have two brothers to avenge. Slain. And only Douglas, I think, Douglas in fullest power, is strong enough to do that. So . . . I am content."

He stared at her, at all the frail and tender beauty of her, as though seeing her anew. Indeed, in that moment, Will Douglas grew in years. He had learned something about essential womanhood which it was as well that he should know.

"I see," he said. There seemed nothing more to be said.

Jamie broke the silence that ensued. "We all would avenge your brothers. Will has commenced to do so. I told you — he has pulled down Crichton's castle of Barnton. He has driven him from the chancellorship. He has drawn Livingstone's teeth . . ."

"Peace, Jamie!" Will ordered. "You know what you are saying. These are nothing. Gestures only. First moves in the game. The real war is yet to be fought. And it will be long and sore. Do not mislead the Lady Margaret . . ."

"I am not misled, sir," that girl assured. "But, if the war is to be long and sore, then you have the greater need of Galloway's aid. Douglas of Borgue, who acts my chamberlain, says that we can muster four thousand men. Many more, given time. And this is a rich province. As is Bothwell. Our coffers are well-filled."

"Aye," Will nodded. "So be it." But he sighed a little, nevertheless.

If Will lacked enthusiasm his brother did not. Jamie, always inclined to hero-worship, now saw Will's exploits as epic achievements, the stuff of sagas. Nothing would do but that the girl should be cognisant of the fact, despite the other's disclaimers and corrections. Margaret Douglas listened with interest — and more than that. Her grey eyes were intent on the younger man's eager face, and though she glanced over at Will's many interpellations and protests, he could not but gain the feeling that it was not the panegyric or its subject that enthralled her so much as the teller himself.

From the first, Will had been uncomfortable about the other young woman's withdrawal. She had not gone far, only sufficient to indicate that she knew her place; almost certainly she had heard all that was said. He called to her now.

"Mistress Meg — my brother would make of me a very paladin in the ears of your lady. Here is treachery, I say — for she will find me out all too soon! How say you that I deal with him?"

"Why, my lord," she called back, nothing loth. "Act the part he makes for you. I wager it should not come so hard!" Laughing, she came sauntering back.

"You would mock me, the Black Douglas!"

"Why no, my lord Earl. But we have long looked to see a paladin come to Threave! You would not disappoint us now?"

"I warn you, Cousin, if you cross swords with Meg, you will require all your paladin's skill," the younger girl declared, with one of her rare smiles.

After that, all was easier. The intensity went out of their talk and they were able to be more natural. Meg Douglas was excellent company, and Margaret obviously looked on her as more friend than servant.

That is, until the Duchess Euphemia came in person seeking them, urging them indoors with the word that food and drink was prepared, and here was no place to entertain such distinguished and handsome visitors. Immediately all was changed, a brittle, artificial atmosphere descended, Will became abrupt and awkward, Jamie gabbled and Meg turned tiring-woman again. The Duchess had her way, and they trailed back to the castle, however reluctantly.

It became no easier thereafter. Despite Margaret's manifest disinclination now, her mother would talk of nothing but the proposed marriage, and the satisfactions of having so puissant a lord, and so goodly a young man, as her son-in-law. She also dwelt upon the excellent qualities of her present husband, Sir James Hamilton, and how notable a chancellor he would make. Her brother, Malise, too, were he ransomed from being hostage in England and restored to his rightful earldom of Strathearn, would do great things for the cause. She herself, being of the royal house, was in a position to influence much. And so on. The young people listened, and sought to forbear comment.

The Duchess kept them company for the rest of the day and evening — as may have been proper, but for Will at least was excessively trying. Jamie was not so concerned, for so long as he was in the Lady Margaret's company he was obviously in some sort of bliss, content to worship. Will, made of different stuff, was apt to look towards Meg Douglas's more substantial charms for relief — but that young woman, in the Duchess's presence, kept herself very much in the background or found reason to be elsewhere.

The day seemed interminable, even though Will found excuse to retire to bed markedly early for an August evening.

Thereafter the elder brother listened to the younger's encomiums on the virtues, perfections and beauty of the Fair Maid of Galloway, and the quite fantastic good fortune of her husband-to-be, until, feigning sleep, he gained silence if not peace.

The Duchess was no early riser, and with something like a conspiracy the four young people hastened to betake themselves, with hawks and hounds, on a mounted expedition up the Dee valley, before ever the great lady showed herself. They made a happy and carefree day of great riding, good companionship and few problems, though only indifferent sport, a day in which statecraft, policies, ambitions and marriage were not once mentioned, and in which Margaret Douglas proved herself to be less fragile than she looked.

When, tired but in good spirit, however, they returned to Threave, it was to find that the Duchess had another and distinctly agitated visitor. It was Robert Fleming. He had ridden long and hard, day and night, all the way from Stirling, sparing neither himself nor a succession of horses. After lying low for so long, Crichton had now struck out from Edinburgh Castle. First attacking and destroying Forrester's castle of Corstorphine, he had proceeded to assail and harry the Douglas lands in the west part of Lothian, Almondale, Strabrock and Avondale. Half a dozen rich manors had fallen to him, and been left smoking deserts. Even now he was besieging Abercorn Castle itself — if it had not already fallen to him. Hay had hurriedly collected a force and gone to its relief — but whether he was in time, or sufficiently strong, was not known. On the word of it, old Sir Alexander Livingstone had left Stirling and gone to his own house of Callendar, leaving the King and the fortress in the care of his son Sir James. Callendar House was near the edge of Lothian, close to the area where Crichton was operating, and clearly Livingstone was preparing to throw in his lot with his former confederate, and deny the Douglas connection, if Abercorn fell and the tide seemed to be flowing that way. He had sent an urgent courier to his grandson, Hamilton, and it was asserted that he was demanding that Hamilton halt any negotiations for the marriage of his stepdaughter and ward with Douglas. He, Fleming, had hastened to be first with the tidings.

Will was shouting for fresh horses before ever the recital was finished. They would ride at once. "Where did Crichton get the men for this?" he demanded of Fleming. "To do all this, he must have gathered many."

The other coughed, and looked away. "It is ill telling, my lord. But they are largely Douglas, they say. *Red* Douglas. The Earl of Angus is with him!"

"Dear God! Angus! Of our own blood!"

There was a shocked hush, with this last revelation still more grievous than the grim news which had preceded it. Will swung on the young woman, who had listened to all.

"You see your paladin now!" he exclaimed hoarsely. "Jamie spoke too soon!"

"No less the paladin, my lord, for other men's misdeeds," Meg Douglas answered quickly. "So be it you make them pay dear!"

The Lady Margaret looked at the other girl thoughtfully.

"You will deal with these jackals in time, Will," his brother declared stoutly.

"If time I am given."

"I wish that I was a man!" Meg cried.

Will found a smile for that, however faint. "You are very well as you are, woman!" he said.

Again the younger girl's heedful glance Then she spoke quietly. "Time you may take, in one matter at least. Before you ride from Threave. A marriage contract. It could be signed. Now."

He passed a hand over his lips.

"It need not be a great, a large writing. Such as a clerk would make," she went on. "Just a few words, declaring the matter. Signed and sealed."

"It would not be signed by Hamilton. And once he had his grandsire's message, he probably will refuse to sign."

"Sir James Hamilton of Cadzow means nothing to me. Or to Galloway. He is my mother's second husband, that is all. Is Douglas to be governed by such?" Although she did not raise it, that was the authentic voice of a long line of warrior earls, of kings indeed — for while her mother was a great-grand-daughter of Robert the Second, her father was a grandson of Robert the Third.

"You are his ward, are you not?"

"Only through his marriage with my mother. He is but a

knight. A Lanark laird. She is the Countess-Duchess. Of the royal house. Let her sign, and he will not dare to deny it!"

That Will could not controvert.

"My mother will sign it, and gladly. And with such paper we could raise Galloway," she added. "Swiftly. From this day. And the word of it, I think, would reach to Edinburgh. And Stirling."

"Very well," he said, levelly. "Before I ride."

CHAPTER SEVEN

As token of things to come, the three young men left Threave with an escort of thirty local men-at-arms, hastily gathered. They pounded northwards across the low green hills to upper Nithsdale, in the failing light, and then on in the August night through the Dalveen Pass amongst the high Lowther mountains to the upper reaches of Clyde and so down, with the dawn, into Douglasdale. At Douglas Castle, changing horses and snatching refreshment, they collected another sixty men, all that could be raised at short notice, and leaving orders for others to follow, pressed on. North by east across the upper ward of Lanarkshire the enlarged party hurried, to Fleming's lairdship of Biggar, where another small troop of men was enlisted. Then, over one hundred strong, they beat west by north now, over the high bleak moorlands flanking the Pentland Hills and so down into Lothian. Weary, travel-stained, saddle-stiff, they came to the high ground above Abercorn and the silver Forth, in the evening light, after over one hundred miles of great and difficult riding — to be confronted by anti-climax. Before them stretched a scene of quiet peace. Some blackened cornfields there were, and on closer inspection burned cot-houses and farmsteads amongst the scattered woodlands, but there was no sign of armies or battle, and Abercorn Castle and monastery lay apparently unthreatened and undamaged in the sunset, only the blue slender columns of evening fires ascending gently from the many chimneys.

In doubt and a sense of unreality, they proceeded down to the coast.

Nearer, there were traces of ravage and rapine, but nothing

of actual battle. In the sea-park below the castle, there was an encampment of armed men, about their cooking-fires, but in no great numbers and mainly wearing the Hay colours. In the castle itself, they found the Constable, with the Countess and the Lady Beatrix, at supper, with the Prior from the monastery — an absurdly domestic scene. Feeling rather foolish, however relieved, the spume-flecked, mud-spattered and bone-weary newcomers, stood about at something of a loss.

They learned that there had been in fact no real fighting. At the approach of Hay and Forrester, Crichton had discreetly retired back to Edinburgh. Possibly he was misinformed as to their strength; possibly he had already over-extended himself; possibly his Red Douglas supporters had come for easy pickings rather than true warfare, and having made their gesture and won much booty were inclined to slip back to East Lothian. Whatever the cause, Hay had met with no opposition, and had been able to act the rescuer to a grateful Countess and daughter at minimum of cost. That morning, Forrester had taken the major part of the force and pressed on eastwards, to see what could be salvaged of his harried domain of Corstorphine. Messages sent back by him reported Crichton to be holed up again in Edinburgh Castle.

All this was less well received by Will Douglas than might have been expected. He saw it not so much as any deliverance, any essential easing of the situation, as a very public demonstration of the flimsiness of the edifice which he was trying to erect, the foundations of sand on which he was building. Whatever else it resulted in, all this could not fail to do his own prestige and position much harm, and therefore gravely hold up, through lack of confidence and support, the further stages of his purpose.

It is to be feared, therefore, that he betrayed only moderate enthusiasm over the further news, which seemed to be exercising his mother and sister much more deeply than these war-like posturings — whatever the reaction from the sober-visaged Sir William — that he and the Lady Beatrix were now happily betrothed, the marriage contract drawn up and only awaiting Will's signature, as head of the house. This information, of course, set off Jamie with the similar glad tidings from Galloway, and great was the acclaim – save from this other designated bridegroom, who seemed to be preoccupied.

The Dowager-Countess was gently radiant. She mentioned that she would have Archie married to Elizabeth Dunbar, the Moray heiress, before the year's end. Without of course admitting it, Will was faced with the contemplation that his mother's methods might succeed where his own did not. He was tired, of course.

Next day he rode for Stirling. He made a circuit to survey his ravished and harried lands of Strabrock and Avondale, as he went — and saw plenty to reinforce his perception of Crichton's essential savagery, in the process, if that was necessary. He could not linger, leaving what solace and promise of both compensation and retribution he could offer.

At Stirling, as the gates opened to receive him, he was well aware that his reception might have been very much otherwise had Crichton not decided to retire to Edinburgh when he did. He had, in fact, been prepared to find the castle barred against him. As it was, Sir James Livingstone greeted his arrival only sourly, and though the young King was welcoming enough, and excited, he was considerably downcast, conceiving his cause to have suffered a severe set-back. That indeed was obviously the general opinion.

Will recognised that he had no one to blame but himself, Through optimism and wishful thinking, allied to inexperience, he had underestimated his enemies, accepted surface appearances for realities, and allowed himself to be partially distracted from the task to which he had set his hand. He had been knocked back sharply, and deserved to be — but he was by no means defeated.

Cudgelling his brains over the situation, and debating it with Rob Fleming — whom he was coming to rely upon and more heavily than on either his brother or brother-in-law-to-be — he decided that certain swift moves were essential if any confidence in his position and efforts was to be re-established — as it must be if the forthcoming parliament called for November, on which so much depended, was to be anything other than an abject failure. Armed sallies must be made, since these were accepted, indeed demanded, by both nobles and people as signs of the right and ability to rule. But they must be successful, and they must be located in strategic areas where they would produce the fullest effects. As well as these, some resounding figure must be found and brought forward, to be Chancellor, some substantial and statesmanlike character who would command respect, especially amongst the more sober folk of the kingdom, and in the Church. Without such, the King's cause must be like a plant without roots.

As to the sallies, there was no point in going to hammer fruitlessly at the impregnable walls of Edinburgh Castle, in present circumstances — so Crichton himself was safe from them. For the rest of the country, the north could be left alone, for Hay, and his traditional collaborators the Gordons, were sound for the King; moreover, the Earl of Crawford, one of the most powerful nobles of the north-east, was father to the Countess Janet, young widow of the murdered Douglas, and so assured in his hatred of Crichton and all his works. The south-west was dominated by the Black Douglases and Galloway. The Highlands, preoccupied with their own affairs, could be ignored, in this. But the west was important and dangerous; and of course the east was in the shadow of Edinburgh, and tended at times to watch the Earl of Angus and the Red Douglases, at Tantallon, one of the mightiest and most secure strongholds in Scotland. West and east then.

One of the lairds in the west who had rallied, earlier, to the Douglas call, was Galbraith of Culcreuch, in Fintry. He had urged, at that time, an attack on Dumbarton Castle, the main royal fortress in the west, but held by Sir Robert Erkine, claimant to the earldom of Mar, a man of doubtful allegiance but thought to favour Crichton, who had appointed him to this lucrative post — which carried with it the custom dues of all Clyde shipping. Galbraith, who had once been deputy-governor of Dumbarton, knew the citadel well, and claimed that given a couple of hundred men and a free hand to methods, he could take it. Will was inclined to let him try, now, for the occupation of this great fortress would resound all over the rich and important Clyde basin.

The east was a different matter, and a major problem. But Rob Fleming was urgent that some move must be made to counter the bad influence of Angus. The sight of the house of Douglas divided against itself was grievously dangerous for the whole cause, and Angus's aid to Crichton in harrying Will's lands had to be answered. The effect on his own people demanded it also. Angus must be taught a lesson.

Fleming advised a sweep of the Angus lands in the east of Lothian, though with no attempt on the Tantallon. Edinburgh must be taught which Douglas to fear.

Will saw the point very well, but recoiled from Douglas attacking Douglas.

The other accepted this, but pleaded that *he* be allowed to lead such a foray, as one of the Lieutenant-General's captains. The Douglas name and colours need not be involved. Let him take as large a force as they could muster, none wearing the Red Heart emblem, and show the east the King's banner.

Will was in two minds. It was dangerous, and meant allowing matters to get out of his hands. But then, were his hands so able and experienced, so capable? Robert Fleming had a level head and a good spirit. And was it not one of the oldest precepts that a good general knew how to delegate authority? Moreover, the east had to be given a demonstration of force somehow — and he himself had other business demanding his attention.

It was agreed, then. Galbraith should have his small force to assail Dumbarton. Fleming should lead as many as could be mustered against East Lothian. Hay should remain, with a reserve, at Stirling, making sure of the King and ready to go to the aid of who might need it. As for Will himself, he would go to St. Andrew's, in Fife, on a very different sort of mission — and alone.

*   *   *

With more trepidation than he had experienced when he had first presented himself before Livingstone's fortress of Stirling, Will Douglas approached the metropolitan see and ecclesiastical capital of Scotland, set right at the tip of the East Neuk of Fife, on a green peninsula thrusting into the North Sea. He had never been to St. Andrews, site of the realm's single and fairly new university, and he was much impressed, almost overawed, by the splendour and magnificence of ecclesiastical wealth displayed on every hand, in Cathedral, palace, churches, priory, monastic buildings, colleges, spires, monuments and shrines. Here was a city ancient and very fair, not so large as Edinburgh, but infinitely more rich, assured, serene. Never before had Will been so much aware of the power and majesty of Holy Church. It was a daunting place, however, for a young man not yet in his twenties, to assail on a mission such as his.

Will had some difficulty in gaining the Bishop's presence, the name of Douglas seeming to mean rather less here than elsewhere — or perhaps it was rather that the episcopal guards could not credit that he *was* Douglas. The palace, which was also the castle, was large, and there were more arrogant flunkeys and underlings to get past than in any lord's fortalice. But when at last he did run his quarry to earth in a bare cell of a room, save for the multitude of books and parchments, in a small flanking tower of the courtyard, it was to find no proud and pompous prelate, richly robed, but a tall, muscular, handsome man in only his mid-thirties, dressed in plain non-clerical clothing. Nor was there anything clerical about his expression, which was strong, stern and direct. He greeted Will courteously but far from effusively, not even laying down the manuscript he had been studying.

"I know not what unlikely chance brings my lord of Douglas to this place," he said, "But whatever it be, you are welcome." He spoke crisply, much more like a man of the field and the saddle than of the cloister.

Will nodded. James Kennedy, Bishop of St. Andrews and Primate of all Scotland, was a major surprise to him, not only much younger than he had realised but different in almost every way. Highly born and a bishop since his twenties, he was nevertheless utterly unlike the image that such a description is apt to conjure up; indeed his reputation was wholly otherwise, that of a sincere, able and honest cleric, a notable administrator and a man of great learning — however little renowned for suffering fools gladly. He was the grandson of Robert the Third, the son of the Princess Mary who had married first the 1st Earl of Angus, and secondly Sir James Kennedy of Dunure, head of that turbulent clan. So that he was cousin of the King, uncle of the present Earl of Angus, and brother of the new Kennedy chief, Sir Gilbert. A protégé of old Bishop Wardlaw, the previous Primate and friend of James the First, he had been raised to the primacy over the heads of numerous senior bishops, in particular over John Cameron, of Glasgow.

"My lord Bishop," Will said, diffidently. "I come on an important errand. An errand that is . . . that means much to Scotland. It is difficult." He swallowed. "It is to ask you to be Chancellor of this realm," he blurted out.

The other raised strong eyebrows. "Indeed?" he said.

"Yes. It is a most serious matter. The chancellorship is vacant. As you will know. With Crichton forfeit. Will you be Chancellor in his room, my lord?"

The Bishop laid down his parchment. "Young man," he said, "Am I hearing aright? Do you, of lesser years than many who study here in my college, come to St. Andrews offering to make *me* the King's chief minister in this land? Do you?"

Will flushed. "I do," he jerked. "In the King's name, of course. I come from His Grace, at Stirling. And I am his Lieutenant-General of the realm."

"Ah, yes. To be sure."

"Does my lack of years count so loud with you, my lord?" That was almost an accusation. "Were you not made bishop younger than most men are made priests?"

Kennedy acknowledged that with just the hint of a smile. "True, sir. Perhaps I am in danger of the tyranny of years, myself. From overmuch hectoring of students, no doubt! Your pardon. But . . . still I am at a loss to understand your mission, my lord."

"It it so strange? You are a man much esteemed. The head of Holy Church in this land. And His Grace's kin. A new Chancellor there must be, to put before the parliament called for November. One whom men will respect. Honour. Learned, and of experience in affairs. Who more likely than you, my lord?"

"Who less likely, rather! I have the Church to govern. And this university. Must I govern the realm as well?"

"What matters how well governed your Church and university if the realm, in which they are, is *mis*governed?"

"H'mm." Kennedy looked at Will with a new interest. "That may be so. But there are many able men who could fill this office, other than myself. And some who indeed seek to do so, I understand! Sir James Hamilton, I am told, esteems himself well fitted to hold the seals of office!"

"*He* may, sir. I do not."

"And you, my lord of Douglas, are to be the judge in this matter?"

"No. Not so. Or . . ." Will hesitated, and shrugged, "Perhaps, yes."

"Ha! You are honest, I see, at least!"

"And why not me?" the young man demanded, suddenly angry. "Why not? Tell me that. Who else in all this land cares? Who has lifted a hand against the rogues who devour the realm? The ruffians who pull the young king this way and that between them, like jackals with a bone! Who else is prepared to challenge these evil men? You, sir? You are the King's kin, and head of Holy Church. What have *you* done? Show me the man who has raised one finger for young James Stewart's realm — and I say let *him* be best judge who should be James Stewart's chief minister!" Will stopped abruptly, on a gasp of breath, appalled at what he had said.

The other inclined his head, but did not speak.

"I am sorry , my lord Bishop. I should not have spoken so. I was carried away. I crave your pardon."

"You need crave no such thing, my friend. What you have said is simplest truth. I have done nothing save tend my own vineyard. As have others. You have the rights of it. But, this matter of the chancellorship is not simple. You and His young Grace may declare Sir William Crichton forfeit and no longer Chancellor. But does he accept that? He has governed this land for long. He still holds the seals. More important, he holds the majority of the Council in his hands. The King is only a minor. Crichton, I think, will claim that he is still Chancellor, in fact."

"Not if a parliament, presided over by the King, appoints another."

"You believe so? Will he not rather declare your parliament void, a fraud? And refuse to give up the seals."

"He may. But the parliament will surely appoint a new Council, as well as a new Chancellor. Shut up in Edinburgh Castle, he can do little. Crichton draws his strength from others. And it is to the others that parliament will speak, not to him. You, sir, would speak loudly in that, if you would. With your own voice, and the voice of Holy Church."

"The Church has other voices than mine. Notably one that speaks from Glasgow! And passing loudly. Loud enough to reach to Rome itself! Calling for a dispensation for one, William Douglas, to wed within the prohibited degree of consanguinity!"

Will blinked. "You are well informed, my lord."

"Little that happens in the Church is not heard of in St. Andrews. My lord of Glasgow, I think, would serve Chancellor, and gladly. He is experienced in the business. He has held the seals before."

"Aye. But would you have John Cameron to govern this realm? Before, he had a strong king to counter him. Would you have him even to govern your Church?"

"The choice is not mine. I would remind you, my lord — for the realm, at least. You it is who choose!"

"I think you mock me, my lord. Myself, I certainly would have other than he. I see him as a self-seeker, not to be trusted. He petitioned the Pope, yes, but not of my asking. I knew nothing of it. Learned only by chance. Bishop Cameron but seeks to use me to gain his own ends. Moreover, he has many enemies. You, I believe, have not."

"I think that I would have, if I became Chancellor!"

"Perhaps, but you could do great service for this realm."

The Bishop stared out of the window, over the blue sea. "You ask, perhaps, more than you know," he said. "This is the life I chose. It was not chosen for me. I sought it. I desire no other. *You* sought otherwise. To fight. To fight for the King, yes. But to fight for Douglas also. You seek vengeance, do you not? Am I to aid you gain it? You would have me fight with you. Take sides. Take sides with Douglas!"

"Is that so ill a fate, sir?"

"Until of late, I would have said so, yes. I fear, my lord, that most of my life I have thought of your house as a pest and a plague on the body of this Scotland. You will forgive my plain speaking? Douglas I have seen as like an overgrown and bloated cloud louring over the land, too powerful by far, seeking only its own, largely by the power of the sword, a threat against the Throne and a menace to all peaceful lieges. If Douglas has changed, I rejoice."

Will drew a long breath. "You speak your mind, my lord, by the Rude!"

"If all men did as much, might not the world be the better? And the happier?"

"All men do not have kings and grandsires and the power of the Church at their elbows!"

"True. But I fear that I was born to speak my mind. And Holy Church mislikes me for it as much as you do!" He smiled.

140

"Although, in fact, I would have thought that you also were a speaker of your mind?"

"Perhaps." Will shrugged. "So you will not work with Douglas?"

"I have not said so. Yet. All I have said is that if Douglas has changed I rejoice."

The younger man sought to keep rein on his temper. "I am not my father. Nor my grandsire," he said shortly. "Any more than you are your nephew, Angus!"

"Ha!" the Bishop said.

"I think that perhaps you confuse the Black Douglas with the Red!"

"Are they so different?"

"Ask Angus that. Who sides with Crichton and defies the King."

"And costs you dear in harried lands?"

"Aye, that also. But that matters less than that the King's cause should suffer, and Douglas be divided in it."

"So you think to use me to bring my nephew Angus to heel?"

"No, sir. This is a Douglas matter. I am Douglas, and will deal with Angus in my own way. You I turn to because you are well-esteemed, an honest man, and of the stature to be Chancellor. I know none other."

"I see. Here is plain speaking also. Almost you disarm me, my lord."

"Then you will do it? Act Chancellor?" Will demanded eagerly.

"Save us, man — not so fast! Say that I will think of it."

"My lord, this realm needs more than thinking. Everywhere men wait to take sides. To discern, if they can, how the balance swings. Your choice, your decision, now, could swing many. Wait, and it may be too late."

Kennedy wagged a rueful head. "You press hard, my friend. See, I will make a compact with you. Give me a day or two. I have to think of much. The Church most of all. Promise me the support of a Council, and I will consider well. A Council of substantial men. Do you that?"

Will tried to make his swallowing inaudible. "Yes," he said flatly.

"Very well, my lord. Give me two or three days, and you shall have an answer."

"Aye — but what sort of an answer?"

"An honest one. A fair decision. I can give you no better than that."

"His Grace the King said to tell his father's sister's son that he relied on him. He . . . he sent you this token." Will, reaching into his doublet pocket, brought out a small folded glove, and handed it to the other.

Kennedy took it, a fragile thing, woven of finest silk, but worn and not over-clean. Two of the fingers had holes in them. On the back, the initials J and J, lovingly intertwined, were embroidered, and surmounted by a crown.

"This is? . . ."

"His Grace has little that is royal to show. Or offer. He has little of anything. This is his mother's glove. The Queen Joanna's. Joanna Beaufort, from England. Given her by the late King when they were wed. The initials are theirs, James and Joanna. The young King has these two gloves. That is all his royal treasure. He sends one to you, in token."

The older man smoothed out the relic gently. "Thank His Grace," he said slowly. "This also I shall remember when I come to my decision."

CHAPTER EIGHT

UNDOUBTEDLY it was one of the poorest, briefest and least representative parliaments that even Scotland, a land not notable for its parliamentary tradition, had ever held. Forty-six men in all attended, almost half of them churchmen, and of these only three were bishops, Cameron's Glasgow faction abstaining. Of the earls, apart from Will himself, there were only Orkney, Crawford and Moray — and Moray was none other than Archie Douglas, hastily married to the heiress Elizabeth Dunbar only two weeks before, and assuming the earldom in her right. Lennox and Ross had promised to come, but did not appear. Of lesser lords, there were but five, and one was only a substitute, Henry Douglas of Borgue, the Galloway chamberlain, who was there as delegate for his idiot brother, the Lord

Dalkeith. The baronage and knights of the shires only sketchily represented the west, south-west and parts of the north of the country. The east, the Highlands and much else, sent no spokesmen. As for the royal burghs, only Stirling and Linlithgow had sent representatives.

Nevertheless, it was a true parliament and no sham, lawfully called, the King present, most of the high officers of state in attendance, and all proper formalities duly observed. Moreover, presiding as Chancellor was the leading churchman and one of the most respected and influential figures of the land. James Kennedy's adherence was Will Douglas's greatest triumph.

Kennedy had conducted the business with dignity, simplicity and expedition. There had been no difficulties, no surprises — indeed, no real opposition. Crichton, of course, had ignored his summons, as had Angus and his other adherents, and old Livingstone had claimed sickness. The latter's son, Sir James, with the parliment being held in the Great Hall of Stirling Castle, could hardly absent himself; moreover, counting him weak if obnoxious, a faulty link in the Livingstone chain, Will had prevailed on the King to make much of the man. Today, parliament had confirmed his appointment as Great Chamberlain, an office of no actual power however resounding. In consequence, he was being pompously helpful.

Most of the business had been of that sort, formal, requiring of little or no debate. First of all the new Chancellor had been accepted and sworn in. Crichton's forfeiture was confirmed and he was convicted of treason, and outlawed for failure to compear and deliver up the seals of office, his family likewise being indicted. Will's own appointment of Lieutenant-General was approved, and Robert Fleming was made royal Cup-bearer, *in absentia* — this because he was unfortunately at present languishing in one of the dungeons of Tantallon Castle, Angus having managed to capture him in the midst of an otherwise successful punitive sweep of East Lothian; this royal appointment was a device to gain his freedom, since if Angus refused to release one of the King's household he could be arraigned for treason.

Some other and more constructive legislation was passed. Strong measures were proclaimed against the spoilers of Church lands — of which there had been a plague, with central

143

authority almost non-existent. Such offenders, however high-placed, were now to be denied any office or employment of government, and even representation at law. The revenues of taxation, customs, Crown lands and the like, were to be much more strictly accounted for by those who had the privilege of collecting them, with the object of cutting down abuse and trying to fill the empty royal treasury. The burghs were to arm, train and maintain not only town guards but train-bands, for their own defence and that of the realm in general.

Three hours after the swearing-in ceremony, Bishop Kennedy closed the session. It had been satisfactory, as far as it went — save in the appointment of a new Privy Council. This was a thorny problem. All the earls for instance, were entitled to be members, even though most seldom attended. Also certain of the senior bishops, Cameron of Glasgow included. Other heads of great families were, by custom, so honoured — and would much resent being excluded. Yet the sympathies of a great many of these were suspect, to say the least of it; and since between parliaments, the Council's power was very great, unwise appointments could form rods to scourge the King's cause. Will's promise to Kennedy to support him with a substantial Council had not been kept, hard as he had tried. He did not doubt that the new Chancellor was very much aware of it.

A banquet was held, after the session, for delegates and their ladies, and most of the Court had come from Linlithgow to attend this. Almost all of Will's own family were present. Archie had his new wife, a pale and unformed child, now thirteen — for whom her husband more than made up, strutting colourfully in his finery as earl, Privy Councillor and spouse. Will had seldom felt less affectionate towards him. Beatrix was there as the Lady Hay of Erroll, already teasing her sober lord and flirting with all and sundry. Their mother had brought Margaret, Hugh and Janet with her from Abercorn, and was now well advanced in negotiating Margaret's marriage to Harry Douglas of Borgue — and however poor a match this might sound for the eldest daughter, the Lordship of Dalkeith was one of the richest in the land, and undoubtedly Harry could be appointed complete controller of it. Jamie, of course, was there in his capacity of henchman and lieutenant to his brother, in which for the time being he had succeeded the incarcerated

Rob Fleming. Only John, Elizabeth, and Henry, were absent.

This banquet was the first such at which the King had been since the grim occasion in Edinburgh Castle almost four years before, when the black bull's head had been served up to the other William Earl of Douglas, and his brother, as earnest of their fate. Will was very concerned that this should be a significant event, demonstrating that a new order prevailed in Scotland, that the King was no longer a mere child, a puppet, in the hands of tyrants. He had had no experience in arranging such affairs, but found a useful assistant in the person of Galbraith of Culcreuch — who had, in fact, succeeded in his attempt on Dumbarton Castle, and now held it for the King. Galbraith had been chamberlain to the Earls of Lennox, who kept up semi-royal state in the west, and he was accustomed to staging entertainments on a major scale. Between them they had organised quite an ambitious evening. Will was a little surprised to discover in himself a taste for spectacle and pageantry.

The proceedings took the form of night-long feasting, interspersed with displays, music, tableaux, contests and dancing. To accommodate all this, the same Great Hall was used, with the King's top table occupying the raised dais area at the head, and other lengthy tabling ranged down the sides, leaving the centre open for spectacles and dancing. The question of precedence, and who should sit at the King's table, was a problem, with no small proportion of the guest believing themselves entitled to the privilege. Will sought to arrange it that a succession of people should be invited up to share this position of honour throughout the evening, with none permanent, save himself and the Chancellor. In theory it was an excellent device, but it worked out less well than might have been expected, and in fact few guests were satisfied.

As course succeeded course — shellfish, salmon, wildfowl, swans, sucking-pig, whole oxen, tongues, soups, cakes and sweetmeats, washed down with ales, wines and the Highlanders' water-of-life — so ever more appreciative, if noisy, grew the reception of the other fare provided, the minstrel's offerings, the cock-fights, the gladiatorial contest with nets and blunted pitchfork, the clowning of jesters, the sham baiting between men wearing the skins of a bull and a bear, and the like. Not only on the part of the guests. Young James Stewart, starved of this sort of thing, grew notably excited, the great birthmark on his cheek becoming crimson as an over-ripe strawberry, and drank, moreover, more than had ever come his way before. As a result, Will and Bishop Kennedy were at pains to soothe him down, distract him from the goblets, and generally steer him on a course of some dignity — no easy task, with an obstreperous and hot-headed monarch of fourteen tasting comparative freedom for almost the first time. James became ever more interested in the women — whose company and charms he had hitherto been almost completely denied — and during the dancing intervals in especial his behaviour became progressively less seemly. Will had not bargained for this. Something of a climax came when, the Constable and his new wife temporarily up at the dais table, James found the Lady Beatrix very much to his taste, and was by no means repulsed by that somewhat forward young woman. Although only a year older than the King, she was becoming very well developed, and wore a gown which did not hide the fact. It was not long before young majesty had his hand down the front of that gown, to the giggling if hardly the protests of the wearer, and the shocked bewilderment of the good Sir William.

It was while Will and the Bishop were seeking to cope with this problem that they were suddenly confronted with another. The company had been waiting for a new spectacle, while they ate, but instead of this, there came in through the great doorway at the foot of the Hall a group of armour-clad men. They were not armed, for nobody would be permitted to come into the presence of the monarch; but they wore breastplates, gorgets and gauntlets of steel however, richly engraved, long riding-boots and carried plumed helmets in their hands — scarcely garb for a royal banquet. The central figure was Sir James Hamilton of Cadzow.

Despite the noisy state of the gathering, by this time, there was something of a hush as the newcomers appeared. Will had not seen Hamilton for seven months, since before that day he was supposed to ride with them to Barnton and Edinburgh. He had kept away from Stirling and the Court both, ever since, taking no part in the struggle for power, waiting to see, presumably, which was likely to be the winning side. He had not attended the parliament. That he had come now, after it, and so soon, must have its significance.

The four men came marching right up the Hall to the dais. Igonoring Will, Hay, and Bishop Kennedy, Sir James addressed himself almost haughtily to the monarch, who had drawn a little away from the Lady Beatrix and was looking somewhat alarmed.

"My lord King," he said, bowing briefly. "I come to greet you. To offer you my sword. And to assure you of the full support of my house." He glanced right and left. "These are — Hamilton of Dechmont. Hamilton of Earnock. And Hamilton of Darngaber. All substantial barons of my kin."

As these three bowed in turn, James coughed. "Aye. Well. Hamilton, aye." He spoke a little thickly, as well as uncertainly.

"The support of my house," the other repeated, as though he was entitled to expect a better reaction than this.

"As is your simple duty, sir," James Kennedy mentioned shortly.

Hamilton turned to look at the Bishop, eyeing him up and down, and curled a distasteful lip, but did not speak.

The King fortified himself with a gulp or two more of ale. "How many men have you? To fight for me?" he demanded.

"I could field seven hundred, Sire."

"S'seven hundred!" James looked at Will. "That is good. Eh, Cousin?"

"Good. Although something late in the day, Your Grace." He turned to Hamilton. "There has been need of Hamilton swords these last months, Sir James. We looked for you, one time, on the road to Edinburgh!"

The other eyed only the King. "I have had much to consider, Sire. My lands are surrounded by those less loyal that I am to Your Grace. I could not leave them defenceless."

Hay spoke. "There was a parliament this day, sir. I did not see you there?"

Still it was the monarch Hamilton addressed. "Alas, I was held back. Hard as we have ridden, we could not be here ere this."

Will eyed the newcomers' attire. There was no sign of hard riding there, no mud of spume stains on those tall riding-boots, no traces of long winter miles. These had ridden only a short distance to come here, he could swear. Which meant that they had been waiting somewhere near by. Why? Presumably for the results of the parliament. Hamilton had not attended, though summoned. And yet he had come, now. It must mean that he did not wish his name to be listed amongst those present. Probably old Livingstone was behind that. They were still thinking that Crichton might win. He might have been afraid that measures would be passed which might injure his interests and which he yet dared not speak openly against. And this was the man who desired the office of Chancellor for himself. It might be that he would by no means sit under Kennedy.

The Bishop may have had the same notion, for he said, "We much missed Sir James's counsel, Sire. He might have ornamented some notable office of the realm. Your Grace might even have had a different Chancellor. To my comfort — if not your realm's!"

"I may yet find the opportunity to serve Your Grace in some useful capacity," the other snapped. "In a fashion, perhaps, that churchmen and clerks cannot!"

"Ah, yes. True. Sir James had undoubted capacities, As ambassador, perhaps? Envoy. Balancing two sides. The ability to weigh advantage, and wait. To bestride two camps . . ."

"What mean you by that?" Hamilton demanded.

"Only that if you have such qualities, sir, His Grace might use them in embassages."

"I think you meant otherwise, Sir Bishop! I . . ."

Will coughed loudly. "Sire — if Sir James and his friends have ridden far, they will be hungry. Weary. They should have meat and drink. May I bid them sit?" Kennedy and Hamilton clearly would continue to hate each other — but the cause was not to be served by such open enmity. He himself had no love for Hamilton, but the man was a powerful baron and better on their side, however reluctantly and belatedly, than on Crichton's. The fact that he had come at all was important, showing surely that his assessment of the parliament was respectful, and that he now felt it wise to be associated. If this careful trimmer so thought, others would not fail to do likewise.

"My lord of Douglas reproves us," the Bishop declared sardonically. "He will, of course, soon be calling Sir James good-sire!"

Will opened his mouth to answer that, and thought better of it. He busied himself seating Hamilton near the King, and finding space for the three lairds at a lower table. The Constable took the opportunity to remove himself and his bride from the danger-zone.

The entertainment was proceeding and fresh platters of smoking meats being brought in, when there was a further unplanned disturbance. Shouting and clash at the bottom of the Hall drew all eyes. There a group of guards were fighting a losing battle with a huge, red-bearded individual whom they appeared to wish to keep out and yet were reluctant to assault. Others seemed to be disputing this, and egging on the giant. Then evidently tiring of this by-play, the big man suddenly bellowed like a bull, and tossing the guards aside as though so many puppies, came stalking in, reeling slightly, shouting incoherently.

Nobody required to be told the identity of that eye-catching figure. There was no one else quite like Beardie Alex, the Tiger, Master of Crawford, heir to the old Earl, and probably the most unruly and wayward character in Scotland. He had attended the parliament, in what capacity was not clear, since his father was present, but nobody had considered themselves called upon to put him out. He had been at the banquet earlier, and then left without leave or explanation, in his typical unpredictable way. Now he was back, and obviously very drunk. Seven feet tall, broad in proportion, and bristling with red hair like any Highland stirk, he made an awesome sight.

More than young James Stewart eyed his approach with apprehension, for he had been known to pick up a man in one hand and shake him until his neck broke. His father was not one of those who worried, however — for the old Earl sprawled fast asleep and snoring at one end of the dais table; anyway, he had long since surrendered any responsibility for his son.

Will and Kennedy, on either side of the King, stood up. The Master, they knew, was utterly capricious. He could be harmless, even docile in certain moods — or crazily berserk. Drunk, they feared the worst. Glancing round, to check the availability of further gurads, Will saw that his brothers Jamie, Archie and Hugh had moved quietly up behind him.

The giant came forward, on an unsteady but determined course, certain cronies some way behind him. He almost fell over the step of the dais platform, but lurched on. Right to the table he came, to lean over on it, his great bristling beard outthrust, eyes strangely and fiercely blue in the congested face.

"I . . . I'll have my rights!" he roared, and smashed down a hamlike hand on the table-top, to set all the dishes and goblets leaping. "You hear? I'll have my rights, by the Lord God!"

The boy James gulped, terrified.

"You shall have your rights, Master of Crawford, never fear," Will said quietly. "Did you not hear parliament promise it, for all men, only today?"

"Quiet, Douglas! Quiet, I say!" the other cried thickly. "It's no' you I seek. It is . . . it is this snivelling priest!" He jabbed a finger at James Kennedy. "Louse! Slug! Crawling clerk!"

"How dare you force your way into the King's presence, unbidden?" the Bishop said coldly. "Were you not drunk, sir, I'd have His Grace put you in ward, for *lèse majesté*, Crawford's heir or no!"

"No, no!" the King croaked.

"Me! Put *me* in ward?" the giant hooted. "You? Or any here? Faugh!" He actually hawked, and spat. "Try, then. You. Any of you. All of you! Try warding Alex Lindsay! I am a man, see you — not one o' your gelded cata . . . catamites!"

"This is beyond all bearing! But if it is myself you are at odds with, then, with His Grace's permission, I will see you elsewhere. Outside this room. At least spare the King's presence this outrage, man!"

"Na, na — I ken the style o' you! You'll no' jouk Alex Lindsay that road! This laddie will hear the truth o' you, and give me my rights — or he'll see how Lindsay looks to his *ain* interests!"

"You threaten the King, sir? To his royal face! This is near to treason! . . . ."

"My lord — let the Master of Crawford make his complaint," Will Douglas intervened urgently, as the big man looked like clambering right over the table itself to get at the Bishop. "Better. Over the sooner. Let us hear it, so that we may judge . . ."

"Judge!" the newcomer roared. "Who judges *me*? When Lindsay is misused, Lindsay judges! No whelps or striplings, Douglas or other! Hold your tongue, I say!"

At his back Will heard Archie growl and Hugh mutter. He signed to them to be quiet. Lindsay must be humoured if serious consequences were not to follow, not only immediate but for the future. For Crawford was one of the most powerful forces in the north east, and hitherto Will had been able to rely on its support. This red savage had been, after all, brother-in-law to the murdered 6th Earl of Douglas. Grievously offend him now and, with his father little more than a cipher, the precarious balance could swing dangerously against them.

"Tell His Grace your complaint, sir," he suggested levelly.

The other snorted. "Lindsay does not complain!" he shouted. "He re . . . retaliates!" Nevertheless, he went on. "I am baillie and justiciar of the Abbey of Arbroath. As my father was before me. Now, these monkish scum have appointed another. They have taken Ogilvy. Oglivy of Inverquharity — God curse him! Against all right and custom. A man of straw and a scoundrel. And this . . . this . . ." He pointed at the Bishop. "This snake supports them! Tells them to disobey me. *Me*, Lindsay! I'll teach churchmen to interfere in my affairs!"

"These are Church affairs, sir." Kennedy snapped.

"They are not. They are mine. The matter is between me and those monks. Until you interfered . . ."

"Again you mistake. I did not interfere. The Abbot sought my advice. After you threatened his life. I told him that he and his brethen have every right to elect their own baillie and justiciar. As they have. That is all."

"Liar! Rogue! Montebank!" The Master lost all control of himself. He had to get at James Kennedy. The dais table was in his way. It was thirty feet long and heavily made of oak, but he grasped it, and tipped it up as though it had been a toy. All the plates, goblets and flagons crashed to the floor. Those sitting behind it, including the King, had to push and struggle backwards, chairs and benches overturning, not all successfully. Chaos reigned.

Beardie Alex was stepping hugely over the upended table when Will Douglas acted, and his brothers with him. Like a pack of terrier-dogs they sprang at him, while he was still unbalanced and astraddle. Will was first, and took a mighty buffet which all but knocked the senses out of him. But he clung on, dizzy, pinioning at least one of the flailing arms until his brothers had the other. The giant, seeking to free his legs from the table between them, as well as the rest of him from his attackers, stumbled and fell headlong. Inevitably the Douglases fell on top of him.

Even then it was difficult to hold the Master down, as they rolled about on the floor amongst the pewter dishes and drinking-vessels. Quickly there was no lack of assistance, though most of it was vocal and advisory.

Hanging on, Will gasped to Kennedy. "Get the King away. And yourself. Quickly."

The Bishop was a man sufficiently sensible not to put dignity and form before common sense. Nodding, he took the alarmed but fascinated monarch by the arm and, without ceremony, led him hurriedly over to the private door at the head of the Hall, and out. He shouted for more guards as he went.

When voices declared that all was clear, Will and his brothers were faced with the problem of disentangling themselves. Fortunately it was less difficult and dangerous than they feared. With guards pointing halberds at him from all around now, Lindsay seemed to regain something of his wits. He went slack. Gingerly the Douglases got up, one by one, watching warily for suddenly lashing fists or feet.

Amidst much shouting, the big man began slowly to rise to his feet. Will, panting, gestured to all to be quiet.

"Master of Crawford," he got out, trying hard to keep his voice calm, level. "I crave your pardon. For laying violent hands on you. We all do. But it was necessary. You understand? Necessary. To save you from seeming to endanger the King. His royal person. Not your intention, I know. But it looked to be so and that is a grave offence. It could have gone ill with you."

The other glowered, from under down-drawn brows, like a dazed bull.

"You take me? Ill with you. And, therefore, with the King's cause. To which you are important. None would ... none would belittle the might of Crawford."

Lindsay, swaying a little, stared around him. The fall seemed to have sobered him somewhat. He was still frowning, but with an aspect of bewilderment rather than fury.

"You understand, sir?" Will persisted. "You may think yourself injured. By me and mine. But it was the work of friends." He even managed to raise a smile. "I swear you should thank us!"

"Kennedy? That Bishop? ... He is gone?" the other demanded hoarsely.

"Yes. Gone. With the King."

"Aye. As well." The big man gave something like a sigh. But for the moment the fight had gone out of him. He peered around him again, as though at a loss.

Will also was glancing round. He pointed. "There is my lord your father," he said. The old Earl had had a rude awakening when the table overturned on him. Now he sat on his righted stool a little way aside from it all, his grey head in his hands, a man who might have been beaten by life. "He is, I think, weary. And a little in drink. Would you . . . would you see my lord to his quarters, sir?"

Without a word, the Tiger pushed through the throng to his father, all moving hastily from his path. He took the Earl's arm and raised him up. When the older man dropped limply, he shook him a little as though he had been a child. Then pulling him after him, he set off. Both had difficulty in negotiating the dais-step, but thereafter huge son led shambling sire behind him down the length of the Hall, with no single word between them. As silent, all watched this strange exodus. The Earl of Crawford, though old-seeming, was but newly sixty, Justice General of the North, Hereditary Sheriff of Aberdeenshire and Lord High Admiral of Scotland.

As they passed out of sight, Sir James Hamilton turned to Will. "You grow wily, my lord. Apace," he said, sarcastically. "Quite the cunning cozener! But yon one will not love you for this, nevertheless."

"Perhaps not," Will admitted shortly. "But I seek not his love. Only his continued support for the King's cause."

"For Douglas's cause, is it not?"

"For the King's cause, sir. The same cause we set out on that day at Linlithgow, before Crichton. Have you forgot?"

The other ignored that. "Whatsoever the cause, think you that you can yoke and drive this team to your plough? With every man's hand against another. Think you to build victory on such foundations?"

"I have no choice. These are all that I have to fight with."

"You had choice, in some measure. And chose Kennedy!"

"He is honest. Able. High-born. And carries much of the Church with him."

"And so his parliament makes edicts favouring his Church! But against all others. We are to be ruled by grasping priests! You will not unite the realm thus, my lord!"

153

"You are well informed, sir, as to today's parliament — though you could not win here in time to attend it."

Hamilton flicked that aside. "Crawford is only one. The first. Other lords suffering from greedy churchmen will turn from you. I swear that you can pay too dear for Kennedy as Chancellor!"

"Who would please all factions? You, sir — had the choice fallen on yourself, would you have had no enemies? None to raise their brows at you?"

Sir James frowned. "I flatter myself that honest men conceive me of their kind. At least you would have Crawford, Livingstone and Hamilton sure at Douglas's back."

Contemplating the thought of these at his back, Will had to repress a shiver. But he could not give voice to such sentiments. "It is my hope that, as His Grace's Lieutenant-General, I shall *have* these, and all leal men, at my back!" he returned stiffly. He jerked a perfunctory bow. "Now. I go to acquaint the King that this mischance is past. Sit to, Sir James — the repast and entertainment will continue." He signed to Jamie to call in the next spectacle.

Making his way thereafter to the King's quarters — no longer in the half-ruined Ballengeich Tower but now in the true royal apartments formerly occupied by Alexander Livingstone — Will Douglas was almost sorry for himself. He had thought that it was a sword, many swords, that the King and his own vengeance required of him; but it seemed that this was the least of it. He had never fancied himself as the realm's peacemaker — Black Douglas! But evidently the smooth tongue, the soft answer, the nimble wits, the scheming mind — these were what his task demanded of him. It was a far cry from Ettrick Forest.

CHAPTER NINE

ALL over Galloway's great and rich province, from the Rhinns to the Machers, from Loch Ryan to the Nith, from the high hills of Merrick and Kells to the Solway marshes, folk went setfaced, men glowered and women clutched their heads against the clangour. Since dawn that summer morning the bells had tolled and jangled and clamoured, every bell and peal and carillon, in every church and chapel, cell and college, in every monastery, nunnery and abbey, in every town, village and hamlet — and Galloway was rich in all of these. The warm still July air throbbed and beat and quivered with the ceaseless tintinnabulation, heads were splitting, tempers fraying — and the bride tended to be cursed instead of blessed and toasted. By noon, many were near to madness.

That is, amongst the common folk of course. All who might aspire to any quality or position had flocked to New Abbey, amongst the green water-meadows where Nith met Solway beneath the tall cone of Criffel, and where the little abbey-town in the shadow of the lovely red-stone splendour of *Dulce Cor* had become a vast pavilioned city with its own streets, avenues and squares, a colourful metropolis amongst the rich pastures, fully a mile square, with the ensigns, banners and colours of half Scotland's chivalry competing with striped and multi-hued tentage, canopies and awnings, and the inevitable men-at-arms encampments, the endless horse-lines and the seething cattle-pens extending all still further. Happily, the noise here at, as it were, the heart of things, was more bearable, for the bells of *Dulce Cor*, or Sweet Heart Abbey, were the sweetest in the land — Devorgilla, Lady of Galloway, had seen to that when she had founded this great minster for the heart of her beloved husband John de Baliol, and for her own when she should eventually join him, two centuries before. Now her young successor of a dozen generations later, moved to her bridal in their mellow, tuneful benison.

The great rose-red abbey had witnessed many a stirring scene in those long years, but assuredly none so compelling as this, wherein the Fair Maid of all Galloway wed the Black Douglas, in the presence of the King of Scots. Ministrels would sing of this day, poets extol it. Today great Douglas was re-united, and the Red Heart and the Sweet Heart were made one.

At noon the bells at last ceased their ringing, and in the vast abbey church, Bishop James Kennedy, Primate and Chancellor of Scotland, raised his voice. Evocative, powerful, sonorous, the rich Latin phrases echoed to the lofty timber roof-work of the nave and the groined stone vaulting of the chancel and transepts. A great choir made the responses, three hundred singing boys and half-men.

Will stood, with Jamie at his shoulder, just within the chancel. He was dressed all in black and silver, doublet and trunks of satin, and long silken hose. With his dark, almost swarthy good looks, he made an eye-catching figure. Jamie, all in grey, looked strangely delicate beside his brother, although in fact they were not so different as to build. On their right, further into the chancel, King James sat in a chair-of-state, very fine in cloth-of-gold, but fidgeting and twisting his legs round those of the chair. Standing a few paces off, on the other side, were the bride and her stepfather, Sir James Hamilton, backed by a bevy of bridal attendants, amongst whom were Will's two remaining unmarried sisters, Janet and Elizabeth. The Lady Margaret of Galloway, in white silk-taffeta worked all over with slender gold filigree, high-throated, her long and lovely neck supported by a tall upstanding collar encrusted with pearls, eschewed all elaborate headdress, such as was the fashion, and wore a simple gold circlet over her long flaxen hair — but it was sufficient to remind all that she was a countess three times over in her own right. She looked heartbreakingly young, innocent and beautiful, but grave. Beside her, Hamilton overdressed in red crammesy, the doublet with great orange bell sleeves, the trunks slashed with emerald, resembled a strutting peacock. Beyond these, and opposite the King, were five more throne-like chairs, one and four. In front sat Abbot Henry Douglas, master of Sweet Heart, and behind four mitred bishops, the first John Cameron of Glasgow, looking sour. These blazed with such a wealth of jewels on copes, stoles, mitres and fingers, as to hurt the eye.

Will had glanced around and behind him, once, over the close-packed ranks of chivalry and beauty, past his mother and brothers and sisters and the Duchess of Touraine — but nowhere did he glimpse her for whom his eyes sought.

When a clash of cymbals intimated the end of the preamble, bride and groom moved together and forward, to a pair of golden cushions placed side by side before the altar-steps. There they knelt, not so much glancing at each other. They had not met since the day, all those months before when Will had left Threave in haste at Rob Fleming's tidings. A sense of complete unreality gripped the bridegroom, at least.

James Kennedy came down to them, and commenced the actual nuptials — which were, in fact, comparatively simple and brief. At the exchange of vows, the girl's voice spoke more clearly than the man's. When the ring was called for, and Jamie brought it forward on a cushion of its own, it was Will who fumbled, all but dropped it, and muttered while Margaret held out a small, slim but steady hand, and indeed aided him to slip it on her finger. On the Bishop's pronouncing of them man and wife, it was she who turned to her new lord and master and dipped a curtsy, gracefully, firmly, though she did not smile, whereas his bow was short to the point of curtness, and the hand that raised her up was almost rough.

Thereafter, as the cymbals clashed again, trumpets flourished, the great congregation shouted, the bells high overhead began to peal again, and the choir burst into the anthem, the two of them stood together, still, silent, her white hand resting lightly on his black arm, almost strangers to each other yet made one in the sight of God, men and the law. Somewhere in Will's head a pulse was hammering.

The paeans of praise and joy seemed to be endless. The bridal couple bore them as best they might, isolated there as the great minster throbbed and shook with thanksgiving. But at last the Primate was able to pronounce the benediction, and then to join the other prelates in heading up the procession of the clergy, led by the Abbot and escorted by acolytes, censer-swingers, crozier-, mace- and staff-bearers, which, after bowing to the King, paced down through the packed nave and out into the midday sunshine where the crowds waited in their laughing and excited thousands. The Lord Lyon King of Arms then signed for his trumpeters to blow, and with his gorgeously tabarded heralds, led the monarch after the clergy, backed by the Constable, the Marischal, the Chamberlain, the Standard-bearer, the Cup-bearer and other officers of state, while everywhere the congregation made obeisance.

Only then did Will and Margaret move, on their long pacing to the great open doors, with pages strewing rose petals before them and the bridal retinue behind, while the colourful and high-born throng commented, nudged and exclaimed.

The tremendous roar of acclaim from the assembled multitude which greeted them as they emerged from the church took Will sufficiently by surprise as to crack his set expression and bring him almost to a halt. The girl, however, pressed his arm a little, and drew him on, smiling slightly.

"My people," she said. "Greeting their new lord. They hail you."

He raised his hand, in answer to the continuing laudation. "You it is they hail," he jerked.

"They hail Douglas. Douglas taking again its power. Girding itself," she amended. "I think perhaps that even Sir William Crichton, in Edinburgh, will hear that shout. Before long!"

He looked at her sidelong, wondering. What had he married?

In the Abbot's library the principals then assembled for what undoubtedly many considered to be the most important feature of the day — the subscribing and witnessing of marriage contracts, charters and portions, whereby literally thousands of square miles of prime land, enormous wealth and the destinies of scores of thousands of people, were transferred and dedicated. By these pen-strokes Will became lawful Lord of Galloway and Bothwell and Earl of Wigtown, master of more territory than any other man in Scotland, including its king.

Refreshment and drinking of healths preceded the adjournment to the huge pavilioned encampment in the meadows, where Douglas was host to all, and whither the great majority of the wedding guests had already repaired. Fortunately the weather was kind, and although thunder-heads mounted and marshalled their cloud phalanxes to the west, the sun shone here.

It made a heartening and astonishing scene, such as had not been seen in Scotland for many a long year, if ever before. Two great squares had been reserved and cordoned off amongst the streets of tentage. One, a tourney-ground, with lists, platforms, raised galleries and boxes, flag-hung and draped with colours and festooned with greenery. Here massed musicians played, meantime, tumblers, acrobats, jesters, dwarfs and other entertainers performed. The other enclosure was set with groaning tables by the score, the hundred, surrounded by tented kitchens, where all might eat and drink their fill, even choosing from sweating cooks and smoking carcases their desired portions of beef and mutton, pork and fowl — for four hundred bullocks alone had been slaughtered for this hospitality and there were as many again waiting the butchers' knives if required. No one knew the actual numbers of the assembled company, but Pate Pringle estimated it as between three and four thousand. The eating enclosure was suitably subdivided, of course, so the nobility, gentry and commonality did not offend each other — but elsewhere there was a great commingling, strolling and good-fellowship.

Only in the smallest and most select enclosure of all, around the royal and bridal tables indeed, were there cold stares, haughty looks and suspicions, this notable day. Here unfortunately there was little love and gaiety evident, with Bishop Cameron refusing to acknowledge the presence of Bishop Kennedy and Sir James Hamilton perceiving neither of them. Others took their cue from these, and the factions were fairly clearly defined. Will, in his capacity of Lieutenant-General rather than bridegroom, sought to associate with all and keep the peace between them. Sir James Livingstone guarded the young monarch from all, like a tigress with one whelp.

The present aspect of the marriage celebrations had engaged Will Douglas's attentions almost to the exclusion of all else — and that was not accidental. Disagreement and suspicion was inevitable, but at least all these had come to his wedding — a matter of which Crichton and others would not be long left in ignorance. But in one respect he was disappointed. Angus had not accepted the olive branch held out to him, so that the Red Douglas was still at open rift with the Black. He had released a thinner and wanner Rob Fleming — but that would be accounted for by the latter's royal appointment as Cup-bearer and the charge of treason which could have followed his continued detention. Fleming was at Sweet Heart with the rest, but not a single Red Douglas notable had accepted invitation. Men spoke significantly of it.

It had been Will's intention to circulate with his new Countess, as far as was possible, amongst all their guests. But problems of mediation, soothing and adjustment tended to distract him; moreover King James was very demanding, only toying with his food and eager for the next stage in the proceedings to commence — and even a bridegroom cannot brush off his monarch. In consequence, Margaret found herself frequently left standing neglected — until Jamie, in attendance, took her off on his own. Will made no protest. Thereafter they circulated apart.

It was when, later, having at last conducted the impatient King to his royal box at the tourney-ground, and then gone in search of his bride, to bring her on as queen of the games, that

Will, in the pavilion set aside for them, came face to face with Meg Douglas. She was looking superb, in a shepherdess costume which allowed her to deck herself out to best effect without seeming to presume above her station, all vital, voluptuous, essential womanhood.

"I have looked for you," he said.

"I saw you," she acknowledged.

He stared at her. "It is done, then," he said, at length.

"Yes. It is done, my lord."

"Aye. Would that it . . . could have been . . . otherwise."

She made no response to that.

"You know?" he asked, almost accused.

"I know," she admitted. "Your eyes talk very plain, Black Douglas!"

"Do they?"

"Aye. You should school them. Lest others see."

"Let them see!"

"No! You have great power, my lord. None may say you nay." She paused. "Save only me, perhaps! But . . . power should be kind, not cruel."

"Meg! . . ." He took a couple of steps towards her.

The young woman shook her head firmly, and held up her hand. "I say no! Not now. Not on this your wedding day. And hers."

He half-turned away, with a sigh. "You are right. Where is she? I came seeking her. For the games, the jousting. All awaits her."

"Your brother, the Lord James, took her. I saw them last amongst the common folk. By the fish-pond. Shall I go fetch her?"

"Aye, Meg. Bring her to the main gateway to the lists. Where we marshal. Or . . . beg my lady's attendance there. With my duty." He grimaced. "And Meg — think on me! Kindly."

"Enough that I think on myself!" she gave back, and fled.

And so, presently, the Earl and Countess of Douglas led the great procession round the circuit of the tourney-ground, under their banners, followed by her ladies, the Douglas brothers, the knight and champions, the swordsmen, equestrians, wrestlers, javelin-throwers, runners, jumpers and the rest, while trumpets blew stirring music. Will conducted Margaret up to the special gallery that jutted out just below the royal box. Here the banners of Douglas and Galloway were set up, the young Countess was seated on a throne-like chair, and a fanfare was sounded. She bowed to left and right, a slight, slender figure but somehow regal, and raised her hand. The stage was set.

First a pursuivant, gallantly attired, rode out into the centre of the tilt-yard, hailed the King, and then at the pitch of his lungs recited the pedigree of the new Countess of Douglas, from the semi-legendary Celtic times down a score of generations to William Long-leg, William le Hardi, James the Good, Hugh the Dull and so to Archibald the Grim. Then, as the cheers for this died away, the Lord Lyon King of Arms appeared in the royal box, to tuck of drum, to announce that the high and mighty prince James, by the grace of God, King of Scots, had of his beneficence and royal favour decided to celebrate this auspicious occasion by bestowing certain honours and appointments. First he nominated his right trusty and well-beloved cousin, William Earl of Douglas, Lieutenant-General of the Kingdom, as Warden of the Border Marches, Keeper of the Great Seal, and Governor of Edinburgh Castle. Such appointments to be confirmed by Privy Council.

An audible gasp rose from the great company at the pronouncement of this last office. Seldom could a clearer and more definite royal challenge have been made under guise of an appointment. Will was, in fact, thereby not only authorised but required to go to Edinburgh and oust William Crichton from that royal fortress. The other offices were key ones and a lot more important; but this represented war to the knife.

Will, standing at his wife's chair-back, turned and bowed to the monarch.

Lyon went on. "His Grace, moveover, hereby appoints his well-beloved Archibald Douglas to be belted Earl of Moray. And his well-beloved Hugh Douglas to be belted Earl of Ormond. And his well-beloved John Douglas to be Lord of Balveny. The said Archibald, Hugh and John Douglas each now to stand before His Grace."

As the hum of exclamation rose, and the three Douglas brothers climbed up to the royal box, Margaret turned her grey eyes on Will.

"What of Jamie?" she asked quietly. "Older. Truer. More kindly your brother than any of these."

"Wait you. Jamie could have been Earl of Ormond if he would. But he would remain rather my assister, my right hand — and no earl could be that. Wait you."

There was much talk as King James fumblingly belted the two new young earls, and gave his hand to be kissed by the new and younger lord. Archie had already been Earl of Moray, but only in right of his wife; now he was truly earl. Most undoubtedly saw all this as merely aggrandisement of the Douglas name and pride — for Ormond was an ancient earldom in the family, long defunct, and Balveny had been James the Gross's lordship before being created Earl of Avondale. But those who understood how the realm was ruled, knew that here were three more assured votes in parliament and two more seats on the Privy Council, to back Will's own.

As the brothers stood down, Lyon raised his voice again. "Further, His Grace raises to the style and dignity of Lords of Parliament his right trusty knights, Sir Laurence Abernethy of Saltoun; Sir Andrew Gray of Foulis; and Sir James Hamilton of Cadzow. Let the Lords Saltoun, Gray and Hamilton approach and kiss His Grace's hand, on appointment."

Again Margaret wondered. "Why these?" she said. "Hamilton? What has *he* done to merit this? You . . . you do not this for *my* sake?"

"I know the measure of your regard for your stepsire!" he told her grimly. "It is much as my own. But he is powerful, and I must bind him to my side. He is still sore over the chancellorship. And it will please your lady-mother! Laurence Abernethy is a sure man, and strong in the north. And Gray is close kin to Rob Fleming, a trimmer that we can thus buy!"

Levelly she eyed him, unspeaking. He looked away.

Once more Lyon cried out. "Lastly, the King's Grace requires his well-beloved James, Master of Douglas, and his trusty Cup-bearer Robert Fleming of Cumbernauld and Biggar, to present themselves."

Will's two lieutenants climbed the steps side by side, and were commanded by Lyon to kneel before the King. James thereupon drew out his sword with a flourish, and performed his first knightings.

"Arise, Sir James!" he said, grinning. "Arise, Sir Robert!"

"Of this I am glad," the girl declared.

"Aye — I thought you would be!"

As the new knights came down, Margaret left her throne to greet and congratulate them prettily. "Sir Jamie!" she exclaimed. "Here is joy!" She took his hands. "A true knight, indeed."

He went down on one knee to her. "*Your* true and most humble knight," he said, his voice catching. "Now, and for all my days."

"Ah, Jamie! . . ." she murmured, raising him up. Still holding one hand, she turned. 'Sir Robert — you better deserve this honour than most who receive it."

"You are too kind, my lady. I value it only that I may the better serve your lord, and mine."

Will cleared his throat. "Aye," he said. "My thanks. And my salutations to you both. But, of a mercy — let us take heed that we grow not too noble, too gallant, altogether! Since our warfare is . . . otherwise!" Abruptly he turned away, and raised an arm, as signal to Pate Pringle at the lists gate.

A long fanfare neighed, and the programme opened to a dramatic start. From either end of the enclosure ten knights in full jousting armour, plumed, helmeted, surcoated in their heraldic colours, shields blazoned, their steel-clad mounts gorgeous in skirted trappings, came thundering in, to the prolonged cheers of the crowd. Spreading out into line abreast, turf flying from their beasts' hooves, the two groups bore down on each other, heavy tilting lances lowered. The entire vicinity shook to the weights of their charge. As the space between narrowed and dwindled there was no slackening of the pace, no pulling aside. As everywhere men shouted and women screeched, the score of contestants and horses crashed into each other at headlong gallop, in mid-ground, with a clatter and clanging of steel, a splintering of lances, and a high whinnying and screaming of horses. In a moment all the colourful gallantry was just a chaos of falling bodies, tossing plumes, flashing armour, flailing limbs and lashing hooves. Out of the resultant shambles that strewed the grass, only eight of the score of knights remained in the saddle, from that initial concussion, five on one side, three on another — and of these some were reeling, and one sagged forward over his horse's neck.

But the survivors all pulled up, and wheeled round as best they could, to drive back at each other, the five against the three, swords being drawn in the process — for only two retained their lances unbroken, and these both on the same side, the three, which helped to balance the fight somewhat. Although some of the jousters were obviously neither ready nor in any state to continue, there was no pause, as the eight hurled themselves at each other again. The two lance-owners now toppled their opponents without difficulty — but the horse of one cannoned into that of his opposite number, and its rider was thrown off beside his victim, lance still in hand. Elsewhere dazed men fell more from the impact than the swording, though the ringing clash of blades on armour did resound. Only two knights remained mounted after this encounter, and this pair proceeded to fight it out. But on foot others were hacking and swiping at each other with their long and heavy two-handed swords, amongst the litter and the cavortings of riderless horses, and now being joined by two or three who had managed to pick themselves up out of the jumbled wreckage of the first mass havoc.

Within three minutes of the trumpets' sounding, only three men still were able to stand upright and wield their massive blades, slow-motion now, shields gone, plumes shorn, surcoats torn. It was difficult to ascertain who attacked whom, or whether all were flailing indifferently; then one man fell, and lay still — for falling in full armour was more apt than not to stun the wearer, irrespective of previous damage. The two were left, windmilling, battering — for there could be no obvious finesse or fencing, weighed down as the battlers were in half a hundredweight of steel.

It was a back-handed swipe which settled the contest, and toppled the smaller of the pair on one knee, sword-point dug into the turf. More or less at his ease, the other raised his brand and brought it down crashing on the unfortunate's helmet. He collapsed in an awkward metallic heap. The victor, swaying, turned and leaning on his sword for support, described a stiff bow towards the queen of the games.

Margaret inclined her head, smiling, and raised her hand with a colourful kerchief. But Will, at her side, was swearing.

"Who that is I do not know. But he is wearing the Hamilton colours, Devil take him!" he fumed though low-voiced. "There were six Douglases in that rout — and see who wins the day! An accursed Hamilton!"

A herald was announcing Sir Patrick Hamilton of Dalserf as

the winner, amidst much cheering. He was helped off with his helmet, to reveal an iron-grey veteran with a lined and scarred face, indeed lacking one eye. While an esquire aided him up to the Douglas gallery, men-at-arms swarmed on to the ground to help the fallen, carry off the still unconscious, catch the riderless horses, despatch one beast with a broken leg, and clear up the mess. Only the Douglases failed to assert that it had been an inspiring occasion. King James was almost beside himself with excitement, and bewailing the fact that, since the winner was already a knight, he could not bestow the accolade on him in admiration.

Margaret congratulated Sir Patrick, and presented him with a rose, as favour — and Will perforce had to express similar sentiments. The new Lord Hamilton came to demonstrate his satisfaction with the day, and to make it clear that he was the power behind the Earl of Douglas and, as stepfather of the bride, real architect of all the day's excellence. Will made but a doubtful success of remaining equable.

Meanwhile eight wrestling matches were in progress in the area, the winners of each bout being thereafter set against each other until again there was one final champion. This proved to be a brawny Carlingwark blacksmith, by name McMin, who, although no Douglas, was at least a Galloway man. Other contests followed, in racing, jumping, quarter-staff, archery, javelin-throwing, heaving weights and tossing tree-trunks. These Will watched with not a little frustration, for he was something of a performer himself in most of them; but today it would be considered unsuitable for him, as host and master, to take part — moreover, as bridegroom, he undoubtedly would be expected to be conserving his strength for other activities.

A bareback horse-race had just finished, with a young Maxwell laird coming first and Douglas lying second and third, when an especially prolonged fanfare sounded, and a herald made the stirring announcement.

"The most noble and puissant Lord Archibald Douglas, Earl of Moray, hereby challenges to single combat ahorse and afoot, any soever for the honour of a favour from the fair Countess Margaret of Douglas and Galloway. Who takes up my lord of Moray's challenge? Who takes it up. I say?"

"The fool!" Will exclaimed hotly. "What does he think he is at? Archie is no champion. He has spirit enough — but too little

165

wit? He is either in drink, or his earldom has gone to his head!"

Margaret smiled. "Perhaps none will dare take up the puissant Earl of Moray's challenge?"

"Would I could think so."

He had barely spoken before a horn blew, and it was announced that the valiant knight, Sir Patrick Hamilton of Dalserf, would fight.

Will groaned, as a loud cheering arose. "He, of all men! I might have known it. Oh, the fool!"

When presently, the two champions rode out from opposite ends of the enclosure, none could fail to remark on the differences between them. Archie was much the better mounted, and clad in magnificent black engraved armour, inlaid with gold, with a splendid and elaborately moulded, extravagantly pointed helm crested with tossing plumes in the Douglas colours. His surcoat was richly gold-embroidered and the red Douglas heart sparkled with garnets. By contrast, Hamilton's armour was plain steel, dented, almost rusty in places, his surcoat tattered, the Hamilton ermine cinquefoils on red only painted on breast and shield, the plumes of his helmet already shorn off in the previous fight. Coming together, they bowed side by side to Margaret, one with a flourish, the other stiff and stocky.

After saluting each other with their lances, they turned and cantered back to their respective bases, to the plaudits of the crowd. Then, at a single trumpet blast, they dug in spurs and hurtled towards each other. This was to be no contest in brute strength like the earlier affray. As they came close, both earl and knight sought to outwit the other. Archie threw up his lancetip, so that it aimed at the older man's gorget. Then, suddenly he dipped it, far down, so that it might slide in well below the great shield and in between the right thigh and saddle. Inserted thus, at speed, a sudden jerk could unseat a man and send him crashing. The Hamilton saw it, of course, but had only instants in which to take avoiding action. The classic recourse to such move was to slew the charger hard round to the left, so that the lance would be taken broadside on by the horse's armoured side or hindquarter, with little likely effect. But Sir Patrick reacted otherwise. Instead, he flung his mount as hard to the right, plumb in the path of his opponent, and too late for the other to change his own direction.

It was a dangerous manoeuvre, for the oncoming horse would have the major impetus behind it, and in a collision the man who tried it might be apt to have the worst of it. But cunning entered into it, as well as impetus. Faced with such drastic collision, and without time for thought, most riders tended automatically to drag back on the reins, if they could not avoid, at least to lessen the impact. Only the experienced and very cool-headed would instead dig in their spurs the harder.

Archie Douglas was not cool-headed. Fiercely he reined back. His high-spirited mount, alarmed itself, strove to reduce speed. Its forefeet scoring long weals in the turf, it all but sat on its haunches, and as the savage pressure on its bit maintained, reared high, forelegs pawing the air.

It was a moment of real danger for the Hamilton, lashing hooves within inches of his head. But wrenching his own mount still further round to the right, out of the way, he performed a most difficult feat of horsemanship and bodily contortion, in his constricting armour. As his charger swung away rightwards, so he swung himself in the opposite direction — and, with himself, the lance couched at his right side. Leftwards the lance swept round in a great arc, with all the man's strength behind it. Striking first the rearing horse's armoured head, it drove on to smash, at three-quarters of its length, just below the gorget, where Archie's helm joined his trunk. The wood snapped like a dead branch. But the sideways force behind it, allied to the younger man's precarious seat on a rearing horse, was irresistible. Over Archie Douglas was flung, convulsively trying to cling to the saddle, hampered by stiff unyielding armour. He failed. Down his mount's right side he fell, to crash to the grass.

Even then he was unfortunate, for it was no simple fall, from which, though shaken, he might have been able to continue the fight on foot. Somehow his right foot jammed in the heavy steel-encased stirrup. Head and shoulders struck the ground heavily, but he remained suspended by the right leg. His horse, crazed with fright and the blow received, pounded off to the other side dragging its rider with it. Bumping and clanking horribly, the young Earl of Moray was carried away from his opponent, who sat still, holding his broken lance. Fifty yards on, Archie's foot was jerked loose. A crumpled heap he lay still, the gold in his armour reflecting the afternoon sun.

"I knew it! I knew it!" Will cried out, smashing a clenched fist on his gallery rail.

The roar of excitement from the spectators swelled and maintained. Used as they were to sudden endings to joustings, it was seldom indeed that in single combat one contestant should be laid completely low at the very first clash.

Margaret had risen to her feet at Archie's downfall. "He is . . . he will be . . . well?" she asked breathlessly.

"He will be sore!" his brother declared callously. "And wiser may be! But . . ."

He was interrupted by the imperious shrilling of another trumpet. A voice followed it. "The right noble and puissant Lord Hugh Douglas, Earl of Ormond, challenges Sir Patrick Hamilton, or any other, for the honour of the Lady Margaret's favour! Does any take up my lord of Ormond's challenge?"

"Dear God!" Will croaked. "Hugh! Hugh, now! Bare sixteen! No! No, I say!" He swung on Jamie, who stood with Fleming behind. "Go, man — stop him. Is he bewitched? Stop him, Jamie. Tell him I forbid it."

Out in the centre of the area the victorious Hamilton was shaking his broken lance in obvious acceptance of the new challenge. An esquire rode out with a new lance.

Before ever Jamie could have delivered his message another fanfare heralded the appearance of the next champion. Notably smaller than Archie, he was not so grandly turned out, but he was very fine, for all that, every item of his equipment new and shining. When he reined up beside the veteran, he looked almost too trim and polished to be real.

For Will to have stepped in and stopped the fight now would have been to humiliate his brother unbearably. If he was old enough for the King to belt as earl, he could scarely be handled like a child before the said King. And with the unfortunate Archie now being led unsteadily off the field, all Douglas credit would be laughed to the winds.

"Does he know how?" Margaret asked. "He *can* joust?"

"We have all jousted since we were bairns," Will told her shortly. "But only against others such as ourselves. Not . . . this. Hugh will make a fighter one day. But . . ."

Hugh Douglas was not entirely foolhardy. He at least had learned a lesson from his brother's fate. When the pair drove at each other in the first charge, he made it clear that he perceived at least two advantages — his own youthful energy and his lighter, nimbler horse. A tired opponent could be halfway to being beaten. So he twisted and turned, jinked and darted, dodging and feinting as much as was possible for a man and a horse both encased in full armour. The other, of course, quickly saw the intention, and sought merely to stand his ground, only touching up his mount this or that at the boy's darting thrusts. So might a rock face the sea's foam and swirl.

"He's too wily for that, laddie!" Will muttered. "You waste your own strength."

Hugh seemed to perceive that, presently, for he pressed home one of his waspish attacks instead of sheering off as before. He drove in low and to the side, with his lance. Whether the other was taken by surprise or not, Hamilton was a trifle slow in his reaction, and in consequence took a blow on his steel-clad thigh. But it was a glancing stroke, and slid off along the horse's protected rump. But at least Hugh was past and out of harm's way before his opponent could bring his own lance to bear on this flank.

It may be that this taste of success made the boy careless; or it could have been just an error of judgment. But whatever it was, Hugh swung his beast round in the tightest turning circle possible, and bore back in, to repeat the manoeuvre while still the Hamilton was shaken from the blow received.

This was where experience told. The older man well knew the danger period after a numbing blow, and was not to be caught so. As his attacker came in, he seemed to be unready, but at the last moment he reined his mount violently round and backwards, so that the brute's frontal armour took the lance-point with major force. But it was the heavy charger that took the impact, not the man, and in that stance it had little effect — save to shiver and split the wood right up its length. And as Hugh reeled, all but unseated by the recoil of his own blow, carefully, almost insolently slowly, the veteran's lance selected its own target and drove in, like a javelin thrust. Struck full in the chest, the youngster was lifted right out of the saddle, and fell like a stone.

With a surprising turn of speed now, Sir Patrick jumped down to the grass, tossing away his lance and drawing his sword. He stood, watching the prostrate boy-earl.

Slowly Hugh, on his back, stirred and strove to raise himself, but could not. He rolled painfully over on to his stomach, and, sadly lacking in dignity, lifted himself on one steel elbow, then on two, on one knee, then on two, and so managed to get stiffly to his feet. As he stood, swaying, he was tugging out his own sword.

The other let him get the heavy blade right out, though the weight of it seemed almost too much for the dizzy youth. Then, quite casually, Hamilton raised his weapon and brought it down with a resounding clang on the top of Hugh's plumed helmet. The boy buckled at the knees and crashed like a log, to lie still.

A great shout of laughter and acclaim went up.

Will was cursing with a fierce intensity — had been, throughout. Margaret, even in her distress for his brother, knew real fear of this man she had married, so savage did he look and sound — more especially when, down in the area, Sir Patrick opened his visor and shouted hollowly, to demand whether any more Douglas heroes cared to cross lances with Hamilton.

The knight had not long to wait for an answer. From the main gate to the lists, the herald made announcement. "The right doughty knight, Sir James, Master of Douglas, will cross a lance with Sir Patrick Hamilton, for a favour of the most fair, gracious and excellent Countess Margaret!"

"In the name of all that is holy — this is beyond all!" Will exploded. "What am I cursed with? A clutch of brothers, or a brood of braying asses! Jamie, now! Less a fighter than any of them! Was there ever such folly? What has got into them? . . ."

"Oh, my lord!" Margaret cried. "Will . . . will Jamie be hurt?" Her sweet calm and assurance was gone. "That evil man! Jamie . . . he could be striken. Slain!" That was a wail. "You must stop it. You hear? You must stop this wickedness."

Will groaned. "How can I, girl? Look!" He pointed. Jamie was already riding on to the field while his young brother was being carried off. Whose armour he had been borrowing while Hugh fought was not evident, but the only Douglas symbol was the heart on the shield.

"You must! You are master here. You must save Jamie. He is not as the others. He is gentle. Mild. Kind. He cannot fight this wicked violent man! He *must* not!"

"Would you have me shame him? In front of all?"

"You could concede the contest. Declare Hamilton victor. Now. Before they start. Say that overmuch time has been spent on this ..."

He shook his dark head. "All would esteem it but base cowardice. Jamie would be a laughing stock. I cannot ..." He shrugged. "There they go."

The two antagonists were galloping out from their bases. What tactics did Jamie think to use, where his more pugnacious brothers had so lamentably failed?

Will Douglas did not wait to see. He turned, to tell Rob Fleming to stay with Margaret. But that man was gone. Only young John, new Lord Balveny, was there now, biting his lips and looking nearly ready to run. "Bide here with her, Johnnie," Will jerked, and without glance at wife, King, or other, slipped away down the steps.

He hurried, almost ran, through the crowd, round the perimeter of the great enclosure, few so much as glancing at him, with all interest fixed on the drama being played out in the arena. At the entry to the lists, there was a long robing-tent, divided inside into booths, where contestants in the games could change from their festive attire into armour, or garb more suited to the ring. Even before he reached this tent, Will could hear upraised voices within.

Pushing past the guards at the entrance, he found a group of men, some in armour, some not, disputing fiercely at the far end. Sir Robert Fleming was amongst them; esquires were buckling armour on to him.

Will strode up. "You can take that off Sir Robert!" he commanded the esquires grimly. "And quickly."

"My lord! ..." Fleming protested.

"Quiet, Rob! I know what you're at. But this is not for you."

"I am a Douglas vassal. Your lieutenant. And no child with a lance!"

"Nevertheless, you shall not fight. You are not a Douglas."

"We told him so, my lord."

"Aye, we need no Fleming to fight our battles for us!"

"Let *me* get at the Hamilton! I will show him Douglas mettle!"

"*You!* I was fighting when you were at your mother's paps!"

"I tell you, I have ridden more tourneys than either of you!

Than any here. It was wicked mischance that my beast stumbled in that first affray . . ."

"Quiet, I say!" Will shouted harshly. At least eight Douglas knights and lairds were there, experienced warriors, each demanding that he should be allowed to redeem the honour of the name. Clearly Will's brothers, youthful as they were, had each had to flourish his rank and standing in order to precede all these. Now Fleming was at the same game. But, at least, the latter was roughly Will's own build. "That armour," he said, pointing to the esquires. "Put it on me, see you."

"Will! My lord!" Rob cried. "You! You cannot do this. Not you. Not today!"

"I can. And shall. Quick, now. Jamie will not last long, I fear. Hurry!"

"But . . . on your wedding-day! Bridegroom! You cannot do it. What of the Countess? And you are host. To all. To Hamilton. Master of the games. You cannot do it, Will. It is against all usage, all form . . ."

"I shall not do it as host. Or master. I ride just as Douglas. *Any* Douglas. A plain helm. A shield, with only the Red Heart. Get me horse, used to the lists. A God's name — hurry fools!"

Despite all protests and doubts, Will had his way. The esquires strapped him into Fleming's armour, over all his bridegroom's finery, but the other's crested and plumed helmet he discarded for a plain and dented casque. A heavy charger was selected for him from the group outside. The last buckles were still being fastened as he strode out to it. A great and almost hysterical shouting from the crowd seemed to tell its own tale.

As Will was hoisted up into the saddle, they heard a herald declaring that Sir Patrick Hamilton prevailed.

"Rob — go tell that herald. Another Douglas challenges Hamilton. No name. Just a Douglas lance. Stay — tell him to say that if Sir Patrick is weary, he will fight any other, on his behalf. Say that. Any soever. You have it? Quickly!" To the others he spoke. "No word of who rides, see you. Just a Douglas. I charge you." He snapped down the rusty visor.

So, a minute or two later, Will Douglas trotted out into the arena, a plainer figure even than Patrick Hamilton, wearing no surcoat at all over the armour, no plumes, no distinguishing mark save the heart painted on the shield. His opponent, of course, had not availed himself of the offer to use a substitute; he was not going to forfeit the glory of being supreme champion, at this stage. Will saw Jamie being aided, limping, off the field. His horse lay still, presumably having been sore injured, and despatched. At least Margaret could swallow her anxiety, now, he reflected, as he drew up at Hamilton's side, to bow to her.

Later, as he thundered forward in the first charge, Will knew what he must seek to do. He was no expert with the lance, any more than were his brothers — and obviously Hamilton was. There was no indication however, as yet, that the other was as proficient with the sword. He might be. But he was an older man, and might well be less swift. Especially on the ground. To get rid of the lances, then.

So as they came up, lances couched, Will quite deliberately pulled his mount out to the right. No doubt it looked a most evident shirking of the clash. He drove by, at a tangent, just too far off for either lance to engage. There was a corporate sigh of disappointment and disapproval from the throng. But even before they were past, the younger man's mount was being wrenched back, with the most savage dragging at its mouth, back and aside, left-handed now, the head forced round. Up on its hind-legs it rose, a good horse abused, fore-hooves waving. Almost it tipped backwards, so abrupt was the reversal of movement, so far round was its head hauled. Half a dozen strange paces forward the brute staggered, on two feet, its rider standing in the stirrups, lance high — but when its forefeet did come down, they were forty-five degrees round from the former direction of advance, and still the fierce pressure was maintained, aided by rowelling spurs, armoured knee, and beating steel gauntlet. Cringing from the attack — for that is what it was — the animal bore round, round, in ungainly, scrabbling panic. But it had made the ninety-degree turn in shorter time than any one there had ever seen at a jousting. It was the sort of turn that a hill-pony required to make if it was, for instance, in the close proximity of a charging wild bull. Everywhere, folk were suddenly holding their breaths.

Will was kicking the beast violently ahead now. Directly in front Sir Patrick was reining up, to pull round in orthodox fashion. Because of the narrow visor-slits in his helm, he could have seen nothing of his opponent's astonishing manoeuvre. Unaware of what was bearing down on him from behind, he was turning left-handed in a wide arc.

The shout of warning that arose from sympathisers all around may have reached him. But nothing could now turn him quickly enough to meet the attack even halfway round. And his lance was useless to him.

Will, intent on his purpose, drove on. He knew just what he was aiming for — under the other's right arm. Try to jerk his mount aside as he would, nothing the Hamilton could do could save him from some blow of Will's lance-point. He braced himself in saddle and stirrups to withstand the impact, half-turning himself, if not his horse, to face the assault, wrenching round his lance with him.

Which was what Will desired. the other could probably withstand any unseating stroke thus — but his right side was wide open. Before the man's lance could be brought to bear, Will's point drove in just to the left of the shield, under the arm, smashing along breastplate and gauntlet. He gave a vicious sideways wrench.

Hamilton somehow retained his seat. But his lance was flung clean out of his grasp, and fell to the turf.

Now there was shouting everywhere, not all of it complimentary to Will. Pulling round, he reined up, unhurriedly now, and brought his sweating, blowing horse to a standstill. He looked across at his disarmed antagonist — and then, after a long moment, tossed his own lance from him.

Pandemonium broke loose amongst the spectators.

Hamilton drew his sword and held it high. Nodding grimly, Will did likewise. He rose in his stirrups, and stiffly lifted his greaved left part-way across his saddle, as though to dismount, and so waited.

But the other was having none of it. Jabbing his sword directly forward, at Will, he kicked his horse into motion again.

Inside his helm Will cursed. Two-handed swording on horseback was a fool's game, unless one was especially expert.

There was nothing expert or edifying in what followed. The pair, after a little preliminary skirmishing, came close — as they must, to achieve anything. They had tossed away their shields, which were now only encumbrances to their left arms.

They commenced what was little more than a clumsy, crude display of swiping and slamming and battering. Little else was possible. The swords were five feet long, broad-bladed and heavy, demanding both hands to wield. Guiding their horses with their knees, they were reduced to mere banging, hackings and pokings. Refinements were impossible.

How long they kept this up Will could not have told — for the heat inside the armour, and his copious sweating, made him dizzy, and the clanging blows of steel on steel, though they scarcely hurt the recipients, affected his head, his eyesight. Even his own hits on the other jarred him. It was his hope that Hamilton, being older, would be still worse affected. He was playing for time, therefore, seeking to tire the man.

But presently it was borne in on Will that weariness was not the only deciding factor in this grievous slogging match — possibly not the most vital. Strength of wrists might well decide the matter. So heavy were these swords. Already his own were aching and weakening. Hamilton was a stocky, thick-set man, and it might well be that he had the tougher, thicker wrists. Time might not be on Will's side, after all.

He tried a few tricks, back-handed swipes, rearing his horse high, seeking to knock the other out of the saddle rather than just to smite him. But all were invalidated by the fact that though the swords were long, as such, they demanded such close in-fighting that there was little room for manoeuvre. Panting, he perceived that his wrists were going numb. He could not go on with this for much longer. He decided to take a major risk, to stake all on a chance.

Noting where his discarded lance lay on the grass, he edged his beast thitherwards. He waited for a suitable blow to strike him, to give him excuse. When one clanged, no stronger than many another, he nevertheless reeled backwards. Retaining his sword with only one hand, he waved the other arm in the air, as though to try retain his balance, swaying drunkenly in the saddle, kicking his feet free of the stirrups. Striving not to make it seem contrived, he rolled over, and fell to the ground, on the right side of his horse, away from the other — one of the most difficult contortions he had ever attempted.

He landed on all fours, jarring himself within the armour, but not seriously. Would Hamilton accept it as a genuine fall? If not, all was probably lost.

With difficulty he got to his feet, and staggered a little nearer to his lance, now only a few feet off. He stood.

The other was clearly at a loss. He circled doubtfully.

Will well knew his problem, since he had deliberately engineered it. To ride down his dismounted opponent obviously would be a temptation, to finish off the fight there and then — although that lance, if snatched up, could still complicate matters. But such a move would be ungallant, unpopular with the onlookers, especially after Will had made the gesture of casting away his lance earlier, when he need not have done.

The gamble came off. Sir Patrick, most evidently reluctant, dismounted. The crowd cheered

And now, Will had the conditions he sought — if only his wrists held out. The champion was dismounted and lanceless. And must be very weary also.

They circled like wary dogs. Quickly Will saw that the other was indeed much less agile on his feet than in the saddle. With a new lease of energy and hope he began to dart and thrust and feint.

Even so he was heavy, of course, weighed down, slow. No man in full armour, however spry, can dance about. But he was a lot swifter, more active, than Hamilton. Soon he was placing his blows almost where he would.

The end came with extraordinary suddenness. In trying to counter, back-handed, a stroke from behind, the older man overbalanced, and went down on one knee, a hand out to save himself. He could still rise fairly quickly, but inevitably his head was bent, his heavy helm aiding. Will had time to aim carefully. One hand gripping his sword half-way down the blade, for greater precision, he thrust the point in between gorget and helm, at the back of the other's neck. With major restraint he held the weapon from deep penetration — for such a thrust could have killed the man beneath him. So he stood.

Hamilton well knew his danger, and the impossibility of doing anything about it. For long moments he crouched there, motionless. Then, slowly, carefully, lest the sword-point be jerked, he lowered himself to the ground and lay still.

With a long sigh, Will raised his steel encased foot and placed it on the other's back. He raised a gauntleted hand also, in the direction of the queen of the games.

Trumpets blared, men shouted, and attendants came running on to the field.

Will withdrew his sword without delay, sheathed it, and with no further glance at his prostrate foe, paced heavily towards his horse. He would have liked to aid Hamilton to rise — but anything such would have meant words, opening visors, recognition. He also should have shouted further challenge to anyone who would still counter Douglas — but did not. An esquire caught his mount for him, and aided him into the saddle, He should have ridden in towards Margaret and the royal box, even made a circuit of the area. Instead, without so much as a hand raised to the storm of applause, exclamation and vilification, he cantered straight across to the lists gate, and out.

Rob Fleming and the Douglas lairds awaited him, looking at him a little strangely. Undoubtedly their respect was increased, but there was something else about them, as well, that tempered their triumph. Will did not have to have it interpreted for him, since he felt the same way himself. In the tent, being aided out of his armour, he cut short congratulations.

"It was bad fighting, but necessary," he jerked. "That was no tilting. It was war. Part of *my* war. Remember that. Now — haste you off with this, of a mercy!"

Jamie came limping into the tent, smiling distinctly shamefacedly. He had a great bruise on his brow and was holding his left arm carefully. Will cut short his mixed praise and apologies ruthlessly.

"You are a fool Jamie!" he declared. "Worse. I sent you to stop folly, not increase it. I require better of you than this!"

"It was . . . it was for . . ."

"I know well what it was for! D'you take me for a bairn? And what of Hugh? What of Archie?"

"Hugh is much shaken, but not hurt. Archie has a bone broke — his shoulder. And cut about the head."

"Aye. And he deserved worse!" Free of the armour, Will glared round at them all. "No word of this, I tell you. It was some unknown wandering knight, giving only the name of Douglas." He dabbed the sweat from his brow, and smoothed down his somewhat limp and crumpled finery. Without a further word to any, he hurried from the tent.

Back through the crowds he pushed his way while a herald was repeating and repeating that the nameless Douglas knight should come forward to receive the Countess Margaret's favour. Everywhere men were discussing, arguing, guessing. Some glanced at him oddly, but none dared question the Earl of Douglas, especially with a scowl on his face.

As he slipped into Margaret's gallery, King James did not fail to see him. "Cousin," he called down. "Who was he? That knight. He has not come. Did you see him? Speak with him?"

"No, Sire," Will returned shortly. "I was asking after my foolish brothers."

"But where is he? He must be presented to me. And to your lady. It was notable fighting. I have never seen jousting like it. Have you?" The boy was almost stammering with excitement.

"I did not see all, Your Grace. My concern was . . . for my brothers. But, if you would have him here, Sire, he shall be summoned. Johnnie — go look for Sir Robert Fleming. He was at the lists. Tell him to find this stranger Douglas and bring him to the King's Grace."

"Sir James . . I mean, my lord of Hamilton, says that he thinks him no true Douglas, Cousin. But some hired bravo, bought to save your name! Sir James Livingstone thinks likewise."

"Then Sire, I cannot congratulate either of them on their wits! Douglas needs not to hire swords. There were a dozen Douglas lairds at itch to get at Hamilton, but held back because of my brothers. This stranger did not."

Hamilton and Livingstone, on either side of the King, exchanged glances. "How know you then, my lord, that the stranger *was* a Douglas?" the former demanded.

"He said that his name was Douglas. And none take that name lightly, in this realm, my lord, I assure you. If you contest that, prove it! Bring the impostor to me."

"He might be under a vow. To keep silence," the romantic monarch suggested. The other two did not speak.

"Aye, Sire," Will conceded. He turned to Margaret. "Jamie is well," he told her, lower-voiced. "A bruise or two, that is all. Hugh is sore. Archie sorer. But no grievous hurt."

She swallowed. "That is good. He — Jamie — fought well." She looked up at him directly. "And you?"

"I?" He shrugged. "What mean you? I am hot. At the folly of my brothers. Their new honours had addled their heads. But they may have learned their lesson."

She turned away, without answer.

The games went on, trials of strength, fleetness, skill. But there was no more jousting. And since the mysterious Douglas champion did not present himself, despite all summons, there was no supreme recipient of the Countess's silken glove — although Sir Patrick Hamilton was brought up to receive a further congratulation on his fighting. Will, watching him closely, added his own compliments, briefly, and perceived nothing to indicate that the other had any suspicions as to the identity of his vanquisher. Will went so far as to declare, then, that the King's cause would well use so doughty a fighter — and meant it.

At last the programme drew to a close. The sky had grown dull and overcast. All were hot and tired. Even King James's enthusiasm wilted. Meg Douglas came to take away her mistress, whom she declared would be too weary for what was to follow if she did not rest. The glance she shot at Will was somehow inimical.

There was more feasting, here in the open, for all and sundry. But for the principal wedding guests there was a great banquet in the Abbey refectory, with music and entertainment. None should claim that Douglas was lacking in hospitality.

Long before that evening was over, Will himself was more than weary of it all, and his bride white-faced and strained. Nevertheless, although most would have forgiven their hosts' defection, in the circumstances, and many all but urged it, they made no move. Will had let it be known, however, that he would frown strongly on any attempt to carry out the traditional bedding of the bride and groom, by whomsoever. Undoubtedly Archie would have been the ringleader in anything such, but he was not present, being a bandaged inmate of the Abbey hospital; and none of his brothers were feeling inclined further to cross swords with Will that day.

At length, with King James asleep in his chair — like many another — and Margaret looking ready to drop, Will could no longer indulge his reluctance. Twice Meg Douglas had come from her lowly place at the foot of the refectory, to behind the dais table, to speak to the younger girl, and to glare at Will, most evidently urging him to take her mistress away and end this ordeal. He rose, and Rob Fleming called for silence.

"Your Grace, my lord Abbot, lords and ladies and

179

gentles all. The night is young, and there are meats, drink and entertainment to sustain you yet for long. But the Lady Margaret is aweary. You would not begrudge her her rest? Nor myself my, my bliss!" Somehow he got it out, the least that he could say. "We bid you all a good night."

There were cheers, laughter and some witticisms. But these were muted, for, whatever the bridegroom's words, his stare was haughty, uninviting, almost challenging. The Black Douglas in that mood, was not a man to cross.

He raised Margaret, bowed to the King, and hand under her arm, paced to door. His countess almost had to run.

"My lord," she murmured. "Less haste ... would be seemly!"

He bit his lip.

CHAPTER TEN

SINCE the Abbey was grossly overcrowded, only two small rooms had been set aside as the bridal chambers. In one of them, Will paced the floor, a man at odds with his fate. Never had he felt less sure of himself.

As he paced, naked but for his furred bed-robe, he eyed the inner door almost askance. He would have had a bed made up in this ante-room, but for the talk that would have followed. All Sweet Heart would know of it before morning, nothing more certain. In any other place than this crowded abbey! ...

Presently that door opened, and Meg Douglas came out. She had her mistress's bridal-gown over her arm. She looked at Will seeming even more toughly muscular and compact than usual in his bed robe, and dipped the sketchy mockery of a curtsy. "All awaits your lordship's pleasure," she said.

He frowned at her. "I' faith, Meg — you at least can spare me this!"

"Spare you, my lord? Who am I to spare the Black Douglas on his wedding-night?"

"Have done!" he said. "You know very well that this is not the wedding-night I would have."

"Did any force you to it?"

Sombrely he looked at her. "I think they did, yes. All of the name of Douglas did!" He inclined his head towards the door. "How . . . how does she?"

"She does very well. Better than you. I think! She is tired, but herself. And very fair. She will not fail you!"

He shook his head. "A child," he said.

"Gentle her, then." Heavily Meg said that, her voice breaking. She hurried to the turnpike stair-head, and away.

The man still avoided that inner door. She was tired, he told himself. She might sleep. He waited, pacing. He wondered where Meg was bedding.

At length, snuffing candles, he tip-toed to the door, and quietly opened it.

A lamp still burned in the inner room, beside the great bed. Margaret was not asleep. She sat upright on the bed, looking very small and slight and great-eyed. The bed-clothes were drawn up to her chin.

"You have been long," she said.

He cleared his throat. "I thought . . . perhaps you slept. You are weary."

"I would not do that, my lord."

"I am not *your* lord!" He almost shouted it.

"Husband, then. And I am none so weary."

"You must be. It had been a long day. Heavy. Trying. I would not have come troubling you. To this room. I would have left you, this night, in peace. But the turnpike opens on to that other. There is no other door. Others, servants, would see. And talk."

"Talk, yes. They would. At such thing. I would not wish such talk."

"No. But I can sleep here, on the floor, very well. Give me but one cover. It will be better than many a night in the field. Or on the hill."

Her eyes widened, if that was possible. "What do you mean?"

"Only that you need fear nothing, Margaret. This night."

"Fear? I . . . I do not fear you." She swallowed, for she was of an honest mind. "Or not, not in this."

"Nevertheless, tonight you may rest. Undisturbed. The bed is yours. All yours."

"What . . . what are you saying?" she whispered. "That you will not bed with me?"

He nodded. "Aye, lass. I will not bed with you."

"But why? Why? What have I done? Do I so displease you, my lord?"

"No, no. Not that. Never think it . . ."

"What, then? I am young, ignorant in this matter. But . . ."

"Aye, you are young," he agreed heavily.

"So that is it! I am too young for you? You think of me as a child? But I am no child. In a few months I shall be sixteen. Many younger than I wed, have children. I am a woman. See — am I a woman, or no?" She flung back the bed-covers, and sat there, completely naked, before him. "I have a woman's body, have I not? These are women's breasts, are they not? I have hair where a woman has hair. Am I a child, Will Douglas? Look at me!"

She was heart-breakingly lovely as she sat there, white, fair, slender, long-limbed. Her breasts were high and round, wide-spaced and sweet, her nipples pink rosebuds, her stomach flat, her hips firmly sculptured, with no hint of fat anywhere — and hair there was, though hardly darker than flaxen. Nevertheless, however exquisite, enticing, fragile, however wistfully eager her display of it — in which her inner shrinking showed in every line of her — it was not a woman's body. Whatever the girl's maturity of mind and spirit, her body was as yet otherwise.

Helplessly the man shook his head "You are most beautiful. Beautiful beyond all words. And desirable. But . . ." He spread his hands. "What can I say? Only that you are young. Too young for this. Too young for me to take. Like this."

"You wed me. Took me for your wife."

"We both know why we wed, girl. It was not, not for this."

"I wed you to be your wife. In all duty."

"Aye, there you have it. In duty. You are dutiful indeed. But you do not, cannot, *want* me. If you had your wish, I swear, it would not be Will Douglas!" If he emphasised the Christian name, it was only very slightly. Worked up as he was, he kept himself from saying the unforgivable thing. "You offer what you have been told it is your duty to offer — offer most generously. I am grateful for your offer. But I cannot accept it."

"You do not want me, then?" Her voice was level now. "You said, there, that I was desirable. But it was not the truth. You do not desire me."

He found no answer for her.

"I am sorry ..." she began. Suddenly she looked up. "Perhaps ... perhaps it is you? That *you* are tired? It was a long day for you also."

"No! No — not so." Almost shocked, he spoke quickly. "I am ... very well."

"I should have thought of it. You must be weary. You have not spared yourself today. It was you, was it not, who beat down the Hamilton knight, this afternoon? I was sure that it was you. Despite all you said. Forgive me — I should have known that you would be tired."

"No — by the Rude! I tell you, it is not true." He glared. "*I* am not tired. I but think of you ..."

They looked at each other helplessly. Then she turned away and flung herself face down on the bed, her back to him, her slender body racked with sobs.

Biting his lip he watched her till he could stand it no longer. He went to sit beside her.

"Margaret, lass — no tears, of a mercy!" he told her. "There is no need. No hurt in this."

"There is," she got out. "Oh, there is."

"No. No. How can there be? You do not, you cannot, love me!"

She did not answer.

"If you do not love, why tears?" he insisted.

"We are wed. You are my husband."

"Aye. But that is not why you weep?"

"It is. It is." Never had she seemed more a child.

Almost he put out a hand to touch, to seek to comfort that white body, but drew back. "See, lass," he said. "You cannot love me, that is certain. And you do not *desire* me, I think? Do you. The flesh, just? You!"

She made a smothered sound, which he took for a negative.

"Aye. Then, what? What is this hurt?"

"It means ... that I have failed. Failed in my first duty as a wife. The first duty of our marriage. To pleasure you. In bed. Failed ..."

"This is folly! You have failed in nothing. This day you have been Countess of Douglas indeed."

"But not now. You do not want me."

183

"And do *you* want me? Tell me that." And as still she did not answer, he did touch her now, reaching out, less than gently, to turn her face to him. "Look at me, girl — tell me if you want me, lacking love? For, if you do, then you shall have me — that I swear!"

She stared at him, gulping, from swimming, blinking eyes, but did not speak. He held her so for silent moments on end. He did not know how fierce he looked.

"Aye," he sighed, at last. "So be it. You do not want me. Only to do your duty. And your duty you have done, in the offering. As in all else. Let it content you."

She made a small moaning noise. "It is not right. She said ... I was assured ... that you were a lusty man. Hot ..."

"Who said so? Who told you your duty?"

"My mother."

If Will had frowned before, he looked black now. The thought of that archly simpering, gaunt and ageing woman, dwelling on this night's bedding, coaching her daughter on pleasuring him, going over it all, having him herself as it were at second hand, sickened him. But at least it had not been Meg Douglas.

"Aye." He stood up. "Give me one cover, then. There has been talk enough, for one night."

Margaret shook her head. "Not that," she urged, almost pleaded. "Not the floor, Come into my bed, at least. On this wedding night. We can share a bed can we not? Husband and wife. Else I am ashamed. Do not touch me. But rest more at ease so ..."

Almost he smiled at that. Only a child would believe that a man, any normal whole man, lusty or not, would rest more at ease in a bed with a naked girl than on the floor alone. But he could scarcely explain this to her, in the circumstances.

"Very well," he agreed shortly. He doused the lamp, threw off his bed-robe, and in the half-dark climbed into the bed beside her, naked as she was. He kept well to his own side, however, so that they did not touch — and he carefully kept his back towards her.

So he lay, silent, stiff, desperately aware of the white body so close to its own, the warmth of which he could feel coming to him. He perceived that she trembled a little, though this could have been the reaction to her former sobbing. He had never felt less like sleep. Every breath she took, every least stir that she made, he was aware of. And every few moments he asked himself if he was a fool.

The longer he lay thus, the more agitated he grew, his masculinity an aching urgency. Almost he willed her to turn, to touch him, to reach out to him — and if she had done, she would have been left, however inexperienced, in small doubt as to his readiness. He sighed and sighed.

But she did not move. As his unease mounted, so hers seemed to diminish. Her breathing evened and became regular. Once or twice she murmured something. After a while he had no doubt that she slept.

He could have cried out on her then, in sheer exasperation and frustration. And on himself. Now he knew his folly. Only a sort of pride saved him.

He made an endless night of it, aware of each hour. It was not that he did not doze over, frequently — but always he was soon fully awake again, tense, aware, demanding. The girl remained quietly asleep, absolutely still, at his side. Almost he hated her, as the night went on — until in the grey light of early morning, an outflung arm and hand came to rest on his chest. With injured, tight-lipped patience he suffered it to lie there — and after a while, strangely enough, a certain pity and regard grew in him for its owner. This, in time, gradually brought him the greatest easement of the night, and presently he fell into an honest sleep.

When he next awoke, the sun was shining into the little chamber, and he was alone in the great bed. He could hear Meg Douglas dressing her mistress in the next room. Long he stared up at the groined ceiling, before reaching for his robe.

CHAPTER ELEVEN

THE little town and the great abbey returned to their accustomed peace and quiet by degrees, wedding-guests and hangers-on of all qualities moving off as and when they would, with unlimited viands and entertainments available for those who chose to linger. Oddly enough, their host was amongst the first to go. It need not have been so — indeed it had not been

arranged thus. But nothing would do that morning but that
Will should be off, without delay, with a small hard-riding
party, for Newark in Ettrick. It had been planned that he
should redeem his early promise to King James to show him
some wild-bull hunting in the forest, after the wedding, and
preparations had to be made for the royal suite. There was no
need, of course, for the Earl of Douglas to go ahead and make
these personally; Pate Pringle, with Jamie or Rob Fleming,
could have done it well enough. But Will insisted. He was concerned to remove himself from his bride of a day and a night.

So, with a tight little company of Fleming, Pate and his
brothers Hugh and John, he set off before noon, on the sixty-
five-mile ride. The royal entourage, with Margaret and the
other ladies, escorted by Jamie, would come on later and more
slowly, halting for the night in upper Annandale, probably at
Moffat.

Will drove the ill humours out of himself that day in sheer,
unrelenting hard riding. If his companions thought it strange
behaviour in a bridegroom, they were not rash enough to say so;
indeed they were given little opportunity for saying anything,
so hot was the pace maintained.

Eleven hours of this, on foundered horses and very weary,
they threaded the quiet night-bound hills to Newark Castle
above the rushing Yarrow. That night, in his own bed in
Newark's lofty garret-chamber within the parapet-walk, Will
Douglas had no sleep problems.

The following evening, when the royal party arrived, all
was in readiness for them. The tall square keep and its out-
buildings were, of course, crowded as never before, and tents
and pavilions had to be pitched for many a knight and gentle
was well as for the men-at-arms. Which provided Will with
excuse for denying himself a bridal chamber, for putting Margaret, her mother and his own, all in one room, the King, alone
of all the company, being allotted a single apartment. If tongues
wagged, their owners had little to go on.

So commenced a week of great hunting, great prowess and
great feeding. As well as the bulls, wolves, boars and the big
woodland stags were sought out, chased and brought low in
large numbers. Will excelled himself, his brothers redeemed
their names — save for Archie, who had to remain a disgruntled
spectator — and King James was kept in an almost continuous

state of excitement. There was little time, or opportunity, for connubial activities.

On only one occasion, when a thunderstorm and heavy rain drove the huntsmen home early, was Will longer than momentarily alone with his wife. Margaret, Meg in attendance, had gone hunting with the men most days, but had tended to turn back for Newark earlier, usually with Jamie as escort. This day, she had remained behind at the castle, and when the hunters were driven back by the rain, it was to discover that Margaret and Meg had gone off by themselves to visit a cave a mile or two off, where the hero Bruce was alleged to have hidden during his wanderings. Jamie at once announced that he would go fetch them home, and Will could hardly do other than accompany him.

The brothers, both soaked to the skin, found the two girls still sheltering in the fern-decked cave under a cliff that overhung the river. Their arrival was greeted with obvious and gratifying pleasure.

"Almost we had started back," Meg told them. "But twice the rain looked about to stop. And I am afraid for the thunder. Or at least, for the lightning . . ."

"That is not true," Margaret declared. "Meg is afraid for nothing. It is *I* am afraid. Always have been."

"You need not be afraid, now we are here," Jamie assured, stoutly.

"Aye — these two valiant knights will protect us from thunder bolts, like all else!" Meg exclaimed, mockingly. "We have naught to fear when they are near. The pity that they are not near more often!" And she looked directly at Will.

He said nothing, though Jamie protested that he was ever at their service, happier in their company than anywhere else soever.

The men had brought heavy hooded riding-cloaks to wrap the girls in, but wet as they were, they neither of them showed any urgent haste to be gone from the cave, for their own different reasons.

It was Meg who presently urged a move — and urged it pointedly on Jamie, not on his brother. "Will you be condescending enough to escort a poor tiring-woman back to the castle, Sir Jamie?" she asked. "And let a new husband and wife have at least a word with each other, in peace! Something rare for this marriage, I vow!"

Will had to bite back his hasty objection. It was not for this that he had waited.

Jamie looked only a little more enthusiastic "Oh, aye. To be sure," he said, eyeing Margaret. "Just that."

"Come, then. I have preparations to make for my lady, in that crowded castle. Dry clothing . . ."

When they were gone, Meg riding pillion behind Jamie, Will found Margaret's calm and steady gaze on him. "Meg does not understand," she said.

He frowned. "There is no great deal to understand."

"Some might think that there was. When, only days married, you avoid me."

"It is not that. I do not avoid you It is only, only that it is best. That we should not sleep together."

"Yes," she agreed. "That *I* understand. But perhaps others do not!"

At her flat tone, he made a gesture towards her. "See you, Margaret — let *us* not misunderstand. I said before, there is no hurt in this. I like you, lassie. I like you very well. I think you are the most beautiful creature that I have ever seen. We are wed, not because we desired each other, but because I am Douglas and you are Galloway. That had to be. You do not love me. I will not take you, young as you are, lacking love. In bed. But . . . that is all. We are still wed. We can be friends. Good friends in all else. You have good wits, a stout heart. Countess of Douglas indeed. Let us be friends, Margaret." That was a long and difficult speech for Will Douglas.

After a moment or so, she nodded. "If you wish it so."

"Not just because I wish it so," he insisted. "It is right. Best. Wise. Is it not, Margaret?"

"Very well."

"Well, aye." He sighed with relief. "And more than well. I need the aid of a wise head and a sound heart. Douglas needs it. This realm needs it."

"And I so young!" she remarked. As his face fell a little, she smiled. "But I will grow older. Nothing more sure. And I will be your friend. Come, then — take me back, Will Douglas."

Will was much eased in his mind — until, that is, later that evening. Margaret and some of the other women had already retired, when a servitor came to murmur in Will's ear, in the

188

Hall, that Mistress Meg would speak with my lord, on my lady's business. A summons form that source did not find him backward, and he followed the man out.

He found Meg waiting at a window alcove of the turnpike stair. She looked him up and down.

"What sort of man are you?" she asked him, without warning.

Surprised, he raised his brows. "A simple man, I think. Ordinary enough."

"I wonder! Since you leave your wife to bed amongst old women! And yourself sleep amongst your brothers."

"The house is full. You know that."

"Aye." She held out her hand. "Come you, my lord."

It was now the man's turn to wonder, but he took her hand, and she led him upwards.

They climbed three full storeys to the stair-head, and there, opposite the door that led into his own garret chamber, which he now shared with his brothers, she passed out on to the open stone-slabbed parapet-walk. Mystified, he was led along this narrow way, in the damp air of night, until, at the angle of the keep, a little gabled cap-house was corbelled out, to overhang the walling. Little more than a roofed-in square turret, it was there to cover the wall-faces below, for defence, and protect the approaches from that side, high above the river. She threw open its door, and entered.

"Well?" she said, turning to look at him.

He followed her in, glancing around him. The place was about eight feet square, with stark stone walls and floor, but it had windows on three sides, to command the walls, and a tiny fireplace, to comfort a sentry of a cold winter's night.

"Well?" he gave back, in turn.

"It is clean. Dry. And could be comfortable enough," she said. She shut the door behind them. "See — a pallet-bed could sit here. Kists there. An eager husband, I think, would not have left this empty, in a crowded house!"

"So! And you would have me an eager husband, Meg?"

"I would have you cherish and comfort my mistress," she said, after a brief pause. "Your wife!"

"Cherish and comfort? These I shall do. Bedding is another matter."

"Bedding is common comfort for a wife, is it not?"

"You make it that she seeks her comfort only between her legs!" he jerked, deliberately coarse.

"I did not say that. She is good. Pure . . ."

"Aye, pure! Too pure for Will Douglas! And young. A child."

"Still you hold to that? I tell you, she is more woman than you know."

"I know enough. Would you call her woman as *you* are woman?"

She moistened her lips. "Perhaps not. Not yet. But . . . what of that?"

"It is all-important. Do you not see? How can I desire half a woman, when you are there? You spoil me for all others, Meg."

She turned away, to peer out of a window into the half-light of the gloaming. "You should not speak so," she said.

"It is the truth."

"Then . . . you shame me."

"Why? How may that be?"

"You make me the cause of my lady's hurt."

"Hurt!" he cried. "This of hurt? What hurt is there? What hurt do I do her because I do not bed with her? She is but fifteen. A child. She does not love me, scarcely knows me. She does not desire my body. Tell me in what I hurt her?"

She turned back to him. "You make her of no attraction. As a woman. Which is something no woman, however young, can suffer."

"I have told her that she is beautiful. She would attract many. I' faith — she attracts my brother Jamie powerfully enough! Even she must see that."

"But it was *you* who wed her."

"The Earl of Douglas wed the Lady of Galloway."

"You wed her . . . intending this?"

It was he who now looked away. "Aye," he said.

"And that first night? Do you mean . . . ? You shared her naked bed . . . and did not touch her?"

He nodded.

"Sakes — are you a man at all, then?"

"Aye, I am a man!" They stood very close together in that confined space, lofty, remote from all. Her vivid woman's presence was like a throbbing challenge to him, her scent, on the hot thundery night air, an almost unbearable incitement. He reached and gripped her. "Need *you* ask that, damn you?"

She did not move within his grasp. Almost she stopped breathing.

Her silence infuriated him. He shook her. And the shaking undid him entirely, the feeling of her rounded bare forearms in his hands, and the swinging of that proud and thrusting bosom against his wrists. Groaning, he pulled her fiercely to him, and clamped his hot lips on hers.

Still she did not stir or respond. But neither did she struggle or seek to turn away from him.

Hungrily he kissed her, on lips, eyes, throat and shoulders, straining her to him, intensely aware of all the warm, curved shape of her against him, his hands urgent, groping. Her lips freed, she made a moaning sound.

"Woman," he ground out, against her soft flesh, "I want you. Have wanted you ... from the moment first ... I saw you. Only you."

"No!" she panted. "No."

"Yes, I say! We are a pair, Meg. You know it. Made for each other. Can you deny it?"

She shook her head. "No," she sobbed. But there were no tears to her sobbing.

Violently he thrust her from him — but only so far, his hands still grasping her shoulders. "You are mine — as I am yours. For always. I want you. I am burning for you. But ... tell me that you do not want *me*! Love me! In honesty. Tell me — and I will go. Leave you. Now. God helping me!" That came forth with strangled vehemence.

She stared into his eyes in the gloom. "I cannot. In honesty. Cannot say it. But — oh, Will ... it is not right ..."

She was wrenched back against him. And this time, when his mouth demandingly sought hers, her lips parted to his, even though still she shook her head slowly, feebly.

Now there was no restraining his masterful hands. The light linen bodice, loose and low-necked as it was, yielded readily, and he had those magnificent breasts, full, firm and hardtipped, to caress and kiss. But these only arrested him for moments — indeed they urged him on. On and downwards he pushed and tore — and if the girl did not aid him, she did not seek to halt him. Quickly enough her clothing all fell away from her to the floor. Partly on it and partly on the bare stone flags, he pressed down her splendid, yielding loveliness.

Now she made no pretence at reluctance. Reaching up, she took him to her. In a storm, a tempest of desire and fulfilment, he sank himself and his clamant need into her warm enclosing embrace.

Long pent up, like many a similar cataclysm, its brevity was on a par with its violence.

Later, passion for the moment spent, the man restrained her when Meg would have risen. "Wait you," he said, and with a new authority, however relaxed. "We are not done yet. You asked if I was a man! You must let me prove it! There is no haste. Not now. None will seek us here."

"I shall not ask again if you are a man!" she told him, a little unsteadily, her breath still coming fast, to the delightful disorder of her person. "Only, I ask myself what sort of a woman I am!"

"I can tell you that. You are *my* woman. The fairest, most kind and wholest woman it has been my joy to know. A man's woman, and true . . ."

"True! Me? When I have betrayed my mistress and my friend! Taken what should be hers."

"No. Only accepted what is not for her. Do not blame yourself, my dear. The blame in this must be mine, and I accept it. But there are forces stronger than priests' words and signed parchments!"

"Aye. But how to tell *her* that? How to face her now?"

He kissed her damp hair. "I' faith — you are of tougher stuff than this, Meg Douglas! Do not tell me that you have not strength enough in you for what must be? I esteemed you otherwise."

"All the strength is run out of me, I think. That is your doing . . ."

"And you misliked the doing of it?"

"No. I will not be dishonest with you, at least."

"Aye! Every sweet inch of you would foreswear you if you declared otherwise, Meg!" He ran his hand lightly over her voluptuous body, which at once began to make its own response. Smiling a little ruefully, he chided her. "Bide you, bide you, just a little, woman! Would you shame me, after all? . . ."

"I am . . . I *am* shameful. Or shameless — I know not which. A wicked woman . . ."

"You are *you*. Just yourself. Not wicked. Outgoing. Kind. Bountiful. Made so. For me! A full woman."

It was not long before her kindness and fullness were sufficient to unite them again. And this time in no fierce storm but in prolonged and joyous fervour, gratification, harmony and mutual completion. Time and all else stood still for them. Physically they were as one.

"Black . . . Douglas!" she murmured at last, exhausted, and slept in his strong arms.

It was late indeed, and very dark of a wet night, when at length they emerged from that watch-chamber and tip-toed hand in hand along the parapet-walk in the rain. There was a guard on the castle by night, of course, but this was centred on the gatehouse and outer curtain-walls. They encountered no one on the way down to the women's quarters — and if any of his brothers perceived Will's belated entry to their garret-chamber, they knew better than to question. Anyway, he was a married man, and could have been with his wife.

Thereafter, for the remainder of the stay at Newark, a pattern in these personal matters developed between the Douglas trio. Will sought to see more of Margaret, by day, and mutual respect and even liking did grow in them, an acceptance of a limited but not unrewarding or sterile relationship; but of a night, Meg and he came together in the little watch-chamber up on the keep-top, for an hour or so of stolen bliss — and all the day was but the waiting for it. All the day, too, Meg had her burden of guilt to bear, with her mistress — and served her the better, more warmly, for it. If Margaret knew, or suspected, she did not say so.

So passed almost two weeks of a notable hot and airless summer. Then, one sultry evening, messengers arrived for the King and Douglas, from Chancellor Kennedy, who had returned directly to Stirling from New Abbey. They brought bad news from an angry man of God. A confederation of his enemies, with a large armed force, had descended upon the church lands in Fife and Angus belonging to the Bishop's see of St. Andrews, and the University there, and with savage and indiscriminate fury had laid them waste, burning and destroying villages, granges and hay crops, plundering whole tracts, wounding and taking captive his vassals and servants, and ruining the richest and best-managed farm lands in the kingdom. The evil men behind this outrage were well known to them all, united in common spleen and hatred against the Chancellor — and most had been his fellow wedding-guests at Sweet Heart just days before; indeed they must have plotted the campaign at the wedding itself, and gone directly north to perpetrate it. Kennedy was informed that the miscreants were under the commands of the new Lord Hamilton, the Tiger Master of Crawford, two sons of Livingstone, and a Highland chieftain named Rob Ruadh of Struan. He demanded immediate action, Douglas's fullest assistance, and, in view of the lofty status of the culprits, an urgent meeting of the Privy Council, at which they be commanded to appear.

That spelt the end of hunting and love-making alike. The sooner authority, in the persons of the King and his Lieutenant and sundry other officers of state, was back at Stirling, the better. But before they left, next morning, Will gave orders to his brothers, and others whom he could trust. The Douglas might, that famed if somewhat vague and sleeping giant, was to be thoroughly awakened at last. Not for this present crisis — although a large supply of armed men would be highly useful for that also; but to tackle the major project of bearding Sir William Crichton in his den at Edinburgh Castle, once and for all, by royal command. All the Douglas man-power was to be raised. North, south, east and west his summons was to go — and all Galloway was now included in the call. The Black Douglas wanted, demanded, every man who could bear arms to be mobilised, equipped and assembled at Stirling, at all speed, those more readily available first, the greater numbers to come on later. No excuses would be accepted, no waverers overlooked. Scores of barons owed Douglas fealty; five hundred lairds were his vassals; many thousands of ordinary men were in man-rent to him, under obligation to answer his call. Let them come now, then — or Douglas would know the reason why, as would the Lieutenant-General of the Realm.

It had had to come, sooner or later.

CHAPTER TWELVE

It was Will's first real Privy Council. He had attended, of course, many brief assemblings of small groups of councillors, called together at short notice to give formal acknowledgment of authority to sundry edicts, charters and the like; but this was the first true conclave of the full Council, called in response to the Chancellor's demand. It was indeed something of a special occasion, on more than one account. There was a much larger attendance than usual, as this was obviously going to be a trial of strength, whatever else it was; and it was the first time in living memory that a Council had been held at St. Andrews — this on Bishop Kennedy's request, so that members, and especially the King's party, might see with their own eyes, en route, the devastation and ruin suffered by the Church lands in Fife, to aid them in their deliberations.

The meeting was taking place in the Guest Hall of the Priory, in case certain of the accused members should refuse to enter the Bishop's own castle here on grounds of possible intimidation or coercion. For, although it was not so described, or conducted in form other than a typical Council meeting, it was in fact a trial in more than strength. Few might have perceived it in any brief and casual inspection of the scene — but here was a trial on which much of the King's and the kingdom's fate might hinge.

The long table in the high timber-roofed, arras-hung hall was littered with flagons, drinking-cups and dishes of meats and cakes, as well as papers and parchments, and men lounged, ate, drank or even dozed thereat — although today there was much less sleeping than usual. In fact, the only man who actually slept, indeed snored slightly, at the moment, was one who had as much at stake in the proceedings as anyone — Alexander, 3rd Earl of Crawford. Crawford was a great sleeper. Possibly he found it as good an escape from the problems of life as any — and to be chief of the lightsome Lindsays, especially with a son and heir like Beardie Alex the Tiger, was to be a magnet for problems.

King James, restless and alternating between tenseness and

sprawling boredom, occupied the head of the long table; and Chancellor Kennedy, the effective chairman, sat upright at the foot. Will was beside the King, with his brothers near by, even Archie summoned, still with his arm in a sling. At the monarch's other side sat his guardian, Sir James Livingstone, the Chamberlain. Halfway down, around the somnolent figure of Crawford, were those councillors whose activities had brought about this meeting — the Lord Hamilton, looking scornful, the Master of Crawford glowering menace, the new Lord Gray of Foulis, black-bearded and grimly amused, and Sir John Lindsay of the Byres, Sheriff of Fife. They made an impressive and confident-seeming phalanx. There were over thirty members present altogether, one of the largest attendances on record. No fewer than ten were bishops or mitred abbots.

Kennedy finished his long list of damages and complaints, and pushed back the sheaf of papers. "There, Your Grace and my lords, is the hurt and evil done," he said. "Done deliberately and in spleen and spite against Your Grace's lieges, against open and defenceless property and lands of Holy Church in this county of Fife. I accuse and indict before this Council the following, as wholly, entirely and flagrantly responsible. First, and most shameful, because he is Your Grace's Sheriff of the county and therefore officer charged with the duty of maintaining the realm's law and peace in Fife — Sir John Lindsay of the Byres. Then, Andrew, Lord Gray, Sheriff of Angus. James, Lord Hamilton. Alexander Lindsay, Master of Crawford. And others, not of this Council. And further I charge as being party and privy to the whole ill proceedings although not in person present — my lord, Earl of Crawford, Justice-General of the North and Admiral of this kingdom." The Bishop suddenly raised a pointing hand. "And Sir James Livingstone, who sits there at His Grace's side, Keeper of the royal castle of Stirling! His father, Sir Alexander Livingstone, Guardian of the King. And Master John Cameron, Bishop of Glasgow, to my sorrow and shame! As Chancellor of this realm and Primate of Holy Church in this land, I demand that His Grace's Privy Council considers, condemns and exacts punishment upon each and every of these disturbers of the King's peace, and commands fullest reparation to be made to God's Church."

There were few, save perhaps amongst the named men themselves, who did not gasp in some measure at the unabashed and bold catalogue of that resounding list, but more especially at the identities of the final four. Even Will, who knew something of Kennedy's intentions, as well as his determination and forthright character, was shaken. Not so much in the revelation as in the deliberate enlargement of the challenge. This was folly — a lack of vision, of statecraft, surely. To provoke all one's enemies at once. The involvement of Bishop Cameron came as a surprise, and, apart from its implication of the Church divided against itself, raised the whole issue of a piece of high-level brigandage to something in the nature of a political conspiracy. And even that was not the worst of it. By publicly naming the Livingstones, father and eldest son, even though they had in fact been concerned, Kennedy was in danger of turning all these separate and almost certainly mutually suspicious elements into a faction, and a powerful faction. Scotland had already two factions — Crichton's and Douglas's. Today's proceedings, Will perceived, could conceivably throw these people, at present all approximately on *his* side, into the arms of Crichton.

King James cleared his throat. "Here is a bad business. Aye, a bad business," he said, looking around him uncertainly. "We'll have to get to the rights of it. But ... but ..." His young voice tailed away.

"The rights are not all on my lord Bishop's side, Sire," Sir James Livingstone declared thinly. Although junior to many present, he was the Chamberlain, and at a Council this gave him added status. "I deny all accusations that I, or my father, have in any way broken the King's peace. As Your Grace knows, I have scarce left your side these months past. And my father is a sick man, and has stirred no more than a mile or two from his house of Callendar. I demand that my lord of St. Andrews withdraws his charges ..."

"Before Sir James finishes his demands, will he deny further?" Kennedy returned strongly. "Deny that his brothers David, Alexander and Robert took active part in these raids? That they were all at Callendar House the night previous to the first raid? That the same night, the Lord Hamilton and Sir John Lindsay of the Byres also arrived at Callendar, direct from New Abbey in Galloway? And that, during the wedding celebrations, Sir James himself shared a bedchamber in the

Abbey of Sweet Heart with Sir John Lindsay and the Master of Crawford?"

"The first I know nothing of. I was with His Grace at Ettrick at the time. The rest I have no reason to deny, since they are nothing to the point. Is it strange that the Lord Hamilton should lodge a night in my father's house on his journey north, since he is his grandson? And all had to share rooms at Sweet Heart — save perhaps my lord Bishop! And, of course, His Grace. If the Abbot chose to put me with the Master of Crawford and Sir John Lindsay, it is his affair . . ."

"And good company too, by Christ's Blood!" Beardie roared abruptly to the alarm of those unready.

Hamilton spoke up smoothly. "Your Grace my lord of St. Andrews is free with his charges. But what crime had been committed? What was done within the jurisdiction of the Sheriff of Fife. In his presence. There has been much unlawful oppression and extortion in that county. Poor folk have been ill-used, driven from their holdings. Honest men made homeless. Taxes, tithes and teinds extorted beyond all right, all bearing. The Sheriff was concerned to put down these evils, and sought our aid. Is it our blame if the worst offenders were monkish clerks and the stewards of Church lands?"

Even James Kennedy was left momentarily speechless by the sheer brazen effrontery of that. His lips moved, but no words came.

"Is it not so, Sir John?" Hamilton pursued his advantage.

"Aye," Lindsay of the Byres was a bull-like man, and sheriff because his father had been so before him. This was the first exercise of his law-enforcement powers to come to Will's notice.

"And my lord of Gray has had similar experience in Angus."

"That is so," Gray, Sheriff of Angus agreed, grinning.

"This is . . . this is beyond all enduring!" the Bishop cried. "To seek to cozen us like bairns! Think you we have neither wits nor any knowledge?" He slammed the sheaf of papers. "Here are burnings and plunderings by the score, ravishings and rapings unnumbered, cattle stolen by the thousand, whole villages destroyed. And you talk of aiding the poor, saving the oppressed, enforcing the laws! My lords — he mocks this Council and His Grace, insults us all! Over and beyond the crimes committed!"

"Not so," Hamilton contended. "Does not my lord Chancellor deny us *our* wits? Is there a noble lord here — a lord *temporal*, that is — who does not well know how the Church grasps at the fruit of honest men's toil? Even the youngest lords know it." And he glaced over at the Douglas brothers. "Do we not know who wrings the last penny out of the land? Who are the hardest taskmasters and hardest bargainers? Aye, and where lie the greatest riches in this kingdom! It is the Church. And the Church owns more land in Fife than in any other county. The bishopric of St. Andrews, swollen with wealth! Is it to be wondered at if the land groans under the oppression?"

"Your Grace — I can only believe that the Lord Hamilton has taken leave of his senses!" Kennedy declared. "He wanders in his mind. And wastes the time of this high Council. These are the maunderings of a man crazed against Holy Church. I will not sit here and listen to them further!"

The other churchmen made noises of agreement.

"Then go, for Christ-God's sake — and a good quittance to the pack o' you!" Beardie shouted.

King James moistened his lips as Kennedy thrust back his chair. "My lords, my lords! . . ." he quavered. He looked at Will.

That young man had seldom been more loth to embroil himself in anything, fighter though he was. Kennedy could declare that Hamilton's mind was wandering, but however absurd these counter-charges, there was no maundering here. It was the age-old and well-proved device of playing off the Church against the rest, the lords temporal against the lords spiritual. The mutual suspicion was always there, latent, ready to smoulder or flame. With the Church owning more than half of the best land in Scotland — and, as it happened, the best managed and therefore most productive — the nobles and lairds could be relied upon to react strongly to any accusations such as Hamilton's, however scantily substantiated. Moreover, by claiming that they did all under the authority of the Sheriff of Fife, and flatly denying any culpability, the miscreants put themselves in a strong position. The Privy Council was not a court of law, and members of it, even though accused of offences, could not be forced into any detailed defence or made to give specific account of their actions. It looked very much as though, on a vote, Hamilton and his friends would get away with it.

Will Douglas was a realist. Perceiving all this, he saw it as no duty of his to fight the Church's battles for it — especially when, in any case, it was likely to lose. His concern was the eventual triumph of the course to which he had set his hand, the King's cause, which he had made the Douglas cause. But for this he needed the Church's support. Just as he needed Crawford's support and, to a lesser extent, Hamilton's and Gray's and the rest. He had no illusions about the size of the task still ahead of him, and recognised that he could afford to lose nothing of the support he had managed to build up. His problem therefore was how to prevent the Crawford-Hamilton faction being thrown into the arms of Crichton, and at the same time keep the regard and sympathy of the Church — which meant, in effect, the Primate, Kennedy. He had little conviction that it was possible.

"Sire," he said, a lot more confidently than he felt. "It seems to me that here is a matter which cannot be decided out of hand, here and now. There is much to enquire into, to establish. And this Council has other grave issues to consider, decisions to make, relative to the safety of the realm. I counsel, therefore, that four lords be appointed, as commissioners, of good faith and not concerned in this issue, to make due enquiry and to report. Two lords temporal and two spiritual. So that we may move to the next business."

"Aye," James agreed relievedly. "Well said, Cousin. You have it right . . ."

The murmurs of agreement from most of the Council were drowned by Kennedy's strong objection. "No!" he cried. "I will not have it. I will not have Holy Church harried and mocked in this realm — and remain this realm's Chancellor! All here know who are guilty, without Lords Commissioners enquiring. I refuse to sit at this table with these foresworn and shameless scorners of the law. Either they go or I go!"

Will moistened his lips, as the Master of Crawford shouted great laughter. "Go then, Churchman — go! Go and pray! We have decisions here for *men* to take — not clerks and half-men! Decisions that require swords, not rosaries!" And the giant shot a quick glance at Will, to remind him as to where lay his hard immediate needs. Beardie Alex Lindsay was not quite such a witless oaf as he sometimes appeared to be.

Will did not really need the warning. "My lord Bishop — I

bid you reconsider. All here are members of His Grace's Privy Council. Here of right. Your hurt is grievous, and must be made good. And lawlessness punished. But these lords have denied your charges against them. My lord of Hamilton's accusations against Holy Church are wrong and should not have been made. But they signify nothing. As to *your* charges, so long as these others deny them, are they not entitled to be here? You cannot turn them away."

"Then I go myself."

"But you are Chancellor. Under His Grace, you preside. Many lords have come far for this Council. And there is much more to decide"

Kennedy did not answer.

"If my lord of St. Andrew goes, we go," the old Bishop of Brechin declared.

As two of the prelates were Douglases, Will doubted if this was certain. But he was faced nevertheless with one of his dreaded situations — the loss of the Church's support. Desperately he played his last poor card.

"Is that wise, my lords? Holy Church's voice undoubtedly will be required. And then, there is the matter of the Bishop of Glasgow! Master Cameron. He was named, was he not, in this charge? He is not here, although summoned. I see that the Bishop of Argyll and the Abbot of Paisley are also absent. In such case, would you leave the word of Holy Church unspoken?"

It was, of course, unscrupulous, almost blackmail. But it was none the less effective for that. It was, in fact, the threat of a division within the Church itself, the raising up of a faction under Bishop Cameron — whom all knew wanted the chancellorship. In that, it was directed against Hamilton also. But none of the churchmen there failed to perceive the danger. Douglas, Bishop of Aberdeen spoke up.

"I hold that we wait," he said briefly.

Others muttered concurrence.

James Kennedy was no fool, however outspoken. He recognised stalemate when he saw it, and the time to change his stance. He stood up.

"I go, then — with Your Grace's permission. But before I go, I declare to you all that Holy Church is not mocked. In token of which I hereby proclaim that I go directly to my cathedral church of St. Andrew here, and after due and holy preparation, present myself before the High Altar. And there I shall pronounce due dire and condign sentence of excommunication upon each, all and every one of those aforementioned and indicted, barring them the Mass and all holy sacraments, all absolutions and dying unction, and all the comforts of religion. The said extremest execration of Holy Church upon all who may harbour, support or cherish them. Furthermore I shall, this day, and every day hereafter, curse them. Curse them solemnly with mitre, bell, book and candle. At the sun's going down each day, before all. Curse them in their waking and their sleeping; their going out and coming in; in their youth and their age; in their wives and sons and daughters, in their manservants and maidservants; in their houses and lands, their cattle and corns, their farms and fields and fisheries. In all that they are, have, and hope for, I shall curse them, until the name of Holy Church is reverenced again in this land. So help me God!"

Raising his hand to the monarch, James Kennedy turned and stalked from the hall.

Stricken dumb, stunned, King and Council sat staring after him, even his fellow-bishops appalled, almost unbelieving. Never had anyone present known anything like this, heard of such cursing, been involved in an excommunication. Even the Tiger looked thoughtful. Only his father slept through it all.

King James was actually trembling, on Will's left — his brothers not so much better on his right. He was affected himself, but less so than the others probably because he had come to know Kennedy passably well and it was more difficult to associate this wholesale malevolence with familiarity.

He cleared his throat. "Your Grace. My lords," he began, a little unsteadily. "We are troubled. Much concerned. By this. By what has happened. But ... there is much to be done. The business of this realm. In especial, the matter of the assault on the castle of Edinburgh. Much has to be considered. Decided. The Chancellor has left us. But His Grace still presides. It is His Grace's Privy Council, not the Chancellor's. Therefore we can and must continue. With Your Grace's agreement?"

None said him nay; indeed none so much as answered. The Primate's spell was on them all still.

"Aye. Well. I move to the matter of Edinburgh. As Lieutenant-General. As to men, I believe that I shall have sufficient. In two weeks time I am assured that I shall have six thousand Douglas men-at-arms assembled. With others, notably those of Hay, Graham, Drummond, Atholl, Maxwell, Montgomery, Borthwick . . ." He nodded towards each of the lords concerned as he named their clans. ". . . and of course, Lindsay and Hamilton, I shall have ten thousand, I hope. Enough."

He had their attention now. To those nobles, fighting-men, swords and lances, by the thousand, spoke louder than anything else in heaven or earth. And six thousand Douglases was something to consider almost with awe. Never had anyone there heard of so large a force fielded under a single name. Here was the sort of discussion in which all felt competent and concerned to join in.

"Crichton cannot muster men to that tune!" King James cried. "Even with my lord of Angus aiding him." He bit that remark off short, looking a little alarmed as he realised the implication that the Red Douglases would fight the Black Douglases might not be popular on his right.

"Aye. But what of cannon?" the practical Sir William Hay put in flatly. "Swords and arrows and lances are of little avail against Edinburgh Castle. A thousand men are scarce worth one cannon. What of them?"

Well Will knew it. "There are cannon to be had. The King's cannon. Some unfortunately are in Edinburgh Castle itself. But there are others. In the royal castles of Stirling, Dumbarton, Doune and Dunbar." He paused, and glanced past the monarch, at Sir James Livingstone.

A faint sigh ran round the table. If any there had wondered before as to Douglas's gentleness and forbearance towards the Livingstones, why the insufferable Sir James had been made Chamberlain and his reprobate old father permitted still to go unpunished, now they perceived it. These four royal fortresses were each in the keepership of one of the Livingstone sons. All the cannon in Scotland which Crichton did not control were in the hands of the Livingstones.

Sir James smirked his sour smile. "No doubt my brothers will do what they can in the matter." He coughed. "Assuming that they are not beset by churchmen and clerks!"

"I will seek my grandfather's good offices," Hamilton said smugly.

"Aye." Into the long quiet, Will's breathing sounded heavy. "Now, as to horseflesh . . ."

CHAPTER THIRTEEN

EDINBURGH had undergone many sieges, invasions and assaults in its day — but undoubtedly never one like this. Will Douglas had been determined on that, from the start. After all, it was not the city that was being besieged, but the citadel. The King's forces had no quarrel with the citizens, except inasmuch as they had acquiesced for long, and too supinely, to Crichton and his friends in the fortress. But even so, the atmosphere now was more than of a weeks-long holiday, an endless gala, than any military campaign. Ten thousand men-at-arms filled the town to bursting-point, with practically nothing to do. In that respect alone, something had to be done to keep them occupied, or there might have been wholesale outrage.

Day after day the green meadows and parkland of Arthur's Seat, the Calton Hill, the Burgh Muir and the banks of the Nor' Loch resounded to the cheers and shouts and laughter, the music, the trumpet-calls and the clash, of organised games, contests, mock-battles, tourney's pageantry and parade. Each night feasting, dancing, baitings, play-acting and minstrelsy prevailed, in every camp and open space amongst the crowded narrow streets of the city. For in it all the townsfolk were included, expected to play their part, even in the great eating. Douglas paid for all — since the royal coffers had long been empty — and anyway, a fair proportion of the beneficiaries were Douglases. Never had Douglas treasure been spent as this Earl spent it.

That there was so little military activity in all this was not Will's fault — who indeed fumed and fretted at the delay. He would have been battering at Edinburgh Castle day and night had he been able. But despite gentle handling and all their promises, the Livingstones had failed him. Some small pieces of artillery they had obtained from Stirling Castle, but nothing as yet from Dumbarton in the west, Doune in the north or Dunbar in the east. For weeks they had waited, urgent couriers had been sent, royal commands, inducements, threats. All to no effect. Excuses in plenty came from Dumbarton and Doune — the cannon were unserviceable; the carriages had broken down; there were no balls of the right calibre; it was too far for oxen to drag them. Excuses, but no cannon. And without sending to besiege these castles likewise, there was no way of forcing the issue. Dunbar, on the Lothian coast, and nearer at hand, might have been different — but soon after the host's arrival at Edinburgh, they heard that the Earl of Angus had sallied out from his nearby stronghold of Tantallon and removed the Dunbar cannon thither, undoubtedly with the connivance of their keeper.

Of cannon-makers Scotland had none. Oddly enough it was Meg Douglas who provided a gleam of hope. She had heard talk years before, to the effect that there was a family of smiths at Carlingwark near Threave in Galloway, who had once made a large cannon for the 5th Earl, which he had taken to the French wars, and which had never come back. That was more than a score of years ago — but in a family, the skills and knowledge might have been preserved. Will sent his brother Hugh hotfoot to Galloway — but cannon were not things which could be wrought in a day, or a score of days, especially the size of weapons that Douglas required. Hugh brought back word that the thing would be attempted, but it would take time. They could only wait.

All this is not to say that there were no gestures made against the castle on the rock. The small cannon they had from Stirling were fired frequently, but really only as a token, and mainly to impress the citizens. The fact was that Crichton's guns up there far outranged them. So they dared not set them up in any established positions, for fear of dire retaliation. The great fortress, skied hundreds of feet high on its crag, could be assailed only from one angle — that covered by its own artillery.

Much more, of course, was required for the reduction of Edinburgh's citadel than just cannon; just as much more was here involved than in the mere siege of a fortress. Crichton had been the real ruler of Scotland for many years, and his power and influence was not readily to be destroyed, whether by hammer-blows or by more subtle undermining. Particularly the fear of him, men's belief that he might yet come out on top, and exact dire vengeance on all who had taken sides against him —

it was this, above all, that had to be defeated. Here was the reason for the ten thousand men — when there was probably fewer than a couple of hundred men in the castle itself; for the displays of splendour, largesse, sheer confidence, in the city beneath its walls. It was a battle for the minds and support and commitment of the people of Scotland. Edinburgh Castle was but one move in that battle.

More was needed, therefore, than cannon and armies. More even than prolonged holiday, feasting and displayed power and might. The King was here in person, lodging in the Abbey of Holyrood, with most of the great officers of state. The Church was represented by as many bishops, abbots and priors as could be persuaded to attend — although Kennedy himself kept his distance, only coming from St. Andrews briefly when the Chancellor's duties demanded. A rift was developing all too evidently between him and Will, despite all the latter could do to heal it. Theirs had been an uneasy partnership from the first, the realist and the idealist.

It was only after two weeks of this ferment that Margaret Douglas brought forth the idea of a parliament, to be held in Edinburgh. A great parliament, more representative than any held for years, sitting here under the walls of the besieged fortress. Surely that would demonstrate, more than anything else, the will of the nation? Crichton would be seen to be isolated, powerless, made to look almost foolish. And Bishop Kennedy, as Chancellor, would necessarily be much involved.

Will saw the force of this, at once. Unfortunately a parliament demanded a statutory calling-period of forty days. Almost six weeks. Yet sieges of fortresses such as this had in the past lasted many months, even years; and it was unlikely that the cannon ordered in Galloway would be made in lesser period — or that Crichton would be apt to yield in the interval. Even if by some miracle he did, a parliament would be useful thereafter to give legality to much that would follow. So the decision had been taken, and the writs and summonses sent out in great numbers. The last parliament had been the least representative for years; this must be otherwise.

Those weeks made long waiting, and a strangely unreal life was forced upon the waiters. The Court established at Holyrood Abbey was brittlely gay. Devices for keeping everybody amused and in good heart waxed almost feverish. Will spared neither himself nor his family, nor yet his purse. Douglas money was poured out like water. Edinburgh had never known anything like this. Will, whose forebears had been named William le Hardi, Hugh the Dull, Archibald the Grim and James the Gross, began to be called William the Magnificent — a title which shocked his practical mind as much as it amused his brothers and Meg.

Meg Douglas was now an integral part of Will's household, accepted by all as vastly more important than any mere tiring-woman. Many undoubtedly suspected that she was the Earl's mistress — indeed, with such an attractive creature constantly in and out of the Countess's bedchamber, such wonderings were inevitable. But the lovers were discreet, and both with their own ideas of duty, and no one — save perhaps Margaret herself — was in a position to know for certain. If that reserved and self-contained young woman did in fact know or suspect, she gave no sign of it. Meg and she remained inseparable companions. In public, the older girl was still the modest and dutiful servitor, but in private she permitted herself a certain latitude with most of the young Douglas family. Which was probably good for them all, if any were in danger of growing swollen-headed, for she had a shrewd wit and only a moderate respect of persons.

The parliament idea, when at last it materialised, proved to be a success. There was a gratifyingly large attendance, representative of all parts of the country — save the Highlands, which always ignored such embroilment. Some lords and lairds of very doubtful allegiance put in an appearance, and even one or two of Crichton's known supporters. Nevertheless, there were some notable absentees, in especial the Earls of Angus, Lennox, Sutherland and Buchan, the Lord of Gordon, and the heads of many of the great eastern and Border houses, such as Hepburn, Home, Kerr and Elliot. These last represented a manpower of mosstroopers, some of the toughest fighting men in the country.

The assembly proceeded to the discussion of various problems of reform and good governance — but these, although vital enough, were largely a show, the real importance of the parliament being as a demonstration against Crichton. Angus and Lennox and some of the lesser men were forfeited for rebellion, as a matter of form — but this meant little against powerful nobles who had the means to repel any attempts at dispossession. The most significant decision was the vote on the resolution requiring the former Chancellor and already-forfeited outlaw, Sir William Crichton, to deliver up forthwith into the King's hands the royal castle of Edinburgh, and also the Great Seal of his former office, the retaining of which was highest treason and punishable by death. The vote was 138 to nil — although a dozen or so careful individuals managed to slip out of the abbey refectory before the vote was taken.

The decision was broadcast throughout the city, and proclaimed by heralds under the Royal Standard before the castle itself, with a peremptory summons to surrender. Crichton did not oblige, of course — but he could not fail to get the message. However, the entire exercise was not so much for its effect on Crichton as on public opinion. In that it was successful, to a large degree. One aspect rather spoiled it all. James Kennedy, at the chairman's table, insisted on breaking off the proceedings at an early hour each day, in order to repair to the abbey chapel, and there, at sundown, before the altar, to go through his daily procedure of ritual cursing, assisted by junior clergy, acolytes and choristers — which, considering that most of the objects of this fulmination were taking part in the parliament, had its effect on the atmosphere. Indeed, the Primate would have had them all banished from attendance, and brought to trial there and then before a properly constituted court of law; but Will Douglas set his face against this. With the Lindsay-Gray-Hamilton contingents a large proportion of the non-Douglas assembled manpower, such a course was just not to be considered. As a consequence, Kennedy's attitude towards Douglas hardened perceptibly.

Will, despite all his organising activities, was preoccupied in more than this. He was basically a single-minded young man, and all the varied and intricate strands of this tapestry-of-state tended to confuse and infuriate him. He increasingly found, strangely enough, that he was considerably helped, guided and comforted in talking matters over, of an evening, with his girl-wife. Margaret Douglas, calm, cool and factual, had in fact a better head on her than almost anyone he knew, certainly better than any of his brothers and close associates. More and more he sought her advice.

The evening after the parliament, they sat together before a flickering log fire in their quarters of the abbey — for it was a wet night of late autumn, and chilly. An outdoor programme of events had had to be cancelled, because of the weather — and they had had their fill of dancings and feastings meantime. It made a cosy, almost a domestic scene, with Will and Margaret on either side of the fireplace, Meg sitting a little back, stitching a seam, and Jamie, who never liked to be far from this company, crouching on a stool and watching the play of the firelight on Margaret's delicate features.

"You are not satisfied with your parliament, then?" she said. "You do not think that Crichton will see it as sufficient? To prove that he now has very little support in the land."

"No. He knows better than that," Will said heavily. "So long as four great earls, and the Border lords, hold aloof from us, he knows our weakness. *Five* earls, if we count Ross, Lord of the Isles. Crichton knows that many who voted for us in this parliament would turn against us tomorrow, if they saw profit in it."

"Perhaps. Lesser men will always follow greater. But they will not move of themselves. And most of these earls are far away, Ross in especial. He is not interested, I think. Concerned only to be king in his own Hebrides. Only one is near. Angus. Of our own kin. And he it is to whom the Border lords all look.'

"Aye. Think you I do not know it!" That came out almost on a groan. "So long as Douglas remains divided, so long as Red hates Black, so long will William Crichton hope. And have reason to hope! But what can I do? I have tried everything. Angus's face is set against me. Offers, pleas, threats. Fair words and foul. He sits secure at Tantallon, and knows that the East March of the Border is his, and therefore the borderline with England. He and his can keep out the English — or let them in! It is a sword he holds over the head of Scotland — and well he knows it."

"There is a truce with England," Jamie pointed out.

"A scrap of parchment! Think you that is enough to keep them on their own soil, if Angus so much as crooked a finger? They still hold our fortresses of Berwick and Roxburgh. They still would have all Scotland in thrall. Angus and his friends could let them in. By sea as well as land — for Tantallon controls the mouth of the Forth."

"But *would* he? That would be black treachery. You do not know him traitor," Jamie would always give the benefit of the doubt.

"He has returned *my* threats with scarce-veiled threats of his own. He is a sour and bitter man. His father treated with the English, against the King's father — even though he was a son of the same King's sister. I do not trust the man."

"How can you say that, Will? You have not so much as spoken with him," Margaret said.

"I have heard sufficient of him. From many. Rob Fleming, in especial!"

"He had no cause to love Sir Robert. Nor you. He is proud. It may be he thinks you prouder."

"What mean you by that?"

"I mean that pride is an ill envoy. Go yourself."

"Go? Go where?"

"Go to Tantallon. Will Douglas to see James Douglas."

"Bravo!" Meg declared, from the shadows.

"You would have me thrust my head into that den?"

"You thrust your head into Livingstone's den, once. Bearded that lion. Is James Douglas more terrible?"

"He would not see me. Let me within his gates."

"Not if you went at the head of a host, no. But if you went alone? . . ."

"And be clapped into his deepest pit! As was Rob."

"Sir Robert was released. When he became the King's Cup-bearer. You are the King's Lieutenant-General. Greater than many cup-bearers. And you are the Black Douglas."

"The richer prize, then."

"At least, he would not imprison the *Countess* of Douglas, I think."

"Eh? . . ."

"Bravo!" Meg said again, laughing.

"My lord of Angus is *my* kinsman, as much as yours," Margaret pointed out. "I will come with you."

"That would be foolishness."

"I think not. You will be the less suspect if you come with your wife."

"It would be worse than foolishness — it would be wicked! To run yourself into danger," Jamie cried. "Do not do it, Will."

"I thought that you deemed Angus less ill than I do?"

"Margaret must not endanger herself, nevertheless. *I* will go with you, Will."

"Na, na. That might be altogether too much for our kinsman! To take Douglas, and Douglas's heir, both! No, if I go, I go alone."

Margaret opened her lips to speak, and then thought better of it. Meg smiled, and went on with her stitching, as the birchlogs spluttered and hissed in the fire.

*　　　*　　　*

In the end, and two days later, three persons rode across the green rabbit-cropped links towards Tantallon — for Margaret had had her quiet way, and Meg had refused to allow her mistress to venture into a possibly difficult situation unattended by another woman. They had ridden the twenty miles eastwards from Edinburgh, with a small convoy of men under Rob Fleming, who knew the territory, but had left these at Sir Walter Haliburton's castle of Dirleton, and proceeded quite unescorted through the rich East Lothian countryside; but they were not unescorted now. At some stage after leaving the little burgh of North Berwick, they had become aware that they were being followed, discreetly at first but gradually more openly and by ever-growing numbers, until at length there were fully a score of horsemen jingling along behind them but keeping their distance. Not a few of these wore red hearts painted on their breastplates, similar to those picked out in rubies on Will's and Margaret's travelling cloaks, and embroidered on Meg's — but they were no people of his.

Tantallon made a sight to hold the eye, more like a vast feature of nature than any work of man. A couple of miles to one side, the great grassy cone of North Berwick Law rose high out of the rolling pastureland, and a mile or so on the other side the mighty mass of the Bass Rock soared out of the blue sea almost as high, gleaming white with the bird-droppings that painted its frowning cliffs. Between the two, this extraordinary castle, unlike any other in the land, reared itself on the cliff edge, a daunting barrier of red stone, high and massive enough to seem on a par with these others. The stronghold was, in fact, a gigantic towering wall cutting off from the land an entire narrow peninsula of cliff. Higher than even the keeps of any normal castle, these walls rose, but at each end of them, and in the centre, three tremendous towers thrust up more than half as high again. From all of these Douglas banners flew proudly, but from the greatest, the central gatehouse tower, flapped a Red Heart standard larger than any flag Will had ever seen. No windows or apertures pierced those curtain-walls, which were crowned by parapets and walks, along which paced many men, seeming puny and skied up there, and from embrasures of which the black mouths of cannon gaped. Landwards of this imperious bastion were two great systems of outer walls, with towers and palisades and gun-ports, fronted by deep and wide ditches, one water-filled. There was no need for defensive works on the other three sides, where two-hundred feet high precipices dropped sheer to the waves.

"Save us — I thought *I* was lord of Douglas!" Will muttered, staring.

However expensively clad, although totally unarmoured, Will at least felt very naked as they trotted forward towards the first of those ditches, drawbridges and gatehouses — especially with that silent cavalcade behind. The women could say what they would about being a source of safety and security, but to him at this moment they represented only additional helplessness — and Will Douglas did not like to feel helpless. But it was too late for second thoughts; they could only go on.

Word of their approach must somehow have preceded them to Tantallon, for the first bridge was down, the gates open, and men-at-arms clustered round, very much on the alert.

"Who comes?" a voice shouted.

"Douglas and his lady. To see the lord of Angus," Will returned, wihout reining in his horse's trot.

There was no reply, but neither was there any attempt to bar their progress. Thudding hollowly over the bridge-timbers, the trio rode through the arched pend beneath the first gatehouse, wary-eyed men flanking them on either side. There was no further word spoken.

At the second gate they were again challenged, this time with the bridge held against them. When Will replied, they were told curtly to wait.

Wait they did, and for long, calling upon their patience under the blank scrutiny of many. The girls chatted quietly together, but the man fumed inwardly, wordless.

At length they were admitted, without any reason proffered

for the delay, to the inner bailey. This was quite unlike any other of their experience, no narrow courtyard or no-man's-land, but a wide open spread of grass, acres in extent, whereon many horses and cattle grazed, a strange sight to see within a fortress. Two large stone dovecots to house fowl-flesh and messenger-birds rose therein. This Tantallon was intended to be self-supporting, if need be. Two men holding each of the horses' heads now, they were led across this by a cobbled causeway to the vast tower in the centre of that daunting curtain-wall.

Here a group awaited them, on the third drawbridge, under the great portcullis arch. A young man, fair-haired, ruddy-complexioned, good-looking in a heavy way, stepped forward. He was carelessly dressed, but had an air of authority.

"You wear an honest emblem, and we have been told that you name yourself Douglas," he said. "But there are Douglases and Douglases! Who do I greet, thus unannounced?" He barely glanced at Will, so interested was he in the young women, Meg in particular.

"Douglas," Will told him briefly.

"Eh? . . ." The sharp succinctness of that brought his regard back to the man. "You mean? . . ."

"Douglas himself, sir. And his lady. Come to call on James Douglas of Angus. Are you he?"

"Douglas? The . . . the earl? Himself? You are Earl William? Here — at Tantallon?"

"Aye. And the Countess Margaret of Galloway. Kept waiting at your gate, my lord, an unconscionable time!"

"God's Name — you say that! I am sorry. But . . . how could we know? And I am not Angus. I am his brother. George Douglas. The Master . . ."

"Aye. Then, if your brother is within, sir, take us to him."

"We are glad to meet the Master of Angus," Margaret intervened gently. To add, smiling. "Cousin."

The other blinked, cleared his throat, and managed a bow. "My lady," he mumbled. "You . . . you are more beautiful even than your fame." He glanced at Meg also, seemed about to say more, and then thought better of it. He turned instead to one of his companions there. "Sanders — conduct my lord and the ladies to the Guest Hall. I go for my brother."

As George Douglas hurried off through the long echoing tunnel beneath the mighty tower, the newcomers dismounted, assisted now by eager hands. Despite the sudden change in the climate of their reception, however, Will felt as though every step into that stone-vaulted entrance passage, flanked by the black gaping mouths of dungeons, was like a succession of doors slamming on his freedom. He was the more grimly unforthcoming in consequence.

But when they emerged from beneath the tower, even he was surprised into exclamation. For suddenly all was changed. The eastwards, seawards side of that tremendous wall could not have been more different from its approach. Abruptly all was light and air and quiet, this sunny autumn afternoon, all signs of castellation and military strength behind them. A spacious open precinct, grass-grown and more pleasance than courtyard, occupied the remainder of the cliff-top, and beyond was only the dizzy immensity of sea and sky. Secondary buildings did flank each side of this, but they were low, quite dwarfed by the bastion behind, and wholly domestic, unfortified, in character, since none might reach their sanctuary save through the serried defences, the cliffs in front being unscaleable. Apart from a well-shaft, protected by a low wall, in the centre, only walks and shrubs and an arbour or two occupied this wide airy quadrangle — admittedly somewhat neglected-seeming and weed-grown. A child, a young girl, played alone in it with a cat.

"Who would have thought it?" Margaret cried. "Such a fair, sweet place to be hidden in this dire stronghold."

"A woman's hands made this," Meg declared. "Here is no man's work. The Princess Mary perhaps? Was she not mother of this earl?"

"Grandmother," Margaret said. "Her son was the last lord, father of this. I like it here. It speaks of peace, not war."

"Yet here were brought the heads of Duke Murdoch of Albany and his sons, to hand to their wife and mother. By the late King James," Will pointed out. "As warning to other traitors. Much evil has been done here."

They were led across the pleasance by their escort, and ushered into a fine apartment with a hammer-beam roof, tapestry hung and with large windows seawards framing a noble prospect of the Bass, the Isle of May and the distant shores of Fife. Here, watching the seas breaking on the reefs and skerries far below, they were presently joined by the Master of Angus. He brought with him a very different young man.

The Earl of Douglas and the Earl of Angus were of similar ages, but there the resemblance ended. James Douglas was very tall, very thin, gaunt-featured, great-eyed, and pale. Dressed with much richness, his clothes hung on him as on a clotheshorse. Yet he had a strange dignity for so young a man, a deal more than had Will, his every movement seeming slow and calculated. He bowed stiffly, formally, to each of his visitors in turn, and said absolutely nothing.

Will stared at the apparition askance, totally unprepared for this. He had heard that Angus was a peculiar man, enjoying only indifferent health, but he had never visualised this long, stalking heron of a creature. If this was the Red Douglas, there looked precious little even of red blood to him.

"Greetings, Cousin," he managed to get out. "I am William Douglas. This is Margaret, of Galloway. And ... and a friend."

"I am no cousin of yours," the other returned, and his speech was slow and grated harshly as a corncrake's. "Nor would wish to be. What brings you to Tantallon, my lord?"

Will bit back the temper which rose within him like a hot tide. "I thought it time that we met," he jerked.

"I met your father once. And misliked what I saw."

His visitor swallowed, and glanced at Margaret. He could not take much of this.

She came to his rescue. "Will is a different man from his sire, my lord," she said quietly. "All the kingdom has had reason to discover that. Have not you? Or do you hide away in this Tantallon, and know naught of what is done in Scotland?"

"Hide, madam? Angus does not hide."

"I would not have thought it, being Douglas. Yet we see naught of you or yours in all the realm. When you could do so much."

"Do much for whom, madam?"

"For the King, sir. Your cousin. And ours."

Her guess, or intuition, proved valid. This strange young man had a name for pride. If he was not prepared to reckon Will as cousin, he was unlikely to deny kinship with the King. His father's mother was a sister of James the First. Strangely

215

enough, these three branches of the house of Douglas here represented were more closely linked by their royal Stewart blood than by that of their own name. Margaret herself was closest to the Throne, with both her mother's mother and her father's mother princesses; Will's link being rather more remote. Whereas the Red Douglases had separated from the Black generations earlier, when on the death of the great 2nd Earl, at Otterburn, for want of legitimate heir, the earldom passed by arrangement to his companion-in-arms and kinsman, Archibald the Grim, son of the Good Sir James by an unknown mother. The fact that there was a closer heir, illegitimate also but a generation nearer, in the Earl's own natural brother, Red George — who had married the Countess of Angus in her own right and so won that earldom — had never failed to rankle, ever since, with his descendants.

"The King I will ever serve," he said. "But not those in whose hands His Grace is held!"

"Unless perhaps their name be Crichton!" Will suggested.

The other looked him up and down mournfully, distastefully, from those great eyes. "Is Crichton greater rogue than Livingstone? Or Hamilton?" he asked slowly. "Yet *you* work with these."

"Only because I have little choice. And for the King's cause."

"He would rather work with you, my lord, I think," Margaret added.

Will moistened his lips, and swallowed. "Aye," he said.

"Yet your parliament had the insolence to declare me forfeit! Me — Angus! You did not vote otherwise, I think? Nor your brothers."

"You rejected the King's summons to attend. Both parliaments."

"The King's summons? *Your* summons!"

"Not mine. The Privy Council's in the King's name. To you, and all others."

"Call it what you will." Angus stalked around the room, more than ever like a great wading-bird. "What did you come to Tantallon to say? It must have been more important than this, to bring you to my house?"

"Is it strange that Douglas should visit Douglas? We are kin. We should work together, not apart. Not against each other.

The Red Douglas and the Black. Together, what might not they achieve."

"It has taken you long to think of this."

"I have had no aid from you."

"You do not want my aid, even now, I wager! You want the Dunbar cannon! And shall not have them."

Will shook his head. "That is not what I came for. Although they should be mine, as the King's Lieutenant-General — for they are the King's cannon. Your taking them and holding them here, against the royal commands, could be deemed treason. But I have taken other steps to gain the cannon we need. They are being made. Are already made, and on their way from Galloway. It is not cannon I seek of you, but . . . but the hand of friendship." Will Douglas found that one of the hardest things he had ever had to say.

"Friendship?" The other looked incredulous, almost alarmed. Friendship undoubtedly was not a state with which he was much experienced. "Why?"

"I have told you. Douglas should be united, not separate. Together we could ensure the triumph of the King's cause."

"The triumph of *your* cause!"

"The King's cause. Douglas is concerned in it, but the cause is the King's."

"I think . . . you are hypocrite . . . as well as . . ." Suddenly Angus began to cough, in great, harsh, rasping barks, sore and deep. He became wholly convulsed. As the paroxysm continued, he staggered over to sit on a bench by the window, his long person hunched and crumpled. On and on it went, the thin frame racked and shaken. Concerned, his visitors eyed each other.

"He gets taken thus. Often," George Douglas told them, looking helplessly at his brother, "Nothing to be done. It will pass."

"Is there nothing we may do?" Margaret demanded. "To aid. Wine? A posset?"

"No avail. Leave him. See — it is easing . . ."

Presently the coughing died away. It left the Earl trembling and exhausted. He did not rise, but quite quickly he spoke, though thickly, huskily.

"What . . . have you . . . to offer me? That I . . . support your cause. Other than . . . empty words? Friendship! Kinsmen! . . ."

It was strange to hear the sufferer launch straight back into the discussion without preamble, comment or explanation. Strange, too, to hear the tenor of his enquiry, the new and blatant note of advantage-seeking.

"You must rest," Margaret urged. "You are unwell. Do not concern yourself, my lord. Not now."

He ignored her. "Did you come empty-handed, man? To Angus?"

Will eyed him thoughtfully. "What do you want?"

"I do not beg. I accept. Or decline. You offer what?"

Will took a deep breath. "The Justiciership, south of Forth. Warden of the East March. Admiral of the Forth," he said flatly.

"Insufficient."

Without change or lift of voice, the other went on. "High Admiral of Scotland. When Crawford goes — and he is a done man. And the great customs of Leith, port of Edinburgh; and Aberlady, port of Haddington."

There was silence in that chamber for a space, save for Angus's heavy breathing. Sweat beaded his high pale brows, from the coughing, but otherwise he seemed unmoved. At length he spoke.

"One matter more." He turned to his brother. "Dod — the lassie," he said.

The Master hesitated, glanced at the others, and then shrugging, went out.

In only a few moments he was back, leading by the hand the girl they had seen playing in the pleasance with the cat. She was a pale, thin, plain child of eleven of twelve, with a frightened look, dressed in what was obviously cut-down women's wear, too large for her frame. She kept her eyes down.

"Aye." Angus barely glanced at her. "Here is the other matter. I would wed."

The gasps of surprise that greeted this announcement were perhaps hardly tactful, much less complimentary. Frowning, the Earl went on, briefly.

"She is Joan Stewart. Or Joanna. The King's sister."

Astonished, they looked from the crouching man to the silent standing child. "Dear God!" Will exclaimed — and then, recollecting himself, made a jerky bow. "Highness! he said. "I . . . ah . . . your servant."

218

Margaret and Meg sketched hurried curtsies. "We did not know the Princess . . ." the former said.

"You may save your breath," Angus told them. "She is deaf and dumb both."

Appalled, they stared, at a loss for words.

This, then, was the third daughter of James the First. They had not known of her whereabouts. Two sisters were safely in France. The late murdered King's unfortunate family had suffered rough usage indeed, the wife mishandled and imprisoned, the only son grabbed and used as a pawn by power-hungry men. That Will had not so much as heard this princess mentioned, by her royal brother or anybody else, for many a month, was perhaps indicative of the sad state of monarchy lacking strength. Yet her father had been Scotland's greatest king since Bruce.

"I had no notion that Her Highness was here," he said.

"I picked her out of Dunbar Castle. With the cannon," James Douglas mentioned. "Her mother had died, and the ruffian Hepburn did not know what to do with her. I deemed her better here."

"Her mother . . . the Queen . . . dead?"

"Aye. Two months back, it seems." Angus sounded indifferent.

"God rest her soul!" Here was the final indignity. Queen Joanna Beaufort, the loveliest woman of her day, her love story with King James the theme of poets and minstrels, thrown by merciless adventurers into the dungeons of a minor royal castle in the keeping of a rough, freebooting Border laird, mistreated and there left to rot and die, while yet under forty years of age, and her son nominally the reigning monarch. Moreover, none informed of her passing, least of all the King. And this deaf-and-dumb child cast adrift, unwanted.

Or not quite unwanted. 'I would wed this princess," Angus informed. "Gain me the royal assent, and that of the Privy Council. And I will make cause with you, my lord."

"Oh — no!" That was Meg. Impulsively she ran forward, to clasp the shrinking child in her arms. "No!"

Their host frowned. "Who is this woman?" he asked.

"Another Margaret Douglas. Grandchild to Earl Archibald the Grim. As am I. Companion to my wife." He paused. "You seek betrothal? To this child? As she is?"

"Wed, I said. Not betrothal — marriage."

"But . . ." he shook his head helplessly. "How old is she?"

"What matters that? Old enough for my purpose."

That purpose at least was sufficiently clear. It was some years before the young King could be married and could produce an heir to the throne. The two elder sisters were in France, one marriedto the Dauphin and the other to the heir to the Duke of Savoy, young as they were. No children they might produce would be acceptable as heirs to the Scots throne. This pathetic waif, however young and mute, might yet give birth to a son. King's lives were notoriously uncertain, especially in Scotland. A Douglas might yet be King of Scots, and his father chief power in the land. And Angus was proud.

Meg still clutched the child protectively, almost glaring challenge. Margaret looked thoughtful.

"Well, man?" Angus demanded. "Will you do this? Or shall I wed her first and seek assent later?"

Will shook his head. What could he say? Angus, holding the girl securely, could most certainly do as he theatened. The thought of the forcible union of this man, consumptive almost certainly, and the deaf-and-dumb child, scarcely bore contemplation. But on the other hand, what better fate would await her otherwise? If it was not Angus, some other would grab her, with like ambitions. Perhaps older, harsher. As Countess of Angus, at least she would be protected from all save her husband's hands.

"It is a hard thing you ask," Will said.

"Why?"

Margaret intervened. "My lord of Angus, I think, would make no ill husband for the Princess Joanna. Later. Meantime, he would succour her. Keep her from others. He would not be demanding on her — that I believe!"

They all looked at her, Will speculatively, Angus approvingly, Meg in sudden resentment. It was George Douglas, the Master who spoke.

"That is true. My lord would not . . . treat the lassie ill. She is kindly used here. He is not . . . not a man for women. It is a matter of what is best."

There was silence for a space. Then Will nodded. "Very well," he said. "I will speak with the King. And the Council."

"That is well. Then there is no more to be said."

"When will you come to Edinburgh?"

"It matters not. When you will."

"Two days hence, then? That will serve. I will have the papers made up."

"Aye. See you to that. And this also . . ." Abruptly he began to cough again. "See you . . . that Crichton . . . is granted . . . fair terms. To yield . . . Edinburgh Castle." Between the bouts he managed to get that out. "Mind it. Or all . . . is by with. I'll not have . . . it said . . . that I sold Crichton!" That was barely intelligible "Dod — away with them . . ."

The coughing went on and on, with the sufferer all but prostrated. But he kept waving them away with a commanding hand, nevertheless. Awkward, embarrassed, the visitors allowed the Master to lead them out without more than hurried bows. The dumb girl sidled out behind them, and scurried back to her cat.

George Douglas had little to say to them as he escorted them back through all the defensive lines of Tantallon. Nor indeed had the trio much to say to each other as they rode away westwards into the setting sun — even though they had gained what they came to seek. What little there was passed between the young woman.

"That was ill done," Meg declared, after a while, tight-voiced. "That poor bairn!"

"Better James Douglas than many I can think on," Margaret answered quietly. "If she is ever wed, she will be a widow soon, I think. And a man sick as that will not have his mind on bedding. She may escape him altogether, and yet be Countess. Wedding and bedding go not always together — eh, my lord?"

That did nothing to ease tongues, and they rode on, silent.

*　　　*　　　*

And so, when two days later the Earl of Angus rode into Edinburgh at the head of one thousand men, it was to join the greatest assembly of Douglas power ever known. Will, well warned of the other's approach, had his own hosts drawn up in their scores and hundreds, their troops and squadrons, companies and cohorts, mile upon mile along the route into the city from the east, through the royal parkland of Arthur's Seat. He calculated that there were fourteen thousand men there — not all Douglases of course, but the majority so. He hoped that Angus might be suitably impressed — although he would swear that the man would not admit it.

There was more than serried thousands to impress the Red Douglas, for the great cannon had at last arrived from Galloway, and fearsome monsters indeed they looked. Angus was in fact treated to a try-out of their effectiveness, and half a dozen huge balls were sent hurtling at the citadel's defences amidst mighty and earth-shaking explosions, almost as alarming for the senders as the receivers. Great was the excitement when the smoke cleared sufficiently to show that one ball had carried away the top of the gatehouse-tower and another smashed the iron gates and portcullis machinery.

Will had organised a banquet and entertainment for that evening, at which a united Douglas theme was emphasised in many ways. After a brief and gabbled announcement by the King that the sentence of forfeiture for treason, passed in misunderstanding, was now removed and expunged, and his well-beloved and trusty cousin, the Earl of Angus, restored to the royal favour and delight, the said Earl's new appointments were announced — omitting in public the reversion to Crawford's High Admiralship which would not have gone down well with the Lindsays — and ending with a proclamation of betrothal to His Grace's dear and exalted sister, the Lady Joan. Angus himself proved to be something of a death's-head at the feast, and King James had difficulty in showing anything but distaste for the man, but apart from that the affair went off very successfully.

Still more successful was the next day's developments. Whether on account of the new cannon, or Angus's change of front, messengers under a white flag issued from Edinburgh Castle, to declare to the King's Grace that Sir William Crichton was prepared to yield the fortress provided that his personal freedom was guaranteed, with that of his family and supporters, and his forfeited house of Crichton, in Lothian, restored to him. Lacking such agreement, he would continue to hold the citadel indefinitely.

Although a hurried Privy Council was convened to consider this proposal, there was in reality little to discuss. Loth as Will Douglas and his colleagues might be to agree to Crichton going free, the alternative was an almost endless prolongation of the siege; for though the new cannon made a difference, none there believed that they could of themselves batter the mighty fortress into submission. Only at the gatehouse approaches could they be brought to bear at all; elsewhere, hundreds of feet high on its rock, the castle was as out-of-range of artillery as it was of slings, swords and arrows. Crichton could probably hold out for months yet, and the encircling host could not be held together for much longer; already men murmured and would be off home — for a feudal army was a civilian army basically. Crichton unseated, discredited and shorn of power, was the main objective; retribution was less vital. So said the Chancellor, so agreed the majority of the Council, so repeated Angus, with threats of complete withdrawal to Tantallon otherwise. Will Douglas acknowledged it in his heart of hearts, and gave in, although with ill grace. Vengeance must wait, on Crichton as on the Livingstones.

So Sir William, in full armour, marched out of Edinburgh Castle at last, with his banner flying and the honours of war, two days later, through the silent ranks of his enemies. He came and made obeisance to the nervous monarch, nodded to Angus and Bishop Kennedy, and blankly ignoring the rest of them, passed on his way, flanked by sons, brothers and supporters, with scarcely a word spoken.

Will watched him ride off into obscurity with mixed feelings. On the face of it, he had done what he had set out to do. The adventurers who had brutally seized Scotland, after the murder of the late King, had been brought low and cast from power. The young monarch was free again, after a fashion, and the realm set on the road to good government — or, at least, passably fair government. And it was almost all his own, Will's, doing. Yet what had primarily set him on his course, the main source of his purpose, revenge for his murdered cousins, remained unfulfilled. Crichton and Livingstone, with their sons and minions, both went free and unpunished. How greatly had he failed then? Douglas was more powerful probably than ever before in its long history. Yet Douglas went unrevenged.

Will was left in no doubts, at least by his wife. He had suffered diminution in Meg's regard over his agreement to support Angus's marriage plans; now he found himself much blamed over Crichton. Margaret, normally so quietly level-headed and wise beyond her years, was, he discovered, im-

223

placably set on vengeance for her brothers. She remained a dutiful wife, as Meg a less dutiful mistress — but Will was made very much aware that in some degree he had failed both women.

As the Siege of Edinburgh broke up, the great hosts dispersed, and the captains and kings departed, the Black Douglas might be architect of it all and supreme in Scotland — but he did not feel it. Nor was he fool enough to imagine for one moment that his warfare was over, his task accomplished, even forgetting the matter of vengeance.

As well that he did not.

PART TWO

CHAPTER FOURTEEN

THREE years will make a great difference to most of us, especially in the earlier part of our lives. On Will Douglas three years had left a greater impression than on many perhaps — three years of uneasy power, of cut-throat political manoeuvring, of maintaining an approximate balance of domination, in 15th-century Scotland. And in living with Margaret and Meg Douglas. He looked now not so much older than his twenty-four years as ageless, as hard, dark, strong, tight-bitten almost taciturn man. Physically he had broadened in the shoulders and chest into a tough, taut and controlled maturity, compact, and fortunately with nothing of his father's weight of flesh. He looked, in fact, what he was, a man accustomed to rule, to take swift, definite and sometimes ruthless decisions, and to see that they were carried out without question or delay. But despite it all, he still retained some hint of the eager youth with the quick shy smile, doubts of his own capacities — especially with women — yet sense of responsibility towards those to whom he was committed. Few would accuse the 8th Earl of Douglas of diffidence, yet somewhere in his character he still struggled against that tendency.

In more ways than one Will Douglas belied his looks. He certainly did not look a man of peace. Peace and he indeed were but little acquainted. Yet he sought peace, more deliberately and actively than most of his kind, sought it with a sort of wistful urgency, even though often with a sword in hand. But this pleasant sun-filled breezy day of May 1448, by the Nith, peace indeed prevailed — and a peace largely of his own making. In the green triangle of meadowland where the Cluden Water joined Nith, a mile or two north of Dumfries, a great and peaceable assembly was in progress. Nothing quite like it had been seen before, in Scotland. It was as much Margaret's idea as his own, but its organisation was all his — and only the Black Douglas could have achieved it. Hundreds of men and women, ordinary folk though mainly elderly, sat on the grass of the bowling-green and pleasance of the College of Lincluden, and some way up the sides of the great tumulus there, with its spiral track to the top — relic of other assemblies long past. Here was really a sort of parliament, a parliament of Borderers. But not of lords and lairds and bishops, although some of these there were also. In the main it was a gathering of the elders of a people, of all types and classes, brought here by Douglas, to collect, discuss and record the ancient laws, customs and traditional usages of the Borderland. There was a distinct culture and way of life belonging to these southern Scottish counties, with their special situation and history, and many immemorial rights, privileges, crimes and punishments — which were not always in accord with the general laws of the realm. As Borderer himself, as Sheriff of Selkirk, and as Warden of the Middle and West Marches, as well as the greatest landowner in the area, Will was interested and concerned.

He sat on the flat top of the tumulus, with Margaret by his side. She had changed less than he had, although she was now a tall and serene young woman of eighteen. Still slender, willowy, delicately-made and fair, of a frail almost breathtaking loveliness, she sometimes frightened her husband by this very fragile beauty.

On the warm grass around them there sat a great concourse of the Douglas kin — for Will was still a notable family man, even though he had no offspring of his own. Jamie was there, faithful as ever, inclining just a little to stoutness, and the only member of the family still unmarried, save for young Henry, who had entered the Church; Hugh, Earl of Ormond and John, Lord Balveny, with their new wives. Archie, Earl of Moray alone of the brothers was absent; he was building an extraordinary new castle up at Darnaway in Moray, in the broad lands he had married, which was to be the finest, most handsome, in the land. All the sisters were present, however, with their husbands; Margaret with Sir Harry Douglas of Borgue, Chamberlain of Galloway and acting Lord of Dalkeith; Beatrix and Sir William Hay, the Constable; Janet, recently married to Rob Fleming, who was now indeed created Lord Fleming; and young Elizabeth, whose wedding to Sir John Wallace of Craigie, chief of that ancient and honourable name, had just been celebrated. With other chiefs and lords of the name of Douglas, they made quite a court around Will.

The discussion was orderly but easy and uninhibited. They were dealing with the subject of the hot trod, whereby a man might pursue a raider of his cattle across the Borderline without having to obtain a formal safe-conduct, and regain his stolen property if he could, if necessary to the effusion of blood — this while the trail was still fresh, or hot, local law acceding. But there were differing interpretations of hotness or freshness, the custom seeming to vary between areas. Two old mosstroopers, one from Eskdale and the other from Jedwater, in especial argued vigorously.

Will raised his hand. "At the Wardens' yearly meeting at the Redswire, we accept that the trod is hot for twelve hours," he said. "No longer."

"That's no' right, my lord," the Eskdalesman objected strongly. "Yon's the Englishry's notion. We've aye held by a day and a night. Aye, and taken it, forby!"

"That is the way I have ever heard it, in Nithsdale and Annandale," Margaret told them.

There were cries of agreement from some, dissent from others.

"Then it seems that there is a difference between the West March and the others," Will declared. "We must discover how and when this change came about. This is a matter . . ."

He stopped, as a disturbance developed from the direction of the redstone College buildings. A small party, in riding-gear of half-armour and thigh-boots, came striding, pushing their way unceremoniously through the sitting crowd, and it did not require the Lindsay colours to identify him.

"Earl Beardie, by the Rude!" Will murmured to Margaret. "Bringing trouble, you may be sure! And bad trouble, to fetch that one so far south as this."

Alex the Tiger was indeed Earl Beardie now, had been for two years. His father, the old Earl of Crawford, was dead. And his dying, a year to the day after Bishop Kennedy's first spectacular cursing of him and his associates at St. Andrews, had resounded loud and long throughout Scotland, not only in the consequent elevation of the wildest character in the land to one of the most powerful positions therein, but as the most dramatically successful piece of cursing and excommunication known for centuries — to the enhancement of Kennedy's reputation, and indeed the advancement of Holy Church. The old earl had died by an arrow, struck down while he was seeking to play peacemaker, at the Battle of Arbroath, when Beardie came to eventual grips with Ogilvy of Inverquharity who had supplanted him as protector of Arbroath Abbey, amidst mighty slaughter. All the land rang with admiration for the Primate's fulminatory and denunciatory powers — although certain members of the Council noted that it was the man who had slept throughout the cursing who had died, and the Hamiltons and the rest were still in excellent health.

Will rose to greet the giant as he came climbing up the tumulus. "Welcome, my lord, to our assembly. It is a far cry from your territories?"

"Aye. Ower far. For hard riding." Though he scowled habitually, he nodded and grinned at Margaret. Strangely enough, she was a favourite of this uncouth character, her exquisiteness seeming to appeal to him. "Aye, lassie."

"You have ridden hard and far, my lord?" she answered. "Then we are the more grateful."

"You'll no' be, by God, when you hear! The English are in! They've struck. Ower into the Merse, Burning and slaying. A great force. It's war!"

"Dear God! The English!"

"But . . . the truce?" Margaret cried. "There is a truce with England."

"There was! A ten-year truce expired last year. A new one is being bargained on now."

"They havena waited for that, i' faith!" Crawford growled. "The word is that it's no bit raid. They're in force. Under Northumberland, their Warden. And Sir John Harrington. Crossed Tweed at Berwick, and are burning their way north through the Merse. And Angus, the rat, has let them in. Done nothing."

"He holds to his brother's policy, then." The Angus referred to was George Douglas, the former Master. Margaret had been right, that day at Tantallon. The Earl had lived a bare eighteen months thereafter, and the Princess Joan was still a virgin. The new Earl, in an effort to keep him friendly, had been given his brother's Wardenship of the East March.

"Aye. The word in Edinburgh is there's none doing battle. The English are running loose. When I heard, I came to tell you mysel'. Rather than send couriers. God — my couriers I sent north! To muster Lindsay!"

"My thanks." As Lieutenant of the Realm this was very

229

much Will's responsibility. And however much of a liability Beardie Alex was normally, where fighting was involved there was none more effective. He turned to those who thronged around him, with his swift decision. "Jamie — all knights, lairds and landed men to attend me in the Provost's room of the College, forthwith. Rob — all horseflesh for five miles around to be brought in. Arms likewise. Hugh — to my lord Maxwell at Caerlaverock, with this word. All his strength . . ."

"Wait a bit, Douglas," Beardie interrupted. "You've no' heard all the tidings from Edinburgh yet. Crichton's up again. Yon ranting priest Kennedy's been raising him. He's been seeing the King. And now he's off to France. Special envoy, no less! To find the laddie a wife."

"Save us — no! Not William Crichton!"

"Aye. The same black devil. And they're saying that if he makes a good match for Jamie, when he comes back Kennedy will resign and give him the chancellorship again."

Will looked at his wife and bit his lip. Her fair features were for the moment strangely hard and set.

After a little Will said, "He is gone, you say?"

"Sailed from Leith three days back. With an embassage of priests and clerks. For France and the Low Countries."

"This is Bishop Kennedy's doing?" Margaret demanded, thin-voiced.

"Aye. He conceives Douglas ower powerful, they say. And with ill friends!" And he grinned. "So he rears up Crichton again."

Will shook his head. "I have long known that Kennedy mistrusts me. Yet — I esteem him an honest man."

'I have never known an honest priest! And an honest bishop would be a miracle, by the Mass!"

"Perhaps. But . . . this can wait. The English will not. You, Johnnie — make ready to lead a scouting party. To find the enemy and keep me informed. Aye, and to rouse some of our people, on the way. Take five score young men, well-horsed. Now — I must send these good folk home . . ."

*   *   *

The news of the invasion of the East March reached Lincluden shortly after noon, and Will rode out eastwards over the Nith ford less than three hours later. He had fewer than two hundred fighting men with him — indeed, his following was largely composed of nobles, knights and lairds, possibly the most top-heavy Scots punitive force ever to ride against the English. The assembly at Lincluden had been a wholly peaceful one, with few men-at-arms present — and in these days Douglases did not have to be protected by armed bands when they rode about South Scotland. It would take time to muster a sizeable force. Jamie would remain at Lincluden, to forward bodies of men as they became available. Hugh would bring on the Dumfries men, the Maxwells, and the main body of local Douglases, just as quickly as possible. Harry the Chamberlain would rouse Galloway. Young Henry, forgetting his priestliness, was already spurring north to muster Douglasdale and Ettrick; while Hay the Constable rode still further north, for Stirling, to mobilise on a national scale — and to keep an eye on fishers in troubled waters. Will was almost thankful that Crichton had sailed for France, for this would have been the sort of situation which he might well have exploited for his own ends. And there were still the Livingstones to consider.

With Earl Beardie on one side of him and the Master of Somerville on the other, Will spurred urgently east by north making for Eskdale and the Mosspaul pass over into Teviot. It would have been more direct to head on a more northerly line, up Annandale, by Moffat and the Ettrick passes and so into Tweeddale — but Will had sent John this way, by Teviot, in order to rouse in passing the Douglases of Drumlanrig and Cavers, who dwelt thereabouts. These were detached branches of the Red house, but, since the compact with Angus, had been co-operating with Will; this invasion must affect them gravely, whatever Angus's own reaction. Will hoped to pick up a substantial contingent of them, en route.

The Morton lands, part of the Dalkeith heritage in Eskdale, yielded useful reinforcements, and then they were into the hills — Armstrong country, whose allegiance was to say the least, doubtful. As Warden of this Middle March, Will called on their aid — but these wild marchmen were a law unto themselves and though Gilnockie, their chief, promised to send a party after them, few expected ever to see it.

In the grey dusk of a May night they clattered down Teviot into Hawick town, where Drumlanrig had his seat, fifty difficult mosspocked miles behind them. John had done his work well, and one hundred and fifty Hawick callants, under Drumlanrig's son, were awaiting them, standing to their shaggy sure-footed horses. Tired as all were, there was no resting. They pressed on down the dale to Cavers, where Douglas thereof, Sheriff of Teviotdale, had another hundred assembled, and after providing food and fodder, accompanied them himself on their shadowy way. Borderers were used to night-time activities.

They headed north now, crossing Teviot by the Denholm ford, and climbing up out of the mists of the valley, over the quiet rounded Minto Hills, to slant down towards Tweed, where, at Leaderfoot ford they were to await the first reports of John's scouts.

It is never really dark of a May night in these latitudes, but the glow which they had been aware of for some time, to the east, was not the sunrise that they looked for. There was no definition to the vista, in that half-light, and no landmarks were to be distinguished, even the great southern barrier of the Cheviot Hills. But for all that, presently, a great spread of lower land became evident below and before them, not so much seen as perceived. And all of it, in a vast arc half-right and front, flickered blood-red as far as eye could see. There were brighter conflagrations amongst the general glow, orange against the dull crimson, representing greater or nearer fires; but what they were seeing was in fact a whole province aflame. All drew up to stare, shocked. Scenes of violence were commonplace to these men; but few there were old enough to have seen before how thoroughly the English behaved when they crossed the Border in strength. Ten years of truce, with the good Regent Gloucester ruling England — and now dead of poison — had spoiled the Scots for this sort of thing.

Anger seething and clouding their minds, with a burst of new energy they hurried down to Tweed. At Leaderfoot, some of the fires appeared to be no great distance off, down-river — although Will realised that the nearest could not in fact be the splendid abbey of Dryburgh, as he had feared. It was further away than that. And Melrose, on the other side, where Bruce's heart was interred amid Douglas tombs, was safe apparently; at least no flames showed in that direction.

Will's first impulse, like that of most of his companions, was to dash off into the stricken Merse, to the aid of the victims,

But that was not what they were here for. Others could attend to that; their task was sterner.

Although many slept, by the broad Tweed at Leaderfoot, Will could not. He paced the river-bank restlessly, a man blaming himself bitterly. He was not Warden of this March — that was Angus's responsibility — but he was of the Middle and West Marches, and he should have been better prepared than this. He had been too concerned with peace and its beguilements. He had done the unforgivable thing; he had continued to trust the English after Gloucester's restraining hand was removed.

Shortly after dawn two couriers arrived from John. They brought challenging news. The main English force had pushed north as far as Dunbar on the edge of Lothian — where, significantly, Angus's territory began — and gone no further. They had burned the town, not attempted its strong castle, and then turned south again. They were even now at Colbrandspath, nine miles on their way back, halted for the night, the Lord Balveny keeping an eye on them. He reckoned the total English numbers as between four and five thousand. There had already been some exchanges with their skirmishers.

Will with not much more than one-tenth of the enemy strength, as yet, was in no position for any head-on clash. But if he could delay them until his summoned reinforcements arrived, he might yet teach the invaders a lesson.

Coldbrandspath lay at a point where the Lammermuir Hills came down to the sea. From there, heading south, the English must either wind their way through the hills, by the Eye Water passes, or climb over the high ground of Coldinghame Moor. Both would take them through difficult country for some ten miles. That country, properly used, might be worth many men.

Will wasted no time. He had his company on the move again within minutes, heading up Lauderdale, the back-door into the Lammermuirs.

Three hours later, but still with the shepherds' cottages only beginning to send up the blue peat-smoke of breakfast fires into the morning air, weary men and beasts climbed the last of the green smooth hills, to pull up just below the gentle ridge of Eweside Hill, with the land dropping steeply before them to the wrinkled sea. Away to the north, a great pall of dirty brown smoke hung over the coastal plain; that would be Dunbar, still burning. Nearer at hand were sundry lesser smokes, to stain a fine morning. Nearest of all, new black smoke was beginning to billow up out of the cleft of one of the many deans which carried rushing streams down off the hills to the sea. That was from no cooking-fires, even for a host. It could only be the village of Colbrandspath itself being set ablaze. Which meant that the enemy, their night's rest over, were leaving their usual token behind them. They had not gone yet, then.

A band of horsemen were spied approaching the ridge from the north-west, out of sight of the low ground — John's advance-party. They came to announce that the English, glutted with the spoils of war, captured cattle, drink and women, had slept long at Colbrandspath. They were only now stirring, preparatory to resuming the march south.

"How do they go, Johnnie? By Eye Water? Or over the moors?" Will demanded, without preamble.

"Who knows? But they came up through the hills. By Eye Water. And the high road is difficult. Steep to climb. Laden as they are with much booty, I would think they would go back as they came, through the valleys."

"Booty, heh? Women?" Beardie snarled. "We'll lighten them o' that! They'll be slow. Who commands? Northumberland himsel'? Or Harrington?'

"Neither. Northumberland is still at Berwick. He grows old. Young Percy, his son, commands here."

"Ha! That pup! The better, then, for an ambush. The Pease Dean?"

"Percy may be young, my lord," the still younger John Douglas gave back. "But he's not a fool. He knows the dangers of Pease Dean. Who does not? I sent scouts down. He has men guarding both sides of it. He'll not be caught there."

"Curse him! . . ."

"Wait," Will said. "If we could force him to take the high road south, by Penmanshiel and Coldinghame Moors — then there is another dean. At the Redheugh. Not so big or so deep as Pease — but it would serve, perhaps. It splits in two, if I mind aright. Home of Dunglass took me hunting there. If we could prevail on them to take that road . . ."

"Aye. But how?"

"If we could block the other. Block it sufficiently to turn them aside . . ."

"Four thousand men are not lightly turned aside by a few hundred, my lord," Cavers said.

"No. Not by men." Will looked away southwards, half-right, towards the upper reaches of the great trough of the Pease Dean, an enormous dog's-leg bent cleft, hundreds of feet deep, which sliced down through the foothills to the rockbound coast. "See — if they go back by the valleys, they must thread that upper end of the Pease Dean, for a mile and more. It is thick grown with whins and broom and scattered pines. And the wind is in the south-west, blowing directly down that leg of the dean. Fire the top of it, the whins and the pines, and it will sweep down there as out of the mouth of hell! I'll wager no host, of however many thousands, will take that road in face of the like!"

"Saints of God!" Crawford roared. "Here's a ploy!" He all but knocked Will out of his saddle by the force of his congratulatory slap on the shoulder.

"They might wait, there," Cavers objected. "Until the first dies out. Expecting an attack."

"I think not. Burning woodland will glow and smoke for days. They could not take that road. And none could attack down it. They will take the other road."

"Aye. To work, then!" Beardie cried. "Who lights the fires?"

They moved off southwards, keeping always below the skylines of ridges. They worked down to near the head of Peace Dean, where amongst the golden gorse-bushes, the heavy-scented hawthorns and the resinous pines, they left John and the Master of Somerville, with a party, to play the incendiaries. But not yet. Then up the other side, the main body rode, and over the shoulder of Aikieside Hill beyond, making for Redheugh Dean, a couple of miles to the east. They left a watch in a niche of the shoulder, where they could observe the advance of the enemy into the Pease Dean from Colbrands path, to signal John when to set whins ablaze.

Halfway to Redheugh they came to the hamlet of Aldcambus, nestling snugly from the sea winds in a hollow of the hillside. This may not have been on the main route of invasion, but it had not escaped all attention. At a farmery, smouldering still, they found three men, part burnt, in the ruins of their cothouses; two old women tossed down a well; three women of middle years, naked, tied face-down and bent double over cart-shafts; and two young girls hanging by their heels from the barn rafters, hay-forks rising from their crutches. Only flies and a door that banged in the morning breeze, moved in that place. At the looted church, near by, the parish priest was crucified to his own door, with daggers.

Only Earl Beardie seemed unaffected, as they pressed on.

The Redheugh Dean was a plunging ravine, grown, like the Pease, with yellow whins and broom, but smaller in all respects. Nevertheless it was almost two hundred feet at its deepest, and comprised in fact two deans, save near the outfall to the shore, where two streams joined. Down one steep side and up the other the high Coldinghame route to Berwick ran, then down again and out once more, on its long climb to Penmanshiel Moor.

Standing on the crest of the spine between the two ravines, Will and Beardie made a swift survey of the place's tactical possibilities. They were very apparent — almost too much so, since any force passing through here would be bound to be on the watch. There were cattle scattered down amongst the young bracken and bushes of the lower slopes, no doubt hidden here from the invaders, and Will thought that he could use these. In a few minutes the force was being split up and sent to various hidden positions. Then, satisfied that the leaders knew what was required of them, he left Crawford in command and rode back whence they had come.

Past the horrors at Aldcambus he went, to rejoin the watchers on the shoulder of Aikieside Hill. He found them debating whether or not to give the signal to the fire-raisers. Horsemen had appeared in some numbers at the far lip of Pease Dean, nearly a mile away, but it was not certain that these represented the main onward movement of the enemy.

Will told them to wait, but when presently banners began to show amongst the riders coming into view, he gave the order for their own little signal fire to be lit.

Quickly results were forthcoming, from a mile on the other side, southwards. Away to his left smoke began to billow up, shot with bursts of flame as individual bushes and trees caught alight. The whins in especial blazed like torches. The crackle of it came down on them on the breeze, quickly developing into a roar. The smoke commenced to pour down the trough of the dean.

Although the fire swiftly became evident to the watchers up on the hill, there was no sign of alarm down in the lower end of the steep valley. At least, ranked horsemen continued to appear over the rise from the north, to dip down and be lost to sight in the trees and shadows. Will was astonished that this continued for so long. Presumably the sound of the conflagration was deadened down there by the noise of the rushing Pease Water. And there was this acute dog-leg bend in the great ravine. The smoke might take a little time to blow down through the woodland . . .

Then, suddenly, there was the high-pitched shrilling of a trumpet. The advance party had no doubt reached the bend in the dean, and was loudly neighing the alarm. Promptly now the trumpeting was taken up from unseen points down the line. The track down there was narrow, on steep-sloping banks; three would be the most that could ride abreast. Major confusion must be rife, however invisible from this angle.

The repercussions began to show at the northern entrance to the valley. The column of men and horses came to a halt, in orderly enough fashion. Then, as those in front came pressing back, order was lost. Something like chaos reigned.

When pennons and banners appeared again on the top of the rise, indicating that the leadership had moved back, there was a pause. The banners halted, congregated, while men milled round. Obviously it was a council-of-war. Scouts rode off up to vantage-points to spy out the land ahead. Then trumpets brayed again, purposeful and prolonged now. The jostling confusion sorted itself out, and the banners moved on once more, down again into the cover of the trees.

Smoke was now filling all the upper dean, thick rolling clouds. The noise of the fire was menacing. It was inconceivable that the English could contemplate trying to force a way up through that. Therefore they must indeed be intending to take the high road, which forked away from the other where the dean made its big bend.

Will waited, however, to make certain, waited until he saw, through a gap in the trees, outriders spurring fast along the track towards Aldcambus, east of the fork. Scouts to prospect the route ahead.

Ordering the watchers to ride to inform Johnnie and Somerville — for they would be unable to see any signals now, in the dense smoke — Will hastened back, unseen from the low ground, to Redheugh Dean.

All now depended on his people keeping themselves completely hidden. To keen eyes there could be no disguising the fact that a fairly large party had passed through Aldcambus recently. But on their way to Redheugh they had deliberately swung upwards, southwards, away from the track, to enter the dean from above, it being hoped that this would give the impression that this party had headed over into the upper Pease Dean, and would be the people responsible for the fire.

Will also had to circuit the dean and make a difficult approach from higher ground, in order to remain hidden. It took time, and he was anxious as to how far he was ahead of the English scouts. But he reached the central spine above the joining of the ravines, in time, and found Earl Beardie and Cavers awaiting him there, in a watch-point disguised by uprooted broom-bushes.

'All is well,' he reported breathlessly. 'They come. Their scouts close. The fire burns mightily. Are all surely hidden? From the track? Well back?'

Aye. They'll no' see any, unless they beat out the whins," Crawford assured. "We've been over it all. We're ready for them . . ."

"Quiet!" Cavers interrupted. "I hear horses."

Listening, they heard the drumming of hooves. In groups, stretched along the flanks of the two ravines, for the best part of half a mile, five hundred men waited.

Over the western lip of the dean a hard-riding group came, spurring fast, young men, but led by a bearded veteran. All the time, as they rode, they were glancing right and left — but they were going too fast for thorough inspection. Clearly they were hurrying to put the accepted and convenient distance between scouting party and main body. About forty men all told, they came thundering down the zigzags of the first long bank, scattering stones and gravel, across the ford at the foot, splashing high, and then up the near side. This was the spine between the ravines, and surmounting it, they passed only some seventy yards beneath Will's hiding-place. But with scarcely a look in their direction they clattered on and down into the next gully. A little later they could be seen mounting the farther slope, speed unchanged and still unchallenged.

When they were out of sight, Beardie slipped away to the left, and Cavers to the right, leaving only Will and a small party above the central spine.

There was only a brief interval before the next company began to appear — the reason for the scout's haste, undoubtedly. This looked like an advance-guard of seasoned soldiers, tough and well-armed and accoutred, but fairly heavily laden with personal booty. Will counted as they came on, three abreast. He was still counting when their leaders were passing directly below him, and had reached one hundred and thirty files of three. This was worrying, for too substantial an advance-guard, permitted to ride on unmolested, could be a real danger when it turned back to the aid of the main body. But there was nothing that he could do about this, meantime. Will reckoned that there were approximately as many, in this grouping, as in his own entire force, as they trotted on and past.

Fortunately there was quite an interval before the next contingent of the English army — clearly the main array this. First came a galaxy of splendidly armoured and mounted knights, their heraldic surcoats, shields and horse-trappings, colourful in the dappled light-and-shade of the morning woodlands, under a forest of banners, foremost and greatest of which was the well-known golden lozenges on blue of Percy of Northumberland. There was a solid group of fifty or sixty of these high-ranking personages and their banner-bearers — and grimly Will Douglas cheered their preference for riding in their own lofty company rather than outspread through the host.

Inevitably, however, Will's glance kept coming back to the tall, slender, fair-headed and proud-featured young man, of approximately his own years, who rode beneath the blue and gold Percy standard. It was his first sight of one of the race with whom he was hereditarily and traditionally at deadly feud. He had, hitherto, done nothing to prosecute this, the most renowned family enmity in the two kingdoms — but undoubtedly it now added a spice to the thing that he attempted. The origins of the Douglas-Percy feud went far back, two centuries, war to the knife between the two great houses which so largely controlled the Border, on their respective sides. The Battles of Otterburn, or Chevy Chase, and Homildon Hill, were but extra dramatic incidents in an unending vendetta. Now the heir of the Earl of Northumberland came riding, all unknowing, to within a few yards of the Black Douglas.

For all that, Douglas let him ride past, fierce as was the temptation to dash out and summon the other to single combat. Will was not here in pursuance of any feud, however hallowed by the centuries. Biting his lip with impatience, he held himself in, waiting until Percy and the other leaders were in fact down into the farther ravine and splashing across the second of the fords. Only then did he give the first signal — an arrow fired by one of his group, burning tow at its tail, which soared high into the air over the heads of the long English column, to fall far down into the low ground.

With only a second or two of delay, shouts and trampling broke out away below there, and frightened cattle went surging off from their hiding-places, spreading out in a wide panic-stricken arc towards the coast. From four or five different points along the lowermost slopes of the double dean the beasts burst — and all along the line of the enemy's march, higher up, heads turned and horses were reined back. To all these, Borderers almost to a man, cattle were wealth, the prime symbol of gain, success, prize. Even in war, indeed particularly in war, the sight of much readily available cattle could be guaranteed to at least distract and preoccupy the attention of men. It did not fail that May day.

The cattle irruption was itself the second signal. As the creatures stampeded off, encouraged by hidden herders, everywhere along the upper sides of that road through the twin deans men rose out of their cover of whin-bush and brake and thicket. They required moments to run to their horses, count, settle themselves in their saddles, and hurl themselves downhill upon the English line — and these vital moments the distraction below provided.

It was a total surprise, and the advantages all with the at-tackers. The English were thinly spread over a great distance, on a narrow track which gave no room for manoeuvre, with a steep slope below them. At this stage their numbers were no advantage. The Scots, yelling the dread slogan of 'A Douglas! A Douglas!', although they too were thinly strung out in little groups over the half-mile of the assault, had the weight of a downhill charge behind them. That first crashing impact did not so much cut up the enemy column as sweep it right off the road and down the hillside, with more men toppling by sheer weight of horseflesh and trampling hooves than by swordery. That came later.

In only a few hectic seconds Redheugh Dean was a shambles of falling, rolling, cursing men and screaming, lashing horses. Only tiny pockets of the English remained on the roadway anywhere, and these so shocked and isolated as to present little threat. Everywhere the Scots drove down, swiping, trampling, shouting — and seeking to pull up their careering mounts on the steep slopes, to turn back and finish off their broken foes. This had been the burden of Will's most urgent command — not to pursue fleeing individuals but to turn back and consolidate and despatch. And to remain a disciplined entity, able to obey further signals. For, of course, although this central half-mile of the enemy column would suffer almost inevitable disintegration, it would represent little more than a quarter of the whole — even though the most important quarter, with the leadership. The advance-party ahead, and fully a couple of thousand men behind, with the baggage and booty, had to be reckoned with.

Once Will, alone now on his vantage-point save for an esquire and his trumpeter-standard-bearer, saw that the first stage was proceeding according to plan. he was able to relinquish his long-held-in patience. Sword out, he spurred down from that broomgrown spine. He did not head straight for the mêlée below him, however, but slanted off half-right, to join the zigzag road itself, at an angle, and pound on down it at full gallop, his two henchmen at his heels. He was, of course, making for Percy.

That young lord, with his knightly group, had survived the first onslaught better than the rest of his people. This Will had anticipated, indeed allowed for — but it had been essential to his plan that at the moment of surprise the English leaders should be in a position where they could exert least control over their forces. So he had waited until Percy was crossing the second stream, in the gut of the eastern ravine, where he could see and be seen by few indeed of his men — even though, by the same token, he was not in a position to be swept off the roadway like the rest.

Percy and his chivalry, then, were still there, upright, horsed in a tight group straddling the ravine floor and the water, being

241

assailed by a circling band of Douglases under Cavers and young Drumlanrig, rather like hounds around a stag at bay. They were plainly at a loss, bewildered — but by no means vanquished. Indeed, here they were in greater numbers than their opponents, and once they had recovered from the numbing effects of surprise, they would not be long in asserting themselves.

As Will thundered down the long slope, cutting the corners of the zigzags, smashing through the bushes, he was waving and shouting to such of his people as he passed, to leave off their harrying of lesser men and fall in at his back. Some understood, and came pounding after him, so that by the time he had reached the bottom of the dean there were perhaps a dozen behind him, and he was gesturing them into a compact arrowhead formation with himself at its apex. With as little slackening of speed as possible for this manoeuvre, he drove on into the stream, heading directly for the centre of Percy's group, lance levelled, sword weaving. Although he did not know it, he was shouting the Douglas war-cry as loud as any of his following.

The English, of course, did not fail to perceive the challenge. The great undifferenced banner of Douglas would have warned them, if nothing else did, that here was the attackers' leader — although whether they realised that it was the Black Douglas himself was another matter. The entire splendid knightly group swung round to face the threat, ignoring for the moment the circling Teviot men. They of course outnumbered Will's arrowhead by five to one — but they were stationary, cramped together, without momentum or room to move, and based on the bad broken stance of stream-bed and high bank.

Will's headlong drive, without the least slackening of speed or change of direction, must have been unnerving to await, in the extreme. His couched lance and himself were as one, the steel-tipped point of an armoured wedge, with men close at either shoulder only half a length behind, and others protecting them in turn. It was an almost invincible formation, given utter fearlessness and determination on the part of the leader, complete discipline in his supporters, and the fierce velocity of a cavalry charge. Lacking these it could be self-annihilating, any faltering or indecision causing either an immediate disastrous pile-up or a break-up of the arrowhead which could then be encircled and demolished piecemeal by the attacked.

The crash of Will's collision with the perimeter of the standing group was appalling, shattering, almost like the effect of cannon-fire. No flesh and blood, human or equine, could stand it. Like ninepins the first and second ranks of the men around Percy went down, amidst a hell of flailing limbs, lashing hooves, splintered lances and spinning swords. The tip of Will's own lance snapped off, but there could be no changing of posture now, so tight-pressed was the driving arrowhead. Still with the broken shaft preceding him, impelled not only by his own momentum but by the weight behind him, he thrust on, sword now swinging right and left in a rhythmic figure-of-eight sweep. For better vision he had not closed the visor of his war-helm, and he saw men rear up before him and fall away below or behind him, remaining scarcely aware of any contact with them. He was aware only of Percy, bareheaded and fair, before him, hemmed in by his supporters so that he could scarcely move, but sitting proudly in his saddle, far from cowering from the assault, coldly arrogant, reputedly a much truer heir of Hotspur than was his somewhat fatuous father.

It was not the Percy's fault, nor Douglas's either, that the two leaders did not in fact come to grips in the single combat which undoubtedly both of them would have sought. It was an old and grizzled English knight a little on the Percy's left who, wise in war and long beyond chivalric posturing, altered the situation. Deliberately, as Will drove on in, he leaned over to his right, almost out of his saddle, and vehemently brought down his sword on the forward portion of the other's broken lance — not the edge of the blade, to shear the wood, but the flat of it. In consequence, the lance end was driven violently downwards, and, tucked under Will's right arm, its butt jerked as violently upwards. almost hoisting its owner off his horse's back. Forward over the beast's arching mane Will was thrown, only saving himself by grasping his sword-arm round the brute's neck, as the lance fell from his grip. The impetus of the charge continued to carry him onwards of course, and his close supporters on either side more or less held him up, sweeping the veteran knight out of their way like stubble. But the immediate danger to Percy was past, with Will swept by only a few feet to his quarry's right, in no position to do more than try to right himself in his saddle and cling to his sword. Indeed, Percy it was who lashed out with a sideways swipe as the Douglas drove by, but this was manfully parried by Will's esquire at his right shoulder.

And now one of the disadvantages of the tight arrowhead charge was demonstrated. The propulsion and direction of its advance was not to be altered swiftly by any sudden decision. On it drove, right through the English ring and up the steep bank beyond. Even with this gradient and the riders savagely dragging back on their reins, a turn and resumed attack could only be achieved by swinging round in formation in a very wide arc, or by pulling up, reforming, and instituting a new charge — no swift proceeding, especially on a steep and broken hillside.

This last Will was seeking to do, nevertheless, when there was a new development. From uphill, behind them, approximately on the same line as he himself had just charged down, another company came thundering, yelling the Douglas slogan with fresh fervour. It was John, Lord Balveny, and the Master of Somerville, with their fire-raisers, arrived on the scene and eager for action. There were not above two score of them — but that was probably not apparent to the English, at first sight.

Percy may have been fearless and arrogant — but he was not a fool. Moreover, despite the havoc made of his knightly company, he had still many old campaigners round him. Whatever may have been his desires in the matter of coming to grips with the Douglas, he was left in no doubts as to his duty as commander of a temporarily scattered and leaderless host. Before Will could turn and reform, or Johnnie could descend upon him from above, he took the wise if unheroic course. Off down the bed of the stream, seawards, he and his companions spurred, splashing and stumbling, leaving the confused shambles of Redheugh Dean for a better, kinder place.

The day was the Scots' — if only for the time being.

Will Douglas, breathless, half-winded by the kick of that lance-butt, shouted gaspingly to Cavers to follow Percy. Keep him in view. Try to head him off to the east. Keep him from rejoining the main body of the English, behind. Drive him in amongst the broken cliffs of the coast, if he could. And keep sending back word . . .

Then seventeen-year-old Johnnie and his party came crashing down, chagrined at having missed the fight. He would have been off after Percy also had his brother not restrained him.

"No, no," Will cried thickly. "Not that. Leave it to Cavers. See — take all the men you can raise here. Up this road. To the east, here. The Coldinghame road. Quickly. Five hundred English of the advance-guard rode that way. Stout men. They would be out of the dean before we struck. They may know naught of what's done. But if they turn back, if Percy reaches them, all could yet be lost. A strong body, and we are scattered. They must be kept away. If they turn back. You understand, Johnnie? A diversion. Lead them off. Seem to flee. Anything. Go now — and quickly."

"And you? Where will you be?"

"I go to aid Beardie. At the rear."

So back up and then down that littered switchback of a track Will and a few followers raced. As he went he gathered all the scattered groups and individuals of his force who yet strewed the twin deans or chased fleeing foes. Mounting the second long slope, there was still no sign of Crawford, or indeed of the mass of the enemy. This was where he had asked the savage giant to take charge, a task for a man who knew neither fear nor scruple, with a mere hundred or so men to face and hold back twenty times that number.

Dead and wounded men and horses dotted this western lip of the dean, but the noise of war only began to sound as the new-comers neared the crest. They were on top, where the trees and bushes thinned out to open rolling pastureland, before the clash, both in sound and sight, was revealed to them. It was an extraordinary scene — and even so it was at some distance, and receding. The entire spreading grassland slopes to the west were a mass of scattered, fleeing men, horses and cattle, that fanned out in ever widening disorder, a panic-stricken rout, like a vast flock of bolting sheep harried and savaged by a few determined and unrelenting wolves. Whatever it had been, it was not a fight now, nothing but a running, crazy slaughter with the best-mounted, the fleetest of foot and the least burdened, winning their lives, riding down their fellows, casting away women, booty, arms, anything that could hamper their flight.

Even though the sight represented totally unexpected and major victory, Will was shocked as he stared, shocked at the shameful sight of utter terror and abject panic — and at the snarling, merciless ferocity of men who killed and killed, mad apparently for blood. Even though this fleeing mob had represented the rear-guard, the commissariat, the drunken riff-raff and hangers-on which disfigures any invading army, burdened with gear and plunder — still this was shame.

He drew rein doubtfully. Clearly there was no need for him to go to Beardie's aid. Moreover, this chase was itself a danger, since it was dispersing the hunters, like the hunted, over an ever-widening area, and taking them further out of control. And behind, to the east, there might well be need of every man and every sword still, if that advance-guard, disciplined and tough, turned back. After a few vexed moments, Will swung on his trumpeter.

"Sound me the recall, man," he ordered. "Bring them back."

High and loud the trumpet brayed, echoing amongst the hillsides. But without other result. No one turned back, no slackening showed in the pursuit of the slaughter.

Will frowned. He turned to his esquire. "Go to him. My word to the Earl of Crawford. To return to me. With all haste. And all his men. *My* men. Enough, say. There is work for us to do. My brother faces yon advance-guard, outnumbered three to one. Cavers trails Percy, outnumbered. Tell him. We have more to do than chase and slay fleeing men. Go!"

But Beardie Alex Lindsay was in his element, at last. He was a killer, and nothing was going to stop him until his thirst was slaked. The esquire, in time, came back to the dean's edge, alone.

Will bowed to the inevitable. He turned his party and rode back south by east now, uphill, above the deans, to gain a high spur as vantage-point. And climbing there, a courier from John came to him presently. Percy and his advance-guard had joined forces again. They were halted now in a strong position on the green turf-grown ramparts of some ancient Roman fort, on the high ground a mile or two ahead. The Lord Balveny and Cavers were keeping them in view, but the enemy were much too strong to attack. What now?

Again it was for Will to bow to the inevitable. There was no more to be done, meantime. His force scattered and tired, surprise no longer possible, and the foe still outnumbering him and with their toughest squadrons unblooded, the thing was not for debate. It had been a notable victory — but enough was enough.

Douglas had longer-term aims than merely to fight it out here with Percy. He was still, after all, Lieutenant-General of the Realm.

"Tell my lord of Balveny and the Sheriff of Teviotdale to retire. To join me. We head south, round the head of Pease Dean. For the Eye Water passes. Tell them that. Leave the English, now. Percy will wait for news of his rear-guard. He will not follow."

"Aye, my lord . . ."

CHAPTER FIFTEEN

THAT evening, Hugh, with twelve hundred men, caught up with his brother's company, at Ayton. More were on the way. There had been no sign of Earl Beardie.

Reinforced, Will was all anxiety to finish what he had successfully begun. His scouts had been watching the high road over Coldinghame Moor all day. They sent back word that Percy, with the remnants of his force to the number of about eighteen hundred, was heading south along it, was in fact near Coldinghame itself, only five miles or so to the north-east, between them and the sea.

But though Will now had the strength to challenge the mauled English in full-scale battle, it was not to be. Not that night, at any rate. His men, who had ridden through two days and a night, were utterly weary — to say nothing of the horses. They must have a night's rest. These newcomers, many of whom had been in the saddle for hours before ever they reached the assembly-point at Lincluden in Nithsdale, had been riding from there since dawn, and were in no state to fight a battle. Moreover, scouts from the south reported that another English force, under Sir John Harrington, was heading north from Berwick, fully one thousand strong.

So the Scots camped for the night outside the blackened walls of what had been the pleasant little town of Ayton, where the Eye took its great turn north to the sea — and where fifty years before, a solemn treaty of eternal peace had been concluded with the English, Archibald the Grim the principal Scots signatory.

The next morning dawned wet and chill, with a grey haar drifting in from the North Sea on an easterly wind. Despite the depressing conditions, there was no delay now in the Scots camp, with Will impatient for action. But just as they were preparing to move, sentinals brought the news that a large body of men was approaching across the Merse from the Chirnside direction, and flying the Douglas colours. They waited.

It proved to be Robert, Lord Fleming, with the first of the Galloway mobilisation — nearly two thousand men. They had ridden all night, spurred on by the Countess Margaret's urgent commands. More would follow, under Jamie.

Will had now a host of thirty-seven hundred, despite Crawford's continued failure to appear. He demanded of Rob whether he was ready to ride on? That faithful stalwart knew better than to suggest otherwise. They set off east by north, into the cold rain.

Alas, they were too late. Too late by hours, Will's forward scouts told him, when they reached the sea at Eyemouth, to prospect the best place on the widening river-line to contest the enemy's southwards movement. Douglas, it seemed, was not the only one who could ride by night. Percy no doubt had had his own scouts out. At any rate, the English had hurried on, through the hours of darkness, even eschewing the tempting opportunity to sack Coldinghame Priory, and leaving both that township and Eyemouth unburned, had crossed the river near Linthill, at first light, fully three hours earlier, and were now well on their way to Berwick — if not there already, for it was a bare ten miles. At least they would have joined up with Harrington's force.

Will's burst of anger was hot but brief. He blamed himself, and the human weakness of men who needed sleep. He cursed that Hugh and Fleming, with their reinforcements, could not have reached him a few hours earlier. He raged at his scouts, for not having come and routed him out of his blanket, at Ayton. Then it was all over, and he was himself again, turning his whole host southwards once more, without delay. Percy was still far from home.

It was not so simple as that, of course. Berwick-on-Tweed lay in the way, a great Scottish fortified town that had been held by the English for many years, one of the strongest citadels in the two kingdoms. The Earl of Northumberland was at Berwick meantime, they said — and Percy would go to his father there. Will had no more hope of attacking and reducing Berwick than of flying in the air, even if he led ten times the numbers that he did. But that was not to say that he could do nothing further against the invaders. He could slip around Berwick, cross Tweed to the west, and then, either attack the Percys on their way south or, if they remained in Berwick, dose the English with some of their own medicine by raiding deep into Northumberland. He believed that was the sort of lesson that they would respect.

They were near Lamberton, half-way to Berwick, when Jamie Douglas arrived from the west, over Mordington Hill, with another fifteen hundred men. And that was not all; Sir Harry, the chamberlain, their brother-in-law, should be leaving Galloway now with the second and main contingent from that province. He had told Jamie that he would be disappointed if he did not bring three thousand. And there were still the men from Douglasdale and Ettrick to come, not to mention what Hay the Constable could raise further north still. Heartened, with five thousand men at his back now instead of five hundred, Will pressed on, although inevitably more slowly. They met with no opposition, Harrington evidently having turned back, with Percy. But no doubt scouts watched their every move.

And then, as they neared the Tweed at Paxton, there was further word from the west — no large body of fighting men this, but two exhausted couriers on foundered sweat-streaked horses. They came from Margaret, who had herself taken over Jamie's position at Lincluden as base commander — only, she was no longer at Lincluden, having been forced to retire westwards to Threave Castle. The English had mounted a further invasion, of the West March, under the Earl of Salisbury, their Warden. Lower Annandale and all the plain of the Solway was theirs, and they had sacked and burned the town of Dumfries. The Countess was holding back all further reinforcements for her husband meantime, and had sent messengers after Sir Harry and his force, six hours gone on the road eastwards. The new invaders' numbers were reckoned at between four and six thousand.

Will was forced to an agonising decision. If he turned back to the relief of the West, he left the already mauled East open to still more savage reprisals of the Percys, smarting under their minor defeat at Redheugh. Moreover, he threw away the advantages of his little victory, and the opportunity to strike a retaliatory blow into Northumberland. On the other hand, he was Warden of the West March, and that was Douglas's own country. He compromised. He ordered Hugh to take two thousand of their force and hasten back to the Solway, picking up the second Galloway contingent on the way. This would give him approximately five thousand — and Margaret might have more awaiting him. Will sent Sir John Wallace, Elisabeth's husband, with him, and the Master of Somerville. None were experienced campaigners — but then, neither were any of them, himself included.

So the host split up again, there on the north bank of Tweed. Hugh, Earl of Ormond and his company hastened off up-river, westwards, and Will led his reduced array of about three thousand splashing across the shallows of the first ford above the estuary, and into England.

The great square pile of Norham Castle guarded that ford — but wisely, in view of the Scots numbers, the keeper thereof did not attempt to contest the crossing. In his turn, Will made no assault on the castle; it was not to squander time on sieges that he had turned invader.

Leaving a screen of scouts behind him, to keep him informed of any movements from Berwick, he drove down fast and far into the somewhat bare Northumbrian country, keeping his force compact and allowing no tentative raiding and slaying *en route*, despite the resentment of his vengeance-hungry followers. Over twenty miles into England, they halted for the night in the valley of the Breamish, near Berwick, taking only sufficient local cattle and supplies to feed them. Well aware of the murmurous discontent of his men, Will ordered strict confinement to camp and a good night's rest for all — no sallies.

Himself, he was late in seeking his blanket, conferring with those of his commanders and veteran mosstroopers who knew anything of this countryside. And he was up before dawn collating the reports of his scouts, arrived throughout the night. When the camp awakened to the sunrise, he was able to address them in terms more to the popular taste.

"My friends," he shouted from an eminence, to men munching a breakfast of cold meat and slaked oatmeal, "ye have been patient. It had to be. I had to wait. Now I know that, up till darkening last night, none of the English had left Berwick, in any numbers, for the south. That word I had to have. Too many Scots raids into this country have ended in disaster because they were cut off from home. Too many of my ancestors have died or been taken prisoner within short miles of this place. But, for today, our rear is secure. We can do what we have come to do."

A ragged cheer went up from chewing men.

"So this day we teach the English their lesson. A teaching that they have earned, my God! But we do it as an ordered host, not a rabble, see you. We divide. I take two thousand, and make for Alnwick, the Percy's town, a dozen miles on. The rest, under my Lord Fleming, will harry this countryside. As the English harried ours. Their towns and villages, farms and homesteads, you will destroy. Their hay you will burn, their cattle slay. Do not burden yourselves with beasts or gear or women — that cost the English dear at Redheugh. Do not, indeed, make war against women and bairns — that is not for men who wear my Red Heart of Douglas. I charge you — mind it! And do not harry the Church. I am scant churchman, but this I command. There is plenty without these, plenty for your swords and torches. You understand? And do not spread too wide and far. Keep touch with the rest. So that you remain a force. We assemble here again, tonight."

None found fault with that programme.

So, with Jamie and Johnnie, with Cavers, as lieutenants, Will took the best two-thirds of his array and headed southeast, down Breamish, fast, through still unroused and unsuspecting country. They wasted no time on pillage and rapine, purposeful, controlled.

In little over an hour they were nearing the Aln valley. The walled town of Alnwick, clustering round the great Percy castle, lay in the valley-floor and climbed the southern bank. Within two or three miles of the place, John and his advance-party were sent on ahead at full gallop. Cavers had been here before, and declared that the northern gate in the walls, captured and held, would not only allow free access to the town but could deny aid coming to the people from the castle, which lay to that side. That the said gate would not be strongly guarded, this breezy May morning, was their hope; this had been the main objective behind Will's prohibition of sack and ravage, hitherto, and consequent delay, which could have allowed the alarm to reach Alnwick.

In consequence, when the main body of the Scots came trotting down the long north slope of the valley, in orderly fashion, to Alnwick Bridge, beneath the dreaded Douglas Red Heart banner, a mile-long column, three abreast, it was to find the town gate standing wide, Johnnie's men in tight control and the cowering townsfolk watching in silent alarm from a discreet distance. There was no move, as yet, from the castle.

The sack of Alnwick, thereafter, proved to be an inglorious, businesslike, almost humdrum affair, thorough, methodical and carefully controlled. There was little or no organised resistance, and only sporadic and short-lived bouts of fighting, where groups of individuals more or less instinctively sought to protect their property. The fact was that a good proportion of the younger and able-bodied men of the town were up at Berwick with their masters, and the remaining citizenry were not sufficiently foolish as to consider that there was any sense in contesting and further infuriating such a powerful attacking host, especially one led by the Black Douglas in person. That they got no lead or help from the castle undoubtedly affected their attitude. Yet for the keeper thereof to have acted otherwise than he did, was scarcely conceivable, with both Northumberland and his son absent, and most of the garrison with them, and the enemy in overwhelming strength in the town. He could hold the castle itself, and that was all.

So Will, after closing and manning all gates, took up his stance at the market cross, and directed the burning of Alnwick almost as though it had been one of his games tournaments. First, all the townspeople, or nearly all, were rounded up and herded into churchyards and other open spaces, and kept under guard. Then, street by street, squads of men were sent through the houses, to collect easily transportable valuables of small bulk. All else was to be left. Thereafter, with due reference to wind direction, the buildings were methodically fired. Most were made of timber and thatched, huddled together in narrow lanes and alleys, and they blazed like tinder. More trouble had to be taken with stone-built constructions, but these were comparatively few.

In a remarkably short time Alnwick was an inferno — though

a well-regulated and directed inferno, the noise of weeping, wailing, cursing townsfolk and yelling children, drowned in the roar and crackle of the flames and the crisp barking orders of Douglas commanders. It would be an exaggeration to say that there was no slaughter, rape or savagery; but such was kept to a minimum, by stern orders, strict supervision and the very tempo of the operation. Will and his brothers were everywhere, co-ordinating, exhorting, watching, restraining, Will grim and vehement, relentless, Jamie hating it all, and Johnnie revelling in every moment.

Presently, with a vast billowing column of black smoke rising hundreds of feet above the town and darkening all the forenoon, they had to drive the frightened, frantic townsfolk out through one of the gates, beyond the walls, where already the invaders' horses had been taken, as all the open spaces became ringed round and engulfed, and showering sparks and embers rained down. There, will took the mayor of the place, himself a Percy by-blow, and wrapping him in a Douglas banner, trussed him up securely and hanged him from the castle's own tall dule-tree, in full view of the garrison — not by the neck, but by his bonds, leaving the man to swing there, and birl, beseeching and imprecating in turns.

Satisfied, Will had his trumpeter assemble his men. He addressed them there, on Percy's green moot-hill before the castle, such as could hear him, with the smoke being carried away in the other direction by the easterly breeze.

"It is well done," he shouted, against the noise of the flames. "The Percy will not forget, for long. But you have kept the name of Douglas bright, as well as feared. You have my thanks. Aye — but there is more to be done. We go back to Breamish. But on the way, we show this fair English country that it is unwise to go north and burn and slay in Scotland. We will spread wide and cut a swathe through this Northumberland that men will point at for many a day! A hundred score of us should cut a fair swathe! We will work in line, myself at the right. Keep you that line."

They left the pyre that was Alnwick, and once out of the trough of the valley, spread out laterally, mainly in little groups of ten or half a dozen, to form a front, facing north by west, with gaps between of up to quarter or even half a mile, depending on the terrain. This took a considerable time to organise, but when at last it began to move forward, the Scots line stretched for some seven miles, and would widen as it it went. Thereafter, in a band that wide, devastation complete and terrible was spread across the fair face of Northumberland, with a thoroughness and method that seemed to make the destruction almost the more dire for its very cold disciplined progress.

On the extreme right, nearest the sea, Will established his controlling position, not in the centre. This was because any attack was likely to come from that direction. No local bands, hurriedly assembled, were going to interfere with such a host as this; but Berwick would not long remain ignorant of what was taking place, and the Percys could be expected to mount some sort of counter-action. Will had sufficiently grim example of what could happen when an invading army, which did not know the terrain intimately, relaxed its vigilance in seeming cowed and prostrate country. He had a screen of fully a hundred scouts out, far in advance, and maintained control and contact personally.

They began to run into already devastated territory before they reached the Breamish in the evening, and ahead of them, as well as behind, all was rolling smoke-clouds. Fleming and Cavers had been busy. In the green dale, gradually the smoke-blackened, hoarse-voiced men assembled, coming in in small groups and large, not a few the worse for liquor, many with more booty than their commands had stipulated. Will was well aware that maintaining a strict discipline in an irregular force such as this, engaged in so heady and scattered a task, was all but impossible; yet he was determined that, as far as was humanly possible, he should remain in effective control. As a consequence, when during one of his many patrols of the camp area in the valley-floor, he distinctly heard a woman's bitten-off scream, he was swift to investigate. Swift also to act thereafter, when he discovered two girls, naked but trussed up and hidden under blankets, amongst the horse-lines of a group of Morton Douglases. Without delay or compunction, he hanged the bonnet-laird in charge and one of his men who protested, as warning to all others who chose to flout the Black Douglas's commands, and took the young women away, giving them clothing and money as some compensation, and sending them under escort to the Vicar of Berwick near by.

That night the sky was vivid red over a great part of Northumbria. Berwick could not fail to see it.

But still no attack developed, the scouts sent no word of approaching forces.

Dawn saw the Scots up and on their stern way, still north by west, their left spreading right to the Cheviot foothills now. There was no opposition, but the land was deserted in their path, flocks driven off and valuables hidden. Undoubtedly many had spent a busy night. Fairly early, word reached Will that a large body of men had left Berwick; but later reports made it clear that this was in fact heading due south at speed, with no diversions right or left — almost certainly Percy and his father making direct for Alnwick. If that was so, it seemed unlikely that there would be any attack mounted for some time; there was plenty to keep the Percys busy in Alnwick.

So the work went on, purposeful but somewhat wearisome now, though with never a moment's relaxation in Will's watchfulness. Jamie and Johnnie he kept riding up and down the long front, seeking to control, to keep it approximately in line, to whip in stragglers, to discourage delaying searches for loot.

Noontide saw Wooler ablaze, and mid-afternoon Doddington, Milfield, Branxton and Etal. They left the castle there unassaulted, like those of Ford, Duddo and Heaten, islands in the blackened sea.

By evening, everywhere the line of the silver Tweed was before them again, and Will at least knew a great relief. Safely across the river, he could base himself securely in a strong defensive position, where he could contest the Tweed crossings, against the inevitable repercussions and reprisals, keep an eye on Berwick, and seek contact with Hugh's force in the West.

The main body crossed again at Norham, leaving some hundreds on the south bank to watch approaches to the various fords. Will, for one, slept the more soundly that night for being on Scottish soil once more.

He was wakened when couriers from Hugh found them. Hugh's news was that he was continuing to harass and dog Salisbury's army, but it was a much larger force than had been reported, and he was not strong enough to challenge it openly. Estimates now put the English in the West at about seven thousand. They were not behaving as Percy had done in the East, but sitting tight in Dumfries and sending out strong raiding columns from there. One of these Hugh had managed to intercept and cut up, but only one. He needed more men.

Will was put in something of a quandary. The obvious course would be, of course, to hurry across to the West with all his strength, and take over from Hugh. But he was quite certain that Northumberland would not lie down under what had been done to him and his, and would strike back in increased fury, with all the force he could muster. And this East March was infinitely more vulnerable than the West, more dangerous for Scotland's safety. Already Percy had been within twenty-five miles of Edinburgh. Will dared not leave this side of the Border.

He had to compromise again, sending a thousand men, under Johnnie, and urging Hugh to make a large-scale feint, possibly across Eskdale to the English side of the Border, burning Longtown or Kirlinton, to entice Salisbury out of Dumfries and into country where he would be disadvantaged. Will would have liked to send Rob Fleming, an older and more experienced man, to take charge — but young Hugh, Earl of Ormond, would take that badly. He sent an urgent courier north to Stirling, however, to demand haste in the national mobilisation, and to suggest that Sir William Hay himself should lead the first contingent down to the Solway. Hugh would hardly feel it contrary to his dignity to serve under the High Constable. Only a little less urgent were Will's requests for reinforcements for himself, in the East.

So, with only moderate patience and good humour, the Lieutenant of the Realm settled down to an unlikely waiting and watching role along Tweed, with his two thousand men — something for him quite out of character when livelier action was building up elsewhere — even though he, like his men, was tired and much in need of a rest. He did find something more active to do than just wait, however. His detachment on the south side of the river reported that they had been shot at from Wark Castle. Wark lay a few miles to the west, across the river not far from Coldstream. Next to Berwick it was the strongest of the Tweed castles. While they waited for Percy, at least they could besiege this. They had no artillery, but mining and sapping were possible. It would keep the men occupied and in trim.

Two days passed. Wark scowled defiance, Berwick made no

move, and there was no sign of Percy coming north again from Alnwick. A small reinforcement reached Will from Teviotdale.

Then the expected news arrived from deep in Northumberland. The Percys had ridden out of Alnwick in force, heading north by west. Numbers were uncertain but believed to be between three and five thousand.

Will waited, in all preparedness, for further news, so that he might gauge, if possible, where the enemy proposed to cross Tweed. For most of its length the river was impassable, and after Berwick itself there was not another bridge until Peebles, seventy miles up. But there were three or four fords, after the river ceased to be tidal some ten miles up, where pebble-banks and shoals allowed mounted men to cross, stirrup-high, when the river was not in spate. These fords Will was guarding.

The next news was also as anticipated. A force had emerged from Berwick, said to be under the command of its fiery governor, Sir Magnus Redmayne, and was proceeding westwards along the north bank of the river. It appeared to foreshadow the traditional pincers-movement. Sitting astride the river at Fishwick, Norham, Dreeper Island and Coldstream, Will dared not concentrate his force until he had some indication as to Percy's objective.

Evening reports put the principal enemy at Wooler, and Redmayne only five or six miles east of Fishwick ford, at Gainslaw.

The Scots stood guard all that night — and waited in vain for reinforcements.

Daylight brought totally unexpected tidings, Redmayne had turned back, during the night, crossed Tweed at West Ord, partly by boats and partly by a little used low-tide ford, and was now heading across open country almost due south. It looked indeed as though he was heading in the Wooler direction, for a link-up with Percy — strange move as this was.

Will puzzled at this. That it had been done under cover of darkness added to the mystery. It seemed like throwing away a good tactical advantage. He could make no sense of it.

All through another day, into June now, they waited, without development of the situation. And through another short night they stood at arms at the fords, anticipating a thrust north in the dark. But nothing eventuated. Dawn found the Scots jaded and more perplexed than ever.

Then, in early forenoon, scouts from the south sent the word. The English had gone, during the night. Burned Wooler was abandoned again. The Percys and Redmayne both, had vanished.

Furiously Will questioned the messengers. But they could tell him little more. Only that signs, tracks and horse-droppings indicated that the united host had moved off south-westwards towards the Cheviots. Men were trailing them, and word would be sent.

Where were they going? It they were heading west into the hills, they must be intending to emerge again somewhere in surprise. To avoid these river crossings, perhaps, outflank them, and drive in behind? Move into Scotland by College, Curr and Kale Waters, it might be? And so into Teviotdale.

In some agitation Will debated. It might all be a ruse. He couldn't make any moves, in reaction, until he was better informed. It would be crazy to leave his present strong positions meantime.

That day, Wark Castle fell, mined from beneath into the inner bailey. They used its own gunpowder to blow up the keep, and set the rest on fire.

Fretting. Will awaited news from his forward scouts. It did not come until nightfall. Percy was now deep in the Cheviots, and still heading westwards, last reported position about the head of Jedwater — actually over into Scotland — and still heading west. A suspicion began to form itself in Will's mind.

By noonday following, the suspicion was confirmed, the verification however having to be brought over fifty miles to him — for now his scouts were working far away indeed. The English had crossed the watershed into upper Liddesdale, not turned north for the Teviot. They were still moving down Liddesdale, south-west. They were going to join Salisbury on the Solway.

Will fretted and delayed no longer. Whatever Percy's reasons for this major cross-country move, it spelt enormous menace to the West, where a united army of over ten thousand could be let loose. He gathered in his companies from all the fords, leaving only small numbers of Teviotdale men to watch them, and with the rest set off for the West with all speed. He sent ahead his swiftest couriers to try to warn Hugh — but feared that it would be too late.

As he pounded up the wide Tweed plain towards Kelso, he cursed himself for not having thought of it earlier. In a way, this was logical. The great Douglas lands all lay in the south-west of Scotland. Percy, hot with rage at what had been done to his capital of Alnwick, was now less concerned with any successful invasion of Scotland than with direst vengeance on Douglas. That was the magnet that drew him to Salisbury's side — hate. Will would wager that his prime objective was Douglasdale. And he had at least a seventy-mile start.

If the Douglases had ridden hard and fast eastwards from Lincluden, they rode now still harder and faster westwards back towards Nithsdale. From Kelso, up Teviotdale they galloped the long, long valley, crossing the breadth of Scotland. Night found them near Hawick, but there was no let up. Stragglers dropped behind and were left, until even Douglas-driven horse-flesh failed them, and they were forced to halt, high amongst the quiet shadowy hills where Teviot was born, and the burns began to flow westwards. They were but half-way to Solway, little more.

It was midday following, down where Liddesdale met Esk, that they saw the first of the fleeing men. Up the valley these came, lashing foam-flecked mounts, frightened men in pairs and groups, who scattered widely on to the hillsides at sight of Will's array. As more appeared, and more, some clearly wounded, Will sent some of his own tired followers to chase and capture one.

This unfortunate proved to be an Englishman, and an Alnwick man at that. He was wounded, exhausted and a little light-headed. All that they could get out of him was that there had been a great battle. They had been surprised. There had been much slaughter. Most of his own troop were dead. Slain by the Scots.

At first, his hearers could hardly credit it. But as ever more fleeing riders appeared, all making for the east — which meant England — it was obvious that there had indeed been a debacle of some sort. They learned the truth of the matter from a party of Armstrongs, in hot pursuit of booty. There had been a great victory. The English hosts, under the Earls of Salisbury and Northumberland, had joined forces at the passage of Sark, near where that river entered the Solway Moss. There the young Earl of Ormond, who had been dogging Salisbury's force from

Dumries, circled through the hills and fell upon the combined English soon after they had joined up and were still in disarray. It had been a savage fight, but the Scots held the higher, firmer ground and the English were driven more and more into the floundering Moss. It was uncertain who was in command, Percy or Salisbury. But they could squabble about it now at their leisure, for both were now prisoners, along with Pennington and Harrington — though old Northumberland himself had escaped, they said, saved by his son. Sir Magnus Redmayne was dead, along with thousands of others, many drowned in Solway. The entire enemy army was broken and dispersed, all within two or three hours . . .

Will Douglas, listening, began to laugh, and went on laughing.

*　　　*　　　*

The Douglases came to Threave two evenings later, tired but well content. Save only in one respect; one of their number was missing. Not actually a Douglas either — Sir John Wallace of Craigie, Sheriff of Ayr, young Elizabeth's husband. Hugh's most able lieutenant at the Battle of Sark, he had saved the day by a magnificent charge on the English right, against enemy mounted bowmen who were bidding fair to change the whole course of the battle. But he had died at the end of it. Their country had always cost the Wallaces dear.

Margaret had all the womenfolk gathered at Threave, and though all were kind to the fifteen-year-old widow, her loss could not wholly spoil the relief and satisfaction of the others. They greeted their husbands and brothers like heroes, and great was the celebration.

Margaret, never effusive, greeted Will with quiet pride, before them all. "My lord," she said, "you have made men proud again to bear the name of Douglas. Women likewise. You come to Threave, this time, a paladin indeed! Lord of a galaxy of such. All paladins! It is my joy to be wife to the Black Douglas."

Embarrassed, he shook his head, but took her in his steel-clad arms and kissed her. Even as he did so, however, his eyes were searching swiftly amongst all the eager women. He saw Meg there, at the back, behind all the high-born ones, biting her lip and smiling, though with a diffidence unusual in that young woman. For a moment their glances locked, and then she turned away. But it was enough.

When he released Margaret, it was to perceive that he was not the only one whose eyes could stray at such a time. She had been looking at Jamie, behind him. Now she went to him, almost at a run.

Jamie was a casualty, in a minor way. At Alnwick a blazing beam had fallen on him, burning his forearm. Receiving no careful treatment thereafter, the burn had suppurated and become very painful and inflamed, and the arm was now bound up in not over-clean linen. The sufferer could have wished that it was an honourable wound sustained in battle; but it was heroic enough for Margaret Douglas. Her non-effusiveness was severely strained as she took Jamie in charge, making only perfunctory acknowledgement when her husband, grinning, pointed out that Hugh was the real hero of the day, the conqueror of Percy and Salisbury both. And what about Sir Harry, properly wounded? And Rob Fleming, stiff from being thrown from a foundered horse? And Johnnie, who had ridden twice as far and as hard as anyone else, as leader of scouts?

There were plenty of other ladies to console these warriors satisfactorily, however, and Margaret was able to devote herself to Jamie.

Later in Margaret's own private bower, which had been her childhood's room, she was alone with her husband. When she had heard all that she desired of the details of the campaign, she changed to a very different aspect of the subject.

"The Douglas name will ring loud from one end of the land to the other, Will," she said thoughtfully. "But there are some, I think, who will sing no praise. You will be wise to remember it. Since these will be powerful voices."

"You mean the Livingstones? And Hamilton?"

"I mean loftier than these. I mean those who should indeed most thank you — but will not, I fear. I mean the Chancellor. And the King."

"James? Why he? His realm is saved, for this present, purged of the English. Indeed, it may be that they will now renew the truce, lesson learned for a little longer. James has reason to rejoice. Kennedy also — even though he does not love me. He is a sound man, with a good head on him. Not, like some, eaten up with hatred."

261

"Perhaps. But have you thought why he has come to mislike you? When you it was who made him Chancellor? He may not hate, but he can fear. It is fear, I swear, that moves James Kennedy against Douglas. Fear that Douglas grows too strong. Too strong for the Stewarts. He is of that kin, mark you, his mother a Stewart princess. My own mother, who moves much in the Court, says that all there know that the Chancellor believes Douglas grown too strong. And tells the King so. This victory must make you stronger, you and your brothers — more highly esteemed. He will not rejoice."

"Is that of any matter? To Douglas."

"I think it could be. It is for this that he has raised up Crichton again. There is danger in that . . ."

'At least he will not turn to the Livingstones again — that I wager! Not after yon cursing!"

"Perhaps not. But his influence with the King grows ever greater. And James is no longer a boy. He is nearly a man now — and a hot-tempered, suspicious man. You are his Lieutenant-General — but I think he would not have the people love you too well."

"But why? He has naught to fear from me."

"No. But does he know it? For certain? Until he is wed, and has a son and heir, who would be king if he died? There is no clear heir-male. No brothers or uncles or cousins of the male line. The closest kin are Douglases and Kennedy himself, sons of princesses. You yourself are of the blood royal, both from your father and your mother. And I, I am closer still. Robert Bruce was less close to the throne he gained than is Will Douglas!"

"Dear God — but this is folly, girl! I would never think of the throne. For me . . ."

"Others might think for you. Your lady-mother, perhaps? And mine! I have heard whispers. And if I, then the Chancellor, who will be well served with spies. Churchmen ever are. Therefore, James himself."

"Damnation! This is too much! Prattling, interfering old women! I'll have none of it. D'you hear? I shall tell James so. And Kennedy."

"They may not believe you. Will. So remember — when all are hailing Douglas as saviour of the realm, the realm's masters may see you something otherwise!"

"You mistake, Margaret — I swear it!"

"I hope that I do. But, see you — there is a matter in which there is no mistake. The name of Douglas may resound on every lip — or most. But the murderers of my Douglas brothers still go free, their blood unavenged. I charge you not to forget it!"

He looked at her steadily. "I have not forgot."

"I hoped not. It is time, I think. Before Crichton rises too high again."

He nodded.

"Yes." She smiled, then, and spoke in a different voice. "You have been very good, Will. Very patient with me. You may go now."

"Go? Go where?"

"Go where you long to go. Where your heart is. To Meg. She waits for you. I am sure."

He drew a deep breath, staring at her, shaken. It was the first time that she had ever admitted that she knew. At a loss, he shook his head.

"Go, I say. Meg has been patient also. And discreet." She spoke calmly, with no hysteria, no hint of reproach even. "She is entirely faithful to you, you understand. She should have her reward. Go, Will."

Biting his lip, but without a word, he did as she bade him.

CHAPTER SIXTEEN

ALL Scotland flocked to Stirling for the King's nuptials, lords and lairds and ladies and landless men, prelates and priests and wandering friars, burgesses, merchants, apprentices and towns-folk, minstrels, tumblers, packmen, pedlars, gipsies and pick-pockets. There had not been a reigning king's wedding in the land for centuries. This Mary of Gueldres whom the former Chancellor Crichton had brought back from the Low Countries as bride for James Fiery-face, was good-looking and moreover a strong and hearty young woman who should bear the King fine lusty sons — which was even more important than beauty. Gueldres did not sound any very lofty dukedom to provide a queen for Scotland, but it seemed that there happened to be a shortage of marriageable young women amongst the ruling houses of Europe just then — and at least she was niece to Burgundy, reputed the richest prince in Christendom.

Of all the companies and trains which wound their way to Stirling that July day of 1449, brilliant, splendid, extravagant as they were, it is safe to say that none nearly rivalled that of Douglas. Not even the bridal train itself, led by her uncle Philip of Burgundy, with seventy counts, barons and knights and their ladies — including his own wife, King James's sister, the Princess Isabella — and three hundred men-at-arms; or that of the King's other brother-in-law, Princess Elizabeth's husband, the Archduke of Austria, in a blaze of Teutonic chivalry; or that of the third princess, Annabella's father-in-law the Duke of Savoy, with a constellation of swarthy, laughing Italian elegants. Douglas outshone all, with three earls, seven Lords of Parliament, four bishops and nearly two hundred barons, knights and lairds, at his back, with no less than six thousand men — not to mention the gorgeous host of ladies who supported Margaret, or indeed the unfortunate captured Percy, heir of Northumberland.

Strangely enough, although this vast, glittering and unwieldy entourage was there by no accident, Will brought it with a very real reluctance. That it would not fail further to alarm those who deemed Douglas as already too powerful, went without saying; but he wanted overwhelming force assembled and at hand for immediate action, for a specific purpose, and this wedding display was the excuse, combining with it something in the nature of a triumphal victory parade for the Border campaign. That all might see it as just Douglas ostentation indeed, and not a tactical mobilisation, was his hope.

There were uses for at least some proportion of the Douglas thousands, for the highlight of the wedding preliminaries was to be an enormous tourney held in the royal park of Stirling Castle, the largest of its kind ever to take place in Scotland. This had been King James's own wish, for he was as enthusiastic over feats of arms as ever, and moreover concerned greatly to outdo the Earl of Douglas's own wedding tournament. For activities such as these, with an influx of folks from far and near to the tune of scores of thousands, major policing was entirely necessary; and by transforming himself into his guise of Lieutenant-General of the Realm and Chief Marshal of the tournament, Will was able to supply and officer this from his host.

Mary of Gueldres was, of course, queen of this tourney, with four Stewart princesses to support her — for even shrinking deaf-and-dumb Joan was brought out of hiding for the occasion. The new Earl of Angus escorted her, but did not want her, having a wife of his own already — and indeed was in process of bartering her with the imbecile Lord of Dalkeith, Sir Harry's brother.

After the usual preliminaries and appetisers, parades, competitions and passages of arms — including a joust wherein King James himself defeated, although only just, another brother-in-law, the Lord of Campvere, from the Low Countries — the highlight of the day was a great challenge, *à l'outrance* that is, to the death, by three Burgundian knights, famous champions and the cream of Continental chivalry, against any three Scots soever — but preferably Douglases. Will was fairly sure that it was King James who had put the Burgundians up to this last, in the hope that a sound beating would be administered to Douglas pride. Be that as it might, there was no lack of Douglases to take up the challenge; indeed the demands to be one of the trio were so numerous, as well as so vociferous, from Will himself down to some of the youngest lairdlings, that it was decided that lots should be drawn for the honour, again the King making the suggestion. The first fell, to fairly universal chagrin, to a man who was only a Douglas through his mother, Sir John Ross of Hawkhead; the second, to James, brother of the powerful Douglas of Lochleven; and the third to another James and another second son — Jamie, Master of Douglas.

Will was as impotent to do anything about this as he was furiously angry. No amount of argument or pleading, or even Margaret's tears, would make Jamie stand down — for despite all his gentleness, he could be notably stubborn. Ross was a veteran, and could be expected to give a good account of himself; Young Lochleven was a totally unknown quantity; but Jamie was not only the least effective fighter of the chiefly Douglas brothers, but one of the least hopeful choices on which the lot could have fallen.

But the die was cast. The champions were armoured and horsed. The trumpets sounded for the lance fight.

Jamie was unhorsed in the first clash. But fortunately, so was his opponent, the Sieur de Longueville, whose horse, shaken after the impact, was cannoned into by Ross's mount, by mischance, and rolled over. Ross himself suffered a broken lance at the hands of one of the Chevalier de Lalain brothers, but the other had his high-decorative shield knocked away by Young Lochleven. Which left honours fairly even, for the first round.

They remounted for the battle-axe encounter. This could be a killer, and Margaret was so overcome that she had to be conducted from the royal box.

Although no one expected it, Jamie did rather better at this, little trained to it as he was, plunging in with a vigorous windmill-like swiping which was very effective at keeping his opponent at a distance, however unorthodox. But it was also very exhausting, and obviously could not be kept up for long. The Burgundian had only to bide his time. But, strangely, de Longueville did not do that; possibly because one of the de Lalain brothers had already toppled Young Lochleven out of his saddle and the other pair were smashing away at each other in titanic fashion, he felt that a waiting game was insufficiently dramatic for one of his fame. At any rate, with a complicated piece of horsemanship he thrust in low, lying almost flat along his beast's neck, to drive upwards with a vicious hooking slash of his axe, that caught Jamie under the left oxter and lifted him right off his horse's back, despite the weight of his armour. He crashed to the ground, and lay still.

De Longueville circled round him. Will groaned. That upwards jerking blow could have broken Jamie's neck. Then the gleaming armoured figure on the grass stirred and slowly, painfully, rose upright. Heavily he moved over to where his fallen battle-axe lay, and stiffly stooped to pick it up.

A great cheer and sigh combined arose from the thousands of spectators. De Longueville reined up his charger and signed his esquire over to aid him to dismount. At the same moment, Sir John Ross fell headlong in clanking ruin, sought to rise on the ground, but sank back again, still.

The Scots were less than expert with the battle-axe, a weapon little used in their tourneys or warfare.

De Longueville advanced upon his reeling opponent. Jamie actually went to meet him, lashing out with a sudden wild blow which almost overbalanced him, and struck the other on the sword-arm, causing the Burgundian's own blow to waver and miss.

As well for Jamie that the other's arm was affected, even if only numbed, and that he had to transfer his axe to the other hand, for the force of Jamie's swipe swung him round and over, and he went down on one knee. A well-aimed chop to the neck then could have killed him; but in the left hand, de Longueville's return stroke was inaccurate, though heavy enough, smashing down on Jamie's shoulder and chest. He pitched forward on his face, and so lay.

The other paced round him twice, and then turning towards the royal gallery, raised his axe on high. The other two Scots lay where they had dropped.

King James stood up.

But not only King James. The battered, sprawling Master of Douglas drew knees up, sideways, and then with grievous deliberation, rose on them. Somehow he got to his feet, using his axe to aid him, and so stood swaying. Then he raised the weapon again, and advanced ploddingly on his foe.

The King jerked out an oath. "No!" he cried. He snatched off the steel gauntlet he still wore from his own joust, and flung it clattering down. "No, I say!" He swung on the Lyon King of Arms near by. "Lyon — an end! Sound an end. I declare Burgundy to win. Quickly, man!"

The trumpeter beside Lyon did not wait for the latter's confirmatory order. He blew his instrument loud and long. The joust was finished.

Jamie dropped the axe promptly enough, as though thankful to be quit of its weight, and stood leaning on it, but still upright. The three Burgundians, two still mounted, one on foot, moved together and bowed. Their esquires ran forward to remove their helms.

Amidst the cheers and jeers and yelling, there was more running than this. A mass of angry and frustrated Douglases burst from the side of the lists and rushed towards the royal enclosure, shouting and gesticulating — not men-at-arms these, but knights and lairds most of whom had put their names in for the lot-drawing. Their anger was natural, their protest legitimate — even if their way of showing it was unsuitable. The King had stopped the contest while their representative was still on his feet — and moreover with two sound arms to wield his axe against his opponent's one. And the contest had been wrong, unfair, from the start. Against the cream of Christendom's fighters the Douglases should have been able to pick their three best, not have to rely on drawn lots. It was all wrong.

Hotly King James glared at the surging Douglases, his red birth-mark flaming. He had grown and thickened into a well-built, compact young man, not handsome but strong-featured, vehement, hot-tempered. His upbringing had been such as to make him wary and suspicious, either cowed or self-assertive. He was not cowed.

"Back! Back, I say!" he cried, pointing imperiously at the Douglases. "This is outrage!" He swung on Will. "Call them off, my lord. Call off your rabble!"

Will was little less angry than the others, although his emotion was complicated by relief that his brother had survived the business alive. He believed that the King had suggested the contest, egged on the Burgundians to demand Douglas opponents, urged the selection by lot, and thus practically ensured the Douglas defeat. Moreover, there was no doubt but that he had called a closure before the accepted end of a joust *à l'outrance*, and while Jamie might have had a belated but slight advantage — however thankful was one part of Will's mind that it had all been called off when it had.

"Rabble, Sire!" he jerked back. "I'd remind Your Grace that these are those who fought at Sark and Colbrandspath, and drove the English from your land!" But he waved his people back, just the same.

James flushed, blinking. "I'd remind *you*, Earl of Douglas, that this is not a battlefield! I will have no brawling here, before my bride, my guests. Have them away." He took a deep breath, and changed his tune a little. Perhaps he recollected that he was speaking to the most powerful man in his realm, and also that these same Douglases were themselves the only policing authority available. "If you please, my lord. That all may proceed without delay."

Will, noting that the royal hand was shaking with barely suppressed passion, nodded coolly. "As Your Grace wills." He signed to the Lord Fleming to go down to the Douglases below — who were, in fact, already lessening their clamour as they realised that this was not the way to make their objections known.

Behind the King, Bishop Kennedy spoke. "His Grace intervened, of his clemency, in time to save your brother, my lord. Would you have had him slain, for the sake of your pride?"

"Aye, you should thank me," the King took him up, quickly. "The Master fought bravely. But he was no match for the Burgundians. None were. I desired no more bloodshed, from brave knights. Go find me how all fare, my lord. Both yours and theirs. I would know."

Thus dismissed, Will strode from the royal gallery. It was his first open clash with James Stewart.

Although there were two days of games and pageantry at Stirling, and two nights of music, feasting, dancing and revelry in the castle thereafter, as part of the marriage celebrations, the wedding itself was not to take place there but in the Abbey of Holyrood at Edinburgh. St. Michael's Chapel in the castle was too small, and Cambuskenneth Abbey deemed insufficiently important; besides, Edinburgh was the capital city, even though Stirling was the royal seat. So, on the third day, all the wedding guests, accompanied by vast number of the holiday-making populace, set out on the thirty-five mile road to Edinburgh, in a sort of prolonged and perambulatory progress and carnival, in which the King halted at every town, village, abbey and castle, showing himself and his bride to the people and receiving hospitality as he went. Three days were devoted to this strange journey, that was normally covered in one; and fortunately the early July weather was kind. Never had such a thing been seen in Scotland. Will Douglas left behind all but a very small proportion of his host at Stirling.

Thereafter, in the grey abbey beneath green Arthur's Seat, amidst great splendour, the hearty, frank and uncomplicated Mary of Gueldres was made wife and queen for the King of Scots, Bishop Kennedy officiating. In close attendance was Sir William Crichton, clearly much in favour. Will at least made no secret of his disapproval and treated the man as he would a leper. Sir Alexander Livingstone, the Justiciar, at least had the grace, or the discretion, to absent himself, pleading age and infirmity. Indeed, of all that faction, only his eldest son, Sir James, and his grandson the Lord Hamilton, were present. Will made a point of watching these two with the utmost care. All was not what it seemed at these royal nuptials, however few were aware of it.

After the ceremony, in the great refectory of the abbey, all the chiefest guests were marshalled to pay their duty and fealty to the new Queen. After the princesses and foreign relatives, the Earl of Douglas, with his Countess, accepted as next in line to the throne, was first of all the Scots to come up, to bend on one knee and kiss Queen Mary's plump hand.

"Your Highness's true and leal servant," Will assured her. "This is a great day for Scotland. His Grace is fortunate, indeed."

'You think so, my lord?" The brown-eyed bride glanced over at Margaret, smiling, "Less fortunate than you, by the Mass! The King should have wed your Countess Margaret, I tell him. Not poor fat Mary of Gueldres. Then he would have the fairest woman in his Scotland to wife, and besides, half of the Douglas strength! Not so?"

It was uncertain who was most disconcerted by this Dutch frankness, the two husbands or Margaret.

Will cleared his throat. "His Grace has no need to marry the Douglas strength. Highness. He has it already. All is his to command."

James looked doubtful, but said nothing.

Margaret spoke quietly. "Your Highness much miscalls yourself. And, who knows — perhaps you will be more successful in giving your lord a son than I have been!"

There were moments of silence. Will's dark features went quite blank, expressionless. The Queen looked from one to the other, opened her widely generous mouth to speak, and then thought better of it. The King frowned and flushed. He flushed easily.

"Perhaps," he said. "And in that day, Cousin, you will bid farewell to any hopes for my throne! For you or yours!" That came out in a rush. "If . . . if such you have."

"By the Rude — such I have not! Nor ever have had." Will's voice grated. "Douglas is well content to remain . . . Douglas!"

The two young men looked at each other, eye to eye, with little of the normal or suitable aspect of monarch and subject. Then Will bowed, almost curtly, and led his countess away with rather longer and swifter pace than was courtly. The Lord Lyon called forward the Earl and Countess of Orkney to greet the Queen's Highness.

Later that evening, after the banquet, Will paced the little chamber in the Abbey Strand where Meg Douglas was installed — for the abbey itself was filled to overflowing, as was all Edinburgh. He threw the words at the young woman who sat on the bed watching him, lovely face troubled.

"Today, she said it! There, before all. Or, to James and his queen. As good as accused me. Of not giving her a son, a child. Proclaimed it! . . ."

"Surely not, Will? Surely not that. She would not do it. She is not of that sort. She is too proud, if nothing else."

"Not in those words, no. She seemed to take it to herself. She said that she had not been successful in giving me a son. Hoped that the Queen would serve her lord better! But . . . the thing was there. For James to see. To hear. And therefore all. She has never done the like. Never spoken of it. Never, even to me . . ."

"She must still feel it. And sorely. I had thought that she had ceased to care. That you would not bed with her. But it must be so. She must care, yet . . ."

"She does not care. Not for me. Does not love me. I know that well. She has never loved me. We are friends, of a sort. Good friends. That is all. Married only for the sake of Douglas. She loves Jamie. You know it. As he loves her."

"But she does not bed with him. And there it is!"

"You are so sure of that? . . ."

"Will — that is unworthy! She is true, honest. You know it."

"Aye. I daresay. But . . . she does not love *me*. Desire me."

"I think . . . I have said it before . . . you should go to her. To her bed. Now. Do it, Will. Take her."

"Why, a God's name? When neither of us desires the other?"

"Because it is her right. She is your wife. She is a woman. Beautiful. Proud. And living a lie. She may want your child, even though she does not want *you*!"

"Dear God — you say this! You, Meg, who are part of me?"

"Aye, I say it. Not wanting to, I say it, my heart! But since she has spoken so, she must wish it so. And it is her right . . ."

He strode over to her, and pushed her back on the bed, his hands urgent on her warm voluptuous body, wrenching down her bodice to free her splendid breasts, then groping lower, his lips eager. But firmly though gently she restrained him, and herself, kept herself from responding, even pushed him from her.

"No, Will. Not *me*, tonight. *Her!* Go to her. Go now. This night, when she has spoken as she did. Tonight you should go. Tonight you have reason to go . . ."

"No! Why should I? It is you I want. How can I go to her, lie with her, wanting *you*?"

"You can, I say. Others have done the like, ere this!"

"After these years? What can I say to her?"

"What matters it what you say? Go to her and she will not need your words. I ask you to do it, Will. For now . . . now I feel that I am robbing her."

"That is folly. You give, do not take. I get from you what she cannot give me. And in all else she has her way, Countess of Douglas . . ."

"You beat the air, Will. It is not so. You have wronged her, in this. From the start. As have I. We cannot shut our eyes to it, longer. Go now, my dear — of a mercy! I am not for you, this night."

Heavily, almost sullenly, he stood up, back from her, staring flushed at all her desirable disorder — made none the less enticing for her efforts to cover herself, with every line and curve of her wanting him also. Without another word, he turned on his heel and strode from that little room.

Back to the abbey itself the man made his way through the thronged night, set-faced, and never had he looked more the Black Douglas. Ignoring the salutations of guards and monks and guests alike, he stalked to the sub-Abbot's quarters where he was lodged, and up the winding stairs. At the Countess's chamber door he paused, but only for a moment, and then threw it open and entered.

Margaret was lying, her back to him, on the bed which faced the window that still admitted the wan gloaming light of a July night. Alarmed, she raised herself on an elbow, to gaze over a white shoulder. She remained thus, gazing, wordless.

He closed the door behind him, less than gently. "I have come," he jerked.

"Will . . .! What . . . what is this? Is aught . . . is aught wrong? Amiss?" It was not often that Margaret of Galloway sounded at a loss, unsure.

"That is for you to say." His voice was harsh, sterner than he knew. "Today you told James Stewart and his queen that I had failed you. Not given you a son. That, I would not have you say."

"I did not say that," she protested. "I said that *I* had failed. To give *you* a son."

"It is the same. So I have come."

"But . . . but . . ."

"You do not want me? Now I am here?"

"No, no. Or, yes. I . . . I do not know. You gave me no warning."

"As much warning as you gave me! That you held this against me. Today. But I will go again. If you wish it. Shall I go?"

For long moments she stared, hesitant. Then she moistened her lips. "No," she said, strangle-voiced.

"Aye, then." Nodding, almost grimly, he began to take off his clothes.

She turned back to face the window, silent.

Presently, naked, he stood looking down at her — and at himself. She had drawn the bed-covers up, over her shoulders, not cast them from her or pushed them down. She did not stir, did not raise her eyes to him. He sensed no hint of any desire in her, for him. And, Heaven knew, his own desire was wholly absent, dead.

But he was committed. Stooping abruptly, he threw back the covers and lay down beside her.

She did not turn to him, did not move, almost she did not breathe.

He lay there on his back, looking up at the ceiling. Their bodies touched in places, inevitably, for this bed, though scarcely monastic in character, had not been made for conjugal abandon; presumably it was the sub-Abbot's couch. There was nothing of need or fire or passion in him.

After a little he put out a tentative hand to touch her — and she jumped as though an adder had stung her. Hastily he withdrew. He lay, waiting. He waited for her, and he waited for himself.

Some time later she stirred, and with tightest, controlled movement, turned on to her back. "I am sorry, Will," she whispered, brokenly. "You must forgive me. Bear with me."

"Yes," he nodded. "Wait you. It is . . . difficult."

"Thank you. You are kind . . ."

He could have snorted a mirthless laugh at that, for the waiting was for himself as much as for her. Crazy as it seemed — indeed he had not thought that it was possible for him — he lay useless to her. He, Will Douglas, whose problem with other women, hitherto, had been quite otherwise. Here he lay, naked, in bed with reputedly the most beautiful woman in the land, and not only did he not want her but could not take her. Admittedly she did not help him — but should Will Douglas require such aid? Humiliated beyond all words, he lay there cursing himself. And her. And Meg Douglas, who had uged him to his folly.

Will-power, it seemed, was of no use to him here. Strangely, this was something that determination could not achieve. But presently anger, sheer ire and resentment boiled up in him, and stirred him physically, curious substitute for the desire and passion that he lacked. In mounting and now cherished wrath, suddenly he began to be all man again.

There could be no more waiting now. Almost feverishly he turned and threw himself upon her. She moaned, and jerked her head from side to side. But she did not actually resist him, however little she did to aid him.

So, after three years, without tenderness or compassion or any joy, Will Douglas took his wife, in haste and violence, hating himself, not allowing himself to pity her, a man at war with himself and his fate.

At least it was over quickly, a travesty of the act of love. He flung himself off her, twisting away — not that he could remove himself far on this narrow couch. He lay thereafter in a turmoil of emotion, none of it pleasant.

Presently he heard her sobbing, at his back.

"I am sorry, lass," he declared harshly. "Sorry."

She did not answer, but turned over on her side, her sobs the deeper.

Though close, and touching, they had never been so far apart. He was waiting again — now only for time to pass.

It was with major relief that, some indefinite time afterwards, Will heard swift footsteps on the stone stairway outside, and a knocking at the door.

"Is my lord there, lady?" an urgent voice demanded. "My lord of Douglas? Is he with you?"

Will sat up. "Aye. What is it, man?"

"It's Wattie. I've sought you a' place, my lord. Livingstone is gone. Sir James. He has ridden off, cloaked and armoured. To the west. Wi' three others. I couldna find you . . ."

"Damnation! Wait, then." Will was off that unhappy bed and dragging on clothing, even as he spoke, his own man again. So it was in his wife's bedchamber that Wattie Scott would look for him last! He strode to the door.

"When was this?" he demanded of the man. A relay of his servants had been watching Sir James Livingstone, the Chamberlain, and the Lord Hamilton, ever since Stirling. "He was at the banquet."

"Aye, lord, I followed him frae there. He went frae the Abbey to my Lord Hamilton's lodging. He bided there a while. Then a messenger came. Ridden hard and long, by the looks o' him. Livingstone came out wi' him soon after. In a right hurry. Near running, he was. Back to his own lodging. Calling for horses . . ."

"He rode west, you say? Three with him? Hamilton? . . ."

"No. Three men-at-arms, just. My Lord Hamilton bided at his house."

"Aye. Well, go get the Master, Wattie. Get all my brothers. And the Lord Fleming." Fleming, though now a lord in his own right, was still master-of-the-horse to Douglas. "To come to my room. My own room. Quickly. Fleming to order horses ready. You have it? Then see to it . . ."

Will turned back to his wife, sitting up great-eyed now in the gloom. "The message has come for James Livingstone. As we guessed it would. He has ridden for the West. It looks to be the attempt we were warned of. I am for Stirling. Forthwith."

"And . . . and Jamie? . . ." she asked.

"Aye. And Jamie with me. All of us. This is a family matter, is it not?"

She nodded her lovely head. "Yes. It is. But . . . you will be careful, Will?"

He grinned suddenly. "I will be careful, never fear. And for your Jamie!" He stepped over the bed, and put out an impulsive hand to touch her long flaxen hair. "Forgive this night's folly, lass. Forget it, if you can. Stay my friend, if you will?"

Wordless she nodded, and gulped, as he left her there.

CHAPTER SEVENTEEN

THE Douglas brothers rode hot-spurred through the night, westwards, by Corstorphine and Abercorn and Linlithgow. For once they were all together, even young Henry, the priest-to-be, at sixteen the youngest archdeacon in the land; and Archie, Earl of Moray, had come down for the royal wedding from his northern fastness, though he had missed the games at Stirling. They rode alone, save for a few servants. Rob Fleming had remained behind at Edinburgh to whip up the remaining Douglas lords and lairds and to bring them on with all expedition.

At sundry points *en route* they checked that four fast-riding travellers had passed this way not long before.

Three hours' hard going brought them to the vicinity of Falkirk. Here was the Livingstones' main seat, Callendar House, where it behoved them to go warily. Already the eastern sky was lightening. Cautiously they circled to the south of the demesne, making for higher ground where, from the cover of trees, they could watch the house.

Will fretted as they waited. But the horses could well do with a rest — as indeed could some of the riders, who had been out of their beds for too long, during current festivities, and were unlikely to be in them again for longer.

An hour's wait, and the Douglases were rewarded. With the sunrise, a fairly large party, perhaps a hundred strong, rode out from Callendar House, westwards, on the road for Castlecary and Kilsyth. No banners or pennons fluttered over it, but the level beams of early sunlight gleamed on much steel and armour.

Johnnie was allotted his accustomed role of scout. With all the serving men they had with them, he was to shadow this Livingstone company and send back what word he could. Only allowing time for the others to get out of sight, Will and his reduced party turned north now, and set off at speed for Stirling by the low plain of Forth, ten miles further.

On the Burghmuir there they found the main Douglas host's encampment just stirring into morning activity, with breakfast fires sending up their smoke columns by the hundred. Their lord's unexpected arrival altered the scale and tempo of activity drastically. Soon trumpets were sounding everywhere, and men were buckling on armour and saddling horses.

Will, impatient as ever, was concerned to get away from Stirling just as quickly as possible. James Livingstone was still Keeper of the castle, and although it was almost certain that he was with the group of his people riding westwards, some of his minions could be replied upon to send him word of any large-scale Douglas movement. Fortunately Rob Fleming turned up, with the bulk of the lairds and officers of the great array, in little over an hour. Now there was no further delay. Each leader went to his own allotted place, and dividing the entire force into three, under the commands of Jamie, Archie and Hugh, with Fleming at his side Will led the way out of Stirling, south-westwards.

They headed directly into the Touch Hills, close at hand. This was the east end of a long range of medium-sized heights which, under the names of the Gargunnock, Kilsyth, and Fintry Hills, and the Campsie Fells, stretched all the way to the Clyde, separating the Forth valley from that of the Clyde's northern tributaries, the Kelvin, the Calder and other waters. In the empty recesses of these green hills, the Douglas host could move westwards hidden save from a few shepherds and moormen. Fleming himself acted as guide here, for this was his country, his paternal property of Cumbernauld lying on the southern slopes.

The trouble was that, though they were well hidden, they were also blind. Their present route and destination was vague in the extreme. Will's information, received from his spies over the last weeks, was that the Livingstones, recognising that their time was now short with the King almost of age and likely to take the rule into his own hands at any time — especially now that he was married and with potent foreign in-laws — had decided on a *coup d'état*. They would marshal all their not inconsiderable strength, and strike while the rest of the realm was preoccupied with the royal wedding festivities at Edinburgh. They already controlled many of the most strategically-placed royal strongholds, as keepers thereof. Lennox, chiefest of the non-royal Stewarts, and ever resentful at alleged indifference to his importance, was known to be in this plot. And Lennox and Hamilton, between them, controlled the entire lower Clyde basin, Glasgow, and therefore the West — as distinct from the Douglas South-West. The attempt, therefore, was almost certain to be made, in the first instance, in the West. Where, was Will's problem.

It need not have come to this, of course. Undoubtedly Will Douglas could have nipped the whole project in the bud, had he so decided — for he had known of it for more than a month. But any precautionary moves would have swiftly got back to the Livingstones, and they would have postponed all until another occasion. There would have been no proof against them, no means of bringing them to book, and they were too powerful to pull down other than by being caught red-handed. So Will had informed neither King, Chancellor nor Council. He had a personal stake in this, of course, as Margaret and others never failed to remind him. He had taken his own precautions, gathered his people under pretext of making a typical ostentatious Douglas show at the wedding, swearing his leaders to secrecy, so that even his own host had no idea that they were in fact mobilised on a war footing. He might officially be moving against the Livingstones in the realm's interest, as Lieutenant-General thereof; it was, in fact, as Black Douglas that he led his thousands through the Stirlingshire hills.

He was waiting now, of course, for a lead from Johnnie. But even so, he believed that he was on the right track, here in these green heights. No faction could intend to take and hold the West without first being sure of Dumbarton Castle, one of the strongest holds in the kingdom, dominating the Clyde estuary. The Livingstones already did that, with one of the sons captain thereof. But in theory at least it was a royal castle. In the event of revolt, it would be one of the first objectives of the loyalist forces. For Livingstone success in the West, it must be shown to all, from the first, as unassailably in their hands; and that would be best achieved by raising the standard of revolt conveniently near by. Dumbarton lay just where the western end of these hills reached the Firth of Clyde. If a secret assembly was visualised, it could hardly be better placed than somewhere in this area.

Johnnie's first courier reached them in mid-afternoon, with the word that the Livingstones from Callendar were on the Kilsyth road still, and past Haggs. They had been joined by a large body of Hamiltons from the Slamannan and Torphichen area. Kilsyth was still west by south of the Douglas's present position in the central Carron valley of the hills. They continued on their way up that river.

The next messenger found them, in the afternoon, near the March Burn in the Kilsyth Hills, vastly spread out now amongst winding narow valleys. He brought the information that the Callendar party was now past Kilsyth and making towards Kirkintilloch. But it was hard to keep them in view, for so many other groups, large and small, were making in the same direction. By the concentration, Johnnie reckoned that the assembly point must be near.

Kirkintilloch lay on the direct road to Dumbarton, and about seventeen miles east of it.

Will slowed his host's pace to a walk, amongst the sheep-dotted braes.

In the early evening, Johnnie himself arrived, weary but excited. He had discovered the actual rendezvous. North of the burgh of Kirkintilloch the shallow strath of the Kelvin was largely flooded and waterlogged. In this boggy desolation were a number of islands of higher ground. The largest of these, seventy acres or so in extent, according to Rob Fleming, was called Inchbelly. Today it was an armed camp, a stronghold without walls but surrounded by mire and swamp.

Fleming knew it and its neighbours well. Livingstone had chosen shrewdly, he admitted. These islands in the moss were approachable only by causeways through the mire. Guard these, and vast numbers could rest secure. A natural fortress.

Will looked at him grimly. "Or a death-trap!" he suggested briefly.

They pressed on through the valleys until they were due north of Kirkintilloch and the Kelvin — only, with a 1500-foot escarpment of hill in between. There, by the head-waters of the Birken Burn they halted, to wait and rest.

Or most of them did. Will himself, with his brothers and some of his captains, continued to ride, due southwards now, up the long green hill, making for a summit viewpoint in the ridge which Fleming called Cort-ma-law. They dismounted well before they reached the skyline, and moved up to it cautiously.

A great spread of country lay below them, south and west, in the evening light, to the far Lanarkshire hills where Clyde was born. In the foreground, patched black and emerald-green with bog, and gleaming with standing water, was the shallow strath of the Kelvin, not so much a valley as a flood plain. The islands in its prolonged morass were very evident from this height, cattle-dotted, for they made good pasture. The largest of them all, that furthest to the west, was now supporting more than cattle, however. Even at this three or four miles range it could be seen to be black with men and horses, a great armed camp, from which the blue smokes of cooking-fires rose into the evening air to rival those of the grey town of Kirkintilloch, which lay on the south shores of the moss a mile or so further off.

For long the Douglases lay and watched it all, eyes busy not so much with the camp area itself as with the approaches thereto, and covered routes through the foothill slopes. Rob Fleming pointed out various features, accesses, advantages to use, problems to avoid. At length, reasonably well satisfied, they turned downhill again.

Hidden in that deep valley the host waited, resting, sleeping, until dusk. Then they moved off, in their companies, not up the hill directly, but still westwards into the side-valley of a subsidiary burn which swung gradually southwards as it climbed towards a deep gap in the long ridge. They had to ride in single-file now, in this narrow, mounting corridor — and six thousand horsemen in single-file form a long, long column. Progress was very slow. But there was little hurry.

It was as dark as it would ever be, for a July night, when the leaders reached the high pass between the north-flowing burn and the south-flowing headstreams of the Antermony Water. Picking their difficult way down the latter's deepening ravine, in the gloom, was a grievous progress; but at least, by following this burn down to its junction with the Kelvin marshes, they were assured of a covered and fool-proof route to their objective.

It was after midnight before they won out of the dark hills and into the pasturelands which slanted down to the great mosses, where shadowy cattle plunged away from them in stiff-legged alarm into the deeper gloom. Will was interested in those cattle. He sent men to round up as many as they might. Presently they moved on, their already difficult progress further complicated by a drove of a hundred or so protesting bullocks.

There could be no hiding their presence now — but Will was

not greatly concerned at the lowing noise. Leaving Hugh and Archie in command, he rode ahead with Johnnie and Fleming. Rob, who hunted here as a youth, for roe and wildfowl, said that the causeway out to Inchbelly stretched from the south side, from the direction of Kirkintilloch. To reach this entailed a fairly wide circuit to the west, to avoid the head of the moss.

Most of the fires on the island itself had now died down, but just ahead one burned brightly, far from the others. Fleming believed this to be on the south shore of the morass — and if so, it probably represented a guard-post at the landward end of the causeway. Circumspectly the trio moved round to inspect. They dismounted, to creep close.

Now there was no question. About a dozen armed men stood or sat around a well-doing fire at a point just above the dark edge of the reed-sea. Every now and again one or a pair would stroll off northwards, into the marsh. Clearly this was a picket to watch the causeway-head. They did not appear to be in the least suspicious or over-watchful — why should they be? They were in the heart of their own country, the merely formal guard at an assembly-point of formidable natural strength.

Leaving Johnnie to watch them, Will and Fleming made their way back to the others, easily found in the darkness by the lowing of uneasy cattle. There Will called together the leaders of the host, to give them strictest instructions.

So when, presently, the long array moved forward again, it was led by a small dismounted group of rough men-at-arms who bore no Red Hearts on their breastplates, herding a drove of cattle-beasts, with much shouting, cursing and whacking. Silently behind came the serried ranks of Douglas. They made for the red pin-point of the watch-fire.

Johnnie joined them, to announce that all was as it had been. The guards were interested in the noise of the approaching cattle, but not evidently alarmed.

Redoubling the herding noises, the drovers pressed on. As they neared the fire and guard-point, two hurried forward into the glow of the flames. One, who was Will's own Wattie Scott, waved and shouted to the guards.

"Hey! You, there. This is the Livingstone's camp? Inchbelly, or siclike ungodly name? Guidsakes — we've been a' place, seeking you! In every devil-damned bog! Whitna place! Is this it? A curse on a' Livingstones!"

"Aye — Inchbelly," somebody answered. "Who a God's name are you? At this hour o' night?"

"Hamiltons. Hamiltons frae Stra'blane. Wi' beasts. Meat. Beef for the camp."

All the time the herd was being pressed on from behind, snorting and protesting, frightened by the fire. And behind that, hidden, shielded, came the Douglases.

The guards were clearly at something of a loss. Little doubt but that they had no orders to deal with such an eventuality as this. "Where you going wi' your beasts?" one of them called.

"Sakes, man," Wattie returned, "we're no' going any place! We've *come*! Guid kens we've come plenty! Been in every accursed hole in the Kelvin! Let's oot to this camp. The laird's there, waiting on us."

"Och, man — there's ower many oot there, a'ready . . ."

But the cattle were now surging forward to the mouth of the causeway. If the guards made further protest, they were not heard in the snorting and puffing and shouting. One of their number, pacing the causeway-stones themselves, decided that he was in an unfortunate position, and turning, hurried away out to the island. After him the bullocks trundled in fine style.

When the first Douglas swords suddenly gleamed red in the firelight, at the back of the herd, the guards were taken completely by surprise and overwhelmed without the least resistance. More important, no sort of warning was shouted islandwards. On after the cattle the horsemen streamed.

The causeway, built of great stones, was perhaps ten yards in width and thirty times that in length. Its course was fairly clear, for tall reeds grew out of the marshland on either side but none grew on the causeway itself. Some of the trotting cattle may possibly have stepped or been pushed off into the deep, quaking mire; but most, certainly, made the crossing. In a compact, jostling, streaming mass they streamed over and on to dry land again — and any surprised folk awake at the far end could do little more than stare and perhaps shout uncertain warning to nearby sleepers. Probably few indeed saw the ranked horsemen who came in tight-packed files behind.

As the bullocks scattered trampling off beyond, to the alarm of various sections of the slumbering camp, the first Douglases across consolidated a secure bridgehead while leaving ample space for their new ranks to pass through. There Will took up his position, directing his squadrons left and right as required. So far, not a drop of blood had been shed.

The awakening of the sleeping host to what had happened was strangely, almost comically, gradual. Will had given orders that there was to be no unprovoked attack. His quarrel was with the Livingstone leaders only; he had no desire for slaughter of the rank and file. These, after all, were not enemies, but fellow-countrymen. So there was no sudden and comprehensive alarm. Trampling beasts rudely awakened some. Others, roused by the noise, peered into the gloom. Some saw shadowy horsemen, some did not. In the centre of the island, farthest from any commotion, tired men slept on. And here were the pavilions of the Livingstone leaders. No trumpets blew, no clash of arms sounded.

In time, of course, it penetrated to all that something was amiss. But by that time Inchbelly's island was entirely ringed with stern steel-clad ranks, facing inwards and sitting their horses in ominous and threatening silence. Even then, many of the awakened force had no idea who these might be, and no certainty that they were in fact enemies. When Will was satisfied that the steel circle was complete, and that sufficient confusion reigned within it, he led a tight group of his knights, pacing through the thronged encampment, to the grassy knoll where the tents of the foremost Livingstones were pitched.

An agitated young man, clothing awry, was slapping on the dew-drenched walls of a tent, shouting, and someone within was demanding what was to do, when Will tapped the shouter on the shoulder.

"Here's what's to do, Davie Livingstone!" he said, quietly, and jerked the other round.

It was the same individual, youngest son of Sir Alexander, who once, at Stirling, had interrupted the swording lesson with the boy King James and haughtily ordered Will to go to his father. He stared, now, in the gloom.

"Douglas!" he gasped.

"Aye, Douglas. Come to call a reckoning. Where is your father?"

"I . . . he is asleep. What . . . what is this? . . ."

'For Livingstones, with ill consciences, you sleep too sound, I think!" Will paused, as a tall thin figure emerged from the tent, with an older man behind. "Ah, Sir James!" he went on.

"We disturb your rest, after your long riding? I vow you would have been better to have bided in Edinburgh. Like my Lord Hamilton!"

"You! . . ." the Chamberlain whispered, starting back as though he had been struck. "God's name — how came you here?"

"Say that I came smelling treason! The stink of it is strong enough, i' faith! Take me to your father."

"I'd counsel you to watch your words, Earl of Douglas . . ."

The older man spoke, William Livingstone of Kilsyth, younger brother of old Sir Alexander. "What do you here? On *my* land!"

"If this is Livingstone land, then it will not be for much longer!" Will told him, briefly. "Where is Sir Alexander?"

"Here's a page says he is in this tent here, Will," Jamie called.

They strode over to a square silken pavilion, more apt for a tournament than a campaign in the field. They heard the thin, high-pitched voice, querulous, angry, within. Without ceremony, Will threw open the flap, pushing aside the page, and entered, his brothers at his back. "Bring light, a torch," he ordered.

A volley of swift-fire and furious obscenity greeted them, shrill, venomous, vehement. Here indeed was the man they sought.

A smoking, flaring pitch-pine brand was brought, to reveal the small, shrunken, twisted figure on the litter, sitting up under plaids, fully clad but wearing a night-cap on his over-large head. But though he might have seemed a figure of fun, none thought to smile. Laughter, other than his own cackle, came but unreadily in the presence of this man, Guardian of the King and principal Justiciar of the realm. He was not cackling now; indeed the sibilant stream of vituperation that issued from Alexander Livingstone, then, had some affinity with the hissing of a sriking snake in its sheer virulence. Even Will Douglas had to draw on his hardihood to withstand the threat of it, unflinching.

"Alexander Livingstone," he said slowly, flatly. "Douglas has come for you. At last."

The other's shrill tirade came to an abrupt stop. For

moments there was silence, save for the hissing splutter of the torch. Then the little man spoke, almost conversationally, in his normal squeaking voice. "Hech, hech — so it's the Douglas laddie again! Uncivil. Aye, uncivil, I call it, breaking in on an auld done man's sleep, this way. Awa' wi' you, now. I'll see you the morn, my lord — no' now."

"You'll see more than me, the morn! You'll see six thousand Douglases, sir! Surrounding all your camp. But meantime, see you me. And my brothers. You'll mind, once I said to you that you would not treat me as you treated my cousin, the Earl William? Him that you murdered, with *his* brother. Because *I* had five brothers — and I had not brought them with me, for you to seize. So that each could be Earl of Douglas after me. Now, Alexander Livingstone, at long last I have brought them. They are all here. Come for you! Jamie. Archie. Hugh. Johnnie. Harry. You have run your bloody course, man. This is the end of Livingstone."

The other's quick throaty breathing rasped. He did not speak.

"I could run you through, here and now. Or hang you from the nearest tree. It would be just, well-earned. But you have a liking for trials, have you not?" Will was speaking now, forcefully, dark eyes narrowed, fists clenched. "You are the Justiciar! Aye, you gave the Earl William a trial. Of a sort. And his brother. Before the King. And *then* murdered them. Then the axe. Your guests. So be it. You shall have your trial. Before the same King. You and yours. And then, again, the axe! Not clean steel, now. That I promise you — on the word of the Black Douglas!"

"Word! Aye, words! Just words — loud, vaunting words!" Livingstone all but screamed, his little, lined ferret's face contorted with hate and fury. "By Christ God — you can do nothing against me! Nothing! Slay me now, if you dare, you braggart loon! For you'll no' do it after. I am still James Stewart's governor. He's no yet of age. I am Justiciar . . ."

"And shall have your justice! You are taken, here, in open and frankest armed rebellion against the King's Grace. In highest treason. I have waited for this, Livingstone, all these years. *You* I have now. Then it will be Crichton's turn. Both the jackals! So prepare yourself. At first light, I, Lieutenant-General of this kingdom, take you bound to the King, and Council,

285

at Edinburgh. You and all your brood. To face your assize."

"Words, I say! Vain belly-rumbling! . . ."

"Enough of words, then." Abruptly, almost savagely, Will swung on the others. "Hold him. As you value your lives! He raised his hand against Douglas! Hold him fast. And all his kin, his crew of sons and brothers and cousins. Bring them all before me, bound. You hear? Forthwith."

Pushing them all aside, his own brothers and friends, William, Earl of Douglas, strode out of that tent, into the night.

Presently, indeed, they were all arrayed before him, in the light of blazing fires — Sir James, the heir, High Chamberlain, and captain of Stirling Castle; Robin, captain of Dumbarton Castle; John, captain of Doune Castle; Alexander, of Dunipace; David, of Greenyards; all sons. Robert, of Westquarter, keeper of Linlithgow; John, of Bonnytoun; William of Kilsyth; brothers. James Dundas of Dundas, son-in-law. And numerous kin less close. Lennox was apparently not in the camp; and though there were not a few Hamilton lairds, there were none close to James, Lord Hamilton himself. Will had intended to berate and harangue them. But suddenly he was tired, sick of them all, a man drained of anger, hate, of any emotion. After staring at them, at his blackest, for long moments, he shrugged and turned away.

"Whelps, lacking the old dog!" he said. "Others can whip them. Hold them, fast bound. I shall sleep. But wake me with the dawn. We ride, with the sun, for Edinburgh . . ."

*　　　*　　　*

James Stewart and James Kennedy, between them, lacked no resolution in this instance. The king had long years of bullying and harsh coercion to wipe out; and the Bishop had not forgotten ravaged Church lands in Fife, St. Andrews, and his famous cursing. And the Privy Council saw clearly on which side its bread was presently buttered; Lennox absented himself and only the Lords Hamilton and Gray spoke up for the Livingstones — and prevailed nothing. Sentence of forfeiture of all property, reduction from all offices, and final execution, was passed on the entire family.

In the end, all were not slain, though not a few went to the block. That two of his sons should have been shortened by a head while old Sir Alexander himself escaped the axe, is perhaps typical of the course of justice in other eras than 15th-century Scotland; however, the old sinner was kept confined in the damp vaults of Blackness Castle, by the Forth, and his death undoubtedly hastened as a result, which was possibly a worse fate. Strangely enough, his eldest son managed to effect his escape from the same grim fortress, it was said with King James's concurrence, and fled to the Hebrides. Many were the wonderings about this eventuality; but it was known that James Livingstone had amassed a large fortune, no doubt hidden away securely — and thereafter the monarch appeared to be much less straitened financially than formerly. But for the rest of the family, it was the end of the road. The Livingstones' fall was of a magnitude and swiftness to satisfy almost all, even Margaret Douglas.

Will Douglas himself took little or no part in this punitive process. His part was played. A moderately grateful monarch and Council bestowed on him three smallish properties of the vast forfeited estates, Blairmakkus, Ogilface and Culter, and these he passed on to his brothers. He found the taste of vengeance somewhat bitter on the tongue.

PART THREE

CHAPTER EIGHTEEN

THERE, in the vast and crowded salon, where five thousand candles in a hundred great glittering crystal chandeliers turned night into day and set the amoretti dancing amongst the archangels and saints of the lofty coved plaster ceiling — there, amongst the crowned heads and the cream of Christendom's aristocracy, chivalry and beauty, in the Grand Salon of the Vatican Palace in Rome, Will Douglas took the two heavily-sealed packets which Rob Fleming had brought him, and turning into a nearby alcove, already filled by the statue of a beckoning naked nymph, there and then broke open one of the letters. Being the man he was, he chose to open first the one sealed with the arms of the Lordship of Balveny.

"The couriers say that they killed nineteen horses bringing these from Scotland," Fleming mentioned, at his back, his homely Scots voice, for all its concern, sounding reassuringly normal and reliable amongst all the high-pitched chatter and jabber around them.

Smoothing out the stiff thick paper from its folds, Will knitted black brows to read Johnnie's strong if uneven, angular script. Johnnie had never been the scribe of the family.

At Threeve of July 9.
Will I cunsal that you cum home. Al is not wel. The king is turned aganst Dugles I think. He has made Criton chancler agen, the Bp Kendy agreing wel. They say you are genral no mor. Your castel of Lochmabin is taken and thron doun. Also Crag Dugles is yaro, his Gce doing this his oun self. I gather much men but best you cum.

Yr loving bro
Jhon of Belvany.

"The fools! The treacherous, damned fools!" Will burst out, smashing letter and fist against the nymph's thigh. "God preserve us from fools in high places! And rogues! I but turn my back! . . ."

"Ill tidings, Will?" Fleming asked, anxiously.

Will thrust the epistle at him, wordlessly. He had left Johnnie behind, in Scotland, as commissioner and representative, in charge of the far-flung Douglas estates and interests, Johnnie being perhaps the most vigorous, single-minded and able of his brothers, although only twenty. But here was work beyond Johnnie. Deadly work. Crichton again! . . .

"James Stewart digs his own grave!" Fleming jerked. "What sort of king is this, who stabs in the back his own friends? And this Bishop! Churchmen I never trust! What does the Lady Margaret say? She has more wits than the Lord Balveny."

Will tore open the seals of the second package. Here was a longer letter, a deal more neatly written. It was also headed from Threave and dated two days earlier than Johnnie's.

My good lord,

It is my hope that you are in good health and find the long journeying none too great weariness. It is now seven long months since you are gone, and for myself I weary for your return.

Perchance that may be more soon than might have been, for I fear I must send you tidings but little to your liking. Much has gone amiss in this realme since you have left it. I misdoubted this embassage from the beginning, you will mind. It is most clear now that the Bp. of Sa. Andrews did envisage it but to get you furth of Scotland. With your friends. And now he has his way. His Grace well pleased, I vow. The more so with her Hieness now big with childe. You are like to be heire but little longer.

His Grace has assumed the full rule and governance, declaring himself of full age, albeit he yet lacks ten months. So that all offices of the crown made in his minority do fall in. Bp. of Sa. Andrews is resygned and given the seales to that evil man and your enemy Crichton, who is now again Chancellor, and very chiefe with His Gce. Did I not tell you, my lord, that you should have dealt well with him long ere this? Now it may be ower late.

His Gce declares now that he has no need for other General than himself. So it is that you are no more Lieutenant of this kingdom. That done, he declares that there is great skaith, robbery and violence done to honest lieges on your lands and by your representers, and that your brother Balveny does permit and condone these and so is in rebellion. Johnnie is less wyse than you are, God knows, and makes mistakes, but this charge is untrue. So His Gce has acted his own General and has struck at your castles of Lochmaben and Craig Douglas, raizing them bothe. What next he will do the good God knows. It is Crichton's work, to be sure. Would that you were here.

I pray you to send me word and your commands, for I esteem this matter gone beyond Johnnie. I constantly do seek God's blessing on you, my lord, and send my true wifely devotion. I beg you give my sisterly affection to Jamie, for whom I also pray. Meg desires that I send you her duty. She sais that you should come home forthwith, for Scotland does have more need of Douglas than does His Holines.

Margaret of Galloway.

Will did not hand this letter to Fleming. Thrusting it into his silken doublet, he said, "It is worse. Worse than Johnnie knows. Seek me an audience of the Pope, Rob. To take our leave. We ride tomorrow."

The other sighed. "Aye. It is necessary. I am sorry."

"Yes. Send the others to me."

Eyeing the gay and glittering throng around him as he waited, Will Douglas pondered on power and what it did to men, to the wielders as much as to those on whom it was wielded. What had power done to him? He knew well that he was not the man that he had been only a few short years before. He had lost something, lost much — eagerness, ardour, faith. hope. Aye, and charity also. Lost faith in himself, as well as in others. Since, in face of the demands of power, he knew that all would crumble, himself and his better desires, with the rest. This was the bitter fruit of power. And what had he gained, beside the power itself? Yet he had not deliberately sought power. It had been thrust upon him. But neither had he rejected it. As Jamie would have done. But with power there were no half-measures. You either wielded it, or were wielded by it.

He was surrounded by power here, God knew. Everywhere he looked he saw it, and something of its effects. Probably seldom before had so much concentrated power, the might of Christendom, been brought together in one place as in this Papal Jubilee of 1450. Here were kings, electors, princes, grand-dukes, rulers of every description, power personified.

Moreover, here was the acme of that other power, almost more dreadful, over the mind as well as the body, in the shape of the Pontiff himself, the Holy Office, the cardinals and archbishops. And what did he actually see? Handsome clothes, colour, magnificence, brilliance everywhere — and darting uneasy eyes, cruel mouths, forced laughter, suspicion, envy, malice, fear. In this Vatican Palace, the Church's heart, he saw more veiled savagery, more nakedness of women, more blatant whoring, concubinage, perversion, more flagrant sins of the flesh, than he had even imagined to exist. In the next alcove to his own a slobbering pimply youth, who could not have been more than seventeen, in the scarlet of a cardinal, had all the upper half of a laughing complaisant woman exposed, save for her sparkling jewellery, and was tugging and biting at her white flesh like an animal — with none caring. Near by, on the floor, when the dancers parted sufficiently for him to see it, lay the over-dressed, bloated and drunken body of the man who had earlier been pointed out to him as the reigning Duke of Tuscany. Not far off, on the marble steps to a gallery, were two exquisites, painted and beribboned, who fondled each other shamelessly before all. One was said to be the love-son of a previous Pope.

These, then, were some of the fruits of power. And now these letters, carried hot-foot to him across Europe, spoke of other fruits. He was not so greatly surprised over James Stewart. Kings were ever a law unto themselves, preoccupied with power, suspecting all — and that young man had served a griev-ous apprenticeship. But Kennedy he had esteemed an honest, able and trustworthy man. Yet Margaret was undoubtedly right. Kennedy it was who, as both Primate and Chancellor, had declared that Scotland must indeed be represented at the Papal Jubilee. And who more suited to do it than the illustrious Earl of Douglas, next in line to the Throne — since priests in Holy Orders, such as himself, might not be so. Who moreover had insisted that, as well as all the Douglas brothers and in-laws, a further brilliant entourage should accompany him, for the honour of Scotland — naming the Lords Hamilton, Graham, Seton, Saltoun and Oliphant, and numerous knights, in fact all the magnates who might have been expected to resist the raising up of Crichton once more, and any assault upon Douglas. Will had accepted the embassage, and the vast expense involved — for it was out of the Douglas purse all had to be paid, the Treasury being, as usual, empty — not because of any special regard for the Papacy but as a patriotic duty, an opportunity to see the world, and perhaps, just a little, to further enhance the name of Douglas. And this had been the reason for it all — a deep-laid assault, conceived in that lofty, reputable episcopal brain, a device to bring down a friend and raise up an enemy — all in the interests of power, and its balance.

Hugh was the first of the Scots party to return to Will's side. Hanging on his arm was a bold-eyed, raven-haired Roman beauty, somewhat older than his twenty-two years, with red-painted nipples peeping provocatively over the top of her pearl-encrusted gown. Even as Hugh asked his brother the reason for the summons, his eyes were straying speculatively to the busy cardinal in the other alcove.

'I'd counsel you to bid the lady goodnight, Hughie — rather than what you contemplate!' Will told him. 'We go to take leave of the Pope. By this hour tomorrow I hope to be in Perugia.'

'Save us — what's this? Take leave? We are here for yet a month . . .'

"Lochmaben and Craig Douglas are smoking ruins. King James himself made them so. Crichton is Chancellor again. So we ride."

"Christ God!" The Earl of Ormond dropped his contessa's arm as though it had bitten him.

"Aye. And we are a thousand miles and more from Scotland! See — go you and help Rob Fleming fetch in the others. Yonder, is Archie, with the Frenchwoman. And Seton, with that fat duke."

It was strange how the Scots did, in fact, stand out in all that crowded company, seeming somehow more taut, stocky, compact, whatever their personal build, more sober of dress — although all were in their best clothing — altogether more self-contained and controlled than almost all the rest of that vivid gesticulating, demonstrative throng.

Fleming was back before all were assembled. His Holiness would see them now, in an ante-chamber.

Will gathered his people round him in a knot and told them briefly of the situation. But he pointed out that whilst he and those closest to him would start the long journey back to Scotland at the earliest possible moment and with all speed, some of their lordships were not so immediately concerned and need not all cut short their visit. However, all looked equally concerned at the news, and none was for remaining behind.

A gorgeously bedecked Papal chamberlain conducted them by marble corridors and statuary-lined galleries to a much-guarded doorway.

There was, Will knew, all sorts of elaborate ceremonial prescribed for Papal audiences, most of it of a sort that no self-respecting Scot would consider for a moment. He had gone as far as he was prepared to do, in this respect, on their initial interview. Now he contented himself with bowing once just inside the anteroom doors, then striding forward to within a few feet of the thronelike chair, and bowing again shortly. Behind him the cluster of Scots lords did exactly likewise.

"Your Holiness," he said, in his stilted student's Latin. "I regret that we must take our leave. Without delay. It is unfortunate. To return to Scotland. We seek your permission to leave Rome." And, as an afterthought. "And your blessing."

Pope Nicholas the Fifth, born Tomasso da Sarzano, was a major improvement on most of his immediate predecessors. A scholar and a bibliophile, he had not filled the Curia with his bastards nor the bishoprics with those of his friends. An ageing, short-sighted, hulking man, with an underhung jaw and long chin, he looked a gentle pedant of farming stock; but he had the name for being strong, shrewd, even cunning, and where necessary, ruthless — indeed no man attained the Chair of St. Peter lacking those qualities.

"If you must go, I regret it also, my son," he said, in a strangely light and musical voice. "It had been my hope to see much more of you, and my other friends from far Scotland. But, alas! Do I understand that you have received a summons from my son in God, King James, your master?"

Will coughed. "In a manner of speaking — yes, you could say that. Serious problems have arisen in the government of our country, and we must return." He gestured around him. "We here are all members of His Grace's Privy Council . . ."

"Ah, yes. So many important lords, far away at one time, could create problems in government, to be sure." However myopic, the Holy Father's eyes did not lack keen discernment.

"But does not the good Bishop of St. Andrews hold the government in sure hands?"

"The Bishop is no longer Chancellor. The office, we hear, is again in the blood-stained hands of Sir William Crichton, whom Your Holiness will know of — a murderer and despoiler."

If Will had hoped to obtain Papal condemnation of Crichton, he was disappointed. "Ah, is that so?" Nicholas said smoothly. "A change of hand on the helm of state can often be unsettling. You have our good wishes, my son."

The Scots had come for more than that. Indeed they had specific requirements still to attain, as some return for the handsome gifts the embassage had brought to the Holy See.

"Yes, I thank you. But, may I remind Your Holiness that there are the two matters outstanding? On which we seek your favour. That of the archbishopric for St. Andrews. And the Bull for a university at Glasgow. We would not wish to leave without these being resolved."

These two issues, developments which only the Pope had authority to sanction, were indeed the primary reason for the entire elaborate and expensive visit, using the Jubilee as an excuse. It went against the grain for Will Douglas to act the petitioner for the advancement of James Kennedy to the status of archbishop, but such move was desirable in order finally to invalidate the long-held, much trumpeted but utterly groundless claim of the Archbishops of York to metropolitan domination over Scotland, as nearest senior churchmen — a convenient excuse for English invasion. The other plea was in the nature of a counter-balance. A second university in the land would undoubtedly be an advantage, but not solely in the interests of education. John Cameron was dead, and the new Bishop, William Turnbull, a very different sort of priest, was almost equally concerned at the growing dominance on the Scottish ecclesiastical scene, of St. Andrews, especially with a king's grandson as Primate. If now made an archbishopric, St. Andrews would indeed dominate all. A new university under the Bishop of Glasgow would be a step in balancing spiritual power — and Will Douglas, as the greatest noble of the South-West, was not averse to the idea.

The Pontiff sat back in his throne. "I have given these questions some thought," he observed genially. "I am prepared to grant my rescript for the founding of a university college at Glasgow, with all accustomed privileges as at my university of Bologna, under the governance of the good Bishop of Glasgow. As to the other matter, my son, I have not yet come to a conclusion." He turned his head. "Aeneas Silvius, my friend — you have the question of the Scots archbishopric clear in your mind, have you not?"

"Yes, Holiness — in so far as anything is clear in that mist-shrouded land!" From the back of the room a man, who had been standing quietly in a corner, limped forward, a dark stooping crow of a man, with a thin, twisted body, a clever face and a mocking sardonic mouth.

Will eyed the speaker curiously. So this was the famous Aeneas Silvius Piccolomini, Bishop of Trieste and Papal aid — indeed some said the mind if not the power behind Nicholas; at any rate, one of the cleverest men in Christendom. An earlier pontiff had sent him as legate to many lands, including Scotland — where unfortunately he had been shipwrecked off Dunbar and, in his extremity, had vowed his Maker and all saints concerned a barefoot pilgrimage to the nearest saint's church if his life was spared. In consequence, thereafter, he found himself faced with a six-mile tramp over frozen ground to the church of Whitekirk, near Tantallon. He had never ceased to blame his chronic rheumatism on that distant and deplorable land — and to eschew the making of rash vows.

"And the situation is, Aeneas? . . ."

"That here is an issue of great complexity, Holiness. St. Andrews, although much the richest see in Scotland, is not the oldest. Its first bishop was consecrated in the year 908; while St. Ninian was consecrated in 397, founding the see of Galloway, at Candida Casa. St. Kentigern founded Glasgow in 543; and the sainted Columba founded the see of The Isles, at Iona, later the same century. So three others claim seniority to St. Andrews."

'Ah," said the Pope.

The Scots were not a little surprised to hear this Italian talking so knowledgeably about their land, apparently with authority. None were in any position to controvert what he said.

"Moreover, despite its riches," Piccolomini went on, "St. Andrews has failed to support the Holy See in duty and treasure, so well as others, failing to pay its annates in full. To raise it above all other twelve sees, therefore, in stature, might well give rise to much question and division within Holy Church."

"You discern the difficulties, my son?' Nicholas said benignly.

Will discerned the message, at least. Until further money was forthcoming, Scotland could do without its archbishopric.

"St. Andrews, being the Primate's see, must spend much of its wealth for the use and benefit of the whole Church in Scotland, sir." That was Jamie Douglas speaking up boldly from the rear — Jamie, who should have been a priest.

"If that is so, Holiness, and an undue proportion of the cost falls upon St. Andrews, then surely this is a matter of poor administration?" the wily Bishop commented. "Moreover, there is the question of *why* this archbishopric is so greatly desired at this juncture? The title of archbishop is not a sacerdotal order. Only an administrative office. The Church in Scotland therefore lacks nothing in ecclesiastical fullness in having no archbishop. Is this request, therefore, for the advancement of God's work and purpose, or merely for political advantage? Or indeed, for the advancement in stature of James Kennedy? . . ."

"Come come, Aeneas we may be sure that the good Bishop's motives are of the highest, concerned only with the better shepherding of his flock. Is that not so, my friends?" The Papal eyes twinkled.

Amongst his hearers, none felt able to stress the true reason for their request — especially as the Archbishops of Canterbury and York were both along there in the Grand Salon, heading the English delegation to the Jubilee, and undoubtedly in close touch with the Pontiff.

Nicholas nodded. "So you will perceive some of the difficulties which beset my decision. You must give me longer to come to a conclusion, my son."

"Or mair siller!" Hughie muttered, sotto voce, in good Scots.

Will inclined his dark head. "I will tell His Grace and the Bishop. They will be much disappointed." He glanced around him. "Have we Your Holiness's permission to retire?"

"But yes. Indeed." The Pope raised two fingers. "Go in

peace. And may God's light illuminate you all, His care enfold you, His strength sustain you, His love keep you. In the name of the Father, Son and Holy Spirit, I confidently commit you and yours to the Almighty. Goodnight to you." And he held out the other hand, for each of them to kiss the Papal ring.

Will caught Piccolomini's amused eye as he turned away. He was frowning blackly, well aware how far out of his depth he was here, a simple man and no diplomat. He should have let James Kennedy come himself, to do his own work, not left him at home to undo his!

*　　　*　　　*

If the gallant and splendid Scots company, consisting of the three Douglas earls, and over a score of lords and knights, escorted by eighty men-at-arms, which rode in a headlong flourish across Europe north-westwards, was not quite so assured and confident as it seemed, then its principals' turmoil of mind was well matched by the state of much of the territory through which it hurried in such princely style; for despite all the apparent amity and accord seen at Rome's Papal Jubilee, Christendom was in fact in a sorry state of internecine strife and savagery that Year of Our Lord 1450. King fought with king, prince with prince, elector with elector, and the Emperor with all and sundry. Even the Papal States themselves were largely at each other's throats, and bishops were as fond of the sword as were dukes. In comparison, Scotland's own upheavals certainly seemed the less dire, even though this by no means slowed down the progress of the home-going embassage. What did slow it down was the frequent and inevitable detours and deviations to avoid areas of open warfare and devastation. By Tuscany, Florence, Bolognia, the plain of Lombardy and Milan, the story was the same. The Alpine passes and the high Bernese Oberland offered a temporary respite from hostilities, even though problems of travel and altitude took their place. But once they started descending again into Lorraine, they were back to the vivid evidences of power politics and man's inhumanity to man. All France not only showed the scars of English Henry the Fifth's wars of conquest, but in the vacuum left by his death and the English withdrawal, every local princeling and count now struggled for territory, for advantage.

Here the Scots learned that the situation had changed even since their outward journey. With the English quarrelling at home as to whether the house of York or Lancaster were to control the imbecile Henry the Sixth, their armies and morale were weakened in France. The news was, now, that they had been driven right out of Guyenne, held by England for three centuries, and even the last toe-hold of Bordeaux fallen. Little as they loved the Auld Enemy, and their sympathies rather with their traditional allies of France, the Scots were much concerned that at least the Pas de Calais was still securely held by the English; for it was here, at Calais, that Hugh Brock's stout ship waited to carry them back to Leith.

By ravaged Hainault they came down to the flat coastal plain, and were relieved to find the English still in uneasy possession. The party held English safe-conducts for this journey, bargained for as part of Hotspur Percy's ransom. Indeed, on the way south, they had actually sailed up the Thames to pay a courtesy call at the English Court, for negotiations were afoot for a new truce between the two countries — after last year's defeats in Scotland, dynastic troubles at home, and this new upsurge of war in France, the English wanted peace on their northern borders. While in England, Will had had a secret meeting with Richard, Duke of York; for his information was that the Yorkists were likely to gain the upper hand eventually in the struggle to control fatuous King Henry — and it happened that King James adhered to the other side, his late unhappy mother, Queen Joanna Beaufort, having been a Lancastrian, indeed sister of their leader, the Duke of Somerset.

Now, at Calais, the English had significant news, encouraging for Douglas even if it was of doubtful joy to the tellers. Somerset and the Queen's party had been overthrown, in England, and York now controlled the King and the destinies of the realm. Will Douglas, in this at least, had outmanoeuvred his monarch.

How much such backing of the right horse might mean was dramatically demonstrated in a remarkably short time thereafter. The north-sailing Scots vessel had passed the North Foreland and was tacking into a stiff north-easterly breeze when a small, fast English vessel put out from the Thames estuary, to quickly overhaul them. To the Scots' surprise. as it

300

drew near, it ran up not the St. George's Cross but the Royal Standard of England, quartering the Lilies of France.

Soon a voice hailed them, in the name of the high and mighty Prince Henry, King of England and France, to know if this was the ship of the illustrious Earl William of Douglas. If so, His Majesty's Garter King of Arms made salutation, and conveyed the greetings of His Royal Highness the Duke of York, with the urgent invitation of His Highness to visit him forthwith at the Palace of Westminster, to their mutual advantage.

Will was not a subject for flattery, but such treatment, amounting almost to the greeting for a reigning sovereign, was surely significant as well as intriguing. And the phrase 'mutual advantage' must mean something. Moreover, to refuse such a summons, in English waters, would be a serious snub. He ordered Hugh Brock to turn back.

The delay caused by the journey up-river to London, and the two days spent thereafter at the English Court, almost certainly was worth while if for nothing more than the information gained. Nevertheless, none of the Scots — except perhaps for the Lord Hamilton — found the visit a cause for joy, and quickly all were concerned to cut it as short as possible.

It was the Duke of York's tidings to Will, imparted glee-fully, that upset them. The Duke, who knew all about the changed Scots situation, and King James's attack on Douglas, had, it seemed, a secret arrangement with John, 10th Lord of the Isles and Earl of Ross. Indeed, not to put too fine a point on it, that chief of Clan Donald, who looked on himself as an independent prince and no vassal of the King of Scots, was in receipt of an English pension as a potential trouble-maker for Scotland. Now, esteeming this an excellent opportunity to fish in troubled water, York had urged him to make a diversion. Nothing loth, for he was allied to the Livingstones by marriage, and had old scores to settle with the house of Stewart, John of the Isles and Ross had struck fiercely and without warning, from his island fastnesses, at the northern mainland. He had taken Inverness, with its fortress, and the castles of Urquhart, commanding the Great Glen, and Ruthven controlling Bad-enoch. All the north was potentially his. And he had a bond of association with the Earl of Crawford, and the Tiger had struck thereafter in the north-east. It now but required Douglas and his friends to rise in the South and West, and King James would quickly learn his folly and mistakes. England would lend her aid in the South and East. Crichton and Kennedy would fall, and James would be forced to seek better counsellors. Douglas could rule Scotland, either behind the throne or on it.

To say that Will was dumbfounded by all is to put it mildly. It is to be feared that he grievously disappointed the ingenious and ambitous Richard Plantagenet by his refusal to take over the rule in Scotland on any such terms — or indeed, to consider taking over the rule at all. Vehemently he pointed out to the Englishman that he was not interested in gaining personal control. He wished to bring Crichton down, but not at the cost of open rebellion against his king — treason. He would reason with James, bring pressure on him if need be — but he would not revolt. The Red Heart that Douglas bore on their arms was Bruce's heart, the King's heart. Douglas did not turn traitor.

York did not hide his mortification and chagrin, almost his disgust, and though they parted on outwardly civil terms, the Scots' departure from the Palace of Westminster was a deal less flattering than had been their welcome.

But, as they continued their interrupted voyage, however much some of his brothers and friends found satisfaction at least in the northern rising and its embarrassment for Crichton, Will himself discovered no cause for contentment. It was Earl Beardie's involvement that worried him. Crawford had a bond with John of the Isles, it seemed. But, unfortunately, he, Douglas, had a bond with Crawford — had had since the time of the Percy invasion. The suspicious might link the two bonds, the suspicious *would* link them. Ross — Crawford — Douglas. An encircling of the realm. Damn Beardie Alex Lindsay!

Arriving unheralded at Leith, the travellers learned that the King was in residence at the Abbey of Holyrood. They made their way there in a body. When citizens in the streets and wynds heard that it was Douglas back from foreign parts, they flocked out to wave and shout and cheer — a heartening sign. It seemed that these, at least, reckoned Scotland safer with Douglas home; changed days from his first visit to Edinburgh.

At the grey abbey beneath Arthur's Seat, however, the reception was different. Armed guards in the Crichton colours of blue and white challenged the party, demanding their business, halberds pointed.

'Fools!' Will snapped. 'Have you no eyes, no wits? I am Douglas!'

Though blinking a little at the fierceness of that, the spokesman held his ground. 'My lord's orders, The Chancellor's. None enter here lacking his express permission. I will inform him . . ."

"By God, you will not!" Wrathfully Will reached out hands to grasp the shafts of the two barring halberds, and jerked them aside strongly. "Douglas has been too long out of Scotland, I see! Out of my way, fools! My business is with the King's Grace, not with your master."

The guards hesitated, as well they might, and were lost. The throng of nobles thrust their way in, and were through. It was a long time since the Black Douglas had had to wait at any man's gate.

King James, however, kept them waiting for their audience. Will would have preferred a private and informal meeting with the monarch, in view of what would have to be said; but this was the return of an official embassage, and all its members should deliver their report together. In answer to their request for audience, James, although in the building apparently, remained out of sight and sent no message for almost two hours. None failed to grasp the implications.

At length, they were summoned to the presence, ominously, by a creature of Crichton's. He led them, to their surprise, to the refectory, the same large hall indeed where the royal wedding feast had been held, to beat slowly, ceremoniously, on the closed doors before entrance — to the snorting of those he escorted.

When the door was thrown open, it was to reveal the great chamber lined with two long rows of armed guards, stiff, silent. Away at the far end a throne had been placed on the abbot's dais. King James sat on it, while a man stood at each shoulder — Chancellor Crichton and Bishop Kennedy. Apart from the newcomers' escort, no person moved or spoke in all that scene.

Will's brows came down like a black bar across his features. As their guide, after a deep obeisance began to pace forward between the inward-facing rows of guards, and some of the

Rome party started to follow, Will, by a brief gesture, held them back, letting the man march on alone. This was quite ridiculous, treating the Douglases and all these other lords, some of the greatest in the land and all members of the Privy Council, to a display of stiff and formal audience-chamber ritual, as though they had been official foreign visitors or burghal suppliants, rather than James's own chief subjects and intimate associates. But however ridiculous, the significance of the thing was evident.

Will let their escort get more than halfway to the trio at the throne, in lonely dignity, before he nodded to his companions and led off at a businesslike stride up the lengthy approach, deliberately unsuitable for any ceremonial occasion. There were more grins than frowns on the faces of the returned embassage.

The King's own features were schooled to what was undoubtedly intended to be the stiffly expressionless. He sat his throne stiffly, too. But being an impulsive and active young man, he only managed to look thoroughly uncomfortable, his facial birthmark flaming, as it always did when he was embarrassed. He was much more richly clad than usual — normally he was careless about clothing — but he gave the impression that the fine wear had been donned especially and hurriedly for the occasion. He might as well have balanced the state crown on his head while he was at it, Will decided. Crichton standing just behind his right velvet-cloaked shoulder, was dressed all in black with silver facings, stooping, hooded-eyed, lined-faced but ageless. Will had not set eyes on him since that day, four years earlier, when he had watched him ride out of surrendered Edinburgh Castle and into ostensible obscurity. He should have struck then, as Margaret had desired, and saved Scotland this. James Kennedy, at the other side, had the grace to look almost as uncomfortable as his monarch and cousin.

The escort, bowing deeply again, began to speak, but Will Douglas cut him short.

"Your Grace — it is good to see you again, hale and well. Though in doubtful company! We greet you. The more joyfully in hearing that you have a fine son. A prince, for your throne. Good tidings to return to, Sire."

There was a polite murmur of agreement from the other lords.

James coughed. Obviously this was not the way the audience was planned to begin. "Yes. To be sure, I thank you, Earl of Douglas. All of you, my lords." He glanced up at Kennedy, uncertainly.

"The Earl of Douglas is the most kind," the Bishop said evenly. "In that he himself is thereby dispossessed as next heir!"

"A position I never sought nor cherished, Sire. And Her Grace? She is well? And the prince!"

"Aye. Well. Both well. But . . . we have other matters to deal with, my lords. You are returned early. From your mission. To the Pope. Months before it was to be. Why?" James brought that out in a rush.

"We heard, Sir, that you had trouble here in Scotland. Unrest. Ill men raising their heads." Will looked directly, if briefly, at Crichton. "Treachery and tumults. We esteemed our place at Your Grace's side. And so returned forthwith."

"And not before time!" Archie supplemented. "We had been gone too long already, it seems!"

"Though not long enough for my lord Bishop, perhaps?" Hamilton put in.

"Who conceived us best out of Scotland, that he might work his will unhindered," Hugh declared.

It was Will's turn to cough. He was no more happy than King James looked about the way the interview was proceeding. "We hastened home, Sire, to place ourselves at your service, as in duty bound. But we did not fail to fulfil our mission, nevertheless. In Rome. And in London."

"Ah, yes — the mission." James sounded relieved. "Your report, my lord. That is the reason for this audience. I hope you have good success to report?"

"Good success, and not so good, Highness. From Rome. His Holiness agrees to the founding of a university at Glasgow, and will grant a Bull to Bishop Turnbull to that end. But he will not yet raise the see of St. Andrews to an archbishopric. He declares the see behind in payment of its Papal dues. And he esteems Galloway, the Isles and even Glasgow, as all more ancient and therefore senior."

"And you accepted that, man?" the King demanded, leaning forward in his chair. "Knowing our will in the matter?"

"I am no churchman, Sire. It was not for me to argue these matters with the Holy Father! For any of us. You should have sent my lord Bishop himself! Then much might have been otherwise. There . . . and here!"

"Aye, by the saints!" Hugh cried, to a murmur of agreement from the others.

James clenched angry fists, making but ineffectual attempts to swallow his wrath. His hot temper undoubtedly was less under control than heretofore. The assumption of full kingship seemed to have had more results than one.

Kennedy spoke, taking the blow well. "It is no such grave matter, Sire," he said. "We are no worse off than before. We shall try again, when perhaps His Holiness more greatly needs Scotland's support! We could scarce expect my lord of Douglas to put himself out over this issue. He considered it a matter for churchmen, it seems — although indeed it is aimed at English claims against us."

A hot response rose to Will's lips, but he restrained it. "That I well understand, Sire. We did what we could. I told the Pope that Your Grace would be much disappointed. But we could scarce say that we sought this as a weapon against the English." He shrugged. "But at least, we did better with the English themselves. At London. They are prepared to discuss terms for another general truce. For a period of years."

"You say so. But what avail is such word now? All is changed there. The Protector, my uncle Somerset, is put down. York now rules. And he loves me not. He is against all my mother's house. My uncle's word of truce is now valueless."

Will cleared his throat again. This required careful speaking. "Aye, Sire. But we went back. Back to London. On our journey home. We had word that the Duke of Somerset had fallen and that York was now Protector. We learned it in France. So I saw the Duke of York. And he accepted the truce." James was bound to learn, sooner or later, of this second visit to London.

There was a moment or two of silence, as this news was digested. "You . . . you were very swift to act, my lord," the King said, distinctly grudgingly.

Will hoped that none of those behind him would blurt out the true circumstances of that second call at Westminster. Nothing would be more liable to make James and his present councillors suspicious and alarmed than York's flattering gesture towards Douglas.

Crichton had so far remained completely aloof, taken no part in the interview. Now, he stooped forward to the King's ear. "The Duke of York's rise may well be but temporary, Sire," he said in his flat, nasal, slightly hesitant voice that was so at odds with his character and performance. "The Duke of Somerset, and the Queen Margaret's party, are like to rise again. In matters of government, men can fall ... but rise again!" His heavy-lidded eyes lifted for a moment to Douglas's. "Was not my lord of Douglas ill-advised thus to recognise York, in the name of Your Grace and this realm? Unauthorised so to do?"

The gasps at his back, and the swift glance Kennedy shot at Crichton were eloquent of the sudden heightening of tension. But King James nodded quickly.

"You are right, my lord. Here was, here was presumption! The Earl of Douglas was given a mission to Somerset, not to York. It is for me to deal with England, and the English moves, not Douglas!"

"Your Grace was sufficiently glad for Douglas to deal with the English but a year ago!" That was jerked out of Will, despite himself, though he bit his lip thereafter.

"Aye — have you forgot Sark?" Hughie cried.

"The Earl of Douglas was then Lieutenant-General. He but did his duty. Here, I think, he exceeded it.' Crichton was cold, exact.

"Sire — this man?" Will demanded. "When last I saw him, he was under sentence for treason and armed rebellion! By what authority does Sir William Crichton now presume to declare Douglas's duty? He was not on the Privy Council which gave this embassage its instructions."

James took a long quivering breath. "He is now Chancellor of this my realm. On Bishop Kennedy's resignment of the office. As my chief minister he has the right and duty to speak in such matters. Of his great experience. And he is no longer Sir William. He is now a Lord of Parliament. Disagreements between him and my, my former advisers, are now overpast and forgotten. I have now taken unto myself the full rule and authority of my kingship — and I have all confidence in my lord of Crichton." If that came out in something of a rush, there was no doubting its determination.

Will looked at his monarch levelly, as the moments passed.

Then he inclined his head slightly. "As Your Grace decides. But there is one matter on which you, Sire, may be mistaken. You say that disagreements between this new lord and your former advisers are overpast and forgotten. It may be true with some. But with *this* former adviser it is not so! Douglas does not forget the murder of his kinsmen, even though Your Grace forgets open rebellion and treason against yourself!"

"God's death, man — you to talk of rebellion and treason! You, Douglas! With the North aflame with the rebellion of your friends and allies, Crawford and Ross!" In his suddenly increased rage, James Stewart rose to his feet threateningly. "Inverness sacked. My castles of Urquhart and Ruthven stormed, my servants slain. Ross, calling himself Lord of the Isles, declares himself independent of my rule! Think you that I do not know why you come home thus early? From Rome? It is because of your treasonable bonds with these rebels, I swear! You say that you return because you heard that I had trouble, tumults. I believe you, my lord! That I do! And who would know better of these troubles than you? You returned not to aid me, your liege lord, but further to injure me!"

Will stared at him. "You believe that?" he demanded. "Of me? What have I ever said, or done, to give you cause for such words? Have I not acted your friend from our first meeting at Stirling Castle, yon day? Who rescued you from the Livingstones' grasp? Who brought down this Crichton for you? Who found you a new Chancellor in this Bishop? Who drove the English invaders from your soil? Who brought Livingstone down at last? And now you would call me traitor?"

The pent-up intensity behind those words, the sheer vehement strength of the dark face confronting him, had their effect on the King — for Will Douglas roused was a more fearsome sight than he knew. James involuntarily stepped back and, his throne in the way, sat down heavily.

"How dare you ... to speak me ... the King ... so!" he panted.

Bishop Kennedy had been looking ever more concerned. Now he spoke up urgently. "Cousin," he said, "this serves no good purpose for any. Save your enemies. My lord of Douglas is no traitor — of this I am certain. Mistaken he can be — as can we all. Rash, indeed. But not treason."

Neither James nor Crichton spoke.

"His Grace knows that I am no traitor, my lord Bishop," Will went on. "What he says is, I think, but to hide other matters. Or another's spleen! I have no bond or alliance with the Isleman. What Crawford may have done is without my knowledge. Ever he was a man apart. But . . . it was not this that sent His Grace against my houses of Lochmaben and Craig Douglas. That was done before ever there was trouble in the North. Here was an unkindly act, unkindly done. But it was not done against a traitor. Else my greater houses would have been attacked and taken. Why it was done I have yet to be informed — although I have little doubt who advised it!"

"It was done, my lord, because these houses of yours were nests of violence and lawlessness," Crichton declared. "Your people were terrorising the country. Your Brother, the Lord Balveny, was warned. But he made no betterment. The King's peace had to be maintained . . ."

" 'Fore God, it was necessary!" James interrupted him. "Necessary. Your people act as though Douglas was king in this realm, not I. They had to be shown, *all* had to be shown, that it is not so."

"Aye," Will saw it all clearly enough, the resentment of a weak monarch for his strongest subject, egged on and played on by the clever malice of this evil man. Kennedy had raised the devil indeed, in his balancing of power. "If Your Grace, and my lord Bishop, saw me and mine as a threat to your throne — which God forbid — the sorrow of it that you had to raise up this man, of all men, against me! A scourge to your own backs! If it is the last counsel your true and leal subject and servant ever gives you — get rid of Crichton while yet you may!"

The Chancellor smiled thinly. "I fear that my lord is weary, Sire. After his long journey. Perhaps a little light of head! Who would wonder at it? Another time, perhaps, Your Grace? . . ."

"Yes," James jumped at the opportunity this offered. "Another time. It is enough for this day. Your reports to the secretaries, my lords. I thank you for your services." He stood up. "This audience is now ended. A good day to you." Turning, as all hastily bowed, he strode from the refectory with more hurry than dignity.

The Lord Crichton was not very far behind him.

"Are you satisfied, James Kennedy?" Will demanded of the Bishop, when the door had closed behind King and Chancellor.

That man spread his hands and then let them fall to his sides. "No," he said.

"Though no doubt you acted for the best!" Will's voice grated harshly.

"That is my hope. My prayer. This had to be, friend. Something of this sort. Douglas was grown too great in Scotland. There was coming to be no room for the King and Douglas both. Do you not see it?"

"I see an evil man raised up, to put me down. And I believe myself honest — as once I believed you to be, my lord."

"Honest? What is honesty, in statecraft? Who can touch it and remain truly honest, I wonder? The single mind and all innocence of heart become shut out by the door of the council chamber and the inner cabinet. If my honesty in this is soiled, my friend — who is to be thanked for it? Who besought me to meddle in affairs of state, who never wished to do so? Who, I say?"

"Aye. Would I had never ridden to St. Andrews, if this is to be the way of it. Ridden with that woman's glove!"

"This *had* to be the way of it! In the end. Can you not see it, man? I said then that Douglas had been for too long like a louring cloud, overgrown, threatening the land. Too powerful. I said, if Douglas had changed, then I rejoiced. But I doubted the change. And I was right. Douglas but grew in power."

"But ... of a mercy — I have not used the power to oppress — whatever Crichton says. I have used it to support the King ..."

"Here's the sorrow of it, my lord. *I* do not accuse you of misusing the power. Almost better if you had, perhaps — God forgive me for saying it! The power itself, it is, that is at fault. Too great a power, in honest hands, can be almost as sore a trial as in ill ones. You have cherished your power, not squandered it, so that it but grows and grows. You have used it to support the King, yes — but now, folk can scarce see the King behind your Douglas lances and swords! Today, the cry of 'A Douglas' in any street, in any field, will speak louder in every ear than will 'A Stewart!' or 'The King's Grace!' And this is, must be, to the realm's hurt — so long as Douglas is not king!"

Will drew a long breath, as the lords behind him stared at the Bishop, at each other, and whispered, at a loss.

"What, then, is to be the end of it?" he exclaimed. "What can I do? I cannot cast away the Douglas power. I cannot change Douglas men into other men. I cannot turn my back on the realm's needs. My father chose sloth — and men blamed him for it. What would you have of me?"

Kennedy spread his hands again. "Would that I knew the answer to that, my friend. If an answer there is. All that I know is that I am the King's servant, not Douglas's. And that the Douglas power must needs be kept from choking the King. For the King is the realm, in the end, and Douglas but a part of it. And the part must remain less than the whole. So in sorrow, I did what I did. And will do what I must do. And you ask me if I am satisfied! *Deus misereatur!*"

For moments the two men eyed each other. Then with a sigh and a shake of the head Will Douglas turned away, to pace slowly down between the double lane of stiffly, silent guards, without another word spoken.

CHAPTER NINETEEN

THREAVE, stern, towering, strong, was not built to look peaceful or gentle. But that late August evening, amidst the green rolling Galloway countryside, bathed with the mellow glow of a quiet sunset that reflected gold from all the lochs and spreading water-meadows which surrounded its island site, and painted purple shadows behind every tree and mound and battlement, it seemed as fair and tranquil a place to the Douglas brothers as any they had seen on their long travels, and a welcome haven to return to — to Will and Jamie, that is; Hugh was not of the sort, as yet, who found tranquillity and havens much to his taste. These three, with their escort of men-at-arms, rode down to it from the north; all the others of the Rome party had dispersed to their own places.

Their coming was known, and Johnnie rode out to meet them, a young man with much on his mind. He greeted them with a nice mixture of relief, indignation and apology, declaiming fervent thanks to his Maker that they were back, inveighing against the wicked ingratitude of their liege lord King James, the villainy of Crichton, Kennedy, Maclellan of Bombie, Herries of Terregles and sundry others, and pointing out that he had done all he could, taken every precaution possible, punished such transgressors as he was able to lay hands on, and salvaged what he could from the ruins of Lochmaben and Craig Douglas. The King's charges of rebellion and violence were false, sheer fabrication, excuses to attack Douglas when they were at a disadvantage. Lacking full authority, he was in no position to take the law into his own hands, and hit back against the royal perfidy. But now! . . .

Will waved his not normally so eloquent young brother to approximate silence. "Aye, Johnnie, aye. Peace lad, peace. Do not fret yourself. The bones of it I know. The rest I shall hear in due course. None blames you — save only those who would hurt us. I blame myself — for ever having gone away. Knowing James Stewart and his realm! I am to blame, not you, Johnnie. You have had an ill road to ride. But peace, now — enough of this meantime. It is good to see Threave again . . ."

Margaret and Meg were awaiting them at the inner Bailey, both looking at their loveliest, the one serenely beautiful joy other radiantly fair. But despite that, and Will's undoubted joy at coming home, there was a constraint, a reserve, at first. Husband and wife were glad to see each other — but each was still more glad to see another, and must try not to show it. So the greetings and welcome, though sincere and underlined with joy, were more formal than might have been. Quick side glances, hand-pressings and the like, had to say what words might not.

But later, well dined, in the cool of the dusk, they all six wandered out by the riverside pleasance to the little watergarden which was the girls' favourite haunt, and there amongst the kindly shadows they could be themselves, at ease, amongst the murmur of flowing water, the sigh of the night wind through the reeds, and the sleepy quacking of mallard from the lochans. Meg, from where she sat behind Will, could slowly stroke the back of his neck with soft fingers, and Jamie could sit close to Margaret and glow quietly in her proximity.

Although they talked mostly of foreign lands and strange sights, of kings and queens and princes, of the wonders of Rome and its follies and sins likewise, inevitably they kept coming back to the situation here at home, where so much was changed from heretofore. None could fail to recognise that the present state of affairs was not only unsatisfactory but dangerous, and must not be allowed to drift.

"The King should fear Douglas less, now that he is of age and has a son — not more," Meg said. "Why does he?"

"The man Crichton poisons his mind," Margaret declared. "But there must be more than that. And James himself has no cause to love Crichton."

"That is what I cannot understand," Jamie agreed. "Crichton has played the King's enemy for years. Why, then, should he now have raised him up?"

"Bishop Kennedy conceives him, I believe, the only man clever enough, strong enough, and willing, to set against Douglas," Margaret told him. "So says my mother. Who else, indeed, would have served?"

"Does he think that such a jackal could bring Douglas down?" Hugh scoffed.

"Jackals do not hunt alone," Johnnie said. "They find other jackals. And there are plenty in this kingdom, by the Rude! Nearer at hand than Crichton. There are vassals of your own, Will."

"Douglases? Siding with Crichton? Against me?"

"Not Douglases, no. But vassals of Douglas. Men who hold their lands of you. Herries, Maclellan . . ."

"Ah, yes. You said something of this when you met us. What is this? Herries is a witless fool. And Bombie but a boy."

"Not Bombie himself. His uncle, Sir Patrick Maclellan, Tutor of Bombie. And not old crazy Herries of Terregles. His brother Herbert, who acts governor to the young laird David. These two are traitors and knaves. They are kin, of course. These it was who provided the excuse for the King to ride against your castles, Will. They are both your sheriffs-deputy, mind, by inheritance. Or Margaret's, it may be. Herries, of Nithsdale and Annandale; Maclellan, of Kirkcudbright."

"What of it? What did they do?"

"They turned jackal, I tell you. Declaring that folk were refusing to pay their rents and dues, and so were rebelling against you in your absence, with one accord they went with fire and sword up and down parts of their sheriffdoms. Maclellan, in the Vale of Urr; Herries in Annandale, slaying and burning and harrying. And under Douglas banners! Claiming that they acted in your name. How many they slew, God knows — but Herries hanged a full score at Lockerbie alone!"

"Save us — but why, man? What had they to gain by this folly?"

"The King's goodwill. He had excuse to ride in wrath against Douglas. But not to Bombie or Terregles, mark you! They went free. He rode against Lochmaben and Craig Douglas . . ."

"But why these? Why Herries and Maclellan? I have never done them hurt, either of them. Why should these turn and betray me?"

It was Margaret who answered him. "Perhaps you do not know, Will. But David Herries, the young laird, is married now to Margaret Crichton of Sanquhar. And the Tutor of Bombie is sister's son to the Lord Gray and Sir Patrick Gray Captain of the King's Guard!"

"So-o-o!"

"I cannot believe this of the King!" Jamie exclaimed. "He is hot of temper. But not this! . . ."

"It may be that he himself did not know the truth of it," Margaret agreed. "It could have been all Crichton's doing, misleading the King. The Grays were ever of his party."

"Aye, Crichton! This sounds like his work. James Stewart is not of this sort. James wishes to pull down Douglas, yes. But not thus, I swear! This takes wits like Crichton's. A snake's cunning — and James is no snake." Will turned on Johnnie. "And you — what did you do? You said that you did what you could? . . ."

"Aye. I went, at once, to Annandale. With five hundred men. I caught Herries at it, red-handed. Up the Dryfe Water. He claimed that he acted as your sheriff-deputy. That I had no authority over him. So I put him in the pit of Lockerbie Tower. To await your return. He is there yet. Despite his folk's clamour."

"Good. I shall deal with Herbert Herries. And Maclellan?"

Johnnie cleared his throat. "Maclellan was . . . more difficult. When I went for Herries, I sent another to Maclellan. To his castle of Raeberry. Pate Pringle. And Pate . . . Pate Maclellan hanged!"

"Lord God!" Will was on his feet in a bound, fists clenched. "Pate Pringle? Dead? Hanged?" That was a whisper. "Hanged by Maclellan! God's curse on him — he slew Pate?"

"I rode to his castle. He shut his gates against me, Raeberry is a strong place. From its gatehouse he told me that I had no authority over him. He said that he had appealed directly to the King. That he demanded trial, for what he had done, before King James himself. He said that he had this right. That the Maclellans had been hereditary sheriffs of Wigtownshire before the Douglases or the Flemings, and though they had lost that office, they had not surrendered the right of trial before the King himself . . ."

"That I deny," Will declared. "*I* am Sheriff of Wigtown. Justiciar. Earl of Wigtown and Lord of Galloway. This man is a vassal under my jurisdiction. And, by the Mass, he shall learn it!"

"What could I do?" John demanded. "I was left your procurator, yes — but in this matter of jurisdiction I knew not where I stood. Moreover, already the King was thundering against Douglas. If Maclellan had put the matter to the King, I dared not make matters worse . . ."

"So Maclellan goes free?"

"Aye. To my shame! What could I do, Will? . . ."

The other was striding up and down the short stretch of path beside the water. "Pate Pringle!" he muttered. "Sir Patrick Maclellan has signed his own death warrant, by the Mass! Quiet, Johnnie! You could do nothing — I know it. But *I* can! And shall. My house needs setting in order, it seems. Tomorrow I shall start to redd it up."

There was silence in that garden for a while, not even of these his nearest kin caring to come between the Black Douglas and his wrath.

It was his Countess who spoke at length. "Here is great evil and sorrow," she said. "Much must be done, much thought of. But . . . it is an ill welcome home. A poor way to spend our first hours together after long parting. Let us talk of happier things, Will?"

"Yes," Meg supported her. "We have waited too long for this night to spoil it so, my lord. This would but please Crichton, I think!"

"You are right." Will took a grip of himself. He halted his

pacing, stood for a moment kicking at the turf, and then went to sit down again. But not, as before, beside Meg. He sat a little apart from them all, now.

Although they talked a while yet, determinedly, of other things, the ease and satisfaction had gone out of the night, and all were aware of it. Fairly soon Margaret rose.

"It grows chill," she said. "And you must be tired. From your long riding. Bed will serve us best now, I think. How say you, my lords?"

None voiced objection, whatever uneasy glances were cast here and there. Margaret, on Will's arm, led the way back to the castle.

In the doorway of the Lesser Hall of Threave, beside the main turnpike stair, the chatelaine supervised the ceremony of handing each guest his candle, and bidding them goodnight, her lord at her side. He saw his wife's hand tremble and the flame flicker as she gave Jamie his candle. Meg stood in the shadows, and when the three younger brothers had gone up, dipped a quick curtsey, murmured something, and taking up her own light hurried away. Husband and wife were left alone.

"Poor Meg," Margaret said quietly.

He looked at her. "And poor Margaret!" he echoed, shaking his head.

"Perhaps. But what of Will Douglas? Poor Will?"

"Aye. Poor Will. And poor Jamie, likewise! We are all agley, lass. God knows why it should be so. Is there a curse on us, think you? Many have cursed Douglas, down the years. Perhaps with cause. Could it be that they have come home to roost? On us?"

She raised her proud fair head. "No," she said firmly. "Not that. Here is no way to talk, Will. You should know better. Leave curses to James Kennedy and his like. What we are and what we do, we cannot blame on curses. We choose our own paths."

"Save those that are chosen for us! Did I choose to be Douglas? Or you to be Galloway? And so . . . this?"

"You chose to come to Threave, one day. Asking that I be your wife. I chose to have it so. Aye, had already willed it. We both could have chosen otherwise. You chose to raise the power of Douglas on high again. And I aided you in it. If there is blame in it, who shall we blame but ourselves?"

"I did not choose to lose my heart to Meg Douglas! Nor you, I think, to my brother Jamie!"

There was a long silence. He had never actually put that in words before.

Margaret lowered her head. But after a moment she looked up steadfastly. "No. That is true. But I have chosen to be an honest and good wife to you, nevertheless. In all that I may."

"Aye. And I . . . I have chosen otherwise!"

"You are a man, and see things differently. Feel them differently."

"Jamie is a man too, is he not?"

"Jamie is a very different man from you. But . . . that is little to the point. I made my choice."

"Then, I wish . . ." he began.

Her hand gripped his arm. "Do not say it, Will," she urged. "Do not say it."

He inclined his head. "Very well. I am made of lesser stuff than you, I think."

"No. You are man, and I am woman. That is all. Different. Now — take your candle. Go to her."

"But . . ."

"Goodnight, Will."

"You would have it so?"

"That you must not ask me to say. But it is best so."

Slowly he reached out to pick up the candlestick. "Meg — she is also a woman," he pointed out. "Different?"

"Only in degree. And so she suffers her own pain. Go, now. Words will not better this matter."

Sighing, he took her hand and kissed it, before turning away along the vaulted passage that led to the lesser, back stairway.

*   *   *

The village of Lockerbie in Annandale sat on its ridge between its two lochs and under its green hill, a sunny open place of scattered red stone thatched-roof houses, turf cabins and timber hovels that had grown up round a square, squat red stone tower of the Johnstones. Many of those houses were roofless, charred and blackened, as Will Douglas, frowning, surveyed the place that August noonday. He sent Jamie to fetch the parish priest, Hugh to round up twelve honest men of the

317

village. and Johnnie to bring out Sir Herbert Herries from the vaults of the tower, over which a Douglas company had kept armed guard for two weeks.

In the open space before the church, Will took up his stance beside the village well, without dismounting. At his back some hundreds of his men-at-arms formed themselves into grimly silent, close-packed ranks. The village people peered round doors and corners, moved nearer diffidently at first, unsure, and then thronging. Loud-voiced women, learning it was the Black Douglas himself, came to clamour at his stirrups, bewailing their dead, recounting their losses, demanding redress and justice and vengeance from their lord. Will nodded briefly, wordless, expressionless.

The old priest was brought, chittering with fright, wringing his hands. Him Will ignored.

Johnnie led Herries out from his cell, a good-looking man though dishevelled, of middle years, heavily built. His fine clothing was stained and torn and he was dirty of person, but he held his head high and his haggard features that had been florid once, were proud still, not to say arrogant, as he was marched between rows of shouting, cursing, spitting, fist-shaking villagers.

Will waited until the knight was brought near. Then he raised his hand for silence. "Herbert Herries," he said, from the saddle, "men say that you have harried and slain and ravished in this Annandale. And in my name, as my sheriff-deputy — an office held by your brother. Many men say it. We lack not for witnesses. What say *you*?"

"I say, my lord, that what I did was within my right to do. Within this jurisdiction of Annandale and Nithsdale. I protest strongly that the Lord Balveny, your brother, has held me here, against all right and decent usage between men of knightly rank. And I demand trial, if trial there is to be, before the King's Grace himself, in accordance with my rank and estate."

"That is all you have to say?"

"Yes."

"Very well. I say that you have no right to trial before the King. Even were you indeed my sheriff-deputy, instead of your brother, you would be deputy to *me*, for I am Sheriff, Justiciar and Lord of Galloway. My jurisdiction here is complete, and you are under it. I elect to try you here and now. I say that in

318

this you acted of your own will. Or another's. But not mine. You acted, indeed, wholly against my known will and interests. You declare that you have no more to say. I will hear any man here who will speak in your favour."

A heavy silence fell on the entire assembly. Even the muttering and murmuring of the angry women died away.

"No man speaks?" Will asked. "I charge you all. If there is aught to be said in this man's cause, any excuse, any plea for mercy, speak now and I shall consider it."

Only the distant barking of a dog broke the hush.

Herries hawked, and spat. "These cattle!" he said contemptuously. "Think you they would speak for any true man? Or that I would have them speak for me?"

"Priest — what have you to say? In this your parish?" Will jerked, not even turning his head.

Out of the mumbling and mowing, the old man found broken words. "God have mercy ... on his soul! I saw ... two score men. Hanging. On those trees. Two score. All ... all of my flock. Two score men! ..."

"They were rogues, thieves, sorners," Herries declared coldly.

There was a great outcry of protest and fury from the villagers. Everywhere people surged forward, fists raised, brandishing sticks. Men-at-arms pushed them back.

"Silence!" Will roared. "There will be no riot in my presence. There are twelve men here to speak. They and they only. This man, Herries, brother to Terregles — is he guilty of the murder of these two score men? And others? Or is he not? I ask you. Think well. Think well, I say. And what you say."

"Aye! Aye!" As from one man came the cry.

"Does none say other? As one day you, with myself, will stand before a higher judgement seat than this! Speak now."

"No! No! Guilty! Away with him!"

"So be it. You hear, Herries? You are judged. By those who best know your crime. By those you have injured. Found guilty. You slew wantonly. Without mercy. In an evil cause. Now you pay the price. As you hanged others on yonder trees, so shall you hang. Now. The priest is here. Make your peace with God. If you can!"

"Hang! ..." The man was shaken, at last. "You ... you cannot *hang* me! Like any scullion! Me — a knight!"

"You have forfeit your knightly standing. By what you have done. By yourself acting the common hangman. You are no longer Sir Herbert Herries. Only a murderer, caught and tried. It is enough. I say no more. Here is the priest . . ."

"I need no snivelling kitchen-bred clerk!"

"Very well." Will reined round his horse, and nodded to one of his captains. "Take him. Hang him. And quickly."

"Aye, lord."

Without another word or glance at the prisoner, at any of them, he rode away.

As men gazed after him, in silence, he turned in the saddle. "Harry," he called, to the Chamberlain of Galloway, his brother-in-law, "have your clerks to write down these people's hurts. Write down the claims of all who have suffered loss by this man. They must be recompensed. Large and small. Then to Nithsdale, to do likewise."

"It will take time, my lord. Days. When do you ride for Raeberry?"

"Tomorrow. Set your clerks to work. Then join me . . ." He rode on.

Bombie was the chief seat of the ancient Galloway family of Maclellan, but Raeberry Castle was the stronger. It lay some five miles to the south of Kirkcudbright, on the crest of a fearsome cliff above the Solway, defended from the landward by wide double ditches, a smaller version of Tantallon. The Douglas host of a thousand men came to it next day, under louring clouds and a smirr of rain. All was shut against them, cattle driven from sight, cot-houses evacuated, drawbridge up. Between the ditches a gibbet stood, and from it a corpse swayed and birled in the breeze. Regularly, as it swung, a splash of scarlet showed on its sagging, rain-sodden ruin — the Red Heart of Douglas painted on a black breastplate.

At Will's elbow, Johnnie pointed. "Pate Pringle, still there. It is six weeks and more! . . ."

Narrow-eyed, his brother stared. "For that, if for naught else, Maclellan dies!" he said, from between clenched teeth. He nodded to his trumpeter. "You speak, Johnnie," he added thickly.

When the trumpet's ringing summons had died away, Johnnie raised his voice. "Here speaks John Douglas of Balveny. Sir Patrick Maclellan, Tutor of Bombie, your lord and mine, the right puissant and noble Earl of Douglas and Lord of Galloway, here present, commands that you open this your house, held in feudal duty. Forthwith and without delay. See you to it."

Raeberry, although strong, was small and did not boast a gatehouse and flanking towers. From one of its upper windows, iron-grated, a man shouted reply. "I open this house only to the King's Grace. Or his Lieutenant. The Earl of Douglas is no longer that. I pay my feudal dues. I owe nothing more to Douglas."

Johnnie almost choked. "You are his vassal, man! You will not deny that you are his vassal?"

"I have never refused vassalage duty and fee. When called on, I have supplied a knight's fee, in men, horse and armour, for Douglas. But this house is my own. I yield it to none."

Will leaned over to touch his red-faced brother's arm. "Maclellan — here *me*, Douglas," he called. "Why does my friend and servant Pate Pringle hang there?"

There was a pause before there was an answer. "Because he *was* a servant. A low-born knave, he came speaking me ill. Me. Maclellan! He offered me insult. In my own house. None does that, and lives!"

"He came here because my brother sent him. In my name. Wearing my colours. And you slew him."

"Your brother, my lord, should choose better who he sends to speak with Maclellan!"

"It is Douglas who speaks to you now. As Justiciar and Lord of Galloway I require you to yield yourself to me, for trial for the murder of this man Pringle. And for other ill deeds. Yield, I say."

"I yield nothing! You cannot require me to do so. I have appealed to the King's Grace. As is my right."

"You have no such right. You are under my jurisdiction."

"Maclellan has alway had that right. Before there were ever Douglases in Galloway! And the King knows it. Accepts it."

"I say you lie. You have no such right. I shall try you, as is my plain duty."

"You are too late. My messengers are even now on their way to Edinburgh. To the King. The issue is in his royal hands. Till he sends me summons, I yield nothing."

"Then I will claw you out of your hold like a fox from a cairn!"

"You may try, my lord!"

"You are a fool, Maclellan. Think you, in your eyrie, to withstand the might of Douglas?"

"There is a greater might than Douglas in this realm!"

"We shall see." Hoarse from shouting, Will turned to Johnnie. "This man must be taught his lesson. And others with him. You will see to it. I have much to do. Too much to sit down outside this Raeberry. Lochmaben and Craig Douglas to visit, and all the lands that for a year have not seen their lord. Pleas to hear, causes to judge. But . . . I want this man, Johnnie. At Threave. And I want him alive. You understand?"

"I will need cannon, Will. For this place . . ."

"I will send you cannon. From Caerlaverock. From Hermitage, if need be." These were the West March fortresses of which, as Warden, Douglas had control. "In two days you shall have your cannon. And as many men as you require. Gunpowder and gear for mining and sapping. But get me Maclellan."

"I will get him, never fear. You are going now, then?"

"Aye. To Lochmaben first. I shall go by Caerlaverock and Dumfries. Then Ettrick. Then Douglasdale. But, first, I have something to do." He looked round him. "I want one man," he called out. "One man. Who does not fear for his skin."

There was a chorus of volunteers, all pushing forward, his brothers foremost.

"No, no. One only. You Wattie." He selected his own body-servant, Wat Scott. "Pate was your friend, also."

"Stand you back, Wattie," Jamie intervened. "*I* will do it."

"That you will not," Will declared. "You are heir to Douglas. If there is risk in this, he shall not have both of us."

"What do you intend?"

"I go for Pate. At least he shall have Christian burial."

" 'Fore God — let some other do that, Will!" Johnnie protested. "Not you."

"Pate taught me much that I know. And he came here in my name."

"They could slay you. Arrows. You will be close under their walls."

"I doubt if even this Maclellan would choose to shoot the

Black Douglas! Before all. But have our own archers command each window. And the parapet. We shall need something. For the body. Give me a saddle-cloth . . ."

Dismounting, for horses could not negotiate the first ditch, dry as it was, Will and Wattie Scott moved forward, to lower themselves down the steep twenty-foot sides of the wide trench, cross its base, and clamber up beyond. There was perhaps thirty yards between the two ditches, and midway rose the gibbet.

Stolidly the two men paced towards the thing, itself no more than another forty yards from the castle walls, a mark that no archer could miss. From in front, as from behind, came no sound, no sign of movement — save only the creaking of the gallows as its burden swayed in the wind.

They reached the gibbet-foot. It was a simple, upright post, twelve feet or so in height, supported at the base by four slant-wise struts. Its top was crossed by a double arm — but only the one side at present bore its grisly fruit.

Will drew his dirk. "Hold him, Wattie," he directed, choking a little, for the stench was horrible. "Wrap the saddle-cloth round him. The legs." Then putting the dirk between his teeth, he grasped the post, set a foot on one of the diagonal struts, and hoisted himself up.

There was no sign, no reaction, from the castle.

When he was high enough, Will gripped the upright pole as tightly as he could, in long riding boots, between thighs, calves and ankles, and steadying himself with one hand, took the knife in the other. Fortunately the hanging had been done with a rope, not a chain. He sawed at the hemp with the sharp blade.

It did not take long. The corpse, hideous now at close quarters, fell, and even the laconic Wattie could not contain his gasp of revulsion as his old friend dropped into his arms. He was not long in lowering the rotting body to the ground and covering it up in the horse-blanket.

Will jumped down, and when the other would have picked up the bundle, thrust him aside and stooped himself to raise his former steward. Across his broad shoulder he hoisted the corpse, and without a glance at the castle, turned and strode back towards his own people. The smell was all but over-powering.

Negotiating the dry ditch was difficult, thus burdened, but now there were other hands to aid them.

"Tie him on a horse, and send him back for burial," Will told Johnnie. "To Douglas. To the Kirk of St. Bride. He was our father's faithful servant. He helped to put him in yon crypt. He shall lie beside him."

Somewhat askance men eyed Will Douglas. He had never looked more grim.

Jamie said, "Thank God they did not shoot!"

"That was folly," Hugh declared. "A live man does not offer his life for the dead. In especial Douglas, whom thousands living need."

Will ignored him. "You know your duty, Johnnie?" he said briefly. "I will take only one troop. The rest see that you use to good purpose! Harry will aid you." To his other brothers he jerked his head. "Come."

*   *   *

Will was holding justice-aires at his castle of Tibbers, in upper Nithsdale, when the Lord Fleming reached him, weary almost to the point of exhaustion. With scant respect for the proceedings, he sank down on the bench at the head of the Hall, beside the Earl.

"God's mercy, Will," he exclaimed, "this is not where you should be, this day! I have ridden from Edinburgh, hot-foot. To Threave. And had to come back here for you. Wasting time. If I had but known . . ." He drew a hand over his sweat-damp hair. "You know that Johnnie has the man Maclellan? Held at Threave?"

"I know it, Rob. Yesterday the word came. I return there tomorrow. What of it?"

"Tomorrow may be too late. That is, if you are set on this matter. As Johnnie and the Lady Margaret say. Indeed, in any case . . ."

"Talk plain, man!"

"Yes. I have come from the Court. Your unfriends have won the day, Will. You have fallen into a trap. A skilful trap. Of Crichton's devising. You know that the Grays are kin to Patrick Maclellan? He is nephew to Gray and his brother. They are kin to me also — little as I rejoice in it. My sister was wed to Sir Patrick Gray when I was a bairn. Patrick Gray is Captain of the King's Guard. Close to the King. And of Crichton's party."

"I know it, man. What of it?"

"They have prevailed on the King to supersede your authority. As Lord of Galloway. And Justiciar. In this matter. To save Maclellan and strike at you. They know that you have sworn that he should die. They willed it thus, indeed. It was all deep planned. You were too quick for them with Herries. But they will have you, with Maclellan. Patrick Gray is even now on his way to Threave. To command that you hand over Maclellan to the King's justice. A royal command. Which you cannot refuse, short of treason. And forfeiture. So you must yield him. Douglas mocked. Made impotent. Before all. Your word, your sworn word set at naught. So you're trapped. Crichton planned it all . . ."

"Not yet, I am not!" Will's table all but overturned with the violence of his uprising. "This court stands adjourned!" he cried, to the surprised assembly. Then he was striding for the door, shouting for horses as he went.

That forty mile dash from Tibbers to Threave was possibly the most furious of all Will Douglas's urgent ridings. Night caught them in the hills east of St. John's Town of Dalry, but there was no slackening of speed, even though hooves slithered and tripped, horses fell and bones were broken. Any of his companions who could not stand the pace were abandoned without comment or apology. Will, in fact, scarcely spoke a word throughout, usually spurring far ahead of all.

They came to Threave just after sunrise, so that its lord had to clamour at his own gatehouse for entry, before sleepy porters lowered the drawbridge for him.

"Is Gray come?" he yelled at them, even as the chains were still clanking down. "Sir Patrick Gray? From Edinburgh."

"No, lord. None such has come . . ."

"The saints be praised!"

A tousle-headed Lord Balveny, drawing on top clothes, met them in the courtyard. Without pausing in his dismounting, Will cut through his greetings and questions. "Johnnie — you have Maclellan safe held? Aye, then. Get me twelve men. Yes, twelve." He grasped his brother's arm, and hurried him along with him. "You hear. Twelve. From the Castleton. Or the Milton. Not any of our men-at-arms — honest, decent men, to

325

make a jury. And quickly. Have them here, decently clad, in the Common Hall, as soon as may be. When you have them assembled, bring me word. Go now. There is no time to lose . . ."

"My lord, my lord!" Margaret cried, from the keep doorway. "Thank God you are come! At last. I feared . . ." She shook her head. "Oh, Will — why, why did you not slay Crichton when you could? When you had opportunity! . . ."

"Because I lacked your strength, woman — that is why! I have told you — I have not your strength. But today — today we shall yet counter Crichton! In this, at least. None mocks Douglas! Get me food. And clothes. For a court . . ."

All Threave was in a stir within minutes, its lord's commands being put into effect. But, though all played their parts, what Will had planned, on that headlong ride through the night, was not to be. They were given insufficient time. Bewildered men, elders of the local community, millers, smiths, masons, foresters and the like, were still being hurried into the Common Hall on the first floor of Threave's great keep, when a shrill high trumpet summons at the gatehouse galvanised all in the castle. The Captain of the King's Guard, and two attendants, was demanding admission thereat in the name of James, King of Scots.

Will's cursing was violent, intense but brief. "He must have ridden with the dawn! Had he but given me another hour, damn him!" Then he drew himself up. "Rob — my greetings to your kinsman, Sir Patrick Gray. All respect and honour to be paid to him. Bid him to my table, after his long riding. You, Jamie — find and fetch me Johnnie. Quickly."

So the tired and travel-stained but palely handsome Sir Patrick Gray was escorted to the castle's Private Hall, one floor above that being prepared for the trial of the other Sir Patrick, with all the ceremony and salutation due to the monarch's personal envoy. Hastily viands, cold meats, ale and wine had been placed upon the dais table, where the Earl and Countess welcomed him, not effusively but at least courteously.

"Here is a notable surprise, Sir Patrick," Will greeted him. "Thus early in the morning. Do you honour us? Or do you ride further, and but visit Douglas in passing?"

Gray was all courtier, bowing with flourish and aplomb, however weary of carriage and strained of feature. "The honour is all mine, my lord," he declared. "His Grace has sent me to Threave to convey to you the assurance of his entire favour, compliments and esteem. That, and to deliver into your hand this letter for your lordship." He produced from within his doublet a paper, folded and heavily sealed with the royal arms.

"Ah, yes." Will took the missive easily. "His Grace is always kind, generous. And to send his greetings by so distinguished a messenger! Coming at this hour, Sir Patrick, I hope that you have not ridden all through the night, while we lay snug in our beds?"

"I stopped for an hour or two at Crossmichael, my lord. The matter is . . . urgent.

"To be sure. It must be, indeed." But Will made no move to open the sealed letter. "You cannot have eaten. broken your fast, I swear. You must be tired. Hungry. Happily, we ourselves are about to eat. You will join us." That was a command and no question.

"Sit in, Sir Patrick," Margaret said. "Your wife? She bears my own name, I think? She is well?"

"Well, my lady. I thank you. But . . . the King's business, my lord." Gray gestured towards the letter. "It concerns my nephew, Sir Patrick Maclellan . . ."

"Then it can wait, sir. Until we have eaten. Hungry men do little honour to anything — in especial a king's letter. It is my experience, Sir Patrick, that all things are the better considered on a full stomach than on an empty. So sit you." Will tossed the unopened letter on the table. "Ah — here is my brother, Balveny. He, now, has broken fast already. But then, he has no wife to keep him late abed! Sit, I say, man!"

Perforce Gray sat, while Margaret offered him food. Taking Johnnie's arm. Will walked him away towards the door again.

'*You* must do what is to be done, Johnnie," he said, his voice low, flat, level. "My vow falls to be kept! Douglas's vow. There is now no time for trial. But then, Pate was given no trial also! You have it?"

"Aye." Johnnie nodded grimly. "And not before time! I would have done this long since. What is it to be, then? The axe? Or the rope?"

"The axe is quickest, is it not? And time, this morning, is a short commodity, it seems."

"Good. I will blow a horn when the thing is done."

"Do that, Johnnie. I shall be listening . . ."

Back at the table, Will sat with his guest, and Margaret, to this second meal of the young day. If his heart was not in his eating, at least he was all attentive host, plying the visitor with meats and drink and questioning him about affairs at Court, Margaret aiding, when he flagged of invention, with queries as to the Queen and the royal baby. If Gray himself was not notably interested in his food, he was kept talking. More than once he attempted to bring the conversation round to the subject of Maclellan, but always he was headed off.

At last, the ululant winding of a horn sounded from the courtyard, and Will let his breath out in a long sigh. Margaret was speaking. He let her finish, and then reached over for the letter.

"Now that we have eaten and are in our right minds, we can better attend the King's business," he declared.

Gray opened his lips to speak, but thought better of it.

Will broke the heavy seals and spread out the paper. Expressionless, he perused the neat penmanship therein, down to James Stewart's untidy signature at the bottom. He looked up, and sighed.

"A pity," he said. "A pity. I fear that it will be difficult. To pay full regard to His Grace's requirements in this matter."

The other leaned forward. "You mean, my lord?"

"Were you advised as to the contents of this letter, sir?"

"I was."

"Then you will understand my regret at being unable . . ." He paused and repeated the word. " . . . *unable* to fall in fully with my royal cousin's wishes, his loyalist subject as I am."

Gray stood up. "Are you saying, my lord, that you will not deliver up to me, on the King's commands, Sir Patrick Maclellan, Tutor of Bombie?"

"No. Not *will* not, sir. Cannot."

"My lord of Douglas, I urge you to think. Think well. This is your plain duty. This knight, my nephew, however you may conceive him to have offended, is no longer in your jurisdicton. The King is supreme in jurisdiction, as in all else. Sir Patrick Maclellan is his prisoner now, since he has taken this matter into his own royal hands. You cannot withhold my nephew's person. Short of outright rebellion against your liege lord."

'M'mm. I see it a̶ _ _ _ _ _ _ _ hat, sir. Much as I would wish to pleasure His Grace.'

"Then I must *command* you, my lord, in the King's name, Command that you hand over to me the person of Sir Patrick, now the King's prisoner. Refusal to do so can only be treated as highest treason. The penalties for which, you my lord, are well aware!"

"You are a bold man, Patrick Gray, to name that word to Douglas. In Douglas's house! But I commend your zeal in the King's service. See you, I do not reject the royal command. I do not refuse to hand over the person of Maclellan to you. I but inform you that there are difficulties."

"Then these difficulties must be overcome. Since it is a royal command. Bring me to Sir Patrick, my lord."

"Very well." Will rose. "Since you insist. Come."

Downstairs Will led his guest, Margaret waiting behind.

In the courtyard, Johnnie was standing in talk with a group of Douglas notables. "My Lord Balveny," Will called, formally. "Sir Patrick Gray, from the King, requests the person of the prisoner Maclellan to be delivered to him. I have explained that this is . . . difficult. But we must do what we can. Since it is the King's command."

"Difficult," Johnnie nodded. "But if it is important. Let Sir Patrick follow me."

They moved out, and into the inner bailey to turn right. Along it they walked until, turning a flanking tower, there before them grew the hanging-tree. And below it, beside a heavy block of wood, a body lay — or the headless trunk of a body. Blood was splashed round about, blood red and not yet black, and there was a buzz of flies.

Johnnie turned, and Will pointed. "You see the difficulty, Sir Patrick? There lies the prisoner. But unfortunately, he lacks a head. It will be somewhere about, I have no doubt. If it is important? . . ."

Gray stared, his pale face quite ashen now. He did not speak.

"A pity that you did not come sooner," his host went on conversationally. "Then His Grace's wishes in this matter might have been met. But justice fell to be done. Else I had failed in my office of Justiciar for this Galloway. This man was a self-confessed murderer. He slew many, without cause.

Defenceless folk. But in especial, one Pate Pringle. You know all this however, I am sure?"

Still the other did not answer, or risk any words. He was biting his lip, his eyes wary, darting now. Never did a man more clearly display fear, personal fear for his own safety now, as he glanced round at all the grim-faced watching Douglases.

"Do you require the prisoner's person, then, sir?" Johnnie demanded. "I am sure that we could find you the head." Even as he spoke, the truncated body twitched oddly at the legs, a macabre sight.

Gray shook his head, and turned abruptly away. "No. Not so " he muttered. "I . . . will go. Now. Since . . . since you have taken the head, my lord, the body is . . . of little avail! I will tell His Grace. My horses, if you please."

"Here is unseemly haste, surely?" Will protested. "You must be weary. Wait awhile, Sir Patrick . . ."

"No. I must be gone." The other's anxious glances were eloquent of urgent desire to be away from that place. "I must not delay. I am on the King's business. You must let me go . . ."

"To be sure, if that is your will."

Gray was obviously having to restrain himself almost from running, as Will walked back with him to the courtyard. Grooms brought the three horses, and he and his attendants mounted there and then.

"You will not even take leave of my wife?" Will asked gravely.

"No. My duty to her. My regrets. It is a long road to Edinburgh, my lord."

"As you will. I charge you to convey my fealty and leal devotion to His Grace. Tell him that, at least, your late-coming has saved him the unpleasing business of a hanging. Go then, if you must."

Sir Patrick wasted no time on further civilities. He clattered out through the inner and outer baileys, and then thudded over the timbers of the drawbridge. But once beyond it, he pulled up and drawing off his gauntlet, hurled it back towards the gatehouse. Then he shook his bare fist.

"You shall pay for this, Douglas!" he shouted. "Do not think that you will not. He was scarce dead! I saw. You had him slain

330

out of hand. He, a knight. And a defenceless man. Coward! You have disgraced the knightly order! You shall suffer for it, 'fore God!" He turned and spurred off furiously.

"Damn him!" Johnnie cried. "That knave needs his own lesson. We can ride him down, with fresher horses . . ."

"No. Let him be," Will said. "Let him ride back to Edinburgh to tell his tale. That is what all was for, is it not? *He* is not the enemy! Let him go back to Crichton, who sent him."

"What think you he will do now?" Jamie wondered. "Crichton. Something he *will* do, that is certain . . ."

CHAPTER TWENTY

DESPITE all the diversions and distractions of the life they now lived, the Douglas brothers — all save Jamie perhaps, that is — still found their truest satisfaction and delight, not in tournaments and knightly pastimes, not in the revels and junketings of the Court, nor even in lordly progresses around their vast domains and the almost princely splendour that was now part and parcel of their circumstances; their prime pleasure was to return to their boyhood haunts in the far-flung and lonely fastnesses of the Ettrick Forest, there to forget the burdens which had been so suddenly thrust upon them, in the chase, hunting happily, as of old, the boars, stags and above all, the wild bulls which roamed that hilly wilderness. After all, they were still young, only eight years having passed since the day when their father's death had pitched them unceremoniously into a new life; and though they all now bore high office and resounding titles, these were superficialities, accretions to be sloughed off when opportunity occurred.

A few weeks after the Maclellan affair, on a crisp golden afternoon of October, the brothers were at Newark hunting northwards amongst the wild hills around Whitehope Rig. Will and Hugh had each slain a bull, and they were now stalking a handsome stag, which Johnnie had declared must be his, in a high corrie where the Gruntly Burn was born, when Jamie, who was less intent on the business than the others, drew Will's attention to movement far down in the valley below.

"A single rider," he whispered. "And a woman, if my eyes do

not deceive me. Margaret, perhaps. Come to join us. I shall go to meet her . . ."

"That you will not!" the other declared, keener of eye. "I know how Margaret sits a horse. That is . . . other. I will go. Bide you here."

Jamie, who had had enough of the chase, was about to protest, but something about Will's expression made him swallow his words. His brother backed away, belly down through the heather to keep out of sight of the deer.

When the curve of the hill hid him from both hunters and hunted. Will rose and strode back to where foresters kept the horses in a hollow of the braeside. Mounting his own shaggy garron, he waved back Wat Scott who would have accompanied him, and rode off downhill.

Meg Douglas waited by the burnside, a hearteningly vital and comely sight, sitting her pony, her red-gold hair blowing in the breeze that moulded her magnificent figure. "Visitors, Will," she called to him. "Important visitors. From the King. The Lady Margaret entertains them. So I came to warn you."

"And a bonny warning you make, my dear! I am glad you came."

"You prefer me to your bulls?"

"Give me but a little opportunity and I will show you how I prefer you, woman! But, this of the King's messengers? It is not Gray again?"

"That mannie will never come seeking Douglas again, I think! No, this time His Grace has sent couriers of a different metal. Your own good-brother, the Lord Hay, the Constable And Bishop Turnbull, of Glasgow. With great sealed letters."

"So! Will Hay and the good Bishop? Here is a changed tune. His Grace has been taking thought. Or, my Lord Crichton, perhaps. To send these. But — I vow it does not mean that they have discovered a new love for me!"

"So deemed your lady! So she would have you warned."

"Aye. Well, we shall see."

They rode together back down the waterside, to the Gruntly Burn's junction with Yarrow. A little above this, at Yarrow Ford, they crossed the river and then turned eastwards again, downstream. Will did not hurry.

Indeed, at a place where the valley narrowed in almost to a gorge, he reined up, and pointed, to a gap at the cliff's base. "You remember that cave, Meg? And what was said, and done, that day?"

"Think you that I could forget it?"

"You ran away from me, once, at that cave. And later that night, you asked me if I was indeed a man! And I proved it to you."

She nodded, unspeaking.

"That day, you might say, we pledged our troth, you and I. Set our course."

"And where is that course leading us, my lord Earl?"

He reached out and took her arm. "Meantime, to yonder cave!" he said, smiling. "Come, lass."

She looked at him, eyebrows raised. "There? Now? Sakes — not now, Will! Not . . . like this. Besides, they await you . . ."

"Let them wait! I' faith, it is seldom enough that I have you alone, to myself, these days. And even then, hurriedly, in a corner, up back stairs!" He was urging his beast on, pulling her with him, as he spoke.

She did not resist, though she shook her head at him.

Within the fern-decked entrance to the cave where they had sheltered from the thunder-storm those seven years before, he jumped from his garron and reached to lift her down from her saddle. In his arms, he could feel already her anticipatory trembling.

"My dear, my heart's darling," he said. "You are lovely. All delight. All joy. My beloved Meg. What would I do lacking you?"

"Be a better husband, may be," she answered, a little breathlessly.

He frowned momentarily, but did not relax his grip. "In this, *you* are my wife!" he said. Though she was no light weight, he picked her up bodily, and carried her towards the dark back of the cave.

"Foolish," she murmured throatily, in his ear. "Save your strength!"

"My strength . . . will serve . . . never fear!"

There was dead bracken on the rock floor, back there, where wayfarers and wanderers had slept ere this. All but falling thereon, he took her with a fierce and explosive passion, cursing cloying clothing. Meg far from passive or quiescent. Indeed it was possibly the most urgent and overwhelming of all their love-makings, a cataclysmic and utterly basic union which left them both exhausted, drained, but joyously satisfied, content.

When, presently, they rode away from that cave, after a few minutes of ruminative silence, Meg spoke.

"Will — have you ever wished for a child? A son? You, the Black Douglas."

He took his time to answer that. "If matters had been other than they are — yes. Every man would have a son to follow him. But, as it is, I care little. I have brothers a-many."

"Brothers are not sons," she said. "Would a son born out of wedlock displease you? Who could not be Earl of Douglas after you?"

"No-o-o. No, I think not. A son is . . . a son!"

"Then, I think perhaps, you have planted a son in me this day, Will Douglas!"

He pulled up. "Dear God — you say so! You mean it? By the powers — can it be so? How can you know? Be sure?"

"I cannot be sure. But I feel that it is so. Feel it in my bones. Back there, I think you made a mother of me!"

"Then I am glad."

"And my lady? And yours? What of her?"

"I do not know. But I believe that she will not be . . . unkind."

They rode on thoughtfully towards Newark.

At the castle, Will found Margaret playing hostess to Hay and the Bishop of Glasgow, in the Upper Hall. Turnbull was a big burly man from the East March of the Borders, more like a farmer than a cleric — but a man of great learning, vigour and character nevertheless, and a notable change from his predecessor, James Cameron. He was reputed to be honest, and gave that impression. He was ambitous however, especially in his plans for his new university at Glasgow, and therewith to assail something of the hegemony of Kennedy, Bishop of St. Andrews. Will had learned to beware of ambitious men, however honest they seemed.

No one would call William Hay ambitious, at least — even though he was now Lord Hay, and soon to be Earl of Erroll. Born to the High Constableship, he fulfilled his function dutifully, and that was all. Will, though long they had been colleagues, brothers-in-arms, and now were brothers by marriage, had never been able to get close to the man. But at least he trusted him. King James had sent two messengers whom Douglas could hardly treat as he had treated Sir Patrick Gray. And Bishop Turnbull owed him much for obtaining the charter for his university from the Pope. But it behoved him, now, to be wary, nevertheless.

They had brought two letters from the King. Unlike Gray's missive, these were both sealed with James's Privy Seal, not with the Great Seal of Scotland, which was in the Chancellor's keeping, and the use of which implied that Crichton was at least involved in some measure in what was written therein.

After a decent interval for civilities, asking after his sister Beatrix, and the progress of the Bishop's college, Will broke the first seal.

This letter surprised him. It was actually a charter, signed by the King, and duly witnessed, regranting to his beloved and traist cousin, William, Earl of Douglas and Avondale, Lord of Galloway and Warden of the Marches, and to his four brothers and their heirs male, all their lands, castles, titles and offices. It was customary, when a young monarch came of age and took over the reins of government into his own hands, for him to renew, confirm — or perhaps reject — charters granted during his minority. This was apt to be something of a formality, although it gave the holders of the lands, all in theory in the King's overlordship, security of tenure. But when a man was out of favour, it presented a notable opportunity for the monarch to express his displeasure and refuse to confirm any or all of the charters, more especially of the offices of responsibility and profit. But here, unsolicited, was a regrant of not only all the vast Douglas territories and superiorities, but of the many positions and offices Will had held — saving only that of Lieutenant-General of the Realm. At a quick glance, Will could see no properties and estates omitted, in ten counties, and no justiciarship, sheriffdom or customship withheld. There was, however, a curious and final phrase, which declared that all this was granted out of the King's true love of the said Earl William, and in despite and notwithstanding all crimes committed by him or by his cousin the deceased Earl Archibald.

Will looked up, brows knitted. There was no need to ask the

two visitors whether they knew of the contents of this letter, for both their names appeared amongst the witnesses to the King's signature. "His Grace appears to be very . . . loving!" he commented slowly. "I had scarce expected this."

"His Grace esteems you very well, my lord. As well he might," the Bishop said.

"Despite my crimes! And those of my cousin Archie. Why his, I wonder? Save in that he was Lieutenant-General before me. Why name him? And not my father? Or even my murdered cousins?" He glanced over at Margaret, the said Earl Archibald's daughter. "There is something strange here."

Neither of his guests had any comment to make.

"His Grace has not always shown his appreciation of my services so warmly," Will went on. "Leaving the crimes, for the moment! This confirms even the Justiciarship of Galloway — about which there was some disagreement! But recently."

"King James regrets that, I think," Turnbull said. "He would let bygones be bygones, my lord."

"Truly noble! Royal! I wonder why? What says Will Hay?"

The Constable shrugged. "You are still His Grace's most powerful subject. Whatever differences you may have had. He needs your support."

"Aye. He assuredly has needed it in the past. And likely will again. Though of late, it seems, he has been thinking otherwise."

"His Grace is inclined to be hot of head," the Bishop mentioned. "But he is of a sound heart. And he will heed good advice, on occasion!"

"And the other sort, also! I know James Stewart as well as you do, I think, my lord Bishop."

"No doubt. But I urge your lordship to read the other letter."

Will opened the second seal. This proved to be a document declaring that in the cause of peace and the welfare of their two realms, the King of England and the King of Scots had ordained that it was right and suitable that the former truce from war-like acts should be renewed and revived between the two said realms, for a period of years. And to this end terms should be discussed and considered at a meeting of commissioners to be held at Durham before the onset of winter this year of grace To which meeting and conference the King's Grace hereby appointed his noble and right well-beloved cousin, William Earl of Douglas and Avondale, in view of his known amity and close association with the Duke of York, Governor to His Grace of England, to be principal represener and negotiator for the realm of Scotland. And to be supported, as colleagues and co-adjutants, by the most noble Lord Alexander, Earl of Crawford. And the most noble Lord George, Earl of Angus. And the leal and excellent Lord Fleming of Cumbernauld. And the pious and learned Lords Bishop of Dunkeld and Brechin. By the King's command.

Will stared at this imposing document, and then from his wife to the two men who watched him. He sighed. "His Grace has forgotten one!" he said. "Or should it be my Lord Crichton who forgot? Forgot John, Lord of the Isles and Earl of Ross!"

Hay shuffled his feet, and the Bishop coughed.

"What . . . what mean you, my lord?" the latter got out.

"I swear that you know very well what I mean. The Constable does, if you do not. Here are notable names. Carefully chosen. But John of the Isles should be amongst them! He took to arms in the North, claiming his rights to the Earldom of Ross. Beardie Alex Crawford supported him in the East. I was falsely accused of supporting both, because of my bond with Crawford. Rob Fleming is my right hand. This mission would get rid of us, out of Scotland. With Angus who would raise Red Douglas on the ruin of Black, to spy on us! This treaty-making would take months, while we haggled with the English at Durham. Think you I have not discovered, and sorely, what happens when I go furth of Scotland? Does James Stewart conceive me a purblind fool?"

"You are unfair, my lord! To His Grace," the Bishop protested. "It is not so, I swear. He honours you, in this. Appoints you his realm's chiefest spokesman. To deal with the English . . ."

"I was honoured to be the realm's chiefest spokesman to deal with the Pope likewise! And came home to planned treachery and evil. Only a fool does not learn, man."

"I do not think that this is the way of it, Will," Hay said unhappily. "I do not think the King intends you ill, in this. You are but the best man for the task. And friendly with York, as is known . . ."

"Aye — there, I swear, we have it. His . . . how does he put it? His known amity and close association with the Duke of York! James Stewart has not forgiven me my visit to the English Court. He does not say that with love, I think. I pay a price for the Protector's amity!"

"You are suspicious . . ."

"I am suspicious, yes. Do you wonder at it? Ask my lady wife. Am I too suspicious of my liege lord James?"

Margaret shook her head. "I think not, Will."

"That he should deem me a traitor, I can perhaps forgive. For this, it seems, is a weakness of kings. But to deem me fool! The thing stinks! To have appointed Crawford to this embassage! A man who loses temper at a gnat. With wits like a weathercock!"

"He is one of the greatest lords in the land," Turnbull pointed out. "You yourself have a bond with him."

"He has three thousand men. That is the reason for my bond. And his sister wed to my cousin, whom Crichton and Livingstone slew. But here is no reason for appointment to negotiate a treaty! And Angus — a fledgling, whose only virtue is that he hates our house! It stinks, I say! First, I am to be won over and softened by the regrant of these charters and offices. Then, to be cozened into leaving Scotland. For why? What plans King James next? Or is it Crichton?" Will turned on his brother-in-law. "Had Crichton any hand in this?"

"Not that I know. We have come from Stirling, not Edinburgh, Crichton comes little to Stirling . . ."

"But as Chancellor he must be concerned in this treaty?"

"That may be. But James spoke as though this was all of his own devising. He spoke of it with us, frankly. I think that you misjudge, Will . . ."

"It is scarce clever enough for Crichton," Margaret put in.

"No. True. Nevertheless, I will not go to Durham."

"But . . . my lord! You cannot say," Turnbull exclaimed. "Here is no request, no plea. It is a royal command. Even Douglas must needs obey."

"Must needs? You think so? See you — this royal command is delivered to me by proxy. Douglas shall obey it the same way — by proxy!" He tapped the letter. "Here is paper. And

338

sealing-wax. James Stewart's seal." From inside his doublet, Will drew a golden trinket on a slender chain, and tossed it on to the paper. "Here is another seal. That of Douglas. This shall go to Durham. In my name and room. As you brought the other to Newark, in the King's. It shall go with my wishes and recommendations for this truce. My authority. The Lord Fleming shall bear it. Beardie can go, if he will. But I bide here, I do not leave Scotland, see you. It is understood?"

The others gazed at him, wordless. None dared enunciate the word rebellion.

Will nodded. "Enough, then. Enough of this folly of kings and governance and the like. Let us be ourselves, my friends. Forget for the once who and what sent you. Accept instead Newark's good fellowship. A plague on all statecraft, say I! Sit you, my lords . . ."

But little relieved, his visitors sat down.

CHAPTER TWENTY-ONE

THE weeks passed, the Scots commissioners went south to Durham minus both Douglas and Crawford, though still nominally under the former's leadership — since King James was too proud to admit that his command had not been complied with — Will returned to Threave, and winter set in. It was a hard winter, of continuing snow and ice, wherein men found it difficult to travel the country however necessary their journeys. As for Will Douglas he was well content to stay at home or at least in the Galloway area; but it was not in the nature of the man to remain inactive, and he and his brothers found plenty to occupy their time without concerning themselves overmuch with affairs of state. They had of course almost one eighth of Scotland to administer, through their chamberlains, stewards and deputies. That winter, for Will, was the most domestic of any since his accession to the earldom, and he found no little satisfaction in the fact. Indeed, he became almost grateful to James Stewart for depriving him of the office of Lieutenant-General, and all the responsibilities that went with it. For a young man of twenty-seven he had had more than his share of responsibilities. He found himself more at ease with Margaret than ever he had been, and yet with pride watched Meg bloom joyously with the motherhood she had prophesied.

It was towards the end of February 1452 that the pattern was changed. As was almost inevitable, it was a messenger from the north who heralded it. Again it was from the monarch, and once more James sent a friend — this time Sir William Lauder of Hatton, a vassel of Douglas, who had indeed accompanied him to Rome, and was, oddly enough, at present under forfeiture for technical rebellion, after trouble with some of Crichton's people.

Lauder repeated the procedure by also bringing two separate letters, both closed with the royal Privy Seal. One was a summons, though in the most friendly terms, requiring the Earl of Douglas to attend upon the King, in person and forthwith, at Stirling, for council and fellowship. The other was much more elaborate, much more strange. It was, in fact, a safe-conduct, in detailed and explicit terms, promising the Earl of Douglas complete security of person and interests during the said visit to Stirling, signed by the monarch himself and countersigned by sundry prominent members of his Privy Council.

They were sitting round the great table in the Upper Hall of Threave, a family gathering, as was normal. Will put the papers down slowly, thoughtfully. Then he pushed them across to Jamie.

"Read these," he said. "Read them aloud. Our friend, Sir William, has brought us interesting tidings. The lesser first, Jamie."

His brother, all eyes upon him, did as he was bid. His voice faltered a little when he came to the safe-conduct wording.

There was almost uproar before he had finished, Hugh and Johnnie vying with each other in question, protest and invective, others little less vociferous. Yet when Margaret opened her lips to speak, all stopped their clamour.

"What is this, Will?" she asked. "It is such as is granted to pass through an enemy's territory, is it not? Or to venture in a foreign land. Such the King of England might grant to Douglas. But not, surely, the King of Scots?"

"Aye — it is an insult!"

"Douglas is his own safe-conduct, by God!"

"James Stewart must be crazed! He to pledge Douglas's safety? In Scotland!"

"Take five thousand men with you to Stirling, Will. And see who needs safe-conduct!"

"Aye. We'll go there. Give him back his piece of paper . . ."

"Peace! Peace!" Will cried. "Of a mercy! My lady-wife asked a question. What is this, she said. Myself, I have never seen the life. Perhaps we should ask Sir William, whom His Grace has sent. What means this paper, my friend?"

The knight was embarrassed. "My lord — do not ask me! I do not know. I knew naught of this safe conduct. The summons, yes — His Grace told me of that. He said he sought your presence with him, in love and affection. Gave me the two letters. But said naught of any safe-conduct. For Douglas . . ."

"Others know of it." Will reached for the paper again, and drew a candelabrum closer. "Here are the signatures and seals of the new-made Earl of Huntly. And the Lord Haliburton. Aye, and Gray — both Grays, my lord and his brother, Sir Patrick! And Darnley, Lennox's son. All assure me, *me*, of my safety!" He barked a laugh. "Here is touching care and kindness! But . . . I wonder why?"

There was a babble of suggestions, few of them complimentary to their liege lord or his present advisers.

"My lord," Lauder only just managed to make himself heard. "Do not too hardly blame His Grace. Here is no insult, I am sure. He would not wish that, since he wishes you to come. To offend you would but keep you away. He much desires your presence, that I know. I think he conceives you as scarce trusting his goodwill. And kingly word. That is why you would not yield the man Maclellan into his hands. Or lead the commissioners to Durham. So, I think, he would assure you that no ill is intended against you, by this safe-conduct."

"Maybe so, friend. But there is more behind it than that. When men think that Douglas could need a safe conduct, in Scotland, and to visit his king, there is something far wrong. Wrong with the thinkers! James may not say it, but it is clear that at heart he considers me enemy. Rebel! This is the behaviour as to a miscreant. Who must be coaxed and cozened."

"I swear it is not so, my lord."

"Perhaps not. But James Stewart may here speak clearer than he himself knows."

"My lord — does Sir William know the reason for the summons?" Margaret put in. "Why does King James so urgently need your presence?"

"That I do not know, lady. But my lord has not attended these last Privy Councils. Nor his brothers. It is much spoken of. It may be that His Grace requires his counsel. And unless he himself comes to Threave seeking it, this is the only way to gain it."

"If the King esteems my counsel so highly, he should not have appointed Crichton to be Chancellor again. He knew my judgement of the man — all honest men's judgement. I will not sit at the council-table under that knave!"

"It may be, I say, that here is part reason for the summons."

"What will you do, Will?" his wife asked, anxiety in her voice.

"Why, I will go, to be sure. It is a royal command."

"It was a royal command that you went to Durham."

"That was different. I cannot refuse the King's summons to his own presence, I have vowed my homage to him. I am no rebel."

"Aye. We will all go. All go to Stirling," Hugh cried. "Douglas will wait on the King, since he wishes it! Douglas, in his thousands!"

"Aye! We will all give of our counsel!" Johnnie agreed. "In a voice that all the realm shall hear. Too long we have sat back. What say you to Jamie, for Chancellor? He is clerkly enough."

"No!" Will snapped. "There shall be no thousands. I go alone. James Stewart asks for *me* to attend him. Myself only. The safe-conduct names only me. I will not ride to Stirling at the head of a host. That would be to show him that I, Douglas, had need to fear. That his safe-conduct had some meaning. Douglas does not need a host, or any escort, to ride to see his liege. I go alone."

All round the table there were murmurings, protests.

"Think you this is wise, Will?" Margaret said, troubled.

"*You* would not deem this paper necessary?"

"No. But . . ."

"Enough, then. I ride with Sir William tomorrow, for Stirling. Alone. And leave this paper behind, for the midden!

342

No — enough, I say. Let us have better entertainment than this. Meg — will you sing for us? . . ."

*   *   *

So Will Douglas presented himself once again before the gates of Stirling Castle, almost as modestly as on that first occasion, eight years before, with no single Douglas at his back — although this time he had Sir William Lauder and three of the King's Guard for company, all looking grander than he. The little party was not kept waiting at the gatehouse — but again King James met him on the way up to the castle's living-quarters, coming hurrying down to greet him, even though the light was fading from the February sky, at the head of a group of wary-eyed courtiers.

James Stewart was affably hearty in a nervous fashion, actually embracing Will and patting his wide shoulder.

"My good Cousin — you have come!" he cried. "It is long since I have seen you. Long since you have honoured my poor Court! Welcome, my lord." He looked behind, and at Lauder. "You . . . you come alone?"

"Aye, Your Grace. Alone." Will was the more restrained for the King's effusiveness. "It is not my host that you sought?"

"No — ah, no. It is yourself. It is well. Very well. Come. You will be weary . . ."

They walked up to the crown of the castle rock, the company falling in behind. Will noted that there were few, if any, of his allies amongst the courtiers — but, on the other hand, neither was Crichton present. Nor Bishop Kennedy. The brothers Gray were there, Haliburton, Darnley, Lennox's son, with Boyd, Cranstoun, and a number of the other new men James had gathered round him. The only friend that Will saw was Sir John Forrester of Corstorphine, now looking a sick man.

Will found the royal apartments much transformed, the woman's hand of Mary of Gueldres in evidence. James presented him again to the smiling sonsy Queen, and proudly showed him the infant heir to the throne, now seven months old and a healthy-looking child.

The King then led his visitor on a tour of the castle, always with the tail of sycophantic supporters, to show him the new works and rebuilding, in which the monarch seemed to be inordinately interested. Will was less so, and could not believe that it was for this that he had been summoned to Stirling. After a while, he indicated as much.

"Your Grace wished to consult me? To ask my counsel?" he said, breaking in on a disquisition on a new audience chamber. "So I came at once. In what can I serve you, Sire?"

James waved a hand. "No, no. Time for that later. Tomorrow. Aye, tomorrow. You shall come and dine and sup with me, Cousin. Tomorrow we shall speak of many matters. Tonight, you are weary with long riding. I will myself show you to your chamber."

Will shook his head. "With Your Grace's permission — no. You are too kind. I shall lodge in the town. And accept your royal invitation to dine. Tomorrow."

Quickly James looked at him, flushing, seeming even younger than his twenty-one years. "Why? There is room for you here. Under my roof. Why lodge in the town, man?"

"You are throng with folk here, Sire. A weary man is better alone. I shall serve Your Grace best when I am rested. I am but ill company, save at my best. I ask you to excuse me."

The King was frowning now, and the murmur of talk behind them had stilled to silence. "I do not understand you, my lord," he said. "Why you seek other roof than mine? Do you . . . do you not trust me? I sent you safe-conduct, did I not?"

"Why did you send Douglas a safe-conduct, Sire? Why did you think Douglas required it?"

James blinked. "It was . . . you had not come. Before. You seemed to keep your distance. As though you feared. Feared for your person. Your safety. So I sent the safe-conduct. On my royal word. That you might be assured."

"What should Douglas fear? In this Scotland?" Slowly, deliberately, Will looked from the monarch round all the watching, listening throng, and back again. "If any fear, surely it should not be Douglas? Whose arm is sufficiently long to assure himself!"

"Yes. Yes. To be sure, Cousin. It was perhaps not necessary."

"Not necessary — no, Sire. So I left your safe-conduct at Threave!"

"You are proud, my lord," the other said, hotly now. "Too proud, too high, for a subject! Do not trust too much to your Douglas strength. To your thousands of men."

"Did I trust to them? To come here, Sire? I came alone, did I not? I trusted not to my thousands — any more than I did to your safe-conduct. I came, as any other leal subject, to your royal summons."

James eyed him doubtfully.

"And now, have I Your Grace's permission to retire?"

The King no longer sought to detain him. "I shall look to see you, to have your counsel, my lord, tomorrow," he said shortly, and turned away.

Will rode thoughtfully down into the town again. He still had not discovered the reason for this summons, but he was convinced that James Stewart was up to something. And he had twice overheard the name of Crawford muttered amongst the courtiers around the King. Could it be another attempt to brand him with treason, linked to Beardie Alex?

Aware that he was being discreetly followed, he found lodging in the establishment of the Grey Friars, below the castle rock. What the friars thought of their unexpected guest they did not reveal.

Confirmation that his movements were being watched reached Will while still abed next morning, when one of the King's gentlemen came bringing an invitation — which, from that source amounted to a command — for the Earl of Douglas to attend His Grace at a hunt in the Cambusbarron area. Horses would be at his door under the hour.

So Will Douglas spent another day in the saddle, a day mercifully free from complications, with the sport only fair, the weather inclement, but King James in genial mood, apparently unconcerned with all but the chase. Tired and wet, but in a much more normal and contented frame of mind, his visitor ended that short February daylight feeling closer to his liege lord than for years.

At dinner in the castle thereafter, the good humour continued, indeed developed into conviviality, as the wine flagons were refilled and filled again. Will was accorded the place of honour between James and his Queen, and had no reason to complain of neglect by the royal pair. Unfortunately the Lord Crichton made his appearance during the meal, presumably having ridden from Edinburgh. Will wondered whether a courier had been sent hotfoot for him the night before. And what his presence now presaged. But meantime the King only nodded casually to the Chancellor's deep obeisance from the doorway, and went on with replenishing Will's goblet as Crichton took a late-comer's lowly seat near the foot of the great table.

Despite James's attention to his guest's cup, Will was drinking only moderately — the more so as his monarch grew ever noisier and still more hearty. James was fond of wine, and apt to be merry of an evening; but Will gained the impression that he was drinking tonight more determinedly than usual, the Queen's frequent and slightly concerned glances over at her husband tending to confirm this. The visitor wondered whether majesty was perhaps priming himself up for an uncongenial task.

The eating was long past, and they were sitting through the third offering of a minstrel with a lute, when James, without warning, rose to his feet, so abruptly as to spill a wine-flagon over the table. Staggering a little as everybody perforce got up, he waved an imperious arm in the direction of a side door. It was uncertain to whom he was gesturing, save that Will was included and his wife was not. Bowing to the Queen, Will followed his sovereign to the ante-room, where a couple of guards with pole-axes stood sentry.

Only a small number of the company presumed to come in after them — but these included Chancellor Crichton, Sir Patrick Gray, the Captain of the Guard, his brother Lord Gray, Lord Darnley and one or two others. The door was shut. Will recognised that he was about to discover the reason for his summons to Stirling.

The room was already lit with candles, so that it appeared that the interview was at least premeditated. James took Will's arm and led him to the far end of the chamber, where a window looked out into the rainy dark. The courtiers remained in a knot near the door.

"Well, Cousin — now I shall have your counsel." The King's voice came thick and loud — loud enough evidently to surprise himself, for he quickly lowered it. "I have awaited it for long. Much troubles me, in this realm. And there are few that I can trust."

"You trust me, Highness?"

"Should I not?"

"I believe that you should. For always I have been leal. I have sought to serve you, and the realm."

346

"And Douglas! You have not failed to serve Douglas also!"

"But not to the realm's hurt. Or yours. Ever."

"You say so?"

"Why not, Sire? I see Douglas as part of the realm. Only that. A limb of the realm. Which should be strong. To work and smite for you, the head of the realm. Would you have it otherwise?"

"Douglas strong to smite for me could be Douglas strong to smite *against* me!"

"That may be so. But so long as *I* am Douglas, that shall not, cannot be. I am your leal man. I vowed my homage, and meant it."

"Yet, when I took Patrick Maclellan under my supreme jurisdiction, you slew him. While my messenger was in your house!" The King's voice had risen again.

"Sire — may I ask *why* you sought to take that jurisdiction to yourself? You had never done the like before. Maclellan was my vassal. Therefore I had feudal right to try him. He had slain my own servant, Pringle, Had him hanging before his door! Moreover, I am Sheriff and Justiciar of Galloway. The jurisdiction, on all counts, was mine. Why should you intervene?"

"Why? Why, man? Save us — must the King of Scots give an answer to Douglas now? As to why he chose to do this or that?"

"Not so. But the King of Scots, I say, should inform the Justiciar of Galloway why he chooses to upset the administration of the law in Galloway!"

"God's blood! I counsel you to watch your tongue, my lord!"

Will was conscious of the incipient forward movement of the throng at the other end of the room. With an effort he kept his own voice calm, steady.

"Your Grace is entitled to choose not to answer my question. But you have my answer to yours. I did but my duty as Justiciar, Before I opened your letter."

James, flushed and hot of eye, glanced towards the others, and back. He changed his stance. "You hanged Herries also. He was Sheriff-Deputy. You, Sheriff and Justiciar, not only took the jurisdiction in your own hands, but hanged the deputy! And

347

you accuse *me*, the King, for taking the higher jurisdiction into *my* hands!"

"Sire — Herries had slain many. Shown himself unfitted to act sheriff. I went to him and, before all, took from him his brother's jurisdiction — for Herries of Terregles was the Deputy, not he. Therefore I hanged no sheriff-deputy but a felon, a murderer. You did not take from *me* my office of Sheriff and Justiciar. Had you done so, I could not have executed Maclellan. If you had no faith in my justice, you should have unseated me."

"Would to God I had! But . . . I swear you would have slain Maclellan, even so!"

Will looked at his choleric young monarch levelly. "If I had, Sire, you would have had reason to condemn me. As it is, I say that you have not."

James tried to outstare him, but he was a little drunk and could not focus his eyes entirely satisfactorily. He turned away, and more than physically.

"You disobeyed my royal command. To go to Durham. To be my chief commissioner to treat with the English," he said heavily.

"I sent my proxy and my seal, Your Grace. Also my advice and instructions."

"That is not what I commanded."

"I obeyed in token, Sire. Being but new back from obeying your command to go to Rome, to have gone furth of Scotland again so soon would have gravely injured my interests."

"Douglas interests! Yet you say that you put your liege lord, and the realm, first."

"I conceived it better service to Your Grace and the realm that Douglas affairs should be put in order, that Douglas should remain a strong arm for your support. For when I came back from Your Grace's business in Rome, it was to discover Douglas affairs much deranged. Douglas strength lessened. So much so that Your Grace had been forced to take action against Douglas during my absence! You would not have had that happen again?"

James's birthmark was not red now, but purple. He looked back into the room, and it was clear that it was to Crichton he looked, appealed. But that man, though attentive of eye, and no doubt straining his ears, made no move forward, nor spoke.

The King burst out, "Aye, I had to act! When I found you traitor. It was time, 'fore God!"

Will took a deep breath. So there it was, out at last. "Not traitor, Sire," he said quietly. "I suggest that you use the wrong word! You did not find me traitor."

"Burn you — do you dare to give *me* the lie? Controvert me to my face!"

"I do, Sire. When you name Will Douglas traitor!"

"You lie! *You* lie, I say!" James raised a hand to point accusingly, a finger to tremble. The watchers now had lost all pretence of standing back and not listening. "You are in bond with Crawford and John of the Isles. He is in rebellion against me. The Islesman. Aided and abetted by Crawford. And by you. Aye, you were absent in Rome. But you planned it so. That you would not seem to be in it. Should it go awry. But we know your guilt. Douglas was to raise the South. Against me. The Islesman the North. Crawford the North-East. Only, John MacDonald struck too soon. Before all was ready. We know it all . . ."

"It is false. There is no truth in it, I say."

"You lie!" James was shouting now, beside himself. "We have uncovered it all."

Will looked from the infuriated young monarch to the cool watching chancellor. "I think you mean that Crichton says he has uncovered it, Sire! Which is a different matter, is it not?"

The older man did not so much as move his thin lips. He left it all to the King.

"You are in league with traitors. Therefore you are traitor!" James cried. "You have bonds with Crawford and John of the Isles. You cannot deny it, man."

"I can and do. I have a bond with Crawford, yes. Have had for years. His sister's husband, and my cousin, was murdered by this forsworn knave whom you have raised up again. But I have no bond with MacDonald. Nor knew of his rebellion. That I swear, on my oath."

"That for your oath!" James Stewart not altogether successfully snapped his fingers. "It is as worthy as your oath of fealty to me. When it comes to obeying my commands. But I command you now. By the living God I do! That you dissolve these wicked traitorous bonds. Here and now. You hear me,

349

Douglas? Before these witnesses. You will abjure them now."

"I cannot dissolve what does not exist. I have no bond with the Islesman. Or any other links with him. Save distantly, of blood. As have you ..."

"That we shall see to. For I have certain intelligence of it. But you do not deny your bond with Crawford. This you shall abjure, at least. Now!"

"No, Sire. It is impossible."

"Impossible? On my command!"

"You know that I cannot. A bond is made by two, or more. Before witnesses. Signed and sealed. No man can dissolve or abjure it alone. It requires both parties. I cannot renounce my bond with Crawford, lacking Crawford's presence. Even at your command."

The King's lips parted. He seemed to gasp for breath, for words. His features contorted spasmodically. Like a man in a seizure, he swayed and panted. Then abruptly he reached down with a groping hand. His words came at least, thick, scarcely intelligible.

'False traitor ... if you will not ... break the bond ... this shall!"

Will stepped back, eyes widening. Steel glittered in the candlelight. The King held a drawn dagger aloft, in shaking hand.

Too astonished for words, Will stared. He could not draw in defence, for none but the High Constable and the Royal Guard might carry arms in the presence of the monarch.

Staggering a little, James Stewart lunged. The first blow struck the other in the throat, a slantwise slash that brought blood spouting like a fountain over the royal hand. Shouting incoherently, he withdrew and stabbed again, low in the body. With a bubbling groan, Will Douglas sank to his knees.

Bedlam reigned in that inner room of Stirling Castle. Sir Patrick Gray sprang to life. He grabbed the pole-axe of one of the guards, and dashing forward, felled the kneeling reeling man to the floor. Then, with the spear-point of the weapon, he began to stab. Darnley, not to be outdone, snatched the other pole-axe and drove in with it, hacking and bludgeoning. Soon the others were fighting with each other for the two axes, and for the dagger that had fallen from the King's grasp, that they might have part in the royal work.

The Black Douglas died without a word spoken.

They tugged open the casement window, James standing back now, bloody hand to open mouth, aghast. They cast out the Eighth Earl of Douglas into the dark February night. And in the courtyard below astonished men-at arms came running, to count twenty-six wounds in the broken body.

William, Lord Crichton, Chancellor of the Realm, watched all distastefully, taking no part. As the candles flickered wildly in the cold night air from the open window, he turned and quietly left the room. He spoke to none, even the Queen, in the Great Hall, but went quickly downstairs, to call for his horses. Of all things, he loathed night riding — but the sooner he was back in Edinburgh and the safety of its rock-skied castle, the better. Before the angry flood submerged Scotland.

THE flood was not long in coming. The Douglas power rose in a tide of fury and vengeance. King James had to be restrained from actually fleeing the country, to France, in panic. The Douglas brothers, now led by Jamie as 9th Earl, came hot-foot to Stirling with an angry host. They brought the royal safe-conduct with them from Threave, tied it to a horse's tail and dragged it through the streets below the castle walls. Then they burned the town under the eyes of the terrified monarch and Court. Civil war raged thereafter, with pitiless fury, for two years, though a furtive parliament met in June, to pronounce the King guiltless of the death of Douglas "because he had publicly and contemptuously renounced the royal protection". Aid, arms and munitions from France had to be sought.

But the Douglas brothers missed Will's strong and sure hand. Their leadership was gallant, but reckless and unco-ordinated, and the new Earl was indeed no warrior. The years of fluctuating warfare ended in disastrous defeat, when Hamilton deserted the Douglas army at a vital moment, and changed sides. The Battle of Arkinholm saw the fall of the Black house of Douglas, with the Earl of Angus, Red Douglas, in command of the royal army. Archibald, Earl of Moray, fell in action; Hugh, Earl of Ormond was captured and executed; James, Earl of Douglas, and John, Lord Balveny, escaped into England and were forfeited. Obtaining English help, and that of John, Lord of the Isles, they continued the struggle for long, but their bolt was shot. John was caught and executed, but Jamie fought on, and thirty years later he was still in rebellion against the Crown, was captured in 1484, and pardoned by James the Third on condition that he entered a monastery. So, though he had married his bereaved sister-in-law and cousin, the Fair Maid of Galloway, soon after Will's death, he died a monk.

Chancellor Crichton died of natural causes only two years after his victim. King James the Second lived six years longer, and was killed, at the age of twenty-nine by a bursting cannon at the siege of Roxburgh. The Earls of Angus, the Red Douglases, grew rich, powerful and traitorous on the ruins of the Black, to be a thorn in the side of Scotland for generations. As so often in their long story the house of Stewart had backed the wrong horse.